ANTI-PAMELA

and

SHAMELA

National Library of Canada Cataloguing in Publication

Haywood, Eliza, 1693?–1756
    Anti-Pamela, or, Feign'd innocence detected / Eliza Haywood. An apology for the life of Mrs. Shamela Andrews / Henry Fielding ; edited by Catherine Ingrassia.

(Broadview literary texts)
On cover and half title page: Anti-Pamela and Shamela.
Includes bibliographical references.
ISBN 1-55111-383-X

    1. Richardson, Samuel, 1689-1761—Parodies, imitations, etc.   2. Richardson, Samuel, 1689-1761. Pamela.   I. Ingrassia, Catherine.   II. Fielding, Henry, 1707-1754. Apology for the life of Mrs Shamela Andrews   III. Title.   IV. Title: Feign'd innocence detected.   V. Title: Anti-Pamela and Shamela.   VI. Series.

PR3506.H94A75 2004   823'.508   C2003-906018-7

Broadview Press Ltd. is an independent, international publishing house, incorporated in 1985. Broadview believes in shared ownership, both with its employees and with the general public; since the year 2000 Broadview shares have traded publicly on the Toronto Venture Exchange under the symbol BDP.

We welcome comments and suggestions regarding any aspect of our publications – please feel free to contact us at the addresses below or at broadview@broadviewpress.com.

North America
Post Office Box 1243, Peterborough, Ontario, Canada K9J 7H5
3576 California Road, Orchard Park, NY, USA 14127
Tel: (705) 743-8990; Fax: (705) 743-8353;
e-mail: customerservice@broadviewpress.com

UK, Ireland, and continental Europe
NBN Plymbridge, Eastover Road, Plymouth PL6 7PY UK
Tel: 44 (0) 1752 202301   Fax: 44 (0) 1752 202331
Fax Order Line: 44 (0) 1752 202333
Customer Service: cserv@plymbridge.com Orders: orders@nbnplymbridge.com

Australia and New Zealand
UNIREPS, University of New South Wales
Sydney, NSW, 2052
Tel: 61 2 9664 0999; Fax: 61 2 9664 5420
email: info.press@unsw.edu.au

www.broadviewpress.com

This book is printed on 100% post-consumer recycled, ancient forest friendly paper.

Series Editor: Professor L.W. Conolly

Typesetting and assembly: True to Type Inc., Mississauga, Canada.

PRINTED IN CANADA

ANTI-PAMELA; or, FEIGN'D INNOCENCE DETECTED

Eliza Haywood

and

AN APOLOGY FOR THE LIFE OF MRS. SHAMELA ANDREWS

Henry Fielding

edited by Catherine Ingrassia

broadview literary texts

Contents

Acknowledgments

A number of people made the completion of this edition possible. When I began the project, my then-chair of the Virginia Commonwealth University English Department, Richard Fine, enabled me to provide students in my graduate courses with facsimile copies of *Anti-Pamela* during the early stages of the editorial process. The responses from those students were quite informative; particular thanks go to Ahsan Chowdhury for his insightful commentary. Subsequently, I taught *Anti-Pamela* in almost every upper-division and graduate course I have conducted at VCU in the last two years; the students carefully read the text and made wonderful suggestions on how to produce a teachable edition. At Virginia Commonwealth University's Medical College of Virginia, Ellen Brock, M.D., answered my questions about the gynecological effects of eighteenth-century herbal abortifacients. Patrick Spedding shared bibliographic information related to *Anti-Pamela*, and part of his *Bibliography of Eliza Haywood*, then in manuscript. Peter Sabor, who has edited a facsimile edition of *Anti-Pamela*, shared his introduction and his special knowledge of the text. Like all Haywood scholars, I am enormously grateful for the tremendous work done by Christine Blouch. For research assistance I thank Matthew Leighty. For valuable commentary on my Introduction, I thank Paula R. Backscheider, Rachel Carnell, Devoney Looser, and Miles McCrimmon. For constructing the map of the London spots Syrena frequents, I thank Richard R. Reed. At Broadview Press, Don Le Pan was unfailingly enthusiastic and Julia Gaunce offered wonderful editorial advice. I also thank the anonymous reviewers of the proposal for this edition.

Despite the academic assistance I acknowledge, my real debts are of a more personal nature. My mother, Roberta Emerson Ingrassia, provided childcare during an important stage of writing. My husband, Miles McCrimmon, unfailingly supported this project with good humor, editorial advice, and the ability to manage all things domestic.

This edition is dedicated to my children Sophia Vita and Paul Paxton McCrimmon who, despite their tender ages, showed great patience with their mother and the amount of time she spent at her computer.

Introduction

One of the eighteenth century's most popular novels, Samuel Richardson's *Pamela; or, Virtue Rewarded* initiated a sustained dialogue between "pro-" and "anti-Pamelists" who published multiple texts designed both to argue their position and, ideally, to profit from the interest in all things related to *Pamela*.[1] The novel's November 6, 1740 publication was quickly followed by *Shamela* (April 4, 1741) and *Anti-Pamela* (June 16, 1741), collected together here for the first time. An epistolary narrative, *Pamela* tells the story of a serving girl who successfully defends her "virtue" from the advances of her sexually aggressive master, Mr. B. Although B. initially thinks Pamela duplicitous, he is ultimately persuaded in the authenticity of her virtue largely by her copious letters and extensive journal which, in a sense, enact that virtue. The "reward" is marriage to B., a union that actually casts her in a more conscripted role. Published anonymously for author Samuel Richardson (1689-1761) who claimed to be the editor of the collection of letters, the novel was phenomenally popular and extremely controversial. Certainly, previous novels such as Daniel Defoe's *Robinson Crusoe* (1719) or Eliza Haywood's *Love in Excess* (1719) suggested the potential readership of the novel as early as 1719. But *Pamela* made clear the novel's cultural possibilities and financial rewards, and established the respectability of the form. *Pamela* amounted to what William Warner terms a "media event." The publication of *Pamela*, according to Warner, cultivated the attention of buyers/readers and critics as well as a broader sustained cultural "curiosity." It also triggered imitations, variations in multiple media, and rewritings of the text such as *Shamela* and *Anti-Pamela*; it "becomes the focus of critical commentary and interpretation." *Pamela* helped change "the cultural location and meaning of novel reading." [2] The book generated excitement about the novel as a genre and ignited a so-called "Pamela-craze" that invigorated the already lively print trade.

---

1 For further discussion of the published responses to *Pamela*, see Bernard Kreissman, *Pamela-Shamela: a study of the criticisms, burlesques, parodies and adaptations of Richardson's Pamela* (Lincoln, NE: U of Nebraska P, 1960).

2 William B. Warner, *Licensing Entertainment: The Elevation of Novel Reading in Britain 1684-1750* (Berkeley: U of California P, 1998) 178, 176. See chapter five, "The *Pamela* Media Event," pp. 176-230.

In the early decades of the eighteenth century, the production of books and the investment of time and money by readers expanded tremendously. Readers, whose numbers were swelling, read from a wide variety of genres, including journalistic texts, devotional texts, various kinds of conduct books and, of course, fiction. Previously, the most widely read books included conduct manuals and books of devotion such as Richard Allestree's *The Whole Duty of Man* (1659, see Appendix D.1). Early prose fiction was consistently greeted with suspicion and some resistance by moralists who felt such a low genre dangerously titillated (typically youthful often female) readers, instilling inappropriate desires and ambitions, and stimulating the imagination rather than appealing to reason. Simultaneously, there was a moral strain of fiction, exemplified by the work of writers such as Penelope Aubin or Elizabeth Singer Rowe, which combined morality and titillation. It is important to remember, as J. Paul Hunter reminds us, that "piety was the most acceptable, most persuasive, and perhaps most fundamental basis for literacy," and reading material corresponded accordingly by being "religious in subject matter, [and] didactic in intent."[1] *Pamela*, which coupled didacticism with entertainment, began to satisfy some critics because of its relentless emphasis on virtue and morality. It attempts to shepherd its readers through the novel's ostensibly unambiguous moral instruction. Yet, as Richardson's critics observed, his didacticism was cloaked by a sexualized almost prurient tone that created a narrative tension. Bearing the residue of the amatory fiction of the 1720s that it both invokes and repudiates,[2] *Pamela* seems to instruct its readers in morality yet it is consistently punctuated with stolen kisses, an attempted rape, calculated disguise, and relentless voyeurism. The responses to *Pamela* parodied precisely that prurience and the utter humorlessness that characterize Richardson's writing.

The two texts in this volume are the most significant responses

---

1   J. Paul Hunter, *Before Novels: The Cultural Contexts of Eighteenth-Century English Fiction* (New York: Norton, 1990) 83, 225.

2   In *Licensing Entertainment*, William Warner suggests that Richardson "overwrites" the amatory fiction of the 1720s (typified by Haywood's work), drawing on its erotic content but cloaking it with a more overt didacticism. Previously, Margaret Doody noted extensive similarities between the fiction of Haywood and Richardson, especially in terms of a common "dialect of sexual passion" (141) and other narrative styles. See *A Natural Passion: A Study of the Novels of Samuel Richardson* (Oxford: Clarendon Press, 1974) 137-150.

to Richardson's fiction. Although distinctly different in their approach, both question his representation of class and work, both interrogate the generic expectations he establishes, and both puncture his representation of sexuality (most potently embodied by Pamela's "virtue"). They also, implicitly, engage in a discussion about what the novel should be and how readers should be treated.

Shamela, Henry Fielding's (1707-1754) satiric response, anticipates the kind of hybrid—the "comic Epic-Poem in Prose"—that he mastered in *Joseph Andrews* (1742) and *Tom Jones* (1749). (It is easy to forget that *Shamela*, like *Pamela*, is a first novel.) As J. Paul Hunter observes, *Shamela* "suggests the expanded possibilities he would find in prose fiction."[1] *Shamela* purports to provide the "true" letters of the real Pamela, who is revealed to be a "sham" who feigns "vartue" in order to mislead and ultimately ensnare the witless Booby. Broadly comic and incisively satiric, *Shamela* reveals the absurdity of certain aspects of Richardson's narrative as it offers linguistically playful and more accurate substitutions for his language. Fielding does not abandon instruction for entertainment; he is, in many ways, more shrewdly insightful into the potential consequences of individual ambition and desire and the dangers of cultural debasement. But his prose is the antithesis of Richardson's overt and relentlessly earnest instruction. Drawing both on his theatrical background and his experience in writing political pamphlets, Fielding maintains a distinctive, knowingly topical voice that punctures the absurdities of Richardson's fiction and a culture that embraced it so fully. Fielding trusts his reader to understand the joke and the cultural implications of the texts they read. *Shamela* foregrounds the narrative, stylistic, and ideological differences between Richardson and Fielding, two writers who were often characterized as manifesting a "feminine" and "masculine" sensibility, respectively. It claims a specific kind of literary territory for Fielding, as he capitalizes in a financial sense on *Pamela*'s popularity while creating a new position for himself as a comic novelist within the marketplace.[2]

1 J. Paul Hunter, *Occasional Form: Henry Fielding and the Chains of Circumstance* (Baltimore: Johns Hopkins UP, 1975) 77.
2 As Allen Michie details in *Richardson and Fielding: The Dynamics of a Critical Rivalry* (Lewisburg: Bucknell UP, 1999), Fielding and Richardson have been read in tandem as representing distinct—and opposing directions— in eighteenth-century fiction. Their own contemporaries, like literary critics of the nineteenth and twentieth centuries, perpetuated a kind of intellectual rivalry that defined not just the two authors, but also the eighteenth-century literary landscape as a whole.

An experienced author with more than fifty-four publications to her name, Eliza Haywood (1693?-1756) also recognized the marketability of a response to *Pamela*. Like Fielding, she was motivated in part by financial interest, and she too satirizes Richardson's tone and representation of a serving girl. But Haywood's novel is a fully developed narrative that responds to Richardson on its way to offering some lessons—and entertainment—of its own. Her "anti-Pamela," Syrena Tricksy, tries to profit financially from the men she encounters as she works in various professions in London. "[T]rain'd up to deceive and betray all those whom her Beauty should allure," Syrena is devoid of any emotional attachments and focuses purely on financial gain in relationships with multiple men. The only "virtue" Syrena is concerned with is the one she feigns. *Anti-Pamela* provides an interesting contrast to the other two texts. Traditionally read in the shadow of the contemporaneous satire, *Shamela, Anti-Pamela's* engagement with Richardson and the literary marketplace has been largely ignored and the text has not previously appeared in an edited modern edition.[1]

Yet Haywood's text is an interesting mix of Richardson and Fielding. Like Richardson, Haywood's prose is informed by the amatory fiction of the 1720s (a genre largely shaped by her earlier fiction), though here in satiric guise—it represents a woman's attempts to gain a measure of economic success and personal autonomy in a culture marked by a regulatory economy of sexuality. Haywood realizes that many of her readers, schooled in her earlier fiction, are resistant to the romantic conclusions of Richardson's text either because of their familiarity with the genre or because of their own life experience. As readers became savvier about the narrative codes, Haywood found it necessary to defy expectations. Haywood's narrative persona engages the reader directly, often through sustained asides, to comment on Syrena's actions, the cultural milieu or the novel as a genre. In that way, *Anti-Pamela* provides instruction (if only through negative example) and anticipates other didactic texts Haywood subsequently wrote, partially in response to the new demand for moralistic fiction. Although *Anti-Pamela* satirizes some specific aspects of *Pamela*, its greater concern

---

1   While *Anti-Pamela* has appeared in two modern facsimile editions (New York: Garland, 1975), and *The Pamela Controversy: Criticisms and Adaptations of Samuel Richardson's Pamela, 1740-1750* in 6 Volumes, edited by Thomas Keymer and Peter Sabor, Volume 2 (London: Pickering and Chatto, 2001), a modern edition has never been published until now.

is to explore that text's construction of gender, its implicit delineation of what fiction should be, and the representation of the material conditions for women. It actively critiques the generic (and gendered) shape of the novel that *Pamela* threatens to solidify. It consistently focuses a shrewd eye on the material realities of women's lives—unlike Pamela or Shamela, Haywood's heroine, Syrena Tricksy, is always seeking a means of financial support, she always has to work. Because Haywood's text engages so many issues related to women's material culture, it goes beyond a mere response to Richardson's *Pamela*. While knowledge of *Pamela* will enrich reading *Anti-Pamela*, it is by no means a prerequisite. Her fully developed fiction can stand alone.

Richardson, Fielding, and Haywood were certainly three of the most commercially astute and well-positioned authors of the early eighteenth century and their texts provide insight into the cultural practices of the print trade. The three texts—*Pamela, Shamela,* and *Anti-Pamela*—illustrate a cultural dialogue that centers around not only the nature of the novel as a genre and the financial and symbolic economies of the print trade, but cultural expectations for and limitations on women. They also provide distinctly different and variously accurate representations of women's work (and suggestive commentary about the author's own literary "work") in a way that illustrates competing models for literary authorship and envisages different narratives for women in both fiction and the material culture of eighteenth-century England. Published within seven months of each other, *Shamela* and *Anti-Pamela*, more than the dozens of other *Pamela*-related publications, implicitly enact the struggle between high and low culture as they demonstrate how the novel and the cultural discourse surrounding it are consistently in dialogue with each other and with the kinds of earlier fiction from which they emerge.

Samuel Richardson, *Pamela*, and the Print Trade

Richardson and the Print Trade

When Samuel Richardson wrote *Pamela*, he initiated what he described to Aaron Hill as "a new species of writing." He thought that certain stories, "if written in an easy and natural manner ... might possibly introduce a new species of writing, that might possibly turn young people into a course of reading different from the pomp and parade of romance-writing, and dismissing the improbable and marvellous, with which novels generally abound, might tend to promote the cause of religion and virtue."[1] Richardson carefully distinguishes his work from "romance writing" and the "novel" with their associations with titillation, intentional deception, and a more "feminized" appeal. In the guise of an editor of a found collection of letters, he tries to produce a text of great morality, didacticism, and cultural authority. These lofty goals sound almost altruistic in nature. But it is important to remember that the "new" species of writing was also designed to position Richardson, a printer by trade, advantageously as a novelist in the literary marketplace.

During the early part of the eighteenth century, the literary marketplace and the profession of authorship expanded tremendously. The nearly exponential rise in the number of books—what John Richetti recently described as an "exploding mass of popular reading matter"[2]—published and sold in the first four decades of the eighteenth century signaled the emergence of a new consumer culture defined, in part, by the commercialization of literature. As Paul Langford observes, "the sheer volume of printed matter produced in this period is striking testimony to the extent of the reading market."[3] Literacy rates, notoriously difficult to measure, increased steadily between 1640 and 1760; by one estimate, 40 per cent of women and 60 per cent of men in London were literate by 1750.[4] The middling classes, with increased income and opportunity, read more extensively and variously in terms of genre. These new readers, typically young, urban, and ambitious, recognized that literacy had pragmatic as well as personal benefits. Literacy provided access not only to fiction, but also self-help books, stock reports, and other discourses relevant to the trade economy. The lower classes, whose literacy rates were typically lower, had access to reading material within the household of their employers or through inexpensive reproductions of texts such as piracies or chapbooks.

---

1 John Carroll, *Selected Letters of Samuel Richardson* (Oxford: Clarendon Press, 1964) 41.

2 John Richetti, *The Cambridge Companion to the Eighteenth-Century Novel* (Cambridge: Cambridge UP, 1996) 6.

3 Paul Langford, *A Polite and Commercial People: England 1727-1783* (Oxford: Clarendon Press, 1989) 91.

4 J. Paul Hunter offers a synthesis of recent demographic work on literacy rates in his essay "The Novel and Social/Cultural History" in the *Cambridge Companion to the Eighteenth-Century Novel*, p. 20. He more expansively discusses literacy rates in *Before Novels*, chapter three, pp. 61-88.

Illiteracy did not preclude an individual from being informed about the latest popular texts. "Through reading aloud in households or coffeehouses," observes Vivien Jones, "or through the reciting of ballads and broadsides by street hawkers, or the reproduction of popular texts like Richardson's *Pamela* (1740) in visual or dramatized forms, print culture profoundly affected the lives of many who could not actually read."[1] When Tickletext recommends *Pamela* to Parson Oliver in the preface to *Shamela*, he urges him to "let your Servant-Maids read it over, or *read it to them*" [emphasis mine], underscoring the accuracy of Jones's comment.

With this expanded market, writers and publishers worked to produce new material that satisfied the reading public's desires. Then, as now, innovation, titillation, and sensationalism could capture a potential purchaser's attention. While, statistically, non-fiction and devotional books actually comprised a larger part of the market, the most vital and dynamic sector was fiction. The kinds of possibilities introduced by fiction—the imaginative displacement of self, the modeling for alternative behavior, access to narratives that often championed social improvement and self-fashioning—all proved alluring to a nascent reading public. Authors and booksellers became increasingly sophisticated about marketing printed material—post-dating texts published at the end of the year so it would appear "new" longer; exaggerating the edition number of a text (claiming "second" or "fifth") to create the illusion of popularity; inserting "puffs" or written praises in the front of books to cultivate credibility and interest in a text. The book trade also remained responsive to the shifting interests of the marketplace, rapidly producing texts that filled a perceived need. As Margaret Doody reminds us, "the press was a lively medium for exchange of knowledge and opinion .... The word gets out—others respond, with questions, annotations, remarks. A new version of the first work is quickly produced, as an answer to the original piece."[2] In little more than a year after the initial publication of *Pamela*, nearly two-dozen pamphlets, continuations, translations and parodies appeared along with Richardson's six editions of the text (all revised to some degree).

---

1 Vivien Jones, "Introduction," *Women and Literature in Britain 1700-1800* (Cambridge: Cambridge UP, 2000) 3.
2 Margaret Anne Doody, "Samuel Richardson: Fiction and Knowledge," *The Cambridge Companion to the Eighteenth-Century Novel*, 96, 95-96.

In this milieu, *Pamela* was tremendously successful—in part because of its original story and accessible narrative, and in part because of Richardson's shrewd understanding of the literary marketplace. The text bears the marks of the epistolary conduct book, *Familiar Letters Written to and for Particular Friends on the Important Occasions* (1741) that was its genesis. As a story "told in letters," the inviting narrative details Pamela's at times harrowing experiences in the colloquial language of a fifteen-year old girl. Upon the death of her mistress, Pamela remains in the household with her lady's son Mr. B. to care for his linen. In a series of encounters he demonstrates his sexual interest in Pamela: he offers her stockings, peeks at her through the keyholes, kisses and fondles her, and secretly reads her letters. Pamela resists his advances to preserve her virtue and good name: "For God's sake, your Honour, pity a poor distressed Creature, that knows nothing of her Duty, but how to cherish her Virtue and good name! ... I have always been taught to value Honesty above my Life"(31).[1] When she wants to return home to her impoverished, debt-ridden parents, B. instead has her transported to his Lincolnshire estate. There, abused by Mrs. Jewkes, Pamela endures B.'s insults, proposals for a settlement, and attempted rape. Finally, he recognizes the sincerity of her resistance and decides to marry her: "you bring me ... an experienc'd Truth, a well-try'd Virtue, and a Wit and Behaviour more than equal to the Station you will be placed in: To say nothing of this sweet Person, that itself might captivate a Monarch; and of the Meekness of a Temper, and Sweetness of Disposition, which make you superior to all the Women I ever saw" (337). Now the narrative of a serving girl (though "better born") who triumphs over oppression from her social superiors seems completely natural even predictable. But in the 1740s, it was

---

1   All references to *Pamela* are to the 1740 edition of *Pamela; or, Virtue Rewarded* (Oxford: Oxford UP, 2001) edited by Thomas Keymer and Alice Wakely. Pamela's sentiment here is consistent not only with the discourse in devotional manuals devoted to women, but also with the earlier strain of women's fiction. For example, in Penelope Aubin's *The Strange Adventures of the Count de Vinevil* (1721), Ardelisa's fiancé admonishes her: "Permit not a vile infidel to dishonor you, resist to death, and let me not be so completely cursed to hear you live and are debauched" (*Popular Fiction By Women 1660-1730: An Anthology*, ed. Paula R. Backscheider and John J. Richetti [Oxford: Oxford UP, 1996] 121).

much more surprising and potentially subversive in a world where "poor Peoples Honesty is to go for nothing" (134). Sir Simon's response to Pamela's appeal for assistance—"Why, what is all this, my Dear, but that the 'Squire our Neighbour has a mind to his Mother's Waiting-maid? And if he takes care she wants for nothing, I don't see any great Injury will be done her. He hurts no Family by this" (134)—captures the cultural perception of the value of "virtue" in women of Pamela's class.

As the excerpts in Appendix C demonstrate more fully, Pamela's language and apparently earnest attitude toward virtue became the basis for everyone's satiric departure. Two camps of readers emerged: the "pro-Pamelists" who read her virtue as sincere and without guile; and the "anti-Pamelists" who thought her virtue was purely of a long-term manipulation to secure an offer of marriage from Mr. B.[1] Her fascination with material goods and her cataloguing of the same roused comments from critics who viewed her as a purely acquisitive, self-interested young woman. Pamela's aspirations for self-improvement, her devotion to virtue in theory and practice, her candid, often rebellious, commentary about the upper classes, and her consumer impulse echo the middling classes' desires and impulses and enhanced the novel's appeal. While it would be reductive to read Pamela primarily as representative of her class—for the narrative reveals a far more complex character— she does suggest many of the desires and contradictions present in a dynamic class structure.

Richardson profited handsomely. As a prosperous printer with considerable standing in the print trade and within his livery, The Stationers' Company, Richardson's position, coupled with his well-documented flair for marketing and self-promotion, enabled him to give *Pamela* a very strong debut. In fact, Alan McKillop asserts that Richardson's connections in the trade gave *Pamela* unusual advantages in advertising that might have contributed to the text's overwhelming popularity. He had "to his credit a large stock of goodwill in the commercial sense ... [and] ... the book was published

---

1 Modern critics' interpretations fall, to some degree, along the same lines. Some scholars describe Pamela as an active and clever participant within a commercial economy; others view her as a marker of the new morality whose virtue is sincere. Obviously, those two approaches are not mutually exclusive.

under conditions much more favorable than those usually enjoyed by works of fiction."[1] A series of well-placed puffs and advertisements, facilitated by Richardson's knowledge of the print trade, contributed to the novel's successful launch.

Pamela went into six revised editions in the first year as well as appearing in serial form in the newspaper *All Alive and Merry*.[2] Despite the text's enormous popularity, Richardson remained concerned about content. Stung by the commentary of some of his critics, he revised the novel to elevate Pamela's language, to add additional moral lessons, and to eliminate some of the alleged prurience. Additionally, insecure about his own clearly middle-class orientation, he worked hard to eliminate colloquialisms from Pamela's speech and to elevate her language generally.[3] Indeed, Richardson, a notoriously compulsive reviser, continued to change *Pamela* throughout his life, and his family posthumously published the last edition in 1801. In the second edition, published on 14 February 1741, Richardson expanded the preface and commendations with a self-congratulatory introduction drawn from letters he had allegedly received from admiring readers. These letters which, as McKillop observes, "are noteworthy for their quantity rather than quality," were largely focused on clergymen praising the text's moral power. In fact, Ronald Paulson suggests that, with these framing devices, "*Pamela* was presented in the second edition as if it were a sacred text."[4]

The introduction, savagely parodied by Fielding, was perhaps designed to compensate for the absence of significant praise from

---

1   Alan D. McKillop, *Samuel Richardson, Printer and Novelist* (Hamden, CT: Shoe String Press, 1960; originally published, Chapel Hill: U of North Carolina P, 1936) 14.

2   McKillop, *Samuel Richardson*, 80. For information concerning other serialized publications of *Pamela*, see Robert D. Mayo, *The English Novel in the Magazines, 1740-1815* (Evanston: Northwestern UP, 1962).

3   Writing of Richardson, Lady Mary Wortley Montagu observed "I beleive [sic] this Author was never admitted into higher Company, and should confine his Pen to the Amours of Housemaids and the conversation at the Steward's Table, where I imagine he has sometimes intruded, thô oftner in the Servants' Hall" (*Complete Letters*, ed. Robert Halsband, 3 volumes [Oxford: Clarendon Press, 1965-67] vol. 3, 96).

4   Ronald Paulson, *The Life of Henry Fielding: A Critical Biography*, (Oxford: Blackwell, 2000) 140.

"important men in literature."[1] George Cheyne and James Leake both wrote to Richardson detailing Alexander Pope's alleged praise for the novel. Cheyne describes him as reading with "great Approbation and Pleasure" and observing "it will do more good than a great many of the new sermons." Yet other voices were notably absent. Given the success of the novel Richardson might be excused for his pride and sense of self-importance.[2] The community of Slough all read (or heard) the book and allegedly rang the church bells when they learned Pamela married B. Dr. Benjamin Slocock recommended the book from the pulpit of St. Saviours Southwark, a gesture that long fueled (unfounded) speculation that Richardson provided him with financial compensation. As an oft-quoted writer in the *Gentleman's Magazine* observes, "it being judged in Town as great a Sign of want of Curiosity not to have read Pamela, as not to have seen the French and Italian dancers." *Pamela* saturated the marketplace.

Like his colleagues in the print trade, Richardson published *Pamela*-related materials to capitalize on his previous success. In 1742, he attempted "to use the success of his first novel" by advertising his edition of *Aesop's Fables* as "'the Aesops quoted in Pamela'."[3] He wrote a sequel to *Pamela*, *Pamela in her Exalted Condition* (published 7 December 1741), compelled by the threats of a sequel planned by "those who knew nothing of the story, nor the Delicacy required in the continuation of the Piece."[4] Throughout his career as a printer-cum-author, Richardson practiced a kind of self-plagiarism, publishing texts such as *A collection of the moral and instructive sentiments, maxims, cautions, and reflexions, contained in the histories of Pamela, Clarissa, and Sir Charles Grandison*, that repackaged moral aphorisms drawn from *Pamela* and his two subsequent novels.

Pamela *and the Development of the Novel*

Pamela's popularity and its presence in multiple media—for the novel was not just a literary event, but a cultural one—increased its

1 McKillop, *Samuel Richardson*, 50.
2 As Terry Eagleton notes, "the modern equivalent of *Pamela* would be ... a phenomenon like Superman." *The Rape of Clarissa: Writing, Sexuality and Class Struggle in Samuel Richardson* (Oxford: Blackwell, 1982) 5.
3 T.C. Eaves and Ben D. Kimpel, *Samuel Richardson: A Biography* (Oxford: Clarendon Press, 1971) 80.
4 Carroll, *Selected Letters*, 43.

powerful appeal. It also heightened its effect on subsequent fiction. Amatory fiction of the 1720s, from which *Pamela* emerges, presented women who, through an "inadvertency," were typically seduced and abandoned by male characters.[1] Women writers such as Aphra Behn, Delarivier Manley, and Haywood wrote fiction with a frank sexuality, created female characters with sexual desires, and represented male-female relationships as often marked by duplicity, manipulation, and disappointment. Similarly, early fiction such as Daniel Defoe's *Moll Flanders* (1722) or *Roxana* (1724) offered female characters whose experiences forced (or allowed) them to circulate sexually, economically, and socially. While these representations of sexually engaged female characters were counterbalanced by the overt morality of the work of someone like Penelope Aubin, they were also underscored by contemporaneous poetic and dramatic representations of women. Thus, the heroine Richardson created marked an important shift in the dominant expectations for female characters. It solidified an idealized construction of women as aggressively virtuous, submissive, and dutiful.[2]

Additionally, *Pamela* established the generic expectations for prose fiction; the courtship novel (with the likely conclusion of marriage), novels of sensibility, and the dilated novel become dominant. Previously, the novel was not a codified genre; indeed, one critic terms it "diffuse, inchoate and tangled."[3] A quick look at texts that called themselves "novels" in the 1720s reveals what an undefined genre it was. Because no one knew what the "novel" was, authors could experiment in terms of plot, characters, and narrative technique. Drawing on multiple contemporaneous discourses simultaneously, the early novel was a truly hybrid form.[4] But after

---

1   For discussion of early fiction, see Ros Ballaster's *Seductive Forms: Women's amatory fiction from 1684-1740* (Oxford: Clarendon Press; New York: Oxford UP, 1992) and John Richetti's *Popular Fiction before Richardson: Narrative patterns 1700-1739* (Oxford: Clarendon Press, 1969).

2   For a discussion of the popular novel after Richardson, see J.M.S. Tompkins, *The Popular Novel in England, 1770-1800* (Lincoln: U of Nebraska P, 1961; originally published 1932).

3   Warner, 177.

4   For example, Lennard J. Davis explores a variety of genres that contribute to the novel, focusing on the nexis between "news" or journalism and the novel in *Factual Fictions: The Origins of the English Novel* (New York: Columbia UP, 1983).

Pamela, which tells an intensely personal story in a readable, first-person vernacular, readers had a sense of what they wanted novels to look like. Subsequently, fiction increasingly focused on the individualized experience, the personal reflections of the writing subject, and the moral relevance of both. Fiction was now more episodic (the division between Pamela's letters serving as *ad hoc* chapters), personally revealing, and, at base, emotional.

While individuals increasingly consumed prose fiction during the century, *Pamela* cultivated groups of readers that transcended the previous boundaries of class, gender, and educational differences. It captured a critical mass of readers who not only embraced the novel but also published reactions to it as well as other attendant cultural—and commercial—representations of it. Consequently, the publication of *Pamela* marks a moment that accelerated the transformation of the print trade. It changed the reading habits of the public, in part, by making the novel both respectable and a subject of cultural conversation; no longer only paper-backed, pocket-sized publications marked as cultural ephemera, fiction—in material form and generic content—could be weighty, significant, and edifying. Yet, despite the "improvement" it offered, it was still regarded as fashionable; women would allegedly display their copies of *Pamela* publicly, purchase Pamela fans, and view the waxworks that presented Pamela's life. The novel appealed to a reading public eager for an overtly didactic and simultaneously titillating narrative. As a result, readers avidly read—and reread—the tale of Richardson's beleaguered heroine. The novel also introduced, but carefully contained, unprecedented class mixing, which appealed to readers. Additionally, Richardson's text redefined (and blurred) the boundaries between high and low culture as the novel tried to find its spot in the eighteenth-century literary hierarchy. These combined factors caused *Pamela* to contribute significantly to the development of the genre that would be known as the novel.

Within this competitive commercial environment, *Shamela* and *Anti-Pamela* appear. Possibly, Fielding and Haywood felt some professional jealousy that fueled their texts. Unlike Fielding and Haywood, Richardson did not have to write to survive because his position as a successful printer provided him with financial security. As writers with consistently ironic perspectives, they might also have resisted Richardson's earnest emotionalism that the public embraced so enthusiastically. Fielding and Haywood each respond to the cultural reverberations of *Pamela*, and their texts simultaneously interrogate its cultural and narrative implications while also underscoring (if not ensuring) its cultural significance.

Henry Fielding and *Shamela*

Fielding's Career and Shifting Literary Hierarchies

By 1740, Fielding was a political journalist and well-known dramatist who had established himself at the Little Theatre in the Haymarket in the 1730s; he was, according to Robert Hume, the "most dominant professional playwright in London since Dryden."[1] Born and raised in the West Country and educated at Eton, Fielding had come to London in 1728 and in the 1730s found great success in a theatrical milieu that was receptive to his innovation, energy, and politically astute texts. Ronald Paulson suggests Fielding also chose the theatre because "the quickest way to earn money was as a successful playwright."[2] Though born to an established family, Fielding had to earn a living his whole life; he was, in John Richetti's words, "culturally privileged but economically deprived."[3] Through the course of his life he was a playwright, novelist, journalist, magistrate, and businessman. His various professional endeavors exposed him to the market dynamics of early eighteenth-century London. Though Fielding wrote for money, he was not a "hackney writer." Instead he "guided as well as followed the market" suggests Paulson, and his "aristocratic ideal of himself, of his own status, education, and abilities ... never abandoned him, only changing registers with changing circumstances."[4] His theatrical work of the 1730s was extremely topical and opportunistically political, satirizing corruption, abuses of power, and the deterioration of public tastes—indeed, throughout the thirties, he excoriates the kind of cultural "dullness" he saw fully realized with *Pamela*.

His attitude and response toward *Pamela* and the attendant cultural preoccupation reveal much about his complicated place in the eighteenth-century literary landscape. In one sense, Fielding espoused an attitude toward cultural practice consistent with the

1 Robert D. Hume, *Henry Fielding and the London Theatre 1728-1737* (Oxford: Clarendon Press, 1988) ix.
2 Ronald Paulson, *Henry Fielding*, x.
3 John Richetti, *The English Novel in History 1700-1780* (London: Routledge, 1999) 123.
4 Paulson, *Henry Fielding*, x.

Augustan satirists Alexander Pope, Jonathan Swift, and John Gay; in fact, in homage to their figure of "Martin Scriblerus," he signed "Scriblerus Secundus" on annotations to some of his plays—*The Author's Farce* (1730) and *The Tragedy of Tragedies* (1731), for example, both of which also parody the commercialization of literature and the aesthetic values that were of increasing appeal to what Fielding perceived as an undiscriminating public.[1] He shared the Augustan's unflinching satiric eye that spotted social, political, or moral corruption, their impatience for cultural debasement, and their anxiety about readers' fascination with texts he considered inappropriate or just aesthetically fraudulent.

Before the advent of a primarily commercial literary marketplace, "literature" was seen as the purview of the leisured and landed gentleman who wrote for improvement not profit. Certain elevated genres (poetry, tragedy, and history) were privileged, and works that appealed to values culturally defined as lofty, universal, and transcendent were perceived as superior. With the rise of the print trade, texts were bought and sold like any other commodity. A wider reading population sought more accessible, exciting, and diverse texts, spurring the market for different kinds of prose (travel literature, newspapers, criminal biography, and amatory fiction) most of which was topical, immediate and, in the eyes of come critics, base. Publishers printed what sold, and what sold often contained, to Fielding's mind, excessive emotionalism, compromised morality, and inauthentic experiences. He preserved a classical sensibility that resisted the erosion of long-standing literary hierarchies. In *The Author's Farce*, for example, Fielding presents the cacophony of disparate literary genres he resisted as personified figures on the stage. Tragedy, comedy, oratory, pantomime, opera— and, notably, the novel in the form of Mrs. Novel, allusive of the early amatory fiction of Eliza Haywood—compete for the audience's attention by appealing to the lowest common denominator.

---

1 The Scriblerus Club—Pope, Swift, Gay, Thomas Parnell, and Arbuthnot— was founded with the desire to ridicule false tastes in learning. The name derives from their fictional creation, Martinus Scriblerus, the learned fool, who provided them with a vehicle with which to satirize professional or "hack" writers lacking in traditional cultural capital. While Pope and the conservative, aristocratic-leaning members of the Scriblerus Club harshly condemned the tribe of scribblers, they also came to be themselves identified *as* Scriblerians. Fielding is deliberately placing himself in this mixed tradition.

This theatrical representation aims to highlight the confused dangers of these highly popular genres.[1]

Although Fielding was concerned about the low standard for popular fiction and the general state of his world, he "considered writing for money a legitimate enterprise."[2] Like his contemporary, Alexander Pope, Fielding depended deeply on the marketplace he critiqued. When his theatrical career was essentially terminated with the Theatre Licensing Act of 1737,[3] out of economic necessity Fielding turned his attention to other genres and began his foray into fiction with *Shamela*. He placed himself squarely in the competitive literary marketplace and sought to profit from works that could both be popular and consistent with his aesthetic values. Certainly Fielding had a financial motivation for *Shamela*. When Richardson, stung by *Shamela*, later learned of Fielding's authorship, he attributed his motives purely to commercial interest ("so long as the world will receive, Mr. Fielding will write"). He also claimed *Pamela* taught Fielding how to write popular material: "*Pamela*, which he abused in his *Shamela*," wrote Richardson to Lady Bradsheigh "taught him how to write to please, tho' his manners are so different. Before his *Joseph Andrews*. . .the poor man wrote without being read."[4]

---

1 Jill Campbell suggests *The Author's Farce* also anticipates the threads of discourse that subsequently appear in Fielding's fiction as well. "Although those novels do not present us with personified embodiments of a handful of genres," writes Campbell, "their language characteristically incorporates the voices of any number of genres." Jill Campbell, "Fielding and the Novel at Mid-Century" in *The Columbia History of the Novel,* edited by John J. Richetti (New York: Columbia UP, 1994) 103. For a discussion of Fielding's treatment of gender, see Campbell's *Natural Masques: Gender and Identity in Fielding's Plays and Novels* (Stanford: Stanford UP, 1995).

2 Brean Hammond, *Professional Imaginative Writing in England, 1670-1740: "Hackney for Bread"* (Oxford: Clarendon Press, 1997) 277.

3 The Theatre Licensing Act of 1737, which some suggest emerged in part because of the political work of Fielding, made it illegal to produce any play that had not first been approved by the Lord Chamberlain through his appointee, the Examiner of Plays. The Licensing Act, a form of censorship, successfully silenced overtly political playwrights such as Fielding. See L.W. Conolly, *The Censorship of English Drama 1737-1824* (San Marino: The Huntington Library, 1976).

4 Carroll, *Selected Letters,* 133. If Fielding had a financial motivation, it was certainly realized: *Shamela* was very popular. Charles Yorke wrote to his brother Philip on 12 April 1741, detailing the positive reception of the text: "Shammela & the Dedications to it, the former as a ridicule on

Yet *Shamela* also reveals Fielding's more consistent concern with tempering the culture's enthusiasm for *Pamela*. Richardson's novel (which he initially did not know was written by Richardson) "roused Fielding's critical and intellectual dislike," asserts Thomas Lockwood, "but also, more importantly, roused a creative desire to rewrite the original."[1] With *Shamela*, his target was Richardson's novel as well as analogous, debased cultural practices. In Fielding's mind, *Pamela* endorses hyperbolic self-justification, the worst kind of moralizing, and what Michael McKeon describes as the "culturally fraught effrontery of the rise of the undeserving."[2] Yet, Pamela (the novel and character) was not the only example of debased cultural practice that comes under Fielding's attack. As J. Paul Hunter suggests, *Shamela* is "the best book report on 1740"; it draws "a revealing miniature of the character of his times."[3] Fielding actively takes on Colley Cibber and his recently published *An Apology for the Life of Colley Cibber* (1740), and Conyers Middleton and his dedication to Lord Hervey in the *Life of Cicero* (1741) (see Appendix C for relevant excerpts of both). These multiple objects of attack complicate Fielding's piece making it about a cultural moment and not just a specific text. Indeed, with its expansive scope and textured presentation, *Shamela*, in many ways, has more in common with Pope's *Dunciad Variorum* (1742) than with *Anti-Pamela*. Fielding and Pope both target the poet laureate, Colley Cibber; both use a hybrid literary form in their response; and both (implicitly) resist what they perceive as a deterioration of culture best exemplified by the popularity of low or otherwise inappropriate texts.[4] This kind of cultural

---

Pamela, & the latter on the Dedication to the Life of Cicero, meet with general Applause.—Your Embassador has not as yet seen the Book, and is credibly informed that it is in such universal Request at the Theatre coffee-house, that unless he were to purchase it for himself (which he has by no means any Intention of doing) it will be impossible for him to gain a sight of it these two months." Quoted in Martin C. Battestin with Ruthe R. Battestin, *Henry Fielding: A Life* (London: Routledge, 1989) 307.

1   Thomas Lockwood, "Theatrical Fielding," *Studies in the Literary Imagination* 32.2 (1999): 105-14.

2   Michael McKeon, *The Origins of the English Novel 1600-1740* (Baltimore and London: Johns Hopkins UP, 1987) 396.

3   J. Paul Hunter, *Occasional Form,* 77.

4   This similarity is not unique to *Anti-Pamela*. Jill Campbell, for instance, notes the continuity between Pope's *Dunciad* and Fielding's *Author's Farce*. See, for example, "'When Men women Turn': Gender Reversals in Fielding's Plays," in *The New Eighteenth-Century: Theory, Politics, English Literature*, edited by Felicity Nussbaum and Laura Brown (New York and London: Methuen, 1987), esp. pages 70-73.

disorder for Fielding bespoke what Martin Battestin describes as "a general social disorder manifest in virtually every area of public life"— the very concerns Pope expresses.[1]

Shamela

Shamela's title, title-page (reproduced in Appendix C), and prefatory material provide a good point of entry for understanding Fielding's complicated project. The title-page parodically echoes that of a conduct book or devotional manual with the phrase "Necessary to be had in all Families," which appears on *The Whole Duty of Man* and any number of other conduct books. It also echoes Richardson's title-page claim for *Pamela*, "Published in order to cultivate the principles of virtue and religion in the minds of the youth of both sexes." Cibber, Middleton, and Richardson all come under assault in the prefatory materials. The letters and "puffs" that frame *Shamela* parody Richardson's prefatory material from the second edition and situate the novel in the literary marketplace; with a commendatory letter titled "the Editor to Himself," Fielding reminds us that Richardson is driven by profit not just didacticism. He also suggests that Richardson, hypocritically disguising himself as editor, wrote some of the letters himself. The framing device introduces the complex political, religious, and theatrical threads of Fielding's satire.

Aside from Richardson, the most pronounced attack is on actor, playwright, and poet laureate Colley Cibber (1671-1757) and *An Apology for the Life of Colley Cibber*. Cibber and Fielding had known each other since Fielding come to London in 1728 and persuaded Cibber, then manager at Drury Lane Theatre, to produce his first London play, *Love in Several Masques*. "The most talented and powerful personality of the London stage,"[2] Cibber embodied the kind of the unmerited success Fielding found so troubling; he humiliated contemporary playwrights, repackaged the work of past playwrights (including Shakespeare), and managed his theatre to ensure his own profit, offering the popular and proven rather than the innovative. He also refused to stage Fielding's next play, *The Temple Beau*, initiating a feud between the two men. His *Apology*, a model

---

1 Martin C. Battestin, *The Moral Basis of Fielding's Art: A Study of Joseph Andrews* (Middleton, CT: Wesleyan UP, 1959) 303.
2 Battestin, *Henry Fielding*, 59.

of textual self-importance, was focused, in Cibber's words, on making his "Follies publick"—"Why not? I have pass'd my Time very pleasantly with them, and I don't recollect that they have ever been hurtful to any other Man living. Even admitting they were injudiciously chosen, would it not be Vanity in me to take Shame to myself for not being found a Wise Man?. . . . Is it for Fame, or Profit to myself, or Use or Delight to others? For all these Considerations I have neither Fondness nor Indifference."[1] *An Apology* shared many of the elements Fielding found objectionable in *Pamela*: both are "written in a totally self-engrossed style," both describe the machinery or personal work behind the public performance; both applaud social elevation due to an alleged moral superiority; and both suggest intimate personal experience has a broader cultural relevance.[2] The full title of *Shamela, An Apology for the Life of Mrs. Shamela Andrews*, like the name of the "author," Conny Keyber, alludes directly to Cibber and his *Apology*. (Indeed, some critics suggest Fielding initially thought Cibber wrote *Pamela*.)

The dedication from "Keyber," or Cibber, to John, Lord Hervey, successful courtier and Walpole supporter, closely parodies Conyers Middleton's unctuous dedication to Hervey in his *Life of Cicero* (1741) (see Appendix C). Middleton's dedication contains the worst kind of obsequious prose commonly used by authors seeking patronage from powerful individuals and, as such, represented the gratuitous marketing of talent Fielding derided. Additionally, its recipient, Hervey, embodied the political debasement Fielding despised. Confidante of prime minister Robert Walpole, Hervey thrived in the self-interested, preferment-based world of eighteenth-century politics. His corruption, coupled with his notoriously transgressive sexual activity, his effeminate behavior, and his political machinations, made him for Fielding, as for Pope, the epitome of skewed cultural values. Finally, Fielding highlights his discomfort with the sexuality of Richardson's text both by his use of Hervey, whose nickname "Fanny" appears through the text, and the name "Conny" which (as footnote 2 on page 229 to *Shamela* indicates) suggests "cunny,"

---

1   *An Apology for the Life of Colley Cibber* edited by Robert W. Lowe (New York, AMS Press, 1966; originally published 1740) 3-4.
2   Fielding initiated his attack on Cibber with his piece in the *Champion* for May 17, 1740, which charged Cibber with the murder of the English language. He also parodied him as Conney Keyber in the revised *Author's Farce* (1734) in ways that anticipate *Shamela*.

a slang term for pudendum. Both contain multiple obscene puns on various slang names for female genitalia.

The series of letters between Parsons Tickletext and Oliver that frame the text alludes to the increasing popularity of Methodism, which, to Fielding's mind, privileged emotions over faith. These letters, like descriptions of Methodism within the text, suggest that religion also depends on a slightly sexualized response rather than on spiritual faith; that too underscores the sexualized, slightly prurient tone of *Pamela*.[1] Tickletext describes his simultaneously physical and emotional reaction to Pamela in terms that underscore the masturbatory connotation of his name: "Oh! I feel an Emotion even while I am relating this: Methinks I see Pamela at this Instant, with all the Pride of Ornament cast off." Fielding slyly hints that Tickletext's "emotion" manifests itself physically as he imagines Pamela shorn of more than just her "pride of ornament." Because *Pamela* was elevated nearly to the level of a new conduct book, Fielding feared its values (literary and social) would be widely emulated. In his prefatory letter, Tickletext, a Pamela enthusiast, claims *Pamela* will be "the only education we intend hence forth to give our daughter."

If Richardson was writing a "new species of writing," Fielding was trying to inoculate against that with his own self-described "new province of writing"; as Battestin observes, he "wished to expose the inherent foolishness of Richardson's book."[2] While Fielding shares Richardson's opinion about the dangers and limitations of the kind of amatory fiction Haywood wrote in the 1720s, his concerns are located more in issues of literary hierarchy and "classical austerity and honour" rather than a desire for didacticism or realism.[3] (Indeed Fielding's novel is no more accurate in its representation of a serving girl than Richardson's.) He found Richardson's technique of "writing to the moment" patently absurd and potentially dangerous and satirized it mercilessly by having Shamela "writing" at ludicrously inappropriate times: "Mrs. Jervis and I are just in Bed, and the Door unlocked; if my Master should come—

---

1 For an excellent and detailed discussion of Fielding's treatment of Methodism and *Shamela*'s connection to the Whitefield sermons, see J. Paul Hunter, *Occasional Form*, 78-81.
2 Battestin, *Moral Basis of Fielding's Art*, 9.
3 Ros Ballaster, "Women and the Rise of the Novel," *Women and Literature in Britain 1700-1800*, ed. Vivien Jones (Cambridge: Cambridge UP, 2000) 207.

Odsbobs! I hear him just coming in at the Door. You see I write in the present Tense, as Parson Williams says. Well, he is in Bed between us, we both shamming Sleep, he steals his Hand into my Bosom, which I, as if in my Sleep, press close to me, with mine, and then pretend to awake." Richardson's unmediated discourse, coupled with the emotional immediacy of the text, troubled Fielding who thought if readers identified too closely with Pamela they would lose what Paulson describes as a sense of "the wholeness of the moral design" of the novel.[1]

Fielding locates much of his satire in the linguistic variance that reveals the fraudulent and ultimately limiting nature of Pamela's "virtue." Thus "virtue" becomes "vartue," a nod to its constructed nature, Shamela's class position, and, likely, her regional rural origins. Not only is Pamela's virtue a concept that exists in passivity and self-generated discourse, it also depends on a performative dimension. Indeed, as Thomas Lockwood suggests, the theatrical nature of the text both reveals Fielding's dramatic origins and highlights the way such extreme virtue could be counterfeited. Virtue to that degree, suggests Fielding, is an act or, equally important, can be "self-dramatized" as it were. In either situation, it is not be trusted. Fielding also mimics the linguistic lapses to focus on Pamela's lower class and its verbal implications (much as Smollett subsequently does with Tabitha Bramble in *Humphry Clinker*).

While he retains the epistolary style, Fielding introduces letters from more correspondents (most notably Williams) to correct the nearly monolithic voice that constitutes *Pamela*. Of the 32 letters in *Pamela* only three are from her parents; the rest of the novel is, of course, Pamela's journal "in captivity" at B.'s Lincolnshire estate. This widening of the narrative provides a more fully developed (or at least fully revealed) Shamela and asks us to complicate our reading of Pamela accordingly. Indeed, Paulson suggests that Shamela is "a humanization of Pamela—or even a sign that Fielding believes that the personification of Virtue in Pamela includes particulars that, beyond Richardson's awareness, contradict the idealization."[2]

Fielding exaggerates in *Shamela* interests Pamela just alludes to, forcing the reader to reassess her as a character. Though Pamela resists the unwanted sexual advances from B., she occasionally betrays her attraction to him with comments on his appearance,

---

1 Paulson, *Henry Fielding*, 141.
2 Paulson, *Henry Fielding*, 143.

concerns for his health, or her admission "I cannot hate him." By contrast, Shamela has an intense sexual appetite; though feigning virtue, she enthusiastically continues her affair with Williams, which previously resulted in an illegitimate child. She critically evaluates Booby's sexual prowess: "Oh Parson Williams; how little are all the Men in the World compared to thee." Shamela's acquisitive nature also includes an avid consumer impulse. Like Pamela, Shamela catalogues her material possessions, her "bundles" when she prepares to leave Booby's home: "two Day-Caps, two Night-Caps, five Shifts, one Sham, a Hoop, a Quilted Petticoat...." Shamela observes "what signifies having Money if one doth not spend it," a sentiment that echoes Pamela's regret that "the Money lies by me, and brings me no Interest....[I] want to make Use upon Use" (498). Shamela is also quite open about her desire to profit, one way or another, from her relationship with Booby. She has transferred her ambitions from mere prostitution to marriage: "I thought once of making a little Fortune by my Person. I now intend to make a great one by my Vartue." In addition to responding to Richardson on specific points of style and language, Fielding also meticulously (albeit in vastly abbreviated form) follows the narrative of *Pamela*. The attempted rape, threatened suicide, and marriage are all included in his response.

Fielding, like Richardson, represents the sexual vulnerability women confronted in domestic service, but, unlike Haywood, he largely ignores the gender politics central to the narratives. If Pamela is able to manufacture a "virtue" that she controls throughout the narrative (and then reconfigures as Mrs. B.), Shamela has little control over her sexuality either in terms of her own appetites or its circulation and appropriation by Booby and Williams. Shamela's mother reminds her daughter to be "well paid beforehand" since women cannot trust a man's promises after "he hath had his wicked will." But there is never the suggestion that Shamela will profit from anything but her sexuality.

Ultimately, *Shamela* functions both as a very focused burlesque of Richardson's novel and a very textured commentary on the culture in which is appeared. It provides insight into the dualism that has characterized Fielding scholarship in the last decades. Do we read him as relentless moralist and cultural critic, outraged by Richardson's novel, or as more pragmatic (and more comic) professional writer capitalizing on a market eager for material related to *Pamela*? Obviously, those two interpretations are not mutually exclusive. As Albert Rivero suggests, while *Shamela* might not fit with the work of the moral novelist that Fielding would become, it is definitely "a work participating in the duplicities of representation it aims to expose and refute."[1] *Shamela*, like Fielding's other work, is characterized by unresolved tensions that examine moral implications but within a suggestive, often overtly risqué narrative. Finally, *Shamela* anticipates the perceived often reductive differences between Richardson and Fielding that have informed the history of the novel. Richardson has consistently been viewed as the moral (perhaps priggish) middle-class novelist who champions texts of emotion, sentiment, and didacticism. Characterized as "feminine" in his sensibilities, Richardson nevertheless acts as a paternalistic voice guiding the reader to correct interpretation and conduct. By contrast, Fielding retains a more jocular (at times rakish) persona consistent with his keenly developed irony, complex plots, and an aristocratic perspective. These often repeated binaries used to characterize the two novelists elide much of the subtlety of their work but accurately highlight the distinct cultural currency and narrative experience each man represented.

Eliza Haywood, *Anti-Pamela*, and the Gender Politics of the Novel

Haywood's Career

Unlike Fielding about whom much has been written and for whom a definitive biography exists, Haywood's life, like her texts, has not been fully explored. Despite being what John Richetti describes as "the most important producer of popular fiction before *Pamela*,"[2] Haywood's personal history remains filled with questions and uncertainties about basic information—when and where she was born, who she married, how she lived. Discussions of Haywood's life have been overly and inaccurately informed by what Paula Backscheider terms "the Story" of Eliza Haywood—a scrappy woman writer transforms herself from scandalous scribbler of

---

1   Albert J. Rivero, "*Pamela/ Shamela/ Joseph Andrews*: Henry Fielding and the Duplicities of Representation," *Augustan Subject: Essays in Honor of Martin C. Battestin*, ed. Albert J. Rivero (Newark: U of Delaware P, 1997) 215.

2   John Richetti, *Popular Fiction Before Richardson*, 179.

immoral novels into a reformed, virtuous novelist.[1] As this introduction, like recent criticism of Haywood, makes clear, that reductive master narrative ignores some of the more complicated aspects of her writing career. The purpose of this introduction is not to provide exhaustive biographical information about her,[2] but rather to position her within the commercial and literary milieu in which she operated and to demonstrate that her professional activities, like her texts, cannot be easily categorized.

Haywood was likely born in London to middle-class parents and was well-educated enough to write prolifically and to author a number of translations. After a brief theatrical career in Dublin that initiated a life-long (and largely unrealized) fascination and professional association with the theatre, Haywood returned to London and published her first novel, the tremendously popular *Love in Excess* (1719). As she later wrote, "The Stage not answering my Expectations, has made me turn my Genius another Way."[3] The enormous popularity of *Love in Excess*, which went through six London and one Dublin editions, anticipated the commercial market for Haywood's fiction. Through her nearly forty-year career, her versatile prose, her political and ideological commitments, and, perhaps, economic necessity caused her to write in multiple genres (poetry, drama, essays/periodicals, political satires, translations), but she most consistently wrote prose fiction. During the period of her greatest productivity, 1719 to 1729, she wrote and published more than fifty texts, more than any other woman author.[4] Books were too expensive to produce except for authors who would sell; Hay-

---

1 Paula R. Backscheider, "The Story of Eliza Haywood's Novels: Caveats and Questions," *The Passionate Fictions of Eliza Haywood: Essays on her Life and Work*, edited by Kirsten T. Saxton and Rebecca P. Bocchicchio (Lexington: UP of Kentucky, 2000) 19-47.

2 For biographical treatment of Haywood see Christine Blouch, "Eliza Haywood," *Selected Works of Eliza Haywood Set I, Volume I,* edited by Alexander Pettit (London: Pickering and Chatto, 2000) xxi-lxxxii; and Blouch, "Eliza Haywood and the Romance of Obscurity," *SEL: Studies in English Literature* 31.3 (1991): 535-52.

3 PRO SP 35 22/54.

4 For a more detailed discussion of Haywood's career see Blouch (cited above); Patrick Spedding, *A Bibliography of Eliza Haywood* (London: Pickering and Chatto, 2004); and Catherine Ingrassia, *Authorship, Commerce and Gender in Eighteenth-Century England* (Cambridge: Cambridge UP, 1998) 77-89 and 104-10.

wood's rate of publication suggests she was enormously popular. She had "a career that was prolific even by the standards of a prolific age" notes Christine Blouch.[1] Like Fielding, she was a professional writer, and observed in the preface to *The Injur'd Husband* that "The press is set to work only to gratify a mercenary end."[2] The nature and number of her texts caused her to have a tremendous influence on the development of the genre we now recognize as the novel.

Haywood consistently wrote about the difficulties women had negotiating the real and symbolic economies that characterized the patriarchal society in which she lived and wrote. Her female characters, typically members of the middling classes, seek some kind of emotional and financial security, but often with disastrous consequences. Many fall victim to men who possess a consumer model of male sexuality. The seducer is sustained by the arousal and then deferral of desire, yet, once sated, it disappears completely. As Melladore in *The City Jilt* (1726) observes, "The very word Desire implies an Impossibility of continuing after the Enjoyment of that which first causes its being. Those Longings, those Impatiences so pleasing to your Sex, cannot but be lost in Possession, for who can wish for what he has already?"[3] Haywood's female characters who do succeed either learn to manipulate male desire to their advantage, or find a way to satisfy their own (sexual or financial) desires which cannot be accommodated by the culture in which they live. Haywood's texts usually possess a frank sexuality, offer alternative models for female behavior, and question some of the assumptions of the patriarchal culture. Yet she always claimed to offer instruction in her texts. As she wrote in the preface to *The Fair Hebrew; or, A True but Secret History of Two Jewish Ladies* (1729), "I found something so particular in the Story, and so much Room for the most useful and moral Reflections to be drawn from it, that I thought I should be guilty of an Injury to the Publick in concealing it. If among all who shall read the following Sheets, any one Person may reap so much Advantage as to avoid the Misfortunes the SUBJECT of...fell into by his Inadvertency, and giving a Loose to Passion; the

1 Blouch, "Eliza Haywood," xxxii.
2 *The Injur'd Husband; or, the Mistaken Resentment* (London: 1723).
3 *The City Jilt; or, the Alderman turn'd Beau: A Secret History* in *Selected Fiction and Drama of Eliza Haywood,* ed. Paula R. Backscheider (New York and Oxford: Oxford UP, 1999) 93.

Little Pains I have been at, will be infinitely recompens'd."[1] These texts and their tremendous popularity created anxiety in some of her male contemporaries who resisted both her alternative constructions of female sexuality and the communities of readers her texts created. The most stunning example of this cultural anxiety is Pope's representation of Haywood in the 1728 *Dunciad*,[2] which solidified her authorial persona as a scandalous female scribbler.

After consistent success and continued publication in the 1720s, Haywood changed the direction of her career in the 1730s focusing more on theatrical and political writing and diminishing the amount of fiction she produced. However, as Blouch notes, nothing "took Haywood very far away from the linked theatrical and literary communities she had inhabited from the start."[3] Previously critics have attributed Haywood's move away from fiction in the 1730s to the negative effects of Pope's excoriating representation of her in the *Dunciad*; yet Haywood worked steadily during the first part of the 1730s trying to capitalize on the growing market for political and theatrical material which were her focus during the decade.[4] She and her

---

1   *The Fair Hebrew; or, a True but Secret History of Two Jewish Ladies* (London: 1729).

2   Pope represents Haywood as a "shameless scribbler," and describes her as follows:

> "See in the circle next, Eliza placed,
> Two babes of love close clinging to her waist;
> Fair as before her works she stands confessed,
> In flowers and pearls by bounteous Kirkall dressed ...
> ... yon Juno of majestic size,
> With cow-like udders, and with ox-like eyes."

His footnote mentions her "profligate licentiousness" and "most scandalous books" and describes her as one of those "shameless scribblers (for the most part of That sex, which ought least to be capable of such malice or impudence) who in libellous Memoirs and Novels, reveal the faults and misfortunes of both sexes, to the ruin of publick fame, or disturbance of private happiness" (Alexander Pope, *The Dunciad* [1728] Book II: 157-64, *The Poems of Alexander Pope: Volume V, The Dunciad*, ed. James Sutherland [London: Methuen, 1952] 119).

3   Blouch, "Introduction," li.

4   While Haywood did have an interruption in her literary production, which Patrick Spedding dates from June 1736 to the publication of *Anti-Pamela* in June 1741, it was certainly not attributable to Pope's commentary. In the *Bibliography of Eliza Haywood*, Spedding attributes

long-time companion William Hatchett had a changing sense of the marketplace and a sustained, if unrealized, desire to have an effect on it. Haywood worked collaboratively with Hatchett as an actress and as a co-author on their successful *Opera of Operas* (1733), which had its genesis in Fielding's *Tom Thumb; or Tragedy of Tragedies* (1730). Haywood and Fielding also clearly had a professional relationship during this period. They both worked in the same highly political, highly satirical theatrical milieu (though Fielding with far greater success). They also shared a profound resistance to prime minister Robert Walpole who was the focus of much of their published work. Additionally, a benefit performance of Fielding's *Historical Register* was held for "Mrs. Haywood the Muse, Author of Love in Excess, and many other entertaining Pieces" on May 23, 1737.[1] Despite Haywood's later comments in *Betsy Thoughtless* (1752) describing the Little Theatre in the Haymarket as Fielding's "scandal shop," their professional lives, if informed by competition, also contained mutual respect and collaboration, particularly in their anti-Walpole efforts. "As exchanges conducted without real invective, at least relative to the period's norms," writes Blouch, "the mutual satires can also be seen as mutually beneficial" (1:lxii). Their relationship suggests how the two authors, despite different styles in terms of both prose and the nature of their satire (although Haywood clearly is more Fieldingesque that Richardsonian), shared an ability to recognize a commercially viable product, manipulate the possibilities of the marketplace, and object to the values and social vision offered by *Pamela*.

Haywood had a finely tuned commercial sensibility that was honed further when she opened her own book-selling shop in 1741 at the Sign of Fame under the Great Piazza in Covent Garden, a venture through which she seemingly sought a greater sense

---

this interruption or "gap" to illness. Dr. Spedding generously shared his manuscript with me and provided me with invaluable information.

1 *The London Stage, 1660-1800; a Calendar of Plays, Entertainments & Afterpieces, together with Casts, Box-receipts and Contemporary Comment. Volume 1, pt. 3. 1729-1747*, edited with a critical introd. by A.H. Scouten (Carbondale: Southern Illinois UP, 1960-68; Part 3, 1960) 674.

of control over her own professional situation.[1] A female bookseller with a small shop would have operated on a very low rung of the print trade; Haywood would not have held copyrights or functioned as a publisher; rather she would likely have had a small stall where she sold a variety of goods ranging from paper products and patent medicines to pamphlets and other printed texts. Operating her shop in Covent Garden, Haywood, notes Patrick Spedding, "would probably also be selling risqué pamphlets, erotic and pornographic prints, as well as 'cundums' and less effective contraceptives."[2] Additionally, Haywood would possibly have been responsible for the assembly of some of the texts herself. For example, after Haywood's 1749 arrest because of an allegedly seditious pamphlet that she wrote, distributed, and sold, her servant, when deposed, detailed how she and Haywood received the pamphlets "in sheets" at Haywood's lodgings, where they "stiched the said sheets into books and ... delivered them to the shops." [3] Haywood was materially as well as imaginatively involved in the production of her texts.

The professional situation Haywood found herself in informs *Anti-Pamela*. Geographically, Haywood was centered in the Covent Garden area, a vital if increasingly disreputable commercial site in

---

1 For a discussion of Haywood's bookselling shop, see Blouch, Spedding, and Ingrassia. See also Patrick Spedding, "Shameless Scribbler or Votary of Virtue? Eliza Haywood, Writing (and) Pornography in 1742," in *Women Writing 1550-1750*, special issue of *Meridian* 18.1 (2001): 237-251. Of course Haywood's heightened awareness of the needs of the marketplace did not necessarily translate into sustained commercial success. "Authors," writes James Raven, "were the very last participants to benefit from the eighteenth-century book bonanza." *Judging New Wealth: Popular Publishing and Responses to Commerce in England, 1750-1800* (Oxford: Clarendon Press, 1992) 60. Throughout her career Haywood alternately drove and chased the market.

2 Spedding, 242. Spedding also speculates that she might have sold her partner William Hatchett's pornographic poem, *Chinese Tale*, published in 1740 (244).

3 PRO SP 36/111 f.213. For a further discussion of Haywood's arrest, see Thomas Lockwood, "Eliza Haywood in 1749: *Dalinda*, and Her Pamphlet on the Pretender," *Notes and Queries* n.s. 36 (1989): 475-77; and Ingrassia, *Authorship, Commerce, and Gender*, 116-128. For more details about women's participation in multiple aspects of the print trade, see Paula McDowell, "Women and the Business of Print" in *Women and Literature in Britain, 1700-1800*, 135-154.

which Syrena spends much of her time. Socially, Haywood existed on the margins or the fringes; as a woman who lived outside the constructed norms of patriarchal culture (as a writer, a bookseller, and a single woman) she skirted the edges of respectability. Though she worked in the book trade, she was unable to fully break into a male culture that was enabled by male friendships and pre-established social relationships. Culturally—as a writer in a commercial marketplace and as a woman forced to support herself—she had a keen awareness of the simultaneous need and difficulty for women to find meaningful work beyond trading on their sexuality (as marriage and prostitution forced them to do). But she also, clearly, was familiar with the kinds of work women had to perform regularly. Whether stitching her pamphlets, tending to her shop, writing any number of texts, or performing unrecorded domestic labors, she existed in a world where women's work is more extensive (and, often, more difficult to escape). It is not surprising that *Anti-Pamela* is so detailed in its depiction of work (as well as its discussion of money) for surely Haywood, of the three authors, had the keenest understanding of women's work and its expectations and limitations.

Though evidence exists that Haywood continued to operate her shop through the decade, clearly it was not enough to sustain her for she wrote consistently during the 1740s. Her chameleon-like ability to change registers rhetorically enabled her to capitalize on the apparent shift in public tastes and to use an event like *Pamela* to publish at least three distinctly different texts that attempted to profit from its appeal. In addition to *Anti-Pamela*, she wrote two "virtuous texts": *A Present for a Servant-Maid* (1743), a conduct book designed for serving girls (see Appendix A), and *The Virtuous Villager; or, Virgin's Victory* (1742), a translation/adaptation of *La Paysanne parvenue; ou les memoires de Madame la Marquise de L.V.* (1735-7) by Charles de Fieux Mouhy which was inspired by *Pamela*. Additionally, as Patrick Spedding has recently detailed, during this period of 1742-3 Haywood also published a translation of Crebillon fils's erotic novel *Le Sopha, conte moral*, a text her contemporaries would have considered pornography. (Horace Walpole described it as "admirable."[1]) The constellation of these four texts demonstrates Haywood's ability to be something of a discursive contortionist who could manipulate her skills to fit the appropriate niche markets. Haywood was also commercially opportunistic; for

1   Spedding, 241

example, as Peter Sabor suggests, she likely appropriated the title *Anti-Pamela* after an advertisement appeared announcing the future publication of *Memoirs of the Life of Mr. James Parry ... being the Anti-Pamela of Monmouthshire* by James Parry. When Haywood's text appeared, Parry published his own work eleven days later under the title *The True Anti-Pamela: or, Memoirs of Mr. James Parry*.[1]

Anti-Pamela

Like *Shamela*, *Anti-Pamela* is an antidote to *Pamela*'s representation of virtue, chastity, and sexual deferral. As Sabor observes, *Anti-Pamela* offers "numerous telling allusions to scenes and incidents from the earlier work" that skillfully re-present "such episodes to [Haywood's] own ends."[2] Throughout, *Anti-Pamela* admonishes the reader against excessive credulity; for example, the title-page claims to teach young men how to resist the snares of women like Syrena: "Publish'd as a necessary Caution to all Young Gentlemen ... A Narrative which has really its Foundation in Truth and Nature; and at the same time that it entertains ... arms again a partial Credulity, by shewing the Mischiefs that frequently arise from a too sudden Admiration." Haywood seems to be offering a cautionary tale to the women—and men—who misread not only *Pamela* but her earlier fiction as well. *Anti-Pamela* suggests from the beginning that all emotions can be feigned, and uncalculated behavior may not exist; Haywood cautions her readers from relying too heavily on their immediate interpretation, urging, instead, that they never take anything at face value.

The interrogation of the presumed motivation of individuals' behavior is just one aspect of *Anti-Pamela*'s didacticism. The text serves as a kind of anti-conduct book or, perhaps, a conduct book for women interested in transgressing convention. Although the novel contains repeated asides that point out the errors Syrena makes, it also provides detailed information on all sorts of practical if unauthorized behavior: how to navigate sites of sexual commerce; how to feign virtue; how to carry on an affair; how to procure an abortion; how to bail a lover out of debtor's prison; how to calculate financial remuneration for a sexual encounter. If Richard-

---

1 Peter Sabor, "Introduction," *The Pamela Controversy: Criticisms and Adaptations of Samuel Richardson's Pamela, 1740-1750*, volume 2, xi. I am grateful to Dr. Sabor for sharing a copy of this introduction.
2 Sabor, xv.

son tutors readers on preserving virtue within a confined domestic space, Haywood extols the virtue of practical knowledge within a complicated urban environment. *Anti-Pamela* is a complex novel that offers an alternative didacticism that teaches cunning, duplicity and, ultimately, self-sufficiency within the treacherous financial and sexual economies women confront.

Anti-Pamela details the adventures of the fifteen-year old Syrena Tricksy who has been raised, from a young age, to believe that she can make her living through the financial gains she can obtain from men; she has been "bred up" in the notion "that a woman who had Beauty to attract the Men, and Cunning to manage them afterwards, was secure of making her Fortune." With her impressive acting ability and the encouragement of her rapacious mother, Syrena engages in a series of relationships (few of them monogamous) with an eye to the financial gain or sexual satisfaction they could provide; "love" or sincere affection never enters the narrative. Syrena gains access to these men primarily through the various kinds of paid employment she must hold because of the "indigence" of her condition. Beginning as an apprentice in a mantua-maker's shop near Covent Garden, Syrena is immediately thrust into the commercial milieu of London. Haywood vividly represents the lived urban culture of eighteenth-century London. Indeed, *Anti-Pamela* is a kind of primer for the social topography of London (a primer Syrena herself could have used). In the colloquial language of the servants and the middling classes, Haywood writes specifically about food, clothing, parks, streets, taverns, and sites of public entertainment. At the beginning of the novel, Syrena can't distinguish between real gold and "pinchbeck" or false gold; by the end of the novel, she can forge letters, evaluate the quality of currency she receives, and recognize the elevated social rank of a Lord at a masquerade. She quickly learns the cultural codes of her complicated milieu.

As an apprentice, Syrena meets the soldier Vardine who uses her ignorance about London to seduce her easily in a private room in a tavern. After abandoning her apprenticeship in part because of a pregnancy that she terminates (with the help of her mother), and in part because she "could not endure the Apprehension of sitting all Day to run Seams," Syrena takes a position in the household of the Baronet Sir Thomas, as a reader to his mother-in-law. Syrena's interactions with Sir Thomas and his twenty-two year old son, Mr. L—— (who "rendered the Place extremely acceptable"), closely parallel *Pamela* in form and content. The fact that Haywood dispenses with this situation rather quickly suggests the limited appeal she saw in that kind of self-generated narrative. Both father and son make sexual overtures toward Syrena, though with different levels of aggression, and Haywood's representation of the situation makes it clear that no female servant was safe from the hazards of sexual harassment—or what Haywood, in another context, terms "Amorous Violence."[1] As Syrena's co-servant Mrs. Mary observes of Mr. L——, "what Designs can such a Gentleman have upon one of us, but to ruin us." Similarly, she describes Sir Thomas as a man who "loves a Girl in a corner." Syrena uses the situation to her advantage and receives financial proposals from Sir Thomas as well as becoming sexually involved with his son (who can't marry without his father's consent). Attempting to compel Mr. L—— to marry her, Syrena and her mother stage a scene of violence and level an accusation of rape. The authorities believe Syrena's story and imprison Mr. L—— until the discovery of a letter detailing the plot compels Syrena and her mother to go briefly to Greenwich before returning to London. While the episode parodies *Pamela* and illustrates Syrena's deceptive powers, it also, more powerfully, illustrates the awkward circumstance for many female domestics who simultaneously have to negotiate both household duties and predatory sexual advances by their employers.

After these two initial unprofitable encounters, Syrena has a series of relationships with men from whom she gains money, but with whom she ultimately can't sustain a relationship. In Haywood's previous fiction, men abandoned women because of their consistent need for new desires and new women. Now men fall prey to their own desires when confronted with a young woman like Syrena who, like an experienced member of the print trade, can successfully market herself to men who possess too much "credulity." Most of the men Syrena encounters are initially seduced by her seeming innocence and virtue. Yet every time Syrena approaches "success"—e.g. marriage or a financial settlement—her own sexual desires undermine her. For example, she successfully bilks thousands of pounds from the Mercer until he discovers she is supporting a lover when the two £50 notes he endorsed to her are used to repay her Gallant's debt to his tailor, the Mercer's close friend. An infatuated Mr. W—— hires Syrena as his housekeeper,

---

1 *Fantomina; or, Love in a Maze* (1724) in *Popular Fiction by Women 1660-1730, An Anthology*, ed. Paula R. Backscheider and John J. Richetti (Oxford: Oxford UP, 1996) 234.

proposes to her, and on the eve of their wedding discovers she's been having an affair with his son. Mr. D——, having fallen in love with Syrena, offers her continued financial support (though not marriage) until he discovers she indirectly contributed to the death of his fiancée and had an affair with a Portuguese merchant. In these relationships, the men do not escape without some cost. Indeed, all the relationships in *Anti-Pamela* demonstrate that all male-female relationships are based on exchange (primarily of a financial nature). As Mr. W—— observes to Syrena, "that Passion that makes us so liberal, makes us also desire something in return— we cannot content ourselves with rendering happy the Object of our Affections, but languish for something more than Gratitude . . . . as charming as you are, you will never find a Man who loves you for your own sake alone."

To that end, *Anti-Pamela* offers lessons in how to circulate sexually while reserving rather than squandering one's (financial and sexual) resources.[1] Syrena accumulates more than £2000 in the course of the novel; "had she liv'd in any frugal decorum, she might have sav'd sufficient to have made her easy for a long time." However, she ends up penniless because she and her mother spend relentlessly, "indulg[ing] themselves in everything they like"; "having nothing now to think on farther than indulging every Luxury." Though Syrena often gains her money through deception and deceit, the narrator remains relatively neutral about the "morality" of those actions. (Indeed, perhaps Haywood expected readers to question the morality of the men in the novel as much as she expected readers to consider Syrena's morals.) What seems more troubling to Haywood is Syrena's lack of self-discipline, her unabated consumer impulse, her misdirected self-interest, and her need for immediate gratification. Syrena, like Shamela, is led largely by her desires and her impulses. While perhaps a better actress than Shamela, and ultimately a more fully developed character, Syrena is ultimately no more successful in her pursuit of financial security. Syrena, like Shamela, is propelled by a relentless kind of multiply directed consumerism—sex, commercial goods, money, entertainment. In addition to actual money, the "cost" to Syrena is her abil-

---

1 For a more extended and slightly different discussion of *Anti-Pamela*, see Ingrassia, *Authorship, Commerce and Gender*, 110-116. See also, Scarlett Bowen, "'A Sawce-box and Boldface Indeed': Refiguring the Female Servant in the Pamela-AntiPamela Debate," *Studies in Eighteenth-Century Culture* 28 (1999): 257-85.

ity to circulate freely in the sites of social and commercial activity that potentially provide long-term associations with men. For example, after her false accusation of rape against Mr. L——, she must flee to Greenwich. After the death of Mr. D——'s fiancée, when Syrena's deception is fully revealed, he "wrote all the Particulars of this fatal Adventure, and desired it might be made publick." She leaves a trail of betrayed lovers until she "durst not go to Plays, Opera's, nor Concerts, because she very well knew, that there was seldom a Night but some or other of that Family she had so grossly imposed upon, were at those Diversions." Indeed, she must resort to attending public masquerades, a much less remunerative location that attracts more disparate groups of men. The masquerade requires an initial investment ("her Tickets, Dress, and Chair-Hire") yet will yield only short-term profits in the form of isolated sexual encounters for pay—a thinly veiled form of prostitution.

Anti-Pamela completely resists the trajectory of the narrative concluding in marriage that organizes much eighteenth-century fiction. Haywood's novel is also more pragmatic (what women have to do to try to earn money) and realistic (virtue is not indefinitely defendable nor, necessarily, should it be). As Syrena negotiates the spatial and social geography of the city, she discovers not only that her "charms" are alluring to men of all classes but that the hazards confronting a young woman are everywhere. The sites of consumer culture that drive England's burgeoning economy are also the sites of the sexual economy in which Syrena must trade. Though Haywood condemns Syrena's inability to save her money and resources, she also implicitly critiques the patriarchal culture where economic and sexual commerce are mutually reinforcing for men. For men, commercial activity provides the opportunity for a sexual union which, in turn, does not usually distract from economic productivity. Pleasure and business can be mutually reinforcing. For Syrena, and women like her, however, her "work" is to provide pleasure to the men she meets; the only kinds of pleasure she receives, either through extracurricular sexual unions or through acquiring consumer goods, ultimately distract her from her work. While I basically agree with Peter Sabor's observation that "Syrena is predator rather than prey,"[1] her predatory nature does not mitigate the effects of the sexual economy that, in the long run, will render women like Syrena—no matter how predatory—ultimately imper-

---

1 Sabor, xiii.

iled unless they gain a measure of financial (and social) security either through marriage or economic self-sufficiency.

By detailing sexualized and commercial interactions, Haywood implicitly critiques both the form and content of Richardson's novel. Haywood also largely abandons Richardson's epistolary form. This shift provides the opportunity for Haywood, a more experienced novelist, to construct a more expansive narrative that is not constrained by the perspective of only one character. When she does use letters, they appear strategically to parody *Pamela*, to advance the plot, or to illustrate either the rapidity of urban postal delivery or the precarious nature of mail delivery to the country. Additionally, the shift in narrative form underscores Haywood's recognition that a servant, no matter how privileged, would never have the time to write so many letters. Indeed, Haywood is much more savvy and realistic in her representation of women's employment and the sexual vulnerability of female servants. With few ways to support themselves independently, women were financially dependent on, and often sexually vulnerable to, those who had social or economic control over them. Underlying the entire novel, and all the work Syrena tries to do, is the fundamental problem facing all women—if they can't capitalize on their sexuality by securing marriage or a financial settlement, they must seek employment in a profoundly unstable market that, at base, does not reward employment for women.

By demonstrating that virtue, arguably Pamela's most pressing work, can be a performative signifier that women can strategically employ to their own ends, Haywood implicitly asks the reader to re-evaluate Pamela and Syrena as well. When Syrena and her mother feign thrift and frugality, which act as markers of feminine decorum, modesty and virtue, Haywood is ostensibly affirming the very gendered construction of female domestic virtue. However, she more profoundly demonstrates the superficiality and meaninglessness of those markets—they are signifiers that can be strategically appropriated and used.

Yet Syrena is not the only woman in *Anti-Pamela*. Syrena's mother, Mrs. Tricksy, "who had been a Woman of Intrigue in her Youth," is, to Haywood's mind, the "first seducer" of Syrena's virtue "by flattering that Pride and Vanity in her Nature, which without some extraordinary Providence, indeed, must render her an easy Prey to the first Temptation that offer'd itself." Just as Pamela's honest parents inculcated the value of virtue, so too Mrs. Tricksy endorsed the value of deception, self-interest, and vice—values she presumably learned from men. As examples from conduct manuals in Appendix D make clear, Mrs. Tricksy's behavior violates the expectations for a good parent. Mrs. Tricksy, Syrena's primary correspondent, is inextricably involved in Syrena's plots, advising her to "let your own Interest be your only Aim." Yet she also occasionally cautions prudence when Syrena's willfulness and sexual desires threaten to undermine her success: "I am far from being an Enemy to your Pleasures; but would have you be a *true Friend* to your *Interest*."

Just as *Pamela* has the "ruined" Sally Godfrey (a woman who succumbed to Mr. B.'s advances) who circulates as a cautionary tale about women who don't protect their virtue, so too *Anti-Pamela* has the obverse of Syrena in a (very) few "virtuous" women who fleetingly appear in the novel. However, in some respects, these women exist in compromised situations as well. For example Mr. D——'s fiancée Maria is a model of female devotion: "this Lady loved Mr. D—— with a Tenderness, which is rarely to be met with in these times of Gallantry ... her Virtue and Duty improving the Inclination she naturally had for him, she had never indulged herself in those Gaieties so many of her Sex are fond of." Yet after receiving Syrena's anonymous note that reveals his affair, she withdraws from everyone and, ultimately, dies. Her virtue and credulity prohibit successful circulation. Similarly, the Mercer's wife, who remains nameless, discovers her husband about to kill himself because his outlays for Syrena have put him deeply in debt. He describes his "guilty Commerce, concealing not the last Article of what he had done for Syrena." A truly virtuous woman, she forgives the adultery (since "there is no true *Penitence* without *Confession*"), offers him her jointure to pay his debts, and retires with him to the country when they conveniently receive an ample financial windfall.

Significantly, a woman "no less cunning, tho' more virtuous than herself," ultimately foils Syrena. Set up as Mr. E——'s mistress with an apartment and a present of £500, Syrena incurs the wrath of Mrs. E—— who arranges for her to be found in a compromising position with another married men, arrested for alienation of affection, and exiled to Wales by her family. While this resolution might, in part, be a marketing device for Haywood (who writes "what befell her, must be the Subject of future Entertainment"), it more powerfully serves as another rejoinder to Richardson. Pamela's narrative primarily records her self-described "captivity" at the hands of Mr. B.—she does not circulate, has few personal freedoms, and records largely her own thoughts. By contrast, Syrena's brief stint in

Newgate was "the first Captivity she had ever been in" and is a moment in the text that goes completely unrecorded. Syrena's ability to circulate (if unadvisedly), interact, and consume, comprise the bulk of Haywood's very lively and entertaining novel. The pointed language Haywood uses clearly suggests that captivity like Pamela's limits a narrative as much as it does an individual. While the text, ultimately, does not endorse Syrena's actions, it illustrates the various strategies women can use to negotiate a world defined by a sexual and financial economy largely controlled by men. Should female readers adopt Syrena's strategies? No, of course not. But they should recognize the dangers and desires of the men who court them, employ them, or, potentially, marry them. Should male readers assume every woman is a potential Syrena? No, but they should hold their credulity (and sexual desires) in check until they really know the individual with whom they're interacting.

Conclusion

Though more readers are probably familiar with *Shamela*, *Anti-Pamela* is an equally if not more significant text. Because it engages more deeply the central issues of the print trade and the novel generally, it has a readability and durability that arguably transcend the more topical, though no less amusing, *Shamela*. Both texts are responding to *Pamela* as well as to the amatory fiction of the 1720s, which made Richardson's text possible. Fielding finds Richardson's narrative implausible and, in its own way, as base and inappropriately low as the amatory fiction it claims to "overwrite" (to use William Warner's term). Indeed, it is potentially more dangerous than amatory fiction for, like Shamela herself, it disguises prurience in the clothes of didacticism. Haywood, whose work largely defined the genre of amatory fiction, deflates the appeal of the heterosexual union and sexuality it depicts. *Anti-Pamela* is, instead, a story of sexual commerce. Syrena negotiates the ephemerality of sexual desire and desirability while also seeking financial gain for her self. Haywood, like her male colleagues in the print trade, similarly depends on the transient nature of readers' desire, both in her response to Richardson's text and in her fiction generally. Each of these writers emerges from a different cultural position and each text is an important step in their process of professional reinvention. The dialogue within these three texts highlights the distinct lines of discourse that contribute to the development of the eighteenth-century novel.

Eliza Haywood and Henry Fielding: A Brief Chronology

1693 Eliza Haywood (née Fowler) born, probably in London

1707 April 22: Henry Fielding born at Sharpham Park, near Glastonbury, Somerset

1715 Haywood arrives at Theatre Royal, Smock Alley, Dublin
Performs Chloe in *Timon of Athens* in Dublin

1717 Haywood leaves Dublin, returns to London
Appears in *The Unhappy Favorite*, Lincoln's Inn Fields

1719 Haywood writes *Love in Excess; or, the Fatal Enquiry*, Parts One and Two.
Fielding begins Eton College

1720 Haywood writes *Love in Excess*, Part Three
Haywood writes *Letters from a Lady of Quality to a Chevalier*, translated from French

1721 Haywood's play, *The Fair Captive*, staged at Lincoln's Inn Fields; she appears in the production
Haywood becomes friends with Aaron Hill, meets Richard Savage

1722 Haywood writes *The British Recluse; or, the Secret History of Cleomira, Suppos'd Dead*, and *The Injur'd Husband; or, the Mistaken Resentment*

1723 Haywood writes *Idalia; or, the Unfortunate Mistress*, *Lasselia; or, the Self-Abandon'd*, and *The Rash Resolve; or, The Untimely Discovery*
Haywood's play, *A Wife to be Lett*, staged at Theatre Royal, Drury Lane
The Works of Mrs. Eliza Haywood, Vol. 1–3, published

1724 Fielding completes Eton; likely comes to London
The Works of Mrs. Eliza Haywood, Vol. 4, published
Haywood writes *The Arragonian Queen: A Secret History*, *Bath Intrigues*, *Le Belle Assemblée*, *Fantomina; or, Love in a Maze*, *The Fatal Secret; or, Constancy in Distress*, *The Force of Nature; or, The Lucky Disappointment*, *The Masqueraders; or Fatal Curiosity*, *Memoirs of the Baron de Brosse*, *Memoirs of a Certain Island*, *Poems on Several Occasions*, *Secret Histories*, *A Spy Upon the Conjurer*, *The Surprise; or, Constancy Rewarded*, and *The Tea-Table* (a periodical)

1725 Haywood writes *The Dumb Projector*, *The Fatal Fondness; or,*

Love its Own Opposer, The Lady's Philosophical Stone, Mary Stuart, Queen of Scots, The Tea-Table, and *The Unequal Conflict; or, Nature Triumphant.*

1726 Haywood writes *The City Jilt; or, the Alderman Turn'd Beau, Cleomelia; or, the Generous Mistress, The Distress'd Orphan; or, Love in a Mad-house, The Double Marriage; or, the Fatal Release, Letters from the Palace of Fame, The Mercenary Lover; or, the Unfortunate Heiress, Reflections on the Various Effects of Love,* and *The Secret History of the Present Intrigues of the Court of Caramania.*

1727 Haywood writes *The Fruitless Enquiry, The Life of Madame de Villesache, Love in its Variety, The Perplex'd Dutchess; or, Treachery Rewarded, Philidore and Placentia; or, L'Amour Trop Delicat,* and *Secret Histories, Novels &, c.* 2 vol.

1728 Fielding's first work published: *The Masquerade,* a Satiric Poem
Fielding's first play, *Love in Several Masques,* produced by Colley Cibber at Drury Lane
Fielding registers as student of literature at University of Leyden, Holland in March
Alexander Pope writes *The Dunciad,* in which Haywood is attacked
Haywood writes *The Agreeable Caledonian; or, Memoirs of Signoriora di Morella, Irish Artifice; or The History of Clarina* (appeared in *The Female Dunciad,* published by Edmund Curll), *The Padlock; or, No Award without Virtue,* and *Persecuted Virtue; or, The Cruel Lover*

1729 Haywood publishes *The Fair Hebrew, The Agreeable Caledonian* (part 2), *The Disguis'd Prince; or the Beautiful Parisian,* and *The City Widow; or, Love in a Butt*
Haywood's play, *Frederick, Duke of Brunswicke-Lunenburg* produced at Lincoln's Inn Fields
Fielding discontinues studies in April and returns to London

1730 Fielding begins theatrical career in earnest, writing comedies for Little Haymarket including *The Author's Farce, Tom Thumb,* and *Rape upon Rape*
Haywood appears in William Hatchett's *The Rival Father* at Little Haymarket
Haywood writes *Love-Letters on All Occasions Lately Passed Between Persons of Distinction*

1732 Fielding writes *The Modern Husband* and *The Lottery*
Haywood writes *Secret Memoirs of the Late Duncan Campbell*

1733   Fielding writes *The Miser*
       Haywood writes *The Opera of Operas*, a musical adaptation
       of Fielding's *Tragedy of Tragedies* (1731), with William
       Hatchett
1734   Haywood writes *L'Entretien des Beaux Esprits, Being the
       Sequel to La Belle Assemblée*
1735   Haywood writes *The Dramatic Historiographer, or The British
       Theatre Delineated*
1736   Haywood writes *The Adventures of Eovaai*, an anti–Walpole
       satire
1737   March: Haywood appears in *A Rehearsal of Kings*, at Little
       Haymarket
       April: Haywood appears in *The Female Free Mason,* at Little
       Haymarket
       21 June: Theatre Licensing Act is passed, ending Fielding's
       theatrical career (and, essentially, Haywood's)
       November: Fielding begins studying law at the Middle
       Temple, London
1739   Fielding begins editing *The Champion*; continues until June
       1741
1740   20 June: Fielding called to the bar at the Middle Temple
       6 November: Samuel Richardson publishes *Pamela; or Virtue
       Rewarded*
1741   Haywood opens book-selling shop at the Sign of Fame in
       Covent Garden
       2 April: *An Apology for the Life of Mrs. Shamela Andrews*
       published
       16 June: Haywood writes and publishes *Anti-Pamela*
       Fielding stops editing *The Champion*
       Fielding publishes *The Opposition*
1742   Fielding writes *Joseph Andrews*
       Haywood writes and publishes *The Virtuous Villager*
1743   Fielding writes *A Journey from this World to the Next* and
       Jonathan Wild
       Haywood writes and publishes *A Present for a Servant-
       Maid*
1744   Haywood writes the monthly periodical *The Female
       Spectator*; it runs until 1746
       Haywood writes *The Fortunate Foundlings*
1745   Fielding edits *The True Patriot,* supporting the Hanoverian
       cause
1746   Haywood writes the weekly periodical *The Parrot,* which

comments on the trials and execution of leaders of failed Jacobite Rebellion of 1745

1747 Haywood writes *Memoirs of a Man of Honour*
Fielding edits *The Jacobite's Journal* until November 1748

1748 Haywood writes *Life's Progress Through the Passions; or, The Adventures of Natura*. Begins *Epistles for the Ladies* (monthly periodical Nov. 1748 – May 1749).
Fielding commissioned as justice of the peace for the district of Westminster, London

1749 Fielding writes *Tom Jones*
Haywood writes *Dalinda; or, The Double Marriage*
Haywood writes, publishes, and likely distributes *A Letter from H—— G——, Esq.*, a pamphlet about the Pretender

1750 Haywood is arrested for seditious libel

1751 Haywood writes *The History of Miss Betsy Thoughtless*
Haywood writes *The Tatler Revived*, a periodical
Fielding writes *An Enquiry into the Causes of the Late Increase of Robbers*
Fielding writes *Amelia*

1752 Fielding edits *The Covent-Garden Journal*
Fielding writes *Examples of the Interposition of Providence in the Detection and Punishment of Murder*

1753 Haywood writes *The History of Jemmy and Jenny Jessamy*
Haywood writes *Modern Characters*
Fielding writes *A Proposal for Making an Effectual Provision for the Poor*

1754 Fielding travels to Lisbon (June–August) and writes *The Journal of a Voyage to Lisbon*, published posthumously (1755)
8 October: Fielding dies
Haywood writes *The Invisible Spy, by "Exploribus"* (4 vol.)

1755 Haywood writes *The Wife*

1756 Haywood writes *The Husband. In Answer to the Wife*
Haywood writes *The Young Lady*
25 February: Haywood dies

A Note on the Text

The first edition and so-called second edition (actually a second imprint) of *Anti-Pamela* are essentially identical. This text is based on the "second edition." *Shamela* is based on the second edition of Fielding's text. In both texts, as well as in any eighteenth-century material used in the appendices, original punctuation, capitalization, and spelling (except for obvious typographical errors) have been retained. Eighteenth-century spelling was not standardized, so departures from modern spelling exist. Both texts, particularly *Anti-Pamela*, have a lot of colloquial language that gives the flavor of the servant classes in which the characters circulate. Additionally, the texts contain extensive references to food, geographic locations, and social customs that might not be immediately recognizable to the general reader. In glossing the texts, I have tried to provide information to make the material world of 1741 more accessible.

No modern, annotated edition of *Anti-Pamela* has previously been published. However, a number of excellent editions of *Shamela* exist and I have been aided particularly by the previous editorial work of Homer Goldberg, Martin Battestin, Sheridan W. Baker, Jr., and Douglas Brooks-Davies. Some standard sources used consistently throughout the footnotes are referenced with the abbreviations below. All references to *Pamela* are to the 1740 edition, edited by Thomas Keymer and Alice Wakely (London: Oxford UP, 2001). I have cited this readily available edition to enable students to easily read further in that originating text.

Partridge	Eric Partridge, *A Dictionary of Slang and Unconventional English* (New York: Macmillan, 1970).
Johnson	Samuel Johnson, *A Dictionary of the English Language* (London: 1756).
OED	*Oxford English Dictionary* (Oxford: Oxford UP, 1993)
Female Spectator	Eliza Haywood, *Selected Works of Eliza Haywood*, Set II, Volumes 2 and 3, *The Female Spectator*, edited by Kathryn King and Alexander Pettit (London: Pickering and Chatto, 2001).
Battestin	Martin C. Battestin, *Joseph Andrews/Shamela* (Boston: Houghton Mifflin, 1961).
Goldberg	Homer Goldberg, *Joseph Andrews/ Shamela* (New York: Norton, 1987).

Porter   Roy Porter, *English Society in the Eighteenth Century*, revised second edition (London: Penguin, 1990).

Other citations appear with bibliographic references in the notes.

A Note on British Money

A variety of British units of currency are mentioned in *Shamela* and *Anti-Pamela*, and they can be divided into gold and silver. The silver currency includes pounds, shillings, and pence, and most divisions of the same. When a character receives coins, they are generally silver coins; typically, a character notes otherwise.

A pound, originally a pound weight of silver, has the value of 20 shillings or 240 pence. It is denoted by an £ before the numeral or by *l.* after it. A shilling, denoted by an *s,* has the value of 12 pence. A pence has the value of 1/12 of a shilling, or 1/240 of a pound; it is denoted by a *d* (for *denarius*) or a *p*. Though the coining of silver pennies for general circulation ceased with the reign of Charles II (1685), silver pence were still in circulation. Halfpence and farthings (a quarter of a pence) were chiefly silver coins, although copper currency in these denominations was in circulation after 1688. A half-crown, also silver, has the value of two shillings and sixpence (2s 6d).

The texts also mention gold coins such as guineas and "broad pieces." A guinea is an old English coin worth 21s. First produced in 1663 with the normal value of 20s, its value was subsequently fixed at 21s—that is a shilling more than a pound. A half-guinea is a gold coin worth 10s 6d. "Broad piece" is the name applied after 1663 to the "Unite" or 20 shilling gold piece made in the earlier part of the seventeenth century. The term refers to the coin's appearance, which was much broader and thinner than the newly minted gold guineas.

In addition to actual currency, the texts also discuss bills of exchange and bank notes, which operate differently. Both of these fall under the category of what was known as "paper credit." A bill of exchange is basically a promissory note between two people — a written order by the writer or "drawer" to the "drawee" (the individual to whom it is addressed) to pay a certain sum on a given date to the "drawer" or the a third person named in the bill, known as the "payee." A bank note is a promissory note issued by a bank payable at a fixed date and to a specified person. Such bills are negotiable, but, in the strict sense of the term, are not currency *per se*. Yet they do provide a kind of narrative of financial (and personal) relationships through the series of names that appear on the bill.

ANTI-PAMELA;
OR,
Feign'd Innocence detected;

In a SERIES of

SYRENA's ADVENTURES.

A NARRATIVE which has really its Foundation in Truth and
Nature; and at the same time that it entertains, by a vast variety of surprising Incidents, arms against a partial Credulity, by
shewing the Mischiefs that frequently arise from a too sudden Admiration.

Publish'd as a necessary Caution to all Young Gentlemen.

Fatally fair they are, and in their Smiles
The Graces, little Loves, and young Desires inhabit;
But all that gaze upon them are undone;
For they are false, luxurious in their Appetites,
And all the Heaven they hope for is Variety.
One Lover to another still succeeds;
Another, and another after that,
And the last Fool is welcome as the former;
Till having lov'd his Hour out, he gives his Place,
And mingles with the Herd that went before him.

ROWE's Fair Penitent.[1]

LONDON:

Printed for *J. Huggonson*, in *Sword-and-Buckler-Court*, over
against the *Crown-Tavern* on *Ludgate-Hill*.

M.DCC.XLI.[2]

---

1 These lines are spoken by Horatio at the end of Act I (lines 382-391) in
  Nicholas Rowe's *The Fair Penitent* (1703).
2 Haywood published the first edition of *Anti-Pamela* on June 16, 1741.
  The "second edition," published October 29, 1741, is in fact a second
  issue of the first edition. The colophon reads: "F. Cogan, near Temple
  Bar." The text was reissued with a new title-leaf, doubtless in an effort to
  increase prospective sales, but the collation, contents, and motto are
  exactly the same. I am grateful to Patrick Spedding for sharing the MS
  of his *Bibliography of Eliza Haywood* (Pickering and Chatto, 2004).

Anti-Pamela,

OR,
MOCK-MODESTY
Display'd and Punish'd.

Syrena was a Girl, who even in her Cradle gave the promise of being
one of the compleatest Beauties of the Age: As her Years encreas'd,
and her Features grew more settled, her Loveliness encreased in Proportion; but what was most to be admired in her was, that the Innocence which is inseparable from Infancy, and which is so charming,
even in the plainest Children, never forsook her Countenance; but
continued to dwell in every little Turn and Gesture long after she
came to Maturity, and had been guilty of Things, which one would
think should have given her the boldest and most audacious Air.

Her Mother, though in very mean Circumstances, when she was
born, flatter'd herself with great Things, from the growing Beauties of
her sweet Babe; and tho' she had other Children, this alone engross'd
her whole Attention: I say her Mother, for her Father, at least him,
whom the Law would have obliged to own her,[1] died soon after she
came into the World; and was incapable of receiving any share either
in the Profits or Disgrace of our little *Syrena's* future Conduct.

Being therefore left entirely to the Care of a Parent, who had
been a Woman of Intrigue[2] in her Youth, was far from repenting
what she had done; and one of the most subtil Mistresses in the Art
of Decoying that ever was; the Girl was not out of her Bib and
Apron,[3] before she instructed her in Lessons, which she had the
wicked Satisfaction to find, her Pupil knew not only how to
observe, but also to improve.

---

1   That is to say, Mrs. Tricksy's husband.

2   A clandestine illicit intimacy between a man and a woman, a liaison of
    sorts. This appellation marks Mrs. Anne Tricksy as a woman of dubious
    reputation.

3   Bibs and aprons were common for boys under the age of three and girls
    until the age of about twelve. "The wearing of an apron without a bib
    was another sign of growing up," writes Anne Buck, "but bib and apron
    was dress wear for younger girls" (*Clothes and the Child: A Handbook of
    Children's Dress in England 1500-1900* [New York: Homes and Meier,
    1996] 190). As Clare Rose notes, "Bibbed aprons shared the symbolic
    role of leading strings" (*Children's Clothes Since 1750* [London: B.T. Bats-
    ford Limited, 1989] 35).

She had not reach'd her thirteenth Year, before she excell'd the most experienc'd Actresses on the Stage, in a lively assuming all the different Passions that find Entrance in a Female Mind. Her young Heart affected with imaginary Accidents (such as her Mother, from time to time, suggested to her might possibly happen) gave her whole Frame Agitations adapted to the Occasion, her Colour would come and go, her Eyes sparkle, grow Languid, or overflow with Tears, her Bosom heave, her Limbs tremble; she would fall into Faintings, or appear transported, and as it were out of herself; and all this so natural, that had the whole College of Physicians[1] been present, they could not have imagin'd it otherwise than real.

Thus was she train'd up to deceive and betray all those whom her Beauty should allure; but she had not so soon as she wish'd an Opportunity of discovering how well she should behave, when what had yet only been Ideal, should come to be real Matter of Fact; for being very little of her Age, the Men took no farther Notice of her, than to say she was an exceeding pretty Miss—a very fine Girl—that she'd soon be a delicate Creature, and such like Compliments, that were nothing to the Purpose at present.

About this Time several of her Mother's Relations, as she had some that lived well, and in good Repute; knowing the Indigence of their Condition, and that they were obliged frequently to have recourse to them, for even the common Necessaries of Life;[2] began to ask what was intended to be done with *Syrena*, for the other Children were all taken away by the Friends[3] of one side or the other; to which finding no determinate Answer, they advised the Mother, to put her to a Milliner or Mantua-maker, tho' the latter they seem'd to think most proper; not only because there required no Stock to set up with, when her Apprenticeship should be expired; but because also they thought that in that Business, having to deal only with Persons of her own Sex, she would be exempt from those Temptations, her Youth and Beauty might expose her to in the Millinary Way. One of these Gentlewomen

---

1 Original text reads "Phycians." The College of Physicians was a chartered professional corporation founded in 1518 that officially licensed doctors who could then legally practice 'physick' in London. It had only 45 members in 1745, evidence of its function as what Roy Porter terms a "closed, oligarchic monopoly" (75).
2 Indispensable, essential or requisite. For Mrs. Tricksy to seek such from her relatives, she is very indigent indeed.
3 Kinsmen or near relations; to seek financial support or to place children in the families of relatives was certainly not unusual.

was so good, as to promise she would give Fifteen or Twenty Pounds with her to a Mistress she should approve.[1] The Mother durst not refuse so kind an Offer, and assured her generous Kinswoman she would enquire about it; but as this was not the manner in which she desired to dispose of *Syrena*, she still found excuses to evade the Matter, and pretended she could not hear of any fit Place.

As there seem'd no room to suspect the Truth of what she said, or that a Parent would not be glad her Child should be in a way of getting a handsome Living; this truly honest and worthy Friend, took upon herself the trouble of looking out for a Mistress, and in a short time was inform'd of one who had very great Business, and was a Woman of a sober and unblemish'd Character. The Mother of *Syrena* had no Objections to make, the Terms between them was soon agreed upon, and the Girl was to go one Month upon Trial; after which the Indenture was to be made, and the Money paid[2] by the

---

1 A milliner sold a wide array of women's clothing and attracted clients of both sexes; a mantua-maker was essentially a dressmaker and catered primarily to women. The clothing trade was second only to domestic service in employing women (Beverly Lemire, *Dress, Culture and Commerce: The English Clothing Trade before the Factory, 1600-1800* [London: Macmillan, 1997] 50). As Ivy Pinchbeck notes, "millinery and mantua-making were the most favored occupations for those in the class 'a little above the vulgar'" (*Women Workers and the Industrial Revolution 1750-1850* [London: Virago, 1981; originally published 1930] 289). Millinery was the most prestigious of all the women's trades and generally attracted women "with capital and some social standing" (Pinchbeck 287). The premium for a seven-year apprenticeship in a milliner's shop could be very high, but was usually around £40, and it subsequently required a large amount of money to "set up" a shop after the apprenticeship— between £100 and 1000, with £400-500 being the average. By contrast, a mantua-maker required a five-year apprenticeship and the fees varied but averaged about the £20 Syrena's family is willing to pay. Mantua-makers had the reputation for paying poor wages; the gender of the employees and the high number of applicants to both trades made low wages inevitable. While Syrena's aims are higher, her family resembles the "aspiring parents of the middle class" for whom, as Bridget Hill details, "these trades represented some possibility of social advancement for their daughters" (*Women, Work and Sexual Politics in Eighteenth-Century England* [Oxford: Basil Blackwell, 1989] 85).

2 The indenture is the contract by which an apprentice is bound to the master who undertakes to teach him or her a trade; the "money paid" is the premium provided to establish the individual in the apprenticeship after the probationary period of one month has passed.

good Gentlewoman,[1] who had taken all this Pains, out of a conscientious regard for the Preservation of a young Creature, who she thought deserv'd it; and who might otherwise be drawn into those Snares, too often laid for Youth and Innocence; especially where there is an Indigence of Circumstances, and which a much better Education than could be expected the poor *Syrena* had been blest with, is not always a sufficient Guard again.

Syrena, who had always been sooth'd with the hopes of living grand, either by Marriage, or a Settlement from some Man of Condition,[2] could not endure the Apprehension of sitting all Day to run Seams;[3] nor was her Mother better pleased at this putting her Girl out of Fortune's way, as she call'd it; but as she resolv'd it should not be for any Continuance,[4] she was the more easy, and made the other so too. Care was to be taken however not to disoblige their Benefactress, and they both affected the highest Gratitude to her, and Satisfaction in what, indeed, was most irksome to them.

Here one cannot forbear reflecting, how shocking it is, when those who should point out the Paths of Virtue, give a wrong Bent to the young and unform'd Mind, and turn the pliant Disposition to Desires unworthy of it; but more especially so in Parents, who seem ordain'd by Heaven and Nature, to instil the first Principles for the future Happiness of those to whom they have given Being; and tho' we cannot suppose there are many, who like the Mother of *Syrena*, breed their Children up with no other Intent than to make them the Slaves of Vice, yet if we look into the World, and consider the number of *unfortunate Women* (as they justly call themselves) I believe we shall find the Miseries these poor Creatures undergo, and frequently involve others in, less owing to their own Inclinations, than to the too great Indulgence and false Tenderness of their

---

1 A woman of good birth or breeding. With this socially marked term, Haywood is signaling the relatively high status of Syrena's near relations, which is underscored by the amount they can afford for her apprenticeship.

2 A settlement is the act of settling property upon a person or persons; in this case, Syrena hopes to become a man's mistress and so be set for life with a large amount of money. A man of condition was a man of wealth, rank, or status.

3 Sewing or "running seams" was obviously a central—and labor intensive—task of a female apprentice in the clothing trade who, during the high season, might work as many as 18-20 hours a day.

4 Duration of time.

Parents; who flattering themselves that by breeding them like Gentlewomen, and setting them forth to the utmost of their Abilities, and often beyond, they shall be able to make their Fortune by Marriage; give them Ideas no way to their Advantage. What Compassion is due to a Mother, who having no Portion to give her Daughter, shall fill her Head with Notions of Quality; give Half a Crown[1] for the cutting her Hair, when perhaps half the Money must serve the whole Family for a Dinner; make her wear Gloves, Night and Day, and scarce suffer her to wash a Tea-Cup for fear of spoiling her Hands;[2] when such one, I say, shall cry out Daughter is undone, and exclaim against the cruel Man that has robb'd her of her Child; who can avoid accusing her as the first Seducer of the Girl's Virtue, by flattering that Pride and Vanity in her Nature, which without some extraordinary Providence, indeed, must render her an easy Prey to the first Temptation that offer'd itself.[3] But as this is an Observation, that must occur to every thinking Person, I ought to beg my Reader's Pardon for the Digression, and return.

The Day prefix'd for the Departure of *Syrena*, the good-natur'd Kinswoman came and took her up in a Hackney-Coach[4] with her Mother, who it was thought proper should go with her, and a Trunk

---

1 Crown, in commerce, is a general name for coins both foreign and domestic, of or near the value of five shillings sterling. Crowns were so called because originally they bore the imprint of a crown. Its value can be gleaned by the fact that a ½ crown could "serve the whole family for a dinner."

2 Soft, white hands marked a woman who did not have to perform domestic labor. Gloves with a softening ointment would be worn at night. For example in Jonathan Swift's "The Lady's Dressing Room" (1732), Celia wears "night-gloves made of Tripsy's hide, /Bequeathed by Tripsy when she died" (lines 30-31).

3 In *The Female Spectator*, Haywood warns of the dangers of overpraising a daughter: such speeches "poison the Mind of the poor Girl, and make her think there is nothing she has to take Care on, but to embellish her Person, so that her better Part is wholly neglected, and every Precept for improving the Mind grows irksome to her Ear, and makes not the least Impression in her Heart" (*The Female Spectator*, Volume 4, *Selected Works of Eliza Haywood, Set II, Volume 3*, ed. Kathryn King and Alexander Pettit [London: Pickering and Chatto, 2001] 380). For an example of cultural expectations for parents, especially mothers, see Appendix D.

4 A four-wheeled, enclosed vehicle kept for hire, drawn by two horses with seats for six people.

with a few Cloaths in it; which the other looking over, told her, it should be better fill'd if she was a good Girl, and behaved herself well. I hope Madam, answer'd the young Dissembler,[1] I shall never do any thing to forfeit the Favour of so kind, so generous a Relation; and if I could be capable of any Pride, it would be to carry myself so, that the Mistress I am going to, should give you such a Character of me, as would convince you I am not unworthy of your Favours. This Speech, accompanied with a thousand modest Graces, so charm'd the Person it was address'd to, that she took her in her Arms, and said, I have not the least doubt about me, that you will deserve much more Encouragement than is in my power to give; but, added she, you may be assur'd I will do all I can. Many such like Expressions of Kindness on the one side, and Gratitude on the other, pass'd between them till they got to the end of their little Journey, where they were very handsomely receiv'd and entertained by *Syrena*'s intended Mistress; and our young Hypocrite so well acted her Part, affecting to be highly pleas'd with the Place and Person she was to be with, and testifying no farther Regret at parting from her Mother, than just so much as served to shew her Duty and Affection, that she was look'd upon as a Prodigy of Sweetness and Prudence.

Thus was she enter'd on a new Stage of Life; but in what Manner she was used, and her Behaviour in it, can be no way so well represented, as by her own Letters to her Mother; the first of which was wrote three Days after their Separation.

THURSDAY Afternoon.

Dear Mamma,

THO' my Mistress has promised I shall go to see you next *Sunday*,[2] if the Weather proves fair, I could not forbear writing to let you know how I go on. I assure you all here are very kind to me in their way. I lie with my Mistress's Sister, and breakfast and dine with them; for they say they see something in me that deserves better Treatment than any

---

1 One who conceals her real purposes under a false appearance; a deceiver or hypocrite. This term is used throughout Haywood's work and marks a character as fundamentally duplicitous.

2 Almost all apprentices—male and female—had Sundays off, partly as a way to further inculcate religious and moral teachings. In this case, Syrena's mistress is also trying to maintain that (allegedly) positive maternal influence Mrs. Tricksy can wield.

they have had before; but all this don't make me easy.[1] I could not live as they do for the World; and I believe I shall find it a hard Matter to stay my Month out, they are such an old-fashion'd sanctify'd Family.—Ah, Mamma, what a difference between this and home! we rise every Morning at Eight o'Clock, have but one Hour allowed for Breakfast, and then to Work—the same for Dinner, and then to Work again—no Tea in the Afternoon, unless Company comes—and then at Night, my Master who has a Place in the Stamp-Office,[2] comes home about Nine; he and my Mistress and her Sister sit down to eat a bit; after that, I and the Maid, and an old Woman that has been a Nurse in the Family, are called into Prayers, and so to Bed——This they call a sober regular Life—my Stars! defend me from such formal Ways—I am quite sick of them already. I pretend, however, to be mighty well pleas'd, and do every thing they bid me with a great deal of Chearfulness, but it goes so against the Grain,[3] that I know I can't do so long. Therefore, dear Mamma, remember your Promise, and contrive some Way to get me as soon as you can out of this Bondage,[4] who am,

Your dutiful Daughter,
SYRENA TRICKSY.[5]

P. S. They don't know of my Writing, so I have no Compliments to send you.

---

1 The "any they have had" refers to previous apprentices. By dining with the family Syrena, like Pamela, is noting her elevated status beyond the average apprentice.

2 An office where government stamps are issued and where stamp duties are received; such an office would be part of the General Post Office, the country's postal system. Because charges were based on distance rather than weight, the fee was relatively high, especially in comparison with the penny post discussed below. This whole paragraph describes a very frugal, "middling" existence without the luxuries (such as tea) increasingly common among the higher classes or those emulating them. It underscores the ways apprentice families were to inculcate values as well as teach a trade.

3 Unwillingly or unpleasantly.

4 Haywood is alluding to Pamela's repeated use of the term "bondage" to describe her situation after she is taken to B.'s Lincolnshire estate.

5 In his *Dictionary*, Johnson notes that "Tricksy," is a term of endearment that means "pretty," which Syrena clearly is. Yet Haywood is obviously also playing on the other meaning of trick or to live by fraud, which Syrena also does well. "Syrena" is perhaps designed to suggest a "Siren," the mythological half woman/half bird who lured sailors to their destruction with their seductive song. "Siren" can also suggest anyone who charms, allures, or deceives, like the Sirens.

MONDAY Morning.

Dear Mamma,

I Fretted myself almost sick that I could not come to you Yesterday; but you saw it rain'd incessantly—indeed I long to see you; and the more, because an Adventure[1] has happened to me, which I don't know but may come to something, if I manage right——I'll tell you exactly how it was, and then you will be the better able to advise me.—You must know, Mrs. *Martin*, my Mistress's Sister, and I, lie in a dark Closet,[2] within the Dining-Room; so I go there as soon as I am up, to comb my Head and put on my Cap in the great Glass; but I am always in such a Hurry to get my things on before my Master and Mistress comes down, that I never minded who observed me.—I was observed however, and all my Motions watch'd, from the first Day I came it seems, as you shall hear——Last *Friday* some Silk[3] being wanting for our Business, and the Maid sent out another Way, my Mistress bade me step for it: I ask'd if she had any particular Place where she bought.—Yes, said she, but that's too far off: for I generally buy a large Quantity together of a wholesale Dealer in the City,[4] so you may go to the Haberdashers[5] at the Corner of the Street, and get a Quarter of an Ounce for the present, but be sure you match the Colour; with these Words she gave me a bit of the Damask,[6] and I said no more, but went on my Errand— The Shop was very full of People when I came in, and among them a fine Gentleman with a lac'd Hat and Cockade,[7] looking over some white Stockings—so I was oblig'd to wait till most of them were dispatch'd;—all the time I could see the Gentleman had his Eye upon me,

---

1 While this term can mean any novel or unexpected event, it also had a specifically sexual connotation (e.g., sexual adventures) that readers of Haywood's earlier fiction would have recognized. The word appears twenty times in the text, almost exclusively with that sexual connotation.
2 Any small room.
3 Silk here sold in the form of thread or twist for sewing. As the rest of the passage indicates, it was typically sold by weight.
4 She means the City of London proper within the original position of the city walls. It is a site of commerce—including the sale of wholesale goods.
5 A dealer in small articles related to dress, such as thread, tape, ribbons and, as the subsequent encounter demonstrates, stockings.
6 A rich silk fabric woven with elaborate designs and figures, often of a variety of colors; this would be an expensive piece of cloth.
7 A cockade was a ribbon or a rosette worn in the hat. The laced hat, likely ornamented or trimmed with braids or cords of gold or silver lace, was part of the required clothing for a member of the military, as was the possession to two cockades.

and when all were gone besides ourselves and the Gentlewoman behind the Counter; How do you do, my pretty Neighbour, said he? Very well thank you, Sir, answered I, blushing and curtsying, as you bid me when any Stranger spoke to me, but I han't the Honour to know you—for that Matter, cry'd he, the Honour would be wholly on my side, if you had found any thing in me to take Notice of; but I assure you I lodge just over against you—I was at my Window when you came out of a Hackney-Coach, accompanied by two grave Gentlewomen, who I suppose were your Relations; I saw too much of you then, not to wish to see more; and I can tell you the Pleasure of looking on you, while you are setting those pretty Locks of yours in Order, has made me an early Riser. As he spoke these Words, he took hold of my Hair as it hung down on my Neck, on which I frowned, and snatched away my Head——I did not know that I had any Over-lookers, said I, but since I have, shall be more careful for the future; then I turned to the Woman of the Shop, and desired she would make haste to weigh me the Silk, for I could not stay. Nay, my sweet Miss, said he, you must not be angry,—I mean no Harm to you,—I have only a small Favour to beg of you, which you must not refuse me. All the Favours I can grant, answered I, must be small indeed. What I have to ask is such said he, it is no more than to chuse a Pair of Stockings; I am obliged to make a Present of a Pair to a young Relation in the Country, and would have your Fancy;—Pray let us see some of your best Women's Silk Stockings, added he, to the Woman; yes Sir, cry'd she, and immediately turn'd to reach a Parcel down. I have no Judgment, upon my Word, Sir, answered I, a little peevishly—so pray Madam let me have the Silk. No, no, I bar that, cry'd he, first come, first serv'd, you know Miss is the Rule; and as I was here before you, I insist on having my Stockings before you have your Silk. I said nothing, but pretended to be mighty uneasy, tho' in my Heart I was well enough pleas'd.—Well! the Stockings were brought, and he would have me chuse; so I pick'd out a pair of white with Pink Clocks, for there was none with Silver.[1]

---

1 Clocks were patterns in hose, knitted or embroidered in. This mention parallels Pamela's description of her own "two pair of ordinary blue worsted hose, that make a smartish appearance, with white clocks, I'll assure you" (77). It also underscores the intimacy of a gift of stockings. In Letter 7 of *Pamela*, Mr. B. gives Pamela "four pair of fine white cotton stockings, and three pair of fine silk ones." Yet Pamela is "inwardly ashamed to take the stockings; for Mrs. Jervis was not there: if she had, it would have been nothing." B. immediately recognizes the cause of her embarrassment, saying "'Don't blush, Pamela: dost think I don't know pretty maids wear shoes and stockings?" (51).

He made me a Compliment on the Genteelness of my Fancy; and having paid for them, and two pair of fine Thread for himself, now, Miss, said he, you must accept of what you have made Choice of, and put them into my Hand with a Squeeze, that made my Fingers ake for an Hour after;—I was very much surprised I confess, not expecting any such thing, but I threw them down on the Counter, and told him, I never took any Presents from Gentlemen: He attempted to force them upon me again and again, but I would not take them all he could do; and there was a great Scuffle between us. At last finding I was resolute, he put them with the others into his Pocket, and went out of the Shop very much out of Humour. After he was gone, the Woman of the Shop began to banter me, and told me, I had made a Conquest; but I seemed to think nothing of it, and went away as soon as I had got my Silk. I prevented my Mistress from asking why I staid so long, by telling her, the Shop was so full of Customers, that I could not get served, at which she seemed not at all surprised. When I began to consider on what had pass'd; I thought I had been a little too rough in the latter part of my Behaviour; for tho' I did not repent my having refused the Stockings (tho' indeed they were very pretty) yet I did, that I had not done it with more Complaisance.—I verily believed he loved me; but then, as it was a Passion of so late a Date, it might want a little Hope to give it Strength; and tho' it was necessary I should seem coy, yet it should have been such a Coyness, as might give him room to fancy I might at last be won; and so have drawn him in by Degrees, till it was not in his power to go back. These Reflections kept me awake all Night, and when Morning came, I dress'd me at the usual Place; but that I might not seem too forward, I put the Window-Shutters a-jar, so that I could see him through the Crack, without his distinguishing me.—I was glad to find he was at his Post, because it look'd as if he had not given over all Thoughts of me;——I wanted to shew myself to him too, but could not tell how to do it, without making him think I did it on Purpose. ——At last I bethought me of our Cutting-Room,[1] which is over the Dining-Room;—I ran up there, and finding the Window open, stood some time; but he not expecting me so high, never lifted up his Eyes; so I took a Bottle with some Mint growing in it, and threw it into the Street; the Clash made him look up; he seem'd pleas'd to find there what he had so long been looking for in another Place, and kiss'd his Hand with a great deal of Gallantry and Tenderness; I seem'd confus'd,

---

1   The place where the primary cutting of fabric is done prior to dress-making.

but made a Bow, and soon after retir'd. I saw him no more that Day, but Yesterday and this Morning we have exchanged Glances several times thro' the Glass.———— Dear Mamma, I am impatient to know if I have behaved hitherto as I should, and how I shall proceed for the future; for I am certain by all his Ways he loves me, and that something may be made of him, for he must be rich; he goes as fine as any Lord, and has a Man that waits upon him: So pray write your Mind with all Speed, and send it by old *Sarah*; but don't let her give it me before any of the Family, for fear they should expect me to shew it them; but she may come as with a Compliment from you to them, and to know how I do:————So dear Mamma, no more at present, but that I am

Your most dutiful Daughter,
SYRENA TRICKSY.

MONDAY *Afternoon.*

Dear Mamma,

As I was coming from putting my Letter to you, into the Post-house;[1] who should I see in the middle of our Street, but my Lover, (for I think I may venture to call him so now) talking to another fine Gentleman————I found he saw me, and it presently came into my Head to make tryal of his Love; so instead of going home, I turn'd down a little Court, I don't know the Name of it, but it goes into *Covent-Garden*,[2] and walk'd slow. I had not gone many paces before

---

1 Syrena primarily uses the penny post, which had more than four hundred locations around London and its environs. In *A Tour Thro' London*, Defoe describes the penny post as a "modern contrivance ... now... come also into so exquisite a Management, that nothing can be more exact, and 'tis with the utmost Safety and Dispatch that Letters are delivered at the remotest Corners of the Town, almost as soon as they could be sent by a Messenger, and that from Four, Five, Six, to Eight Times a Day, according as the Distance of the Place makes it practicable; and you may send a Letter from *Ratcliff* or *Limehouse* in the East, to the farthest Part of Westminster for a Penny, and that several Times in the same Day" (39). A post house is a house or shop where postal business is carried on, where postage stamps are sold, letters are registered and posted for transmission to their destinations, and from some of which letters received from places at home and abroad are delivered.

2 By the time of *Anti-Pamela*, Covent Garden, once a fashionable residential area, instead housed taverns, bagnios, and houses of prostitution. While the area was the site of the city's largest commercial market, specializing in fruit, flowers, and vegetables, Covent Garden was renowned for its numerous prostitutes.

I heard somebody come very fast behind me, I did not doubt but it was my Gentleman; and so indeed it proved; for having overtaken me, so my little cruel Dear, said he, taking hold of my Shoulder, have I caught you abroad once more.——I pretended a great Fright and Confusion, and desired him to take his Hand away; not without you'll tell me where you are going, and permit me to accompany you said he. Lord, Sir, cry'd I, trembling, I am only going to—to— where my Dear, again demanded He? Only to *Covent-Garden*, answered I, for a little Fruit. Well, said he, and where's the mighty Business if I go and buy a little Fruit too——I beg'd he would not— told him we should be taken notice of—and said all I could, but he swore he would go with me, and go with me he did.——When we came among the Stalls he would needs fill my Pockets with the best the Market afforded; I would have paid for them, but he would not let me, and I thought it would be carrying the thing too far, to make a bustle[1] in that publick Place; so I thank'd him, and was going to take my leave——No, said he, since Opportunities of speaking to you are so scarce, I am resolv'd you shan't quit me now, till you have heard what I have to say; and with these Words took hold of my Hand, and attempted to pull me into the Tavern, at the End of the Piazza.[2]——I was frighted now in good earnest; and snatching my Hand away with more Strength than could be expected from me; what do you mean, Sir, said I, what do you take me for? For every thing that's charming, answered he—By Heaven! I would rather die than offer any thing should give you cause of Offence; therefore, dear Angel, oblige me so far, as to go in for one Quarter of an Hour only. Not for a Minute, cried I, I would not set my Foot in a nasty Tavern for the World. Fie, fie, said he, I shall suspect you for a little Prude if you talk at this rate, and look'd I thought as if he took me to be silly. I don't care what you suspect me for, answered I, and turn'd away as if I was going home; but he came after me, and beg'd that since I would not go into a Tavern, I would take a little walk with him in the Church-Yard,[3] just to let him tell me something.

---

1 A commotion or disturbance.
2 "Piazza" refers to the open space that constitutes Covent Garden. Taverns sold primarily wine and were slightly higher priced than ale houses; generally, they were not locations where respectable young women would be found. Taverns often had private rooms for sexual encounters and some hosted brothels.
3 Syrena is referring the churchyard surrounding St. Paul's, Covent Garden, located at the west side of the Piazza.

This I was not averse to in my Mind, for I long'd to hear what he had to say, and so after some seeming Reluctance I comply'd.——— Dear Mamma, 'tis impossible for me to repeat the fine Things he said to me, and much more to express the Tenderness with which he spoke them. He swore that his Intentions were perfectly honourable, that his Heart told him the first Moment he saw my Face, that I was the Person that must make him happy or miserable for ever—that he could not live without me, and that if he had Millions he would lay them at my Feet; and sigh'd at every word as if his Heart were breaking———I reply'd very little to all this, and seemed to think him not in earnest; but then he swore a Thousand Oaths, and offer'd to give me any proof I ask'd, tho' 'twere his Life.———Indeed Mamma, I never read more moving Things in a Play,[1] but I did not seem to believe him for all that, and was for hurrying away; but he would not let me go till I had promised to meet him on *Wednesday* at the same Place—So pray let me have your Advice before then, whither I shall keep my word or not, and how I shall behave, for I am quite at a loss—Let old *Sarah* come by all Means[2]—I am,

Dear Mamma,
Your most Dutiful Daughter,
SYRENA TRICKSY.

The Answer to these two Letters came to her on *Wednesday* Morning by old *Sarah*, as she had desired, and contained as follows.

WEDNESDAY Morning.

Dear Child,
I Received your Letters, and am very much surprized to find you have gone so far in a Love Intrigue, in so short a Time: I perceive nothing, however, to condemn in your Behaviour hitherto—your Refusal of the Stockings, your giving him an Opportunity to speak to you a second Time, and the Confusion you affected were all perfectly right; but I am a little angry that you so readily believe what he says, and seem assured of his Affection———I doubt not, but he

---

1   Like Polly Peachum, the naïve heroine of John Gay's *The Beggar's Opera*, Syrena has been schooled in the codes of playbooks and is susceptible to Vardine's flattery.

2   By using her mother's servant ("Sarah" being a generic name for a serving woman), Syrena and her mother are spending even less than a penny a letter.

likes you, but my Girl there is a wide Difference between *Love* and *Likeing*; the chief aim of the *one* is to make the *beloved Object* happy: That of the *other*, only to gratify *itself*.[1]——Now your Business is by an artful Management to bring this *Likeing* up to *Love*, and then it will be in your power to do with him as you please.——But after all, I am afraid he is not worth taking much pains about—if he be only an Officer, as I guess by his Cockade, 'tis not in his Power to make you any Settlement as a *Mistress*—and as a *Wife*; when Children come, what is a Commission![2]— Or what a Pension to the Widow, left perhaps in an advanced Age, when 'tis out of one's power to mend one's Fortune any way.——No, Child! 'Tis your Business to make Hay while the Sun shines[3]—for when Youth and Beauty are no more—Farewell Hope—I could wish notwithstanding you knew his Name, and what Family he is of. He may be born to an Estate, and if so, his Passion must be cultivated.—It won't therefore be improper to give him the meeting to-night, but continue your Shyness; yet so as to give him some little Encouragement too, that you may the easier get out of him what he is; for there is no advising you how to proceed till we know that.——Be sure you write me a full Account of what passes between you, on *Thursday* Morning; and if you come on *Sunday*, shall then give you Instructions suitable to the Occasion.—I hope you do not stand in need of any Caution against indulging a secret Inclination for him; for if it once comes to that you are ruin'd!—No Woman ever made her Fortune by the Man she had a sincere Value for.—Depend upon it in a little time you will see finer Gentlemen than he, be he as fine as he will—let your own Interest be your only Aim—think of nothing, but how to be fine

---

1 Throughout most of her work, Haywood consistently sounds this theme of desire rather than love being the predominant motivation of men, an idea distinctly in contrast with the sentiments of the aforementioned playbooks.

2 As we later learn, Vardine is only a lieutenant in the army, a position he later reveals was purchased for him by a "person of quality." All commissions in the army could be bought or sold (subsequently, Syrena hopes he will raise some money for her by selling his commission). Most officers relied on the army for their livelihood and an officer's pay little exceeded the interest on the price of his commission. Thus, as Mrs. Tricksy shrewdly recognizes, Vardine lacks any equity except the value of his commission itself. Because of the limited value of the commission, the pension for a widow would be equally small.

3 To employ one's time profitably.

yourself; and by keeping in that Mind you will be happy, and also make so,

> *Your Affectionate Mother,*
> ANN TRICKSY.

P. S. I charge you not to be prevail'd upon to go into any House[1] with him—I don't like his asking you to go into the Tavern.

Syrena was rejoiced to find by this, that her Mother approved of her keeping the Assignation, and had before prepared an Excuse to her Mistress for going out——Her Lover had detain'd her so long on *Monday*, that she was oblig'd to say when she came home, that in stepping out to buy a few Apples, she had met with a Relation who was very glad to see her, and to hear she was so well put out; and added, that she had bid her come to see her on *Wednesday* in the Afternoon, for she had something to make her a Present of. Well, said Mrs. *Martin*, to whom all this was spoke; I'll prevail on my Sister to give you leave, for 'tis pity you should lose any thing for not going for it. The good Gentlewoman performed her Promise, little suspecting the Truth, and *Syrena* put a handsome *Paris* Cap[2] in her Pocket, which at her Return, she pretended had been given her by her Cousin; but in what Manner she had in reality been engaged, she gave her Mother a faithful Account of, the next Morning, in these Words.

THURSDAY *Morning.*

Dear Mamma,

HAVING your Permission I went at the appointed time, which was Four o'Clock, to the Church-Yard.——My Gentleman was there before me, and his Eyes sparkled with Joy as soon as he saw me coming: He ran to meet me; my dear Angel said he, the Place we are in will not permit me to throw myself at your Feet, as I ought to do, to thank you for this Favour; but be assured, my Heart is more your Slave than ever by this Goodness. Sir, I have been taught, answer'd I, that to be guilty of a breach of Promise, is the worst thing almost that a Person can be guilty of, so have always been careful to avoid

---

1 A building for the entertainment of travelers or of the public generally; it can be an inn or tavern, although by the nineteenth century it is associated primarily with a brothel.
2 A Paris Cap fitted the head closely with a jeweled band running over the top of the head and ending in a point on the cheeks.

that Fault with every Body. But may I not hope, returned he, that you make some Distinction between me and others, and that I owe this Blessing to something more than meerly a Punctilio[1] of Honour.——I wish, Sir, said I, that I have not given you too much Cause to think so; for as the Promise I made you was upon a sort of Compulsion, I might have dispensed with it. This I spoke, Mamma, in a more tender Air than ever I had done before; in Hopes by seeming open and unguarded to him, he might in reality be so to me; and indeed it answer'd my Expectation, for on my representing the Hazard I run in my Reputation, for meeting by Appointment with a Gentleman, who was a perfect Stranger to me, he readily told me his Name was *Vardine*, that he was of *French* Extraction, and his Parents among those who quitted their Estates and Country for the Sake of Religion;[2] and that they being dead, a Person of Quality, but who he did not mention, had been so good to procure him a Commission in the Army: He concluded this Narrative of himself with telling me, he expected to be preferr'd, for at present he was only a Lieutenant;[3] and that if I could once be brought to love him, he would make me a happy Woman.—I thought of you then, Mamma, and how lucky it was for me, that I had not set my Heart upon him.——I took no Notice however of the Baulk[4] it was to me, but seem'd very civil and obliging.—He press'd me again to go and take a Glass of Wine with him, but I absolutely refused that; however, being afraid somebody might happen to come through the Church-yard that might know me, we cross'd, at my Request, the Garden, and struck down *Southampton-street*, and so into the *Savoy*,[5] where we walk'd about an Hour: he all the time entertaining me with Praises of my Beauty, and the Impression it had made on him. Indeed I staid with him more to accustom myself to hear fine things said to me, and to practice an agreeable manner of receiving them, than any thing else—for as you say, Mamma, he is neither fit to make either

---

1   A minute detail of action or conduct; a small or petty formality.
2   A Huguenot or French Protestant.
3   In the army, the officer next in rank to the captain, though clearly Vardine expects promotion (something he would actually have to purchase).
4   A disappointment. A word Richardson uses in *Pamela*, 1741 I. viii. 244: "It was a great baulk to her, that you did not comply with my request."
5   Syrena and Vardine head east out of St. Paul's Churchyard, cross southeast through Covent Garden, and head South on Southampton Street; then they go east on the Strand, an area of commercial activity. The Savoy is the area around the Savoy Palace. See map in Appendix E.

Husband or Gallant to one in my Circumstances; so I am resolv'd to think no more on him.——I am a little vex'd tho' now, that I did not take the Stockings, for as there is nothing to be done with him, 'twould have been clear Gains; but I did not know then, his fine Cloaths deceiv'd me; and methinks I am sorry he has not an Estate, for he has Wit at Will, and I am sure loves me to Distraction; and so you would say, if you heard him as I have done——but that's nothing to the Purpose—let him love on—I shall trouble my Head no more about him, but wait with Patience 'till something offers more to my Advantage.—He wou'd fain have exacted another Promise to meet him again; but I told him it was not in my power, if even I had an Inclination, I was much so confined; and if ever he had an Opportunity of speaking to me again, it must be Chance that gave it him.——He complain'd bitterly of my Cruelty; but I was not to be persuaded, and left him as much mortified as the Account he had given me of himself had made me.—I shall see you on *Sunday*, and if any Thing should happen before, then, shall not fail to let you know it—till then I am,

Dear Mamma,
Your Dutiful, but
Disappointed Daughter,
SYRENA TRICKSY.

Hitherto *Syrena* had disguised nothing either of her Behaviour or Sentiments from her Mother; but a very little Time made her alter her Conduct in that Point, and practice on her some of those Lessons of Deceit, she had so well instructed her in. *Friday* in the Afternoon, as she was sitting at Work, old *Sarah* came in: She was surpris'd to see her, and ask'd hastily if her *Mamma* was well. Yes, Miss, said *Sarah*, very well; but hearing me say, I was coming this way, she desired me to call and give you her Blessing, with these three Yards and a half of Dimitty;[1] she says, if your Mistress will be so good to cut it out, and give you leave to run it up at a leisure Time, it will serve you in a Morning to comb your Head and wash in, and save your other Cloaths; as she deliver'd this Message, she gave her the Bundle, and at the same time slipt a Letter into her Hand unperceiv'd by any Body. The Mistress who was present, said Mrs. *Tricksy*

---

1 A cloth made of linen and cotton (or cotton alone), woven with raised stripes or fancy figures; usually employed undyed for beds and bedroom hangings, and sometimes for garments. From the subsequent description, Syrena is to make a dressing gown of it.

was a very good Mother; and she might be sure, the Girl should find time to make her Gown very soon. *Sarah* then told her, they hoped to see her on *Sunday*, which the other promised, and the old Emissary went away.

Syrena could not imagine the reason of her Mother's writing again, when she expected to see her so soon, and as she thought had no farther Advice to give her, concerning the Lieutenant; being full of Impatience to see what it contain'd, she soon made a pretence for going out of the Room, and read these Lines.

FRIDAY Noon.

Dear Child,

THO' I hope to see you on *Sunday*, I could not refrain giving you some Remonstrance, which every Hour's Delay of, may render less effectual.——I have not slept all Night for thinking on some Passages in your Letter. Ah, *Syrena!*—*Syrena!* I am afraid you like this poor idle Fellow, more than it may be you are yet sensible of yourself—why else are you sorry he has not an Estate?—If he has not an Estate others have, that, perhaps, may find you as agreeable as he has done.—You have a very great Opinion too of his *Wit*, and of his *Love*; suppose you are not mistaken, he is only the more dangerous, and you ought the less to trust yourself with him.——I charge you, therefore, to shun him henceforward—be as industrious to avoid all Opportunities of seeing him, as 'tis probable he will be in seeking them.——You already believe all the fine Things (as you call them) that he says to you; and knowing by Experience, how susceptible the Heart is at your Years, I tremble lest all the Counsel I have given you, should not be sufficient to guard you from the Temptation.—— Don't think Child, that I want to lay you under any unreasonable Restraints.——No, if we were rich and above Censure, I should be far from putting any curb to Nature; but as all our Hopes depend on your making your Fortune, either by Marriage or a Settlement equal to it, you must be extremely cautious of your Character till that Point is gain'd, and when once it is, you may freely indulge your Inclinations with this, or any other Man.——You see, I do not like most Parents, want to deprive you of the Pleasures of Life; I would only have you first attain, that which alone can give them a true Relish; for Love in Rags *Syrena*, is a most despicable Thing. Therefore, I once more lay my Commands upon you, to speak no more to this paltry *Vardine*; and to endeavour with all your Might, to conquer whatever Sentiments you may be possest of in his Favour, which is all that can restore Peace of Mind to her, who is at present,

Your most discontented Mother,
ANN TRICKSY.

P. S. Come as early as you can on *Sunday.*

Syrena was not very well pleas'd at the Contents of this Letter: She thought there was no Occasion for this Caution; and that she had said enough to convince her Mother, that she had no regard for any Thing in Competition with her Interest.—Why then, said she, must I be debarr'd from speaking to a Man that loves me? A little Conversation with him sometimes would certainly instruct me better how to behave to the Sex, than a thousand Lessons—besides, I might get some small Presents from him——but she will needs have it that I am in love, forsooth.—Not I, indeed, I did not care if he was hang'd for that Matter; but there is something pleasingly amusing, in being address'd by a Man that admires one, and can talk well—in the insipid Life I lead here, 'tis necessary I should have some Diversion to keep up my Spirits.—She owns my Conduct has been perfectly right hitherto—why then should it not be so still?—why must I run away whenever I see him, as if I were afraid he would devour me? Indeed, I shan't make myself such a Fool——if Fortune or his own Endeavours throw him in my way, I shall hear what he has to say, and it may be manage, so as to get something of him——poor as she thinks him.

Thus did Vanity, Self-Conceit and Avarice, tempt her to despise the Admonitions of her crafty Mother, and make her resolve to act henceforward of herself.

When *Sunday* Morning came, as she stood drawing on her Gloves at the Window, she saw him at his ready drest; she presently imagin'd he was ready so early, for no other Reason than to watch her going abroad; but she had not indulg'd herself with this Idea above three Minutes, before it was entirely dash'd: He took up his Hat and Cane and went out of Doors, without so much as looking up.——Ha! cryed she in a Pet,[1] is it so—you are strangely alter'd methinks.——Mamma, need not have been so fearful. The Coldness of my Behaviour last time, has certainly made him resolve to give over all Thoughts of me.

---

1 Offence at being (or feeling) slighted or not made enough of; a fit of ill humor or peevishness from this cause: now usually implying one of a slight or childish kind.

So instead of thinking she had been too kind, she was beginning to repent of not having been kind enough; and in the room of avoiding her Man, was fearful of nothing so much, as not being pursued by him,——in this Ill-Humour she went out of her Mistress's House; but was no sooner in the Street than she perceived the Person who had occasion'd it, at the Corner of that Court, where he had once before overtaken her.—Her Heart bounded with Joy at the Sight of him, not doubting if he stood there for any other Purpose, than to observe which way she went. She deceived not herself in this; he soon came up with her, and accosted her with more Gallantry than ever.— She pretended to be greatly alarm'd at seeing him—entreated he would leave her, and told him she had suffered enough already by the little Acquaintance she had with him.——Some body, said she, saw us together in the Church-yard, and told my *Mamma*, who is so angry, that she vows she won't own me as her Child, if ever I speak to you again. Your Mamma, answered he, is ignorant of the Respect I have for you——besides all old People have odd Notions in their Heads— But, my Charmer, continued he, this might have been avoided if you had complied with my Request, and gone into a Tavern. O! that might have been worse, cried she. Much better for us both, said he; at least if I am not the Object of your Aversion; for you would have been convinced of the Sincerity of my Passion, and I should have been happy in your being so; but I'll warrant, added he, the same scrupulous Modesty that made you refuse me then, will not suffer you now to accept of a Coach where you are going. Not for the World, replied she hastily, I am going to my *Mamma*, who expects me; and if she should send any body to meet me (as 'tis likely she may, for she is violently suspicious since she heard that Story) I should be undone; so pray, Sir, don't go any farther with me. He seem'd to believe what she said; but swore that whatever was the Consequence he would not quit her, till she promised to meet him in the Afternoon. O dear! cried she, then we may be seen again. No, said he, I'll be in the *Birdcage-Walk* in *St. James's* Park, about Four o'Clock, and if you'll come we'll strike up into the Fields behind *Buckingham-house*,[1]

---

1   Syrena and Vardine are using the area in and beyond St. James's Park and Buckingham House which was built in 1707 and is adjacent to St. James's Park. Birdcage Walk, originally the site of James I's aviary, was a walk created as part of the post-Restoration remodeling of St. James's Park. It was a popular place for couples seeking a private location. The whole area beyond would have been more akin to a country meadow than the manicured site of St. James's Park.

where we may be private enough. Well, said she, I like this better than going into a Tavern, and if I can get away from Mamma, I will do thus much to oblige you. He call'd this but a half Assurance, nor would leave her till she protested in the most solemn manner, that she would be at the Place he mentioned. Had he known her Mind, he might have spared himself the trouble of exacting a Vow from her, for the fear of losing the first Lover she ever had, render'd her in so complying a Humour, that she was ready to grant almost any Thing to secure him.

The Reception she had from Mother, was such as she expected from her Letter; but by telling part of the Truth, she so cunningly conceal'd the rest, that artful as the Person she had to deal with was, there remain'd not the least Suspicion in her Breast. The foolish Fellow watch'd me out, said she, but I gave him such Looks, as I believe put half what he intended to say to me, out of his Head; but yet he would come with me, and talk his Stuff, so I told him we had been seen together in the Church-yard, and you had been made acquainted with it, and were very angry; and for my own Part I did not like to be followed about, and did not know what he meant by it; but whatever Designs he had upon me, he should find himself disappointed; that I could neither like him nor love him, nor desired to be lov'd by him, and a great deal more to the same Purpose. And at last he said, he had been a Fool to trouble himself about me, that I was a proud, pert Minx, and so went strutting away highly affronted. I dare say, Mamma, I am quite rid of him now, and I hope you will be so of all your Fears for me. Mrs. Tricksy was perfectly well satisfied with this Account, and after a little ridicule on the Folly of Women, who suffer themselves to be seduced by fine Speeches only, they fell into other Conversation, such as the Affairs of the Family Syrena was in, and the Methods that were to be taken for her coming away at the Month's End; till the young Gipsy remembring her Assignation, said what a sad Thing it is to be confined, Mamma, now I have not seen you for almost for a Fortnight, and must not stay with you but a small Part of the Day. How so Child, cried the Mother? why said the other, my Mistress dines abroad on an Engagement made long ago, and poor Mrs. Martin is almost dead with the Headach, so she begg'd I would come home soon, for 'tis our Maid's Sunday to go out, and she should be alone. I thought you had an old Nurse in the House, said Mrs. Tricksy; yes, answered Syrena, but she has been these two Days with her Grandson who has the Small-Pox. Well then, returned the Mother, I would not have you do any thing to disoblige Mrs. Martin, or any of them, because they may give you a bad Word to your Cousin——you shall go as soon as Dinner is over.——When the time grew near, *Syrena* played *loth to depart* to the Life, and seemed ready to whimper, but her Mother forced her away; and she departed laughing in her Sleeve, and applauding her own Ingenuity in outwitting so penetrating a Judgment.

Vardine was in the Park before the Hour prefix'd, and *Syrena* scarce exceeded it; the Afternoon being gloomy, there was but little Company, especially on that side, so they chose to entertain each other there, rather than walk farther; but this was no sooner agreed upon, than there fell so violent a Shower, that had it continued, the Trees under which they stood for Shelter, would not have defended them from being wet: Happily however for them, and all that were abroad, the Sky cleared up, yet not enough to give any Prospect of a fair Evening, so he could not desire her to stay, without shewing he had little Regard of her Health; they walked pretty fast till they came to *Spring-Garden*,[1] when it began to rain again: He called a Coach, but there was none in hearing, and they were oblig'd to stand up in a Tavern Entry, tho' when she ran in, she knew it not for such; and when she did, would have quitted it, tho' all the Doors beside being shut, she saw no other Refuge from the Storm. Nothing could have happened more lucky for *Vardine's* Designs: He had now a very plausible Pretence for persuading her to go into a Room.[2]——It would be a piece of strange Affectation, said he, to chuse to stand in a Place where we are exposed to the View of every body; (and you see how many People pass) rather than go with a Man who loves you, and whose every Action you may command. With such like Arguments she was at last prevail'd upon, and he order'd some Wine to be made hot with Spice and Sugar. After they had drank a Glass or two, now, said he, where is the mighty Business of going into a Tavern—is it not better sitting here than strolling the Streets, as if no House would receive us?—— 'Twould be more comfortable indeed, answered she, if it were not for the Scandal; there is no Scandal in it, cry'd he; beside, who need know it, unless we tell it ourselves, for the Drawers[3] here are as secret as Confessors. That may be, said she, in a sort of Childish Tone; but methinks I am ashamed to know I am here myself. That's for want of knowing the World, my Dear, replied he; in such Weather as this the veriest Puritan would have made no Scruple. Did not *Dido*, tho' a great

---

1 Haywood refers here to gardens in the vicinity of Charing Cross, originally part of St. James's Park but in public use after 1634. The surrounding area is populated by shops and taverns.
2 A private room within a tavern.
3 One who draws liquor for customers; a tapster at a tavern.

Queen, run into a Cave with a wandring Soldier to avoid a Storm.[1]
Great Folks may do any thing, said she, but pray what is that Story? I'll
tell you anon, my Dear, answered he, but first pray ease me of this Luggage;—I have had your Stockings in my Pocket all Day, and now I
desire you'll take charge of them yourself;—with these Words he laid
them on the Table before her:—My Stockings, said she, indeed they are
none of mine;—and I won't have them;—but you shall, and you must,
reply'd he; you chose them, and they are bought and paid for;—but
may be you think they won't fit;—I should know that, because they
may be changed;—I can tell in a Moment, by grasping your pretty
Leg:—Here he made an offer of doing as he said, but she resisted with
all her Strength, crying out at the same time— hold! hold! I will have
them—they will fit; and glad enough she was to take them, tho' in reality a little frightened at the manner in which he forced them upon her.
He found she trembled, and would not alarm her Modesty too much
at once, so drawing back his Hand, don't be under any Apprehensions
my sweet Innocence, said he; upon my Soul I mean no hurt to you, and
did this only to oblige you to accept my little Present.——Well, I'll
believe you this time, answer'd she, but pray don't offer such Freedoms
any more, for if you do, I'll never speak to you again. He then made her
drink another Glass of Wine in token of Forgiveness; and that being followed by several others, her young Brain unaccustomed to such an
Encrease of Heat, began to grow confused, and she lost all Memory of
the Place, or Danger she was in: He ply'd her all the time with Protestations of Love, and sometimes by way of Parenthesis gave her a Kiss,
which he had the Satisfaction to find she less and less resisted.

How ought, therefore, the Fair-Sex to beware of indulging even
the very Temptation of a Vice,[2] which I am sorry to say is at present

---

1   Vardine is referring to the episode in Book IV of the *Aeneid* in which
    Dido and Aeneas seek shelter in a cave during a thunderstorm and con-
    summate their relationship. Dido, like Syrena, is abandoned by her soldier.
2   Haywood discusses the "pernicious Consequence" of "Dram-drinking"
    in *A Present for a Servant-Maid* (1743): "I have known several who have
    loath'd the very Smell of any spirituous Liquor, become at last to love
    them to their Ruin . . . You begin with a little, and think you will never
    exceed a certain Bound, but by degrees increase the Proportion; you
    crave still for more, till by frequent Use it becomes too habitual to be
    refrained. The Consequences of these intoxicating Spirits, none of you
    but have Sense enough to see, if you would give yourselves the Trouble
    of considering, and the horrible Objects which the Streets every Day
    afford you, methinks, should make it impossible for you not to do so"
    (Vol. 1.1, 216). Also see Appendix A.

too prevalent among them. I need not say I mean that of Drinking, which indeed opens the way to all others; the Example before us of a Girl train'd up in Precepts directly opposite, to giving Way to any tender Inclinations, and taught that the only thing she had to avoid, was the bestowing any Favours but where Interest directed; now, by the meer Force of Liquor, betray'd to yield to the Impulse of Nature, and resign that Jewel,[1] on which all her Hopes of living great in the World depended, to a Person from whom she could have no Expectations, and for whom what she felt could not justly be called Love; this, I say, may be a Warning to all of what Principles and Station whatever; since there are Dangers arising from this pernicious Custom, as well in the Closet as in the Street, tho' perhaps of a different Nature.

The young Officer perceiving the Ground he gain'd, did not fail pursuing the Attack, and bombarded her so fast with Speeches out of Plays, tender Pressures, Kisses, and the more intoxicating Juice of the Grape, that at length the Town was wholly his;——the momentary Rapture over, the Power of Reflection return'd to this unhappy ruin'd Girl—she reproach'd him and herself;—she wept;—she exclaim'd;—but it was now too late. He said a good many fond things to her, but he made a Jest of her Complaints; why, my Dear, cry'd he, you desir'd to know the Story of *Dido* and *Æneas*, and I have more than *told* it to you, for I have *acted* it to the Life. O wicked! wicked Man! cry'd she, and sobb'd most bitterly:——He then endeavour'd all he could to set her Mind at ease: He made a thousand Vows of everlasting Constancy, and that when his Affairs were once settled, he would make her his Wife; at last she grew a little more composed; and it being now dark, began to think what Excuse she should make at home for being out so late; her ready Invention soon supplied her with one, and a Coach being call'd, he set her down at the end of the Street, after having made her promise to meet him again the first Opportunity, which she was to let him know by a Sign from the Window.

The good People at home were very much frighted at her staying so late, for it was near Nine, and as much rejoiced to see her safe returned: She told them, that being just coming away, the Rain oblig-ed her to stay; and that afterwards a Person who happened to dine that Day with a Lodger in the same House, offer'd to set her down if she would stay her Time; so Madam said she, I accepted her Favour, as it was a bad Evening; and hope you would not be offended; not in the least, answered her mistress, I am very glad it happened so.

---

1 Pamela repeatedly refers to "the best Jewel, my Virtue" (190), a phrase Haywood is echoing.

As *Syrena* had a Share of Understanding uncommon for her Years, she could not recollect what had pass'd between her and *Vardine*, without a great deal of Uneasiness; but her Vivacity and Strength of Spirits soon threw it off; she consider'd that as it was past recall, to hurt her Eyes and Complexion, by crying and fretting, would encrease not diminish her Misfortune; and therefore resolved to be entirely secret in the Matter, and get as much as she could from him, in recompence for what he had robb'd her of. How she should contrive any future Meetings with him, was now the chief Employment of her Thoughts; but tho' she rack'd Invention to the utmost Pitch, she could not hit on any thing that had not some Danger of Discovery. She saw her Lover the next Morning at his Window as usual, but had no Sign to make but a melancholy shaking her Head, accompanied with a Look that told him, it was not owing to her Inclinations, that they had not a nearer Intercourse. The next Day it was the same, and probably would have continued so till *Sunday*, had not Fortune befriended her Endeavours.

A Gown being in hand, *Syrena* was ordered to go to the Lady's House for Silver Lace to trim it;——what would she not have given to have known this in the Morning,— but it was now too late.—— *Vardine* was abroad, and she knew not where to send to him;— it came into her Head however as she was in the Street, not to go, but to walk about a little, and return home, pretending the Lady had not bought the Trimming, and had bid her come for it the next Day at three in the Afternoon: This was feasible enough, and passed current with People that had not the least Suspicion of her Conduct.

Possession had not so far abated the Fervour of her Gallant's Affections, but that he attended the Window as before—and she had the Opportunity of making him know he might see her in the Afternoon; which was done by pointing to the Street, and holding up three Fingers, in signification that Three o'Clock was the time. He express'd his Satisfaction by a thousand tender Gestures; but she was oblig'd to leave him in the midst of them, fancying she heard somebody coming up Stairs. She had indeed more than ordinary Reason now for being cautious, not only because Guilt naturally makes People so, but also, because his standing so much at the Window had been taken Notice of: The Maid told her one Day as she was washing her Hands in the Kitchen, that she was sure she had got a Sweetheart since she came;——a Sweetheart, said *Syrena*! what do you mean, *Margaret*? I mean as I say, answer'd *Margaret*;——the Gentleman that lodges over the Way is as surely in love with you, as I am alive.—I never go to the Door or into the Parlour in a Morning, but

I see him staring at our Windows, as if he'd lose his Eyes; and it must be for you, for there's no other young Body in the House;—why not yourself, said Syrena, you are not old;—no, no, I am not so vain, cry'd *Margaret*; but if I were, he takes care to undeceive me; for the Minute he sees me he pops his Head in. *Syrena* laugh'd, and the Maid being call'd, there pass'd no more between them; but this serv'd her as a good Warning to be circumspect; for she very well knew that if her Conversation with him were once but so much as suspected, it would break the Neck of her Designs every way.

When it grew near three Syrena reminded her Mistress, that it was the time for her to go; and received the Praise her supposed Dilligence seem'd to deserve.—*Vardine* was at the usual Corner, and having a Coach in waiting at the end of the Street, they both stept into it, and drove immediately to the same Tavern they had been in before.

The pains she took for this Interview may very well be taken for the Effect of Love, as indeed it was; but not of the Man, tho' something belonging to him. She had seen a very genteel Snuff-Box in his Hand of *Pinchbeck's* Metal,[1] which she mistook for Gold: This Box had run in her head ever since *Sunday*; and she languished with Impatience for an Opportunity, which she hoped would make her Mistress of it.

She was not deceiv'd in the Complaisance of her Lover, tho' she was in the Value of the thing she had set her Heart upon; for by praising and looking earnestly on it, she so artfully insinuated she had a mind to it, that he soon made her a Present of it. They past about an Hour together, in the manner Persons usually do, who see each other on the Terms they did; and parted with a Promise of meeting at the same Place at four o'Clock, as she came from her Mother's next *Sunday*. After which she went on the Business she was sent, and was dispatch'd time enough not to make her Mistress think she loiter'd; tho', to excuse her stay, she pretended she had waited a good while before the Lady could be spoke with.

She had now nothing to think on, but what she should wheedle him out of next: He had no Ring on his Finger, no lac'd Ruffles, or any thing fit for her to ask.—She therefore contriv'd a Stratagem to get a small Sum of Money from him (for she did not imagine he could spare a large one) and executed it in this manner.

When she came to the Tavern, where he was ready to receive her,

---

1　A false gold. Syrena's gullibility shows her inexperience.

she put on so wild confused a Countenance, as made him, when about to take her in his Arms, start back and ask if she were not well——Yes, said she, I am well enough in Health—but the saddest Accident—O that I had been sick, or dead, or any thing, so that I had not come out this Day!——Then she threw her self into a Chair, and burst into Tears. He prest her very endearingly to tell him the Occasion; but all the Answer she gave him was, O! I must never look my *Mamma* in the Face again—O! I am undone—I durst not go home—I cannot tell what to say, that will pacify my Mistress—Sure I am the most unfortunate Creature in the World.——What, my Dear, said he, nothing concerning me, I hope, is discovered? No, reply'd she sobbing, but I'll tell you the whole Business. You must know, continued she, that my *Mamma*, borrow'd five Guineas[1] of my Mistress, upon a very great Exigence:[2] She gave her a Note for it, and a time was prefix'd for the Payment;—it became due Yesterday, and my *Mamma* having the Money ready, desired the Note might be sent by me, as I was to come this Day.—O! unhappy Day that it is to me, I'm sure.——Here she feigned as if she could not speak again; but then seeming to recover a little——In short, said she, I carry'd the Note—My *Mamma* gave the Money to me, and I put it into my Purse, where I had a few Pieces of Silver of my own;[3]—but they are all gone together—Either some Rogue has picked my Pocket, or I have pull'd out the Purse with my Handkerchief.——An ugly Accident indeed, my Dear, reply'd he gravely, but might have happen'd to any body—You must ev'n tell the Truth——O! cry'd she, 'tis a sign you don't know their Tempers; they would tear me in Pieces—My Mistress would think it a Trick between *Mamma* and me, because I carry'd the Note; and *Mamma* beside would be obliged to pay—O! what shall I do? I'll never go home again, unless I have the Money—She run on in this manner for a good while, without his offering to interrupt her; which she had cunning enough to look on as no good

---

1 Five guineas would be more than a year's wages for a domestic servant. The average annual national income in England at this time was little more than twice that amount.
2 A pressing state of circumstances, or one demanding immediate action or remedy; an emergency.
3 This whole encounter depends on the new instruments of credit-based finance (which largely escape Syrena). She claims to have lost the promissory note (and final payment for the same) her mother allegedly signed in her moment of exigency. Mrs. Tricksy is allegedly returning the note so she can mark her loan as paid.

Omen of Success; and finding she must speak more plain—O! if you loved me half so well as I do you, said she, you would not see me fret so—you'd give me or lend me such a Trifle. I protest, Child, reply'd he, I have not so much about me—Well, said she, you may leave me at the Corner of our Street while you fetch it——That I would willingly do, return'd he, but if you must know, I am not at present Master of so much.——But you can borrow it, cry'd she; nor can I borrow it any where that I know of, answer'd he; I never ask'd such a Favour of any body but our Agent,[1] and he happens to be out of Town—so you had better own the Truth.——I dare not, said she, and you only perswade me to run the risque of it, because you don't care to part with your Money.—Upon my Soul, answered he, I have it not—See here, continued he, pulling out his Purse, and throwing two Guineas[2] on the Table; this is my whole Stock, besides a little Silver in my Pockets——But you have a gold Watch, returned she, and any Body—the very People of this House, I'll warrant you, would lend you five Pounds upon it till your Agent comes to Town——Excuse me, my Dear, reply'd he somewhat haughtily, I never pawn,—nor can I part with my Watch on any Consideration—we in the Army are oblig'd to observe time——[3] Well, cry'd she, sobbing again, I see that I am miserable—you have ruin'd me, and now neither love nor pity me. That's unkind, said he, I would serve you if it were in my power, but this you ask is not—if these two Pieces, added he, would make your Mistress easy—Give them to me, interrupted she, I'll tell her, *Mamma* receiv'd but half what she expected, and could send no more than two, but she should have the other three some Day this Week—but then you must be sure to get them for me. He would fain have perswaded her to have told the

---

1 Vardine is referring to the regimental agent, a civilian who took care of the bulk of regimental accounts and also served largely as the personal servant of the colonel. Agents, who were often thought to profit from the arcane qualities of regimental finance, also acted for the colonel and other officers in numerous regimental and private concerns.

2 A guinea is an English gold coin worth 21s, or 1 shilling more than a pound.

3 Captain Thomas Simes's *The Military Medley* (1768) includes "the List of Things Necessary for a Young Gentleman to be furnished with upon obtaining his first commission in the Infantry," which details that "it is essential that he have a watch, that he may mark the hour exactly" (quoted in Alan J. Guy, *Oeconomy and Discipline: Officership and Administration in the British Army 1714-1763* [Manchester: Manchester UP, 1985] 96).

Accident—He said he could not be assured of receiving Money so soon, and would be loth to disappoint her—In fine,[1] they had many Arguments, he to keep, and she to get the two Guineas:—At length he found himself forced in a manner to recede, and she pocketed the two Pieces——Well, said she, I'll tell my Mistress, that I forgot to bring back the Note—but, my dear, dear *Vardine*, don't fail to procure me the other three by *Tuesday*——I can't promise it so soon as then, reply'd he, you must say *Thursday* or *Friday*—Ay, let it be *Friday*——Since she found she could do no better, she urg'd it no farther, and began to grow more chearful—but the young Officer could not so readily dissipate his Gloom: He was not quite satisfy'd with the Story she told him, and began to fear his little Mistress would become too expensive to him. He conceal'd his Sentiments, however, as well as he was able, and when the Close of Day reminded them of parting, ordered a Coach, and set her down at the same Place where he had taken her up.—As she took her leave, remember *Friday*, and the three Guineas, said she, I shall look for you at the Corner of the Court, about Ten in the Morning, and if you fail, will never speak to you again——And if I do, Child, answer'd he, I'll never venture to look thee in the Face again.

Now did *Syrena* Glory in the Power of her Beauty and Invention, she thought it impossible for Mankind to refuse her any thing; and tho' it was with Difficulty she had gain'd her Point with *Vardine*, she imputed it only to the Scantiness of his Fortune; and did not doubt but to find Articles to get greater Sums of him, tho' he even sold his Commission to raise them for her: But her Triumph lasted not long.—*Friday* Morning happening to come into the Dining-Room, before the Maid had quite finished putting it in order—O Miss! cry'd she, you have lost your Admirer——I did not know I ever had any, answer'd *Syrena*; but what do you mean, *Margaret?*——Why, said she, the Gentleman that I told you of over the way, that used to stare up so.——*Syrena*'s Heart flutter'd at these Words, and in the present Confusion, she cry'd hastily, well what of him? He has left our Neighbourhood, reply'd *Margaret*; as I was washing our Steps about an Hour ago, I saw a Hackney Coach at the Door with a Portmanteau[2] and other Luggage before it, and presently in stept the Beau, and cry'd, Drive away Coachman. Pish! said *Syrena*, thou art always troubling one with some Stuff or other—What was the Fellow to us,

---

1 In short.
2 A case or bag for carrying clothing and other necessaries when traveling; originally of a form suitable for carrying on horseback.

I wonder. She said no more, nor, indeed, was she able, nor to stay any longer in the Room, without discovering her Disorder. She ran up Stairs, tho' she knew not why, she doubted not the Truth of what the Maid had said—She saw the Window open, but no Lover appear—She sat down, pondering on this Adventure, at last recollected herself——Well, said she, a thousand Accidents may have obliged him to quit his Lodging, but that does not follow, that he must therefore quit me.—He will certainly be at the Place he promised at the appointed time——I will at least make my self easy till then.

Soon as she heard the Clock strike ten she ran out, pretending she had broke her Lace, and must go to buy another; but no *Vardine* could she see.——She stay'd a few Minutes walking about the Court, flattering herself still with the Hope that he would come; but instead of him, a sort of ill-look'd Fellow came up to her, and ask'd if her Name was not *Syrena Tricksy*, and on her saying it was, gave her a Letter, which she hastily opening, found in it these few, and little pleasing Lines.

Dear Girl,
OUR Regiment[1] is ordered to the *West*, and thence, I believe, to *Ireland*: I was too lately apprized of it to take my leave of you—make yourself as easy as you can—when I come back I shall with pleasure renew my Acquaintance with you,

Yours, &c.
J. Vardine.

P. S. I am sorry I could not comply with your Request.

Rage did not so far bereave her of her Senses, but that she ask'd the Fellow a great many Questions, but he either could not or would not answer any thing to the purpose; and all she could get from him was, that the Letter was given him by a Gentleman at a Coffee-House, who ordered him to wait in that Court till she came, and deliver it to her.

It must be confessed, this Action of *Vardine's* was cruel and ungrateful——what must have become of the undone and forsaken *Syrena*, had she been possest of that Softness and Tenderness which some are; but as she was capable of loving in reality nothing but her-

---

1   The specific name of the largest permanent unit of the cavalry, infantry, and foot-guards of the British Army.

self, and carried on a Correspondence with him merely on a mercenary View, she was not much to be pitied. The Mortification of her Pride and Avarice, however, gave her Agonies which she before had no notion of; and made her the more easily counterfeit an Indisposition, which was the Pretence agreed on between her and her Mother, for her going Home at the Month's end——and it is certain, she grew so thin and pale, that the Mistress herself imagined that sitting so close to her Work had prejudiced her Health. She had the Good-nature to offer her the Advice of a Physician, but could not help agreeing with every body who were consulted about it, that it was most proper she should be with her Mother, as best acquainted with her Constitution. In fine, home she was brought, nor could that Kinswoman who had recommended her, take it amiss, when she saw how ill she looked—a violent Pain in her Head and Stomach was the Complaint; and it seemed reasonable to believe, that stooping forward to her Work, had occasioned it. There was again some talk of putting her to a Milliner, which was indeed what Mrs. *Tricksy* aimed at; but the Reasons before alledged against that Business, being now repeated, stopped her Mouth; and nothing seemed now so proper for her, as to wait upon a Lady.[1] All the Relations in general approved of this, and promised to enquire among their Acquaintance for a Place for her.

In the mean time *Syrena* was so far from recovering her former Colour and Vivacity, that she look'd worse and worse; and had sometimes such sick Fits, that her Mother began to be afraid she had counterfeited a Disorder so well, as to bring it upon her in good earnest: But her Penetration did not permit her to continue long in the dark as to the Cause. She soon discover'd, that a too near Conversation with a Man had made the Alteration;[2] and not doubting but it was *Vardine*, accused her in such plain and positive Terms, that the Girl had not Courage to deny it. She search'd her Trunk, and found the Stockings, Snuff-Box, and two Guineas, with the Letter, which not only let her into the whole Mystery of her undoing, but her being forsaken also. It would be tiresome to repeat the Exclamations she made, or the Reproaches poor *Syrena* was oblig'd to bear; 'tis sufficient to say, that the first Fury of her Resentment over Reason resumed its Place, and as what was past could not be recal-

---

1   By preventing Syrena from going into millinery and learning a trade, her kinswoman is essentially ensuring that she will never have the opportunity to be financially independent.
2   That is to say that Syrena is pregnant.

I'd, all that could be done, was to endeavour to alleviate the Misfortune as much as possible: To that end, she prepared a strong Potion, which the Girl very willing drank, and being so timely given, had the desired Effect, and caused an Abortion, to the great Joy of both Mother and Daughter.[1] After all was over, and *Syrena* pretty well recovered, Mrs. *Tricksy* could not forbear renewing her upbraidings; but the other confessing herself to blame, and professing her future Conduct should retrieve all, at length mollify'd her Passion; and the more so, because tho' she had suffered herself to be beguiled by that young Officer, yet her Management of him afterwards shewed the Instructions given her had not been thrown away; and that she had both a Genius and Inclination to make the most of her Men, and now an Opportunity offered to prove her Abilities that way.

She was recommended to the Service of an old Lady, who wanted one chiefly to attend her in her Chamber, and read to her till she fell asleep. Such an Employment would have afforded little Hope of advancing *Syrena* in the manner she had desired, had it not been for the

---

1 For women in the eighteenth century, the most popular means for a successful abortion were the use of herbal potions like the one Syrena uses here. As Angus McLaren observes, "women in pursuit of abortifacients had recourse to almost every type of toxic and non-toxic substance" (102). The most frequently prescribed herbs were ergot of rye, pennyroyal, and savin. Ergot of rye is created from rye afflicted with a fungal disease that transforms of the seed of rye and other grasses. Pennyroyal is a species of mint formerly much cultivated and esteemed for its supposed medicinal abilities to treat flatulence, intestinal colic, and delayed menstruation, the latter being the primary use here. Savin, the most popular of the herbs used, is derived from the brownish-blue seed-bearing cones and young shoots of cones from a common evergreen shrub. "Savin enjoyed the reputation of being the most powerful of abortifacients," notes McLaren (104), which doubtlessly accounted for its popularity. Savin is strongly poisonous and possesses emmenagogic agents which increase or renew the menstrual discharge. It was under this guise, of renewing the menses, that abortifacients were frequently marketed (Angus McLaren, *Reproductive Rituals: the perception of fertility in England from the sixteenth century to the nineteenth century* [London and New York: Methuen, 1984]). It is interesting to note that, despite continued sexual activity, Syrena never gets pregnant again. Complications from a medicinally induced abortion could render someone sterile. Such abortions generally happened rather gradually and sometimes the gestational tissue was not completely expelled so that there was continued bleeding and increased susceptibility to infection.

Family the old Gentlewoman was in; which consisted of her Daughter, who was married to a Baronet,[1] and Their Son, a fine young Gentleman of about twenty-two. This last Article rendered the Place extremely acceptable, and our young Deceiver being introduced to the Ladies, her feigned Innocence immediately gained their Favour; and she was received into the House, with the promise of being used very kindly. The second Day after her coming, she wrote to her Mother as full an Account of the Family, as she was able to give in so short a Time.

FRIDAY.

Dear Mamma,

HOW happy would some young Women think themselves to be in my Place, I have so little to do, and am so much respected by the inferior Servants, that I can scarce think I am a Servant myself [2]——it is not required of me to rise till nine or ten o'Clock, and then I go into my Lady's Room, enquire after her Health, and give her her Chocolate,[3] which is ready made and brought up by the upper House-maid:[4] After

---

1 A baronet is a commoner, the principle of the order being to give rank, precedence, and title without privilege. The L——s are clearly a prosperous family and enjoy all the activities their status and geographic location afford them, frequently going to the theatre, shopping, dining out, and having a visiting day.

2 Within a household like the one Syrena has entered, a fine distinction between upper and lower or "inferior" servants would likely exist. Upper servants occupied an executive and supervisory position, and they often had special skills. Lower servants, by contrast, were relatively unskilled manual laborers. Upper servants had a greater degree of visibility than inferior servants. As Lady S——'s lady's maid, Syrena occupies a high position within the household—one enhanced by her literacy, her appearance, and her connection with persons of position. Status within the servant hierarchy was determined, in part, by personal background (e.g. birth and education). As a lady's maid, Syrena attends to the personal needs of her lady—laying out and mending her clothes, dressing her hair, reading to her, etc. Because Syrena's lady is older, fewer demands are placed on her (hence the late rising time and leisurely start to her day).

3 A hot beverage made by dissolving a paste or cake composed of the seeds of the cacao-fruit roasted and ground, sweetened and flavored with vanilla and other substances.

4 A housemaid would be one of the "inferior" servants to which Syrena refers. A housemaid, who ranked below a chambermaid, needed no special training, only industriousness. She served a utilitarian rather than an ornamental function.

this, I am my own Mistress till about one, when she rises, and I help her on with her Clothes, and see her no more till about eleven, which is the time she generally goes to Bed. I sit down and read to her till she falls asleep, and this compleats the Work of the Day—Her Daughter's Woman has ten times more fatigue than I, tho' her Ladyship is reckoned very good too;[1] but I heard by the by that she is horribly jealous of Sir *Thomas*; and that makes her a little cross sometimes to those about her; so I am glad I have nothing to do with her: I lie with Mrs. *Mary* her Chamber maid, who is a mighty good-natur'd Creature, and likes me prodigiously;[2] it was she gave me the hint about Sir *Thomas*, and bid me avoid him as much as I could; for says she, if he should take any notice of you, my Lady would never rest till you were out of the House; and her Mother is so fond of her, that she would part from any body rather than give her a Minute's uneasiness—and I can tell you he loves a Girl in a corner—so I find, Mamma, I must take care of my Behaviour[3]—As for the young Gentleman, I never saw him

---

1 Mrs. Brown, her Ladyship's personal maid, obviously has a more taxing schedule in part because her Ladyship is a more active individual, requiring more attention to her clothing and a companion when she goes out (for example, she later accompanies Lady S—— and Lady L—— when they go shopping). As the personal maid to the lady of the house, Mrs. Brown would have had more status than any other female servant except the housekeeper. A lady's maid was "used with more respect and accorded a greater degree of formal courtesy as is indicated by the 'Mrs.' generally placed before her surname when she was addressed" (J. Jean Hecht, *The Domestic Servant Class in Eighteenth-Century England* [London: Routledge, 1956] 63). Even Mr. L—— addresses her as Mrs. Brown.

2 Syrena and Mrs. Mary share quarters as was typical for servants of comparable status. As a chambermaid, Mrs. Mary (who was above the inferior servants) would answer to both the lady of the house and the lady's maid (e.g., Mrs. Brown). Her responsibilities would include taking care of clothes and taking care of the bedroom (dusting, starting the fire, etc.).

3 Haywood is highlighting one of the consistent dangers for women in domestic service: their sexual vulnerability to all the men who live in the same household. As Bridget Hill details, "the very characteristics which distinguished female domestic servants made them particularly prone to sexual exploitation" (44). Alone in a strange household, they lacked familial or parental protection. Additionally, their daily routine would be known to everyone; thus "any predatory male in the house would know where they could be found at any time of the day—and night." That knowledge, coupled with "the intimate services maidservants often performed for their masters," provided "ample opportunity for sexual advances." Female servants' physical accessibility was underscored by the

till this Morning as I was coming up Stairs—I assure you he is not at all handsome—you need not fear I shall lose my Heart.—He did not speak a Word, but stared at me when I stopped to let him pass, and I made him a Curtesy—so how things will happen I can't tell; but if any thing material occurs, you may be sure of being immediately acquainted with it, by

Dear Mamma,
Your most Obedient Daughter,
SYRENA TRICKSY.

P. S. Just as I had finish'd the above, my Lady's Bell rung; so not having time to seal it then, I have the opportunity to tell you, that as I was crossing the passage, I saw the young Gentleman again, coming out of his Father's Closet; I made him another Curtesy, and blush'd, and I thought he look'd a little red too, but did not speak a Word—I hope soon to have more to acquaint you with.

MONDAY.

Dear Mamma,

I Long'd to see you Yesterday, but did not think it would look well to ask to go out the very first *Sunday* I came. So I write to inform you, what has happen'd since my last. On *Saturday* Morning, as I was in a Room joining to my Lady's Chamber, tacking a Pair of three-double Ruffles on her Sleeves (for she goes as fine and as gay as her Daughter, tho' she is so very old)[1] Mr. L—— came thro' to pay his Duty to his Grandmother, as it seems he does every Morning, tho' I never happen'd to be in the way before. He took no notice of me as he went, but when he came back, So my pretty Lass, said he, you wait upon my Grandmother, I think? Yes, Sir, replied I, rising and curtesying, I am so happy. I hope you'll have cause to think yourself so, returned he, she is a very good Mistress, and you look as if you would deserve her Favours. This was all that past, and he went directly down stairs.——Now whether he had any Meaning in what he said I can't tell, but I could not help thinking it a lucky Omen, that the first thing he said to me should be, that *he hoped I should have*

---

dominant attitude toward them "For many in the eighteenth century it seemed very natural that masters—and their sons—should regard their servants as sexually available" (50). *Servants: English Domestics in the Eighteenth Century* (Oxford: Clarendon Press, 1996).

1 Syrena's experience at the mantua-maker's probably heightened her desirability as a servant for she (allegedly) possessed solid skills as a seamstress.

Cause to think myself happy.—I should think myself happy indeed, if I could get a Husband with such an Estate as he will have——O, what Splendor does my Lady L—— live in!——How every body worships her—tho' I must not set my Heart too much upon it, for fear of a Disappointment—but I have something more to tell you still, *Mamma*—Yesterday in the Afternoon my Lady, and Sir *Thomas* and his Lady, and Mr. L—— went all out a visiting—So it being an idle time Mrs. *Brown* Lady L——'s Woman, and the Chambermaid and I were got all together over a Pot of Coffee in the Back-Parlour; and tho' I believe none of us are silly enough to give any Credit to what one may fancy is to be seen in throwing the Grounds, yet to amuse ourselves we toss'd the Cups, as they call it, and were telling one another our Fortunes[1]—when, to our great Surprize, in comes Mr. L——: we were so busy, that we never heard him, till he was just upon us—it seems some of the Under-Maids[2] happen'd to be standing at the Door, and he came in without knocking—He found what we were at, and fell a laughing most prodigiously; but the Confusion we were all in is not to be express'd——Nay, nay, said he, I won't disturb you; and since I have caught you, am resolved to make one among you—Come, which of you is the Artist?——I believe, Sir, replied Mrs. *Brown*, who had the most Courage, our Skill is pretty equal; tho' I think *Mary* is rather the best at Invention——Then *Mary* shall be my Conjurer,[3] said he; and with these Words turn'd down a Cup. Poor Mrs. *Mary* was sadly asham'd, and begg'd his Honour would excuse her; but he would needs carry on the Jest, and forced her to take the Cup——Well then, said she, here is a great House, and a fine Lady at the Gate, that seems to expect a Visit from your Honour; and a great deal more such Stuff she run on with. He laugh'd again, and said, as you observed Mrs. *Brown* I find *Mary* is a great Visionary; but she has not happen'd to hit upon my Humour ——I don't regard fine Ladies; Beauty and Innocence have more Charms for me than Grandeur——He look'd full at me as he spoke

---

1   Reading coffee grounds and tea leaves were common forms of prognostication (and entertainment) at the time. Note too that these three servants are usually segregated from the inferior servants in duties, accommodations, eating, and leisure activities.

2   An undermaid was a general household maid and the least skilled within the house.

3   While a conjurer can mean one who conjures spirits and possesses some sort of supernatural power, it can also more broadly mean an individual who can tell fortunes (or an imposter who pretends to).

these last Words:——then, I thank you for my Fortune, however, *Mary*, continued he; and I think I ought to pay for it. With this he gave us every one a Kiss, beginning with Mrs. *Brown*, and ending with me. But indeed, Mamma, I am very much mistaken, if there was not a great deal of difference between his manner of saluting them and me; he seem'd, I thought, only to touch their Lips, but press'd mine so hard that he made them smart. After this, Well, said he, I won't stay to be a Restraint upon you—pray pursue your Diversion, and so went up stairs.

This Accident is very trifling, but every thing must have a Beginning; and therefore I thought fit to let you know it, as you shall most faithfully all that happens to, my dear Mamma,

Your most Dutiful Daughter,
SYRENA TRICKSY.

WEDNESDAY.

Dear Mamma,

I AM not half so easy as when I wrote to you last—I am afraid, I have made a Conquest in the wrong Place.—I find what Mrs. *Mary* told me is true.—Sir *Thomas* can't be content with his own Lady, tho' she is allow'd to be one of the finest Women in the Kingdom, and is not old now; for they say, she was a perfect Girl when Mr. *L——* was born: Well, if I were a Woman of Fortune, I'd marry none of them.—But I'll tell you, *Mamma*; Lady *L——* went with some Company to the Play on *Monday*; after she was gone, Sir *Thomas* came up into my Lady's Room, and staid about an Hour, and drank Wine and eat some Jelly with her, which I serv'd, as it being in her Chamber; when he took his leave I was order'd to light him down;[1] I did so, and when we came to the Door of his Study, he took hold of my Hand and pull'd me in: I was so confounded, not expecting any such Thing from him, who had never before seem'd to look at me, that I had not power to make any Resistance.—Pretty Mrs. *Syrena*, said he, I would not have given you this Trouble; but for an Opportunity to tell you how much I am charmed with your Person and Behaviour——in speaking this he clapped the Door, but did not lock it. I beg your Honour would not talk so to me, answered I, endeavouring to get from him; but he held me fast, and in spite of all I could do, forced a hundred Kisses from me.——The more I struggled, the

---

1 Lady S——'s room is upstairs and Syrena illuminates or "lights down" the stairway for Sir Thomas.

closer he press'd me to him; and I don't know how far the old Goat might have proceeded, if I had not protested, I would cry out and alarm the House: he then desisted; but still held me with one Hand, and with the other took five Guineas out of his Pocket, and would have put them down my Bosom;[1] say nothing to any body, cried he, and I'll be a Friend to you: Sir, said I, resolutely, I desire no Friendship, but what I shall endeavour to merit by my Honesty; and as I am Madam S———'s Servant, shall take no Presents from any of her Relations, without acquainting her with it. You are young, cried he, and don't know the World yet; nor do I desire to be inform'd of it by such Means, replied I; and giving a sudden Spring got loose, and ran up Stairs. I thought that I had thrown all the Pieces down, that he attempted to put into my Bosom; but when I came to unlace me, I found one Guinea had slipt in unknown to me.—Indeed, I was a little tempted to keep it, as believing he would not miss it, in the hurry of Spirits he seemed to have been; but then again I thought that if he did, it would look like an Encouragement: So it came into my Head to make a merit to the Ladies of restoring it, and at the time shew him, that any future Attempts he should think to make upon me would be in vain. When I went into my Lady's Chamber in the Morning; Madam, said I, after I had read you to sleep last Night, I saw this Guinea lying on the Carpet, so I took it up, fearing it might be lost, when the Carpet was taken up to be shook, I suppose you happen'd to drop it. No, answer'd she, I never carry Money loose in my Pocket.—I believe, my Son in pulling out some Papers, might let it fall. I beg then, Madam, said I, you will be so good to return it to him. No, replied she, you shall do it yourself. When we go to Dinner, I'll send for you into the Parlour: She did so, and having told Sir *Thomas*, what I had said concerning the Guinea; I went to him, and made him a low Curtesy, offering it to him. No, Mrs. *Syrena*, said he, pray keep it yourself, as a Reward for your Honesty. I humbly thank'd his Honour, and went away; but as I went out of the Room, I heard Lady L——— say, Sir *Thomas*, I am glad you have given it to her; and the Butler[2] told me afterwards, that they all were full of my

---

1 It is worth noting that Syrena considered this a handsome sum in her dealings with Vardine. In 1750, the average annual income in England was £12-13—little more than twice what Syrena is offered here.

2 Though technically a butler was the male servant responsible for keeping the wine cellar, realistically his job would be more expansive including everything from cleaning shoes and knives and forks to the cellar management.

Praises. Sir *Thomas* himself, I find is not disobliged at this Action, for as I went through the Dining-Room this Morning, to ask how Lady *L*—— had slept, she being a little ill with the Head-Ach last Night, he was sitting at the Window, and as soon as he saw me, he rose, and in a low Voice, said, I see you have a Discretion above your Years. ——I will offer nothing that shall alarm you; but I must have a Moment's Discourse with you soon. I was vex'd he was there, and only answer'd, I beg your Honour will not think on't, and so left him. As to Mr. *L*——, I have not seen him since *Sunday*, but at Table when I carried in the Guinea, and once in my Lady's Chamber; so I can form no Judgment, how far I am in his good Graces, any farther than my last made mention of.—It is very unlucky that his Father likes me; but I shall shun him as much as I can, without being taken Notice on by the Family.——I am afraid I shan't be able to see you next *Sunday* neither, for my Lady talks of taking Physick;[1] but I am not certain yet, and shall write to you again before then, for I have time enough, if I have but an agreeable Subject. I am,

Dear Mamma,
Your most dutiful Daughter,
SYRENA TRICKSY.

THURSDAY Evening.

Dear Mamma,

STRANGE Adventures have happen'd since yesterday Morning; but don't be alarm'd for the Consequence of them, in all Probability will turn out highly to Advantage, one Way or another. But I will not keep you in Suspence. As soon as Dinner was over, the Coach was order'd, and my Lady and Lady *L*——, and Mrs. *Brown* went among the Shops as they call it, that is to make all the Tradesmen in their Way pull down their Goods;[2] tell them what Lady bought of such a Pattern, and what of such a one; in fine to hear News, and buy Pennyworths[3] if they meet with any. But this is nothing to my Purpose.——After they were gone, I went up into my Lady's Room, to lay her Night-Things ready, as I always did, against she undrest, and was a humming a new Tune to myself, little thinking any Body was behind me, when turning about, I saw Sir *Thomas* just coming into

---

1 To dose or treat with physic or medicine, especially with a purgative.
2 It is likely they are going to the Royal Exchange.
3 The amount of anything that is or may be bought for a penny; or, according to Johnson, "any purchase; anything bought or sold for money."

the Chamber; I was very much startled, but had not time to speak, before he said Mrs. *Syrena*, I have a Favour to beg of you; in any Thing I can, and ought to do, I shall obey your Honour, answer'd I; it is only to mend a Hole in my Stocking, that is just now broke, return'd he; and then looking round the Room, I see you are alone, cried he: These Words frighted me very much, and I would have given any Thing to have been out of the Chamber, or that somebody had come up; but he knew well enough the Under-Servants were all at Dinner; and he had left Mrs. *Mary* busy in her Lady's Room, or else he would not have ventured to come into me in that Manner. He saw I was uneasy, and to dissipate my Fears.——Don't be under Apprehensions, said he, I shall do you no Hurt—you don't think I wou'd ravish you sure.——I hope, Sir, answer'd I, you would not harbour any Thoughts of ruining a poor Girl, who has nothing but her good Character to depend upon.[1] No Child, said he, your Character can run no risque with a Man, who would not forfeit his own—and it is on this Head, I want to talk with you.——He then told me, that he liked and loved me above any Woman he had ever seen; that if I would consent to be his, he would put it out, even of his own power to use me ill, by making me a handsome Settlement.—All which Offers I rejected with (I think, I may say without Vanity) a well-affected vertuous Pride.——I told him, I preferr'd my Honesty in Rags, to all the Splendor in the World, when it must be the Purchase of Vice and Infamy; and desired he would desist making me any such Offers; for as I looked upon it, as a Crime even to listen to them, I must be obliged to leave the House.[2]——Well, said he, I will endeavour to conquer myself, if I am able.—But, how is it possible, continued he, sighing, and looking full in my Face, when I see those Eyes.——Then I must hide them, cried I, turning away. ——No resumed he, I must not, cannot lose the Pleasure of seeing you—cruel Girl as you are—but still I hope, you will one Day be

---

1   The term "character" suggests both the more abstract sense of one's moral worth, value or reputation as well as the more immediate sense of the term as the formal testimony given by an employer as to the qualities and habits of one that has been in his employ. As Hill notes, without a character "obtaining another place might be difficult if not impossible" (98).

2   Pamela writes, "I can so contentedly return to my Poverty again, and think it less Disgrace to be oblig'd to wear Rags, and live upon Rye-bread and Water, as I use to do, than to be a Harlot to the greatest Man in the World" (41).

kinder.—Yes you will.—You must, continued he, catching hold of both Hands, and pressing them between his——then perceiving I began to tremble again, why are you so alarm'd, added he? tho' Opportunities are so scarce, that perhaps, I was a little too precipitate in seizing the first; yet you see I now behave to you in a different Manner. Every thing that has a Tendency to corrupt my Innocence, said I, is alike alarming; and I against protest, I will not stay in a House where I cannot be secure.——Well, Mrs. *Syrena*, replied he, letting go my Hands, you judge my Intentions with too much Severity.—I assure you, that the short time you have been in my Family, has made an Impression on me, that would not suffer me to injure you.—Only think on what I have said, and command any thing in my power: With these Words he kiss'd me, and left the Room. I presently lock'd the Door to prevent his Return; and was sitting down to consider how I should behave in this Affair, when the Closet-Door behind me open'd, and out came Mr. *L*——. Never was Surprize equal to mine, of seeing him there: I had not Presence enough of Mind to forbear shrieking, which I am since heartily glad, nobody heard. Hush! cried he, or you'll bring my Father back again. For Heaven's sake, Sir, said I, what brought you into that Closet? Not Curiosity, upon my Word, answer'd he, for I little expected the Scene I have been witness of; but whatever Motive induced me to conceal myself here, you ought not to be dissatisfy'd, since by it I have proved your Virtue and Prudence equal to your Beauty. I beseech you, Sir, said I, don't rally a poor silly Girl, who has nothing to boast of, but the Resolution of keeping herself honest. No, Mrs. *Syrena*, reply'd he, I never was more serious in my Life than I am this Moment—I was less so, I confess when I went into that Closet, but my Father's Behaviour has been such a Surprize upon me that——He was going to say something, but a sudden Thought made him break off, and after a little Pause, But sure, resum'd he, you do not in earnest intend to quit my Grandmother? I should think it the greatest Blessing of Life, answer'd I, to continue in the Service of so good a Lady; but the Persecutions I am like to receive from Sir *Thomas*, are of a Nature I neither can or ought to bear, for any Consideration. I am sorry to say, returned he, that amorous Addresses are not very becoming in a Man of fifty to a Girl of your Years; but if ever it should be discover'd, 'tis his own, not your Character, would suffer by it—You may depend, that whatever his Inclinations are, he has too much Honour to make use of Force to gain you; and if you should leave us, you can go into no Family, but where those Eyes of yours will lay you under the same Temptations you receive from him. On this I hung down my Head, and kept looking on the Ground to avoid seeing how he look'd when he spoke. Don't be asham'd, pursued he, taking me by the Hand, I tell you nothing but Truth—So, pretty Mrs. *Syrena*, you must not think of going out of the House, at least yet a while. If I could be safe, said I, nothing could give me greater Pleasure than to continue here—but——You shall be safe, interrupted he, Come, dry those lovely Eyes—(for I was just then squeezing out some Tears) I had something to say to you, but will take another Opportunity, and leave you now to compose your self: He concluded with giving me a Kiss, accompanied with a most tender Pressure of my Hand, and then went out of the Chamber; but had not been gone above three Steps, before he return'd; I believe, said he, you are too discreet and good-natur'd to expose my Father's Folly? I should be very sorry, answer'd I, to do any thing that might create Uneasiness in a Family, for the greatest part of whom I have the most perfect Love and Veneration. Those of us who enjoy that are happy, cry'd he, and methought his Eyes struck Fire as he spoke these Words; but he went on, I have one thing more to desire of you, and that is, that you will let me know from time to time what Sollicitations you receive from my Father——My Advice may be of some Service to you; and such a Mark of your Confidence highly obliging to me. Sir, reply'd I, tho' such a Confidence to a Person of a different Sex, must cover me with the utmost Confusion; yet you seem too good, and too full of Pity to me, for me to refuse. You cannot have too great an Opinion of my Good-will towards you, said he, and so you shall find. Here he took me in his Arms, and gave me three or four hearty Kisses, tho' with all the Modesty in the World, and then ran down Stairs.

Now, *Mamma*, what can I think of all this, but that he conceal'd himself in the Closet for no other purpose, than to attempt me in the manner Sir *Thomas* has done; but that my resolute Behaviour to the *Father*, made a Convert of the *Son*; and turned the Inclinations he felt for me, into others of a more respectful Nature.—I would be loath to flatter my self too far—but I think I am right—Time will discover——This Morning, after he came down from Breakfast, as he always does, with Sir *Thomas* and his Lady in their Chamber, he tarry'd walking backwards and forwards in the great Parlour, for, I believe, three Hours; and every time I pass'd him, as I was oblig'd to do very often, there being no other way from my Lady's Room, he gave me Looks which told me, he had the kindest Thoughts of me; and once, no Body being in Sight, came to me and kiss'd me, with these Words, Dear Mrs. *Syrena* be easy. He dined abroad to Day with

Sir *Thomas*, so I have seen neither of them since; but I don't doubt now, but I shall have Matter sufficient to employ my Pen to you very often. Dear *Mamma*, with good Success to,

Your dutiful Daughter,
SYRENA TRICKSY.

FRIDAY Morning.

Dear Mamma,

I Am now eased of the Suspence I was in when I wrote to you Yesterday: Mr. L—— has broke his Mind to me——I'll tell you in what manner—*Thursday* being what they call my Lady's Visiting Day,[1] there was a vast deal of Company; but I had nothing to do with them, for Mrs. *Brown* and the Chambermaid attend in a little Room within the Drawing-Room, as the Groom of the Chambers and Butler do in one without;[2] so having no Body to converse with, I sat in my own Lady's Room, meditating on my Affairs—I think I mention'd in my former, that the two Gentlemen dined abroad——Sir *Thomas*, after he had quitted his Company, it seems, went to the Play, but Mr. L—— came Home—He did not stay five Minutes in the Drawing Room, but knowing how the Family were engag'd, and expecting to find me where he did, came directly up. I rose to pay my Respects to him, but he made me sit down immediately, and placing himself near me, I desire, said he, that there may be no Distance observ'd between us when we are alone, and could wish our Circumstances would admit of an Equality in publick—But Fortune is not always just to Merit. I was about to make him some Compliment in return, but he prevent-

---

1 The Lady's visiting day is the day that is signified as the one in which an individual would receive guests; an at-home day.
2 The location of the servants during this social occasion illustrates how the upper servants were visible during social or public events while the lower servants, generally, were not. The groom of chambers was the lowest among male servants and would have been responsible for maintaining the furniture and other household items, and would also have been expected "to attend in the Hall when there [was] company" (Hecht 63). Since Syrena is not Lady L——'s servant, she is not required to be present. While the presence of servants was a way of demonstrating rank and assuring personal convenience, it often resulted in tips or "vails" for those servants as well. As John Burnett notes, "even in middle-class households it was usual to give the maid 1s. after a visit" (*A History of the Cost of Living* [Aldershot, UK; Brookfield, VT: Gregg Revivals, 1993; originally published: Harmondsworth, UK: Penguin, 1969] 184.)

ed me by going on——I have a great deal to say to you Mrs. *Syrena*, pursued he, but if you desire I should be a sincere Friend to you, you must be sincere to me in answering a few Questions I shall ask. I should be altogether unworthy of the Honour you do me, Sir, reply'd I, if I should make any Attempt to impose on your Belief—I say an Attempt, for being bred up in a perfect Abhorrence of Lying, and all kind of Deceit, I should go about the Practice of it in so aukward a manner, that a very little Share of Judgment would be sufficient to detect me. But, Sir, continued I, thank Heaven, I yet am conscious of nothing I would wish to conceal from the Knowledge of any Body. (There, I think, I followed your Instructions to a nicety, *Mamma*.) I dare answer for you to my self, said he, that you have been guilty of nothing that can be call'd a Crime; but Love is not so; and my sweet *Syrena*, have you never yet seen the Man happy enough to make an Impression on you? Never, indeed, Sir, reply'd I, nor do I boast it as a Virtue; because till the dreadful Declaration made by Sir *Thomas*, I never heard the Sound of Love from any Man in the World. Well, resumed he, and was it owing, examine well your Heart before you answer, to a Detestation of his Offers, or a Dislike to his Person and Years, that made you so resolutely repulse him? To a Detestation of his Offers, said I, for I consider'd nothing farther. Then, cry'd he, you would equally hate any other should address you on the same score? I think so, answer'd I; but, Sir, I beseech you question me no farther.— I know my Heart at present, but know not what it may be hereafter.— I have heard of Women, that have an hundred Times my Understanding, and yet made a false Step, as they call it.—'Tis Heaven alone must keep me, and by depending on that only Guard, I hope to be secure. Well, but there is no harm, said he, in indulging a Tenderness, for a generous faithful Lover. No, Sir, replied I, not when his Designs are virtuous and honourable. The World, cry'd he, is not well agreed about the true Signification of those Words, *Virtuous* and *Honourable*; but for my Part, I think that what tends to make the Happiness of the beloved Object is both *Virtuous* and *Honourable*.—But, we'll leave the Defini- tion to the Casuists:[1] I have one Thing more, my charming *Syrena*, to be inform'd of, and then I have done.——Suppose, continued he, I loved you, and loved you with a Passion, which it was utterly impos- sible for me to subdue, must I for that Reason, be the Object of your Aversion?—(I expected this, so had prepared myself for it, as you will

---

1 A theologian (or other person) who studies and resolves cases of conscience or doubtful questions regarding duty and conduct.

find *Mamma*.) Heaven forbid, cry'd I, that I should ever be brought into so terrible Dilemma.——I know what I ought to do—but—(here I seem'd to faulter in my Speech) but I beseech you, Sir, do not talk in this Manner to a poor silly Creature, that knows not how to answer you. Dear lovely Innocence! cry'd he, pulling me to him, and kissing me an hundred Times, I believe in spite of all my Struggling, I do love you, pursued he; the very first Minute I saw you, I loved you.——But your Wit, your Prudence, your unaffected Modesty, has made me now almost adore you. Here, he began to kiss me again with more Vehemence than before, and I could not get leave to speak for a good while; at last bursting from him, and pretending to weep, Ah, Sir! said I, if you lov'd me, you would not use me in this Manner. By Heaven, I do, said he, and to prove it will——here he stopped, and then, will do almost any thing. I was going to reply, but heard somebody coming up Stairs; it was the Groom of the Chambers for a Sheet of gilt Paper out of my Lady's 'Scrutore,[1] for one of the Company to write a Song; he seem'd surpriz'd to find Mr. *L*—— with me, as was he at his coming up; but to take off all Suspicion, I came a begging too, said he, for a Stick of Wax; I happening to be out, and I know my Grandmother is a great Clerk,[2] but Mrs. *Syrena* tells me there is none, have you any in your Charge, for I want to seal some Letters? I think I have, Sir, answer'd the other, where shall I bring it your Honour? Into my Chamber, said Mr. *L*——, and went with him down Stairs. I have not seen him since, nor indeed was there any Opportunity, for the Company taking leave soon after, they went to Supper; and he is not stirring yet;——a thousand to one but this Day will produce something more; if it does, I'll write Tomorrow, for my Lady persists in her Design of taking Physick, and I can't come out on *Sunday*. If you find any thing amiss in my Management, let me know it by old *Sarah*, for I would not have you trust the Penny Post;[3] but if I have behaved according to your Mind, defer writing

---

1 An abbreviation of escritoire, a writing-desk constructed to contain stationery and documents; in early use, often one of a portable size; more recently, chiefly applied to a larger piece of furniture, a bureau or secretary.

2 Mr. *L*—— claims to need wax for sealing a letter. Originally, a clerk was a person of book learning, one able to read and write often more generally synonymous with scholar. By this time, however, the term often refers to a penman.

3 Letters sent by penny post were not delivered directly to the person but rather were left at the post office until called for. For that reason, Syrena wants to use "old Sarah" to be sure that her letter does not get misdirected.

till a more material Occasion, for I would not have any Body come after me too often. I am, dear Mamma, as ever,

Your most obedient Daughter,
SYRENA TRICKSY.

P. S. I had forgot to tell you that Mr. *Groves*, the Groom of the Chambers, has been vastly diligent to oblige me ever since I came into the House; and I am afraid guesses somewhat by seeing Mr. *L——* in the Chamber with me last Night, for this Morning he looks very sullen, and did not speak to me as he used to do.

MONDAY Morning.

Dear Mamma,
FRIDAY pass'd over, without any thing happening worth acquainting you with; tho' both Sir *Thomas* and his Son were at home the greatest part of the Day; not that I believe it owing to the Inclinations of either; but that the Presence of the one was a hindrance to the other, in any Design they might have of speaking to me. On *Saturday* Morning I saw Mr. *L——* in my Lady's Chamber; as he went out, I happened to be pretty near the Door, and he took the Opportunity of snatching a Kiss from me behind a great Screen, that stands to shelter that part of the Room where my Lady sits from the Air. This was all the Place would give him leave to do, but he afterwards watch'd my coming down Stairs, and the Coast being clear, my dear *Syrena*, said he, that impertinent Fellow (meaning *Groves*) interrupted our Conversation the other Night, before I had told you half what I had to say;—my Father will be engaged for the whole Evening, and the Ladies are to be at the Assembly;[1]—don't be frighten'd if I conceal myself again in the same Closet, nor shun the Place because you know I shall be there. I had no Opportunity of making any Answer, if I had been prepared for one, which indeed I was not, he took me so unawares; for the Moment he left off speaking, he turned upon his Heel, fell a singing an *Italian* Air,[2] and went up Stairs. Indeed, Mamma, I was very uneasy at this.—I thought to be there would have too much the Air of an Assignation;[3] and not to

---

1 An evening gathering for persons of quality of both sexes. It provides a sharp contrast to the kind of gatherings to which Syrena has access.

2 Italian song, likely from an opera, which underscores Mr. L——'s educational and financial status.

3 The arrangement of the time and place for an interview or tryst.

be there when I knew he was waiting for me, would be an Affront, not befitting one of my Station to one of his, and might turn the Love he had for me into hate; so I resolv'd on the former, but how to carry myself, so as that my complying should not give too much Encouragement, employed my Thoughts the whole Day: But I might have saved myself that Trouble, if I could have guessed what would happen. Sir *Thomas* went out at four o'Clock, and the Chariot was order'd for the Ladies at seven; as soon as they were gone, Mrs. *Brown* comes jumping into the Parlour, where Mrs. *Mary* and I were talking of some silly Stuff or another; so, said she, now we have the House to ourselves for one while: Mr. *L——* is gone out, is he not? pursued she, to Mrs. *Mary*; I believe a good while since, answered she, for I saw him with his Hat on presently after Sir *Thomas* went, and his Man is snoring on the Dresser below.[1] Well then, we'll enjoy ourselves, cry'd the other, I'll treat you two with a Bottle of *French*[2] and a *Seville* Orange,[3] and then we'll have a Pot of Tea: What say you, Mrs. *Syrena*? I thank you, Madam, answer'd I, but I have so much Business to do——O you are greatly employed, you would make one believe, cry'd Mrs. *Brown*, but we'll have you for all your Excuses. Well then, said I, I will only put my Lady's things in Order, and come down; with that I ran up Stairs in a great Hurry, not doubting but my Lover was at his Appointment; as indeed he was; for pretending he was going out when they rose from Table, he took his Hat and went into his Chamber, where locking himself in till the Ladies were gone, he slipp'd up the Back-stairs, and so into the Closet. When I came into the Chamber, after he had peeped thro' the Key-hole, that he might not be mistaken in the Person, he opened the Door, and catching me in his Arms, dear Girl, said he, what Pains do I take for a Moment's Pleasure, and that too I fear you grudge me;—but with your Leave, my Dear, I'll shut the Door for fear of Mr. *Groves*, added he, with a Smile, and immediately bolted it. O, Sir, cry'd I, I shall be soon obliged to open it, if I make any Stay here. I then told him of Mrs. *Brown*'s Invitation, and how I had promised to go down; on which he gave her two or three hearty Curses; he had not time to utter much more, for Mrs. *Mary* came up,

---

1 That is, Mr. *L——*'s man servant is asleep on the kitchen table or sideboard ("dresser") down in the kitchen. As this text makes clear, personal servants were essentially off duty when their master was not in the house.

2 French wine or brandy.

3 A bitter orange used for making marmalade.

and finding the Door fastened, cry'd, Hey-day! what have you bolted yourself in;—open the Door, Mrs. *Syrena*, Mrs. *Brown* sent me for you. On this Mr. *L*—— was compell'd to return to his Concealment, and I let in the Intruder;——come said she, what are you doing; I was going, answer'd I, to pin up a Head[1] for my Lady;—— Pish, return'd the other, you know she does not go out Tomorrow— therefore you may let it alone till another time;——come, come, Mrs. *Brown* is making the Bishop[2] herself, and 'tis ready by now—— I'll follow you in a Moment, said I. No, no, cry'd she, I'll have you go with me;—come, who knows but the young Squire may surprize us as he did over the Coffee. If I thought so, answer'd I, you should have none of my Company, for I never was so much asham'd in my Life;— there's no Danger, said she, and pull'd me along with her; when we came into my Lady *L*——'s Dressing-Room, for it was there Mrs. *Brown* made this Regale,[3] you are so fond of mewing yourself up[4] in that Chamber above, said she to me, that one would imagine you met a *Sweetheart* there;——I believe, Mamma, that in spight of all the Lessons you gave me to the contrary, I could not quite overcome my Confusion at these Words; but putting on as composed a Look as I could, if no body thought no more of *Sweethearts* than I do, answered I, the *Parsons* would have little Business—— O! one may have a *Sweetheart*, resumed she laughing, without having any Occasion for a *Parson*: Ay, cry'd I; for my part I always thought entertaining a *Sweetheart*, was in order to make a *Husband* of him. That's as it falls out, said she, for there are *Sweethearts* of different kinds. She seemed, methought, to speak this with a sort of malicious Sneer, and what I have since heard, convinces me I was not mistaken. I took no Notice, however, but laugh'd as they did, and we were very merry over our Bishop. At last, I can't remember for my Life how she introduced it, but she cry'd all on a sudden, So, Mrs. *Syrena*, you would have us think you never had a Lover yet; I don't care what any Body thinks, answer'd I, but sure if I had one, we

---

1 Head dress.
2 A sweet, warm drink made of red wine mixed with sugar and oranges or lemons. It is a drink often found in taverns, and Johnson describes it as a "cant" word, or a dialect word that marks its lower social location.
3 Food or refreshment.
4 To "mew yourself up" is to confine, hide or conceal one's self. Syrena later says she won't conceal herself in the closet any more. To mew up can also mean to change one's hair or clothes, which may also be intended here.

should see one another sometimes, and all the House knows, that since I have been here, I have never been once abroad, nor has any Man or Woman either come to visit me——yes, said Mrs. Brown, to my certain Knowledge you have had a *Visitor*, I won't say a *Lover*. Me! cry'd I, in some Astonishment; yes, you, for all your demure Looks, resumed she, pray was not Mr. L—— once with you in your Lady's Chamber? Here, Mamma, I had enough to do to contain myself; but I believe I behaved pretty tolerably; Mr. L—— said I, yes, he came up one Evening for a Stick of Wax,—but what of that? Nay, nothing, answer'd she, but I had a Mind to banter you a little; she said no more, but I perceived by this that *Groves* had been tatling, and also, that there was some Suspicion that the Stick of Wax was but a Pretence. I resolved therefore to consent to no more Concealments in the Closet, for fear of a Discovery, which would infallibly ruin all our Projects. When Mrs. *Mary* and I were in Bed, she told me as a great Secret, that both Mr. *Groves* and Mrs. *Brown* imagined Mr. L—— had a more than ordinary liking to me; but said she, she has told my Lady nothing of it yet, nor won't, I heard her say, till she had found all out, and I fancy she made the Treat[1] on purpose to try if she could pump you out of any thing;——so, Mrs. *Syrena*, as I wish you well from my Heart, I would advice you to take care, if there be any thing in it; for Mrs. *Brown* is a very good Woman, but a little prying, and loves to meddle—you understand me. I do, answer'd I, and thank you for your Caution, tho' I assure you there is no need of it, Mr. L—— never chang'd ten Words with me in his Life. I am glad of it, said she, for what Designs can such a Gentleman as he have upon one of us, but to ruin us.[2] Very true, reply'd I; she again conjured me to Secrecy, which I as firmly promised, and that put an end to our Discourse; but I was so nettled, that I did not sleep all Night. Yesterday I did not stir out of my Lady's Chamber the whole Day, not even to Dinner, for she made me eat a bit of boil'd Chicken with her: and Mrs. *Mary*, and one or other of the House-Maids, brought up and carry'd down every thing that was wanted; among other things Mrs. *Brown* told me on *Saturday*, that there was a talk of going out of Town this Week: My Lady also mentioned something of it to me herself; but on what Day, or who of the Family are to go, I know not as yet; but am very sure I shall be one, whoever

---

1 An entertainment of food and drink given without expense to the recipient.
2 See Appendix A for examples of the sexual vulnerability of female servants.

is left behind, for my Lady likes nothing but what I do for her. If their Resolution holds of going this Week, I shall ask to come and take my leave of you; but I suppose you will hear from me before that, who am, dear Mamma,

Your Dutiful Daughter,
SYRENA TRICKSY.

WEDNESDAY Afternoon.

Dear Mamma,
SUNDAY being fix'd for our Country Journey,[1] I send this to acquaint you, that I hope to be with you on *Friday*, for To-morrow my Lady dresses early to go out, and on *Saturday* we shall all be busy packing up; but I mentioned *Friday* to my Lady, who has promised I shall have the whole Day to myself. Nothing worthy of writing has happened since my last, except that seeing Mr. *L——* in the Parlour, waiting for a Chair[2] to go out, I ventured to run to him, and acquainted him with what Mrs. *Brown* had said to me, and the Hints given me by the Chambermaid;——he bit his Lips all the time I was speaking, and seemed very much out of Humour; I know not whether at me or the News I told him; for just as he was about to reply, we heard somebody coming, and he cry'd, Curse on it, there's no speaking in this House, and I ran as fast as I could into the Back-Parlour, and so down Stairs; the Person who gave us this Interruption was Sir *Thomas*, as I afterwards found, for my Lady's Bell ringing, I was obliged to return, and saw him talking to his Son as I pass'd the Door. If (as they say) *Difficulties encrease Inclination*, both Father and Son meet with enough in their Designs on me, to make them grow violent at last. But, dear Mamma, I hope we shall have Opportunity on *Friday* to talk over all our Affairs, and consult what future Measures are proper to be taken by

Your most obedient Daughter,
SYRENA TRICKSY.

---

1 The household is preparing to go to L—— Hall, the L——'s house in the country, likely marking the end of the London season in April or May.
2 An enclosed chair or covered vehicle for one person, carried on poles by two men.

SATURDAY Morning, Eight o'Clock.

Dear Mamma,

YOU little think by what Means I was prevented waiting on you Yesterday, as I intended, and how greatly your poor Daughter stood in need of all the Admonitions you have given her, to defend the Hope of making her Fortune in this Family, from being totally destroyed at once.—But you shall have the whole History of what has befallen me since my last.——My Lady being abroad on *Thursday*, I was afraid Mr. *L*—— would take the Advantage of her Absence, to slip again into that dangerous Closet; and as I was resolved not to venture holding any more Discourses with him in that Place, kept as much as I could below Stairs; but in avoiding him, I fell into Sir *Thomas*'s way, who seeing me pass by the Parlour-door, boldly called me to him, under Pretence of asking, whether my Lady took me down into the Country or not; tho' to be sure he knew well enough. He ask'd me the Question loud enough to be heard into the next Room, if any body had been there; but then, with the same Breath, said in a low Voice, my Charmer, 'tis an Age since I have touch'd these dear Lips—and kiss'd me violently;——I resisted with all my Strength; still unkind! return'd he, but I don't wonder at it;— you don't yet know the Good I intend for you; but when we get into the Country, I shall have more time to shew——he could say no more, for Mr. *L*—— came into the Room; and I could perceive by his Countenance, was not very well pleas'd at finding me with his Father. As I was going away, don't forget Mrs. *Syrena*, said Sir *Thomas*, very gravely, which I suppose was to make Mr. *L*—— imagine he had been speaking to me on some Affairs of the Family: My Lady came home in the Evening, and went directly into the Drawing-Room, which was very full of Company; I kept with Mrs. *Brown* the whole time, and did not go up till I knew my Lady was near coming to Bed. Not but I long'd to hear what Mr. *L*—— had to say to me, and believed he waited for me, but durst not run the risque of meeting him there, after what had been said to me—I reflected on what Sir *Thomas* had hinted, that in the Country there would be more Opportunities; and if so, did not doubt but his Son would make his Advantage of them, therefore was determined his Designs upon me, whatever they were, should stand still till then. But he was too cunning for me; tho' as things have happened, I think 'tis better for me that he was so, now I know his Mind.——Yesterday Morning I went into my Lady's Chamber, to know if she had any Commands for me before I went out, for she had given me leave the Night before. She told me she had not, and I might have the whole

Day to myself. Mr. *L*—— was with her, and I left him there when I went to my own Room to put on another Gown: He hardly looked toward me, and I found he was angry. While I was dressing, Mrs. *Mary* came up for something, and I prayed her to send one of the Men for a Coach, which she promised, and when I came down I found one at the Door; so in I stepp'd, full of Joy to think I should have so much Time with you—but I was not two Streets beyond the Square,[1] when the Coach stopp'd; I look'd out to see if any thing was in the way, and the mean time the Door on the other side was opened, and in comes Mr. *L*——; never was Surprize equal to mine at being serv'd this Trick——O! Sir, cry'd I, why do you do this?— he made me to Answer, but call'd to the Coachman to drive to *Blackheath*,[2] and immediately drew up the Window;—I expected nothing less now than to meet a second *Vardine*, and begg'd, and pray'd and would have thrown myself upon my knees to him in the Coach; ——no, *Syrena*, said he, I have you now, and will not part with you, till I have told you all my Sentiments concerning you, and know how far yours are influenced in my Favour.—I waited for you in my Grandmother's Closet three Hours Yesterday, but you took care to avoid me, tho' I found you had not the same Caution with Regard to Sir *Thomas*. I then repeated to him the true Reason that made me act in that manner, and also what Sir *Thomas* had said to me, which put him into a better Humour; but all I could say would not prevail upon him to go out of the Coach, or let me do so;—the Fears of what might happen, and the Vexation of my Disappointment of seeing you, made me burst into real Tears;——he endeavoured to compose me as much as possible, protesting he would offer nothing I should not approve of; and indeed during the whole time of our little Journey, he attempted no greater Freedoms than a Kiss. As soon as he found I seemed a little better satisfy'd, my dear *Syrena* said he, I need not tell you that I love you; the Pains I have taken to gain even a Moment's Sight of you, is the greatest Proof of it that can be given; but there are others not in my power to give, which perhaps

---

1 That Sir Thomas and his family live on a square suggests they are in the newer, more fashionable part of London, which was carefully laid out.

2 Blackheath is a district south of Greenwich Park (in what is now southeast London) and would indeed be a "little journey" as Syrena subsequently describes it. The name is derived from "bleak heath," for the area is a windswept table. Blackheath was the location for the welcome of Charles II when he returned to England from exile in 1660; it was also used for military reviews and recreational purposes.

you would think more convincing: I mean, continued he, making you the offer of a Settlement for Life, and a handsome Provision for any Children that might be the Consequence of our Intimacy.[1]— This, Sir *Thomas* can do for you; and I believe by what he said to you, is what he intends to do for you, if you'll accept it. But you know, *Syrena*, that while he lives, I have no Estate, and am a meer Dependant on his Pleasure, for my present Expences; indeed my Allowance is not so scanty, but that out of it I could support you in a Fashion, that, with a little Love on your side, would make you easy;—what Answer, cry'd he, perceiving I was silent, does my dear *Syrena* make? Alas, Sir! said I what Answer can I make, that will not be displeasing to you? I have already told you I prefer my Honesty to every thing, and I hope shall always be of the same Mind. Here he brought all the Arguments, and indeed many more than I thought the Cause would bear, to prove, that to resign oneself to a Man of Honour, and who loved one, was no breach of Virtue; brought a thousand Examples of Women in past ages, and in foreign Countries, whose Love was never imputed to them as a Crime; and in fine, left nothing unsaid that he imagined might make me think as he would have me. I did not pretend to argue with him, only cried, as often as he gave me Opportunity to speak, good Sir, don't talk so to a poor simple Creature, that does not know how to answer you—I am very unhappy that you should think on me on this Score and such like; but tho' I feign'd a World of Ignorance, I took care still to let him see I kept up to my Resolution, and that nothing should persuade me out of my Virtue. This Discourse lasted till we came to *Blackheath*, where we alighted at a House, which I suppose he knew to be a proper one for the Purpose he brought me there upon. We had a very elegant Dinner, and fine Wine; but I remember'd *Vardine*, and drank very sparingly; when the Cloth was taken away, and the Waiters gone, I see, *Syrena*, said he, the Source of my ill Success in all I have urged to you——it is because my *Person* has made no Impression on you, that my *Arguments* have fail'd;——but believe me, continued he, taking my Hand, and tenderly pressing it to his Heart, that you will one Day see some happier Man, whom to oblige, you will

---

1 He offers to provide not only for Syrena's comfort, but for that of any subsequent children. As we discover later from Syrena's encounter with Lord R——, this arrangement was not unusual. In *Pamela*, Mr. B. supports and ultimately adopts his child by Sally Godfrey. Increasingly, gentlemen took financial responsibility for their illegitimate offspring.

think nothing a Crime. Indeed, Sir, I never shall I'm sure, return'd I with a Sigh. How are you sure you could refuse a Man you lov'd, cry'd he? were you ever try'd by one you loved?— with these Words he look'd full in my Face: (I saw his Drift[1] was to find out if I had any liking to him, and thought that to seem as if I had, would give him the greater Opinion of my Virtue, in so resolutely withstanding his Offers) so feigned to be in a great Confusion—trembled—set my Breasts a heaving—and in a faultering Voice cry'd, I don't know what you call Love, Sir,——but I am sure I could refuse giving up my Virtue to one that I would give my Life to oblige in any thing else ——and I would give my Life, return'd he hastily, to be that happy Man you speak of, even tho' you should continue to refuse me the Proof of it; I desire—tell me—tell me, my little Angel, pursued he, throwing his Arms about my Waist, am I so blest to be thought well on by you? O! do not, Sir, cry'd I more and more confused, endeavour to pry into the little Secrets of a silly innocent Maid, that knows not how to disguise, nor to confess them as she ought;——but if I were a great Lady, I should not be asham'd to let you see into my very Heart;—but don't, added I, hiding my Face in his Bosom,— don't, Sir, talk to me any more of Settlements and Provision.—Poor as I am, I scorn the Thoughts of any Thing, but——Love, interrupted he, in a kind of Rapture, say Love my Charmer; if I were to be won from the Principles I have been bred in, said I, Love, since you will have it so, would be all that could induce me. Now, Mamma, I fancy you'll think I carry'd the Feint[2] too far, and brought myself in a Snare, I should not know how to get out of; but I had all my Wits about me, as you'll find. He called me his Life, his Soul, Cherubim— Goddess, and I know not what.——We'll talk of nothing then, but Love, cry'd he, do nothing but Love——and having me in his Arms, was about to carry me to a Settee[3] at the other End of the Room.— —I begg'd him to let me go, but he was deaf to all I said; till at length I broke from him, and throwing myself at his Feet, beseech'd him with a Flood of Tears, not to ruin me; but this proving ineffectual, and he still persisting in his Endeavours to raise me from the Posture I was in; I counterfeited Faintings, fell dying on the Floor, and between every pretended Agony, lifting up my Eyes, cry'd, O! Sir, you have kill'd me—but, I forgive you. This Piece of Dissimulation

---

1 The conscious direction of action or speech to some end.
2 An assumed appearance or pretence.
3 A seat (for indoors) holding two or more persons, with a back and (usually) arms.

had the Success I wish'd: He vow'd no more to shock my Modesty—said a thousand tender Things, and, I believe, was truly concern'd to see me in that Condition—by little, and little, I seem'd to recover my Spirits, and when I had; how shamefully, said I, have I betray'd myself.—How dare I encounter the Artifices of Mankind, with my plain simple Innocence:——How could I flatter myself such a Gentleman as you, could have any Inclinations for such a Creature as myself; but such as would demean me more: O! infinitely more, than Fortune has done. You wrong yourself and me, reply'd he; you know very well I could not marry you, without entailing Ruin on us both—but any Thing else.—I beg you, Sir, said I, let us talk no more of Love or Ruin.—I know the Difference between us in all Respects—I am unhappy, and I must be so——then I began to weep again, and appear'd so wild and discomposed, that he was afraid my Fits would return.—He led me into the Garden for Air, and the whole Time we were together afterwards, which was till quite Night, neither said, or did any Thing, but what would become the most respectful Lover.

Now *Mamma* by this, you may see into the bottom of his Heart.——He loves me, but will not marry me: Nor can he make a Settlement till his Father dies, and who knows how his Mind may alter before then; so I think it would be better for me to break quite off with him, and see what Proposals, Sir *Thomas* designs to make me. I send this by a Porter, because the Penny-Post would not be Time enough for your Answer, which pray send directly;[1] for I want your Advice what to do, especially, as I shan't see you, till we come to Town again. I am,

Dear Mamma,
Your ever dutiful Daughter,
SYRENA TRICKSY.

The Messenger by whom this was sent brought an Answer to it, the Contents whereof were as follows.

Dear Syrena,
YOU have very well attoned for the Vexation I suffer'd Yesterday, through your not coming; by the full Account you give me of the

---

1 The Penny Post, with its multiple sites for delivery and pickup could in fact get Syrena a response within less than twenty-four hours, but she doubtless desires the security and even quicker response ensured by a porter who would take the message directly to her mother and wait for a written response to take back to Syrena. Also, since Syrena is leaving for the country the next day, she can't risk the delay.

Cause that detain'd you: I am highly pleas'd with every particular in your Conduct, and, especially, that you have such just Notions of what is your real Interest; and make no Distinction between Youth and Age, but as either is most advantageous.——As Mr. *L*—— can settle nothing upon you, and drawing him into Marriage, seems attended with many Difficulties; I would have you receive Sir *Thomas*'s Proposals with somewhat less Severity, than you have done; but not so much, as to make him too secure of your yielding neither; for as I believe, by all Circumstances, that Mr. *L*—— has a strong Passion for you, there is a Possibility you may have him at last your own Way.——Only, my dear Child, stick to this Maxim, to make nothing of him, if you can't make him a Husband.——I doubt not but before you come back, you'll know what Sir *Thomas* intends to do for you;—till then there is no resolving on any thing.——I perceive neither of them have, as yet made you any Presents, which I much wonder at—if any should be offer'd, accept of nothing from the *Father*; but you may receive any Proof of the *Son*'s Affection, because it will also confirm him in the Hope you have given him of yours; which is the only thing you have for bringing him to the Point we aim at.——I wish you a good Journey, my dear Girl, and safe Return; write as often as any thing occurs, to

Your Affectionate Mother,
ANN TRICKSY.

Sir *Thomas* and his Family went as they intended to his Country-Seat;[1] where they had not been above seven Days, before *Syrena* had Matter to inform her Mother of, which she did in these Terms.

LETTER I.

L—— *Hall,*

Dear Mamma,
I Won't fill up my Letter with any Particulars of our Journey, 'tis sufficient to tell you, we all got safe down; and that People with Heads, not so taken up as mine is, might find every Thing here, they could desire for their Entertainment. I dare say you are Impatient to know how my Love-Affairs go on.——As to Mr. *L*—— he behaves to me with an inexpressible Tenderness, mixed with more Respect than before our Conversation at *Blackheath*; but still gives me not the least room to hope, he has any Intentions of making me his Wife——on

---

1 The residence of a country gentleman or nobleman; a country-house.

the contrary, he rather seems afraid I should flatter myself so far; for being one Day with him in an Arbour a good Distance from the House, after he had said a thousand passionate Things, and taken some Liberties which I permitted with an Air, which seem'd to tell him, I was too much lost in Softness to know what I did, I started suddenly from his Knee, where he had made me sit, and cry'd, O! to what does my fond artless Heart betray me.——Cruel! Cruel Mr. L——, can you pretend to love me truly, and use me in this Manner? And then fell a weeping in so extravagant Manner, that he look'd quite confounded——but putting his Face to mine, and wiping with his Cheeks my Tears away: My dear *Syrena*, said he, what can I do in the Circumstances we both are?—I wish to God there were less Inequality between us.[1]—You know I am not Master of myself.—Sir *Thomas* likes you as a Mistress, but would never forgive me for making you his Daughter.——My Mother, Grandmother, and all our Kindred, are full of your Praises as a Servant; but would despise and hate you as a Relation.—In fine, you must be sensible, there is no coming together for us in the way you would approve; and therefore if you lov'd me, would not see me wretched merely for a Ceremony, which sometimes instead of joining Hearts more closely, serves but to estrange them. I said nothing to all this, but kept on weeping and sobbing, as if my Heart would burst; but tho' he said all he could to comfort me, I could not perceive that he receded at all from the Declaration he had made.——Nay did not even pretend, that when his Father died, he would marry me—all he talk'd on was the Violence, and Constancy of his Affection, for me; that when he came to his Estate, I should vie with the greatest Ladies in the Town, in fine Cloaths and Equipage;[2] and that if Duty or Convenience ever oblig'd him to marry, I should still be the sole Mistress of his Heart; but as I knew better than to depend on Promises, I had not any occasion for dissembling to shew my Contempt for them. Company coming into the Garden we were oblig'd to separate, which, indeed, I was very glad of, as our being together had made so little for my Purpose.——He made me promise, however, to meet

---

1   In *Pamela*, Mr. B. similarly asks "How then, with the Distance between us, and in the World's Judgment, can I think of making you my Wife?" (213).
2   While equipage can refer to a carriage and horses, with the attendant servants (likely what is meant here), it can also refer to small articles of domestic furniture, especially china, glass, and earthenware, something else Syrena would desire.

him the next Day, in a Lane on the back of the House; I kept my Word, but that produced no more than a Repetition of those Arguments he had made use of in the Arbour.—So I doubt *Mamma*, that all the Advantage I shall make by his Addresses, is a more thorough Knowledge of the Passions of Mankind. As for Sir *Thomas*, according to your Directions, I appear less and less reserved, whenever Chance or his own Endeavours throw him in my Way, which, indeed, is very seldom; for what with Company, and what with his Son's Watchfulness, he can hardly get an Opportunity of speaking three Words to me. I believe he was going to say something very material to me Yesterday, but was interrupted by Mr. *L*—— coming into the Room. So, my dear Mamma, this is all at present from,

Your most Obedient Daughter,
SYRENA TRICKSY.

LETTER II.

L—— *Hall.*

Dear Mamma,

I WAS not mistaken when I told you in my former, that I thought Sir *Thomas*, had something extraordinary to say me; for this Morning he watch'd for me, in a Part of the House that he knew I must pass to go into my Lady's Chamber, and as it was too public a Place to hold any Discourse in, he only put a Paper into my Hand and said, I hope this will convince you, that my Designs are such as you cannot disapprove, without being an Enemy to your own Interest. And then went away directly, without staying for any Answer. I was quite impatient to see what it contain'd, and made haste into my own Room, and lock'd myself in, that I might not be interrupted in reading it. I send you an exact Copy of the Contents; because I thought best to keep the Original in my own Hands, for fear he should ask for it again.

PROPOSALS *offered to Mrs.* SYRENA TRICKSY'*s Consideration, by one who would be her faithful Friend.*

    I. The Person will engage himself to pay, or order to be paid to her, the annual Sum of One Hundred Pound, either Monthly, Quarterly, or Yearly, as she shall think fit, during his Natural Life.[1]

---

1 Mr. B.'s proposals to Pamela, which these echo, appear in Appendix C. By offering Syrena £100 a year, Sir Thomas would provide her with an income comparable to a member of what Daniel Defoe termed the "middle station."

II. The said Person will enter into Articles, and settle, out of what Part of his Estate she shall chuse, upon her, during her Natural Life, the Annual Sum of Fifty Pounds to be paid her in like Manner, as the former.

III. That in case she shall have any Children, they shall be taken care of, and educated without any Expence to her.

IV. This Agreement to be drawn up by a Lawyer of her own Nomination, and sign'd and seal'd according to Form.

I leave it to you, *Mamma*, to judge of these Conditions, and will avoid Sir *Thomas* as much as possible, till I have your Answer, which I desire may be soon: Direct for me to be left at the Post-House, in —— 'till call'd for; because if it should be brought to the House, and I not just in the way, who knows but the Curiosity of Mrs. *Brown*, *Groves*, or even Mr. *L*—— himself, might tempt them to open it; and as it is but a little Mile, I can easily go to fetch it.

Nothing worth acquainting you concerning Mr. *L*—— has happen'd since my last; nor has he been able to get one Opportunity of talking to me in private, tho' I can see he is very uneasy, and more passionate than ever, since he thinks I love him.——If I am in the Chamber when he comes to my Lady, he talks, indeed, to her, but has Eyes continually on me; and if she does but turn her Back one Moment, I am sure to have a Kiss, or a Squeeze by the Hand—— the same in the Gallery,[1] or the Stairs, or wherever we meet——but what signifies all his Love, if he won't make me his Wife, nor can do any Thing handsome for me.——I take care, however, to look upon him, and receive the Proofs he gives of his Fondness; so as to make him think I have as great an Affection for him as he can have for me——Because who knows how far one may be able to work him up at last, when he is once convinced he can get me on no other Terms—I had a Stratagem come into my Head, but I know not how you will approve of it, and that is to pretend to him, that I could not bear to be continually in the Sight of a Person, whom I could not keep my self from having the tenderest regard for, yet knew never could be mine, but by a way I would rather die than yield to; and that I was determined to quit my Lady's Service, and endeavour by Absence to lose the Memory of him. I'll try what Effect this will have, if you think fit, *Mamma*; it can be no Prejudice to me at least, and if it comes to nothing, I can accept Sir *Thomas's* Offers at last. Pray give me your Opinion in full, on both these Affairs; for you may

---

1 A long narrow apartment, sometimes serving as a means of access to other parts of a house or a corridor.

depend upon it, I will do nothing for the future without consulting you. Who am,

Dear Mamma,
Your most dutiful Daughter,
SYRENA TRICKSY.

LETTER III.

L—— Hall.

Dear Mamma,

NOT hearing from you as I expected was a very great Disappointment and Vexation to me, and the more because I was afraid you were sick or dead, or something extraordinary had fallen out; but we are inform'd that the Mail has been robb'd, all the Bills taken out, and the Letters thrown away;[1] so hope the want of your Advice so soon as I could have wish'd, is all the Misfortune of it; and as things have happen'd, I have the less Occasion; for I shall very shortly be in Town. A Man and Horse came last Night with the News that Lady G——, Sir *Thomas*'s Sister, is dead, and having left him sole Executor and Trustee for her Children, he is oblig'd to go directly for *London*. He talks of setting out To-morrow, with his Son in the Chariot, and the Ladies in two or three Day's after; so you will hear no more from me till I see you——We are all in a vast Confusion and Hurry here, so have time for no more than to tell you, I am,

Dear Mamma,
Your most dutiful Daughter,
SYRENA TRICKSY.

P. S. Since I wrote the above, Mrs. *Brown* told me the Ladies were resolved to follow Sir *Thomas* the next Day.

The Family came to Town as *Syrena* had wrote, and the Mother and Daughter soon after meeting, concerted a Design the most abominable that ever was invented, and which in a short time they carry'd into Execution in the following manner.

Sir *Thomas*, either through Grief for the Loss of a Sister whom he had tenderly loved, or the Hurry of Affairs her Death had involved

---

1   "Bills" or bills of exchange were negotiable; they were a "note ordering the payment of a sum of money in one place to some person assigned by the drawer or remitter in consideration of the value paid to him at another place" (Johnson). Although Syrena (whose understanding of paper credit is limited) might also mean paper money, it is unlikely those would be sent through the mail.

him in, had no Leisure immediately to prosecute his Amour with *Syrena*; but the young Gentleman, less affected, omitted no Opportunity of testifying the regard he had for her, and she, by a thousand different Artifices, every Day improved it, till his Passion for her arrived at that height, that for the Gratification of it, he would probably have given her the Proof she aim'd at, and become her Husband, had not the Fear of being disinherited, and rendering her as unhappy as himself, prevented him.——Her Mother having told her, she approved of her pretending to quit the House, she terrify'd him with that, and one Day, when he was saying all the tender things that Love could suggest, in order to prevail on her to quit that cruel Resolution, as he call'd it——O! said she, could you, Sir, be sensible how much I shall suffer when separated from you, you would acknowledge, I was much more cruel to my self than you. And gave him, while she was speaking this, a Look, which made him think it might still be in his power to prevail on her. On which he began to reiterate all the Promises he before had made her; adding, that if she would be his, he would use her in all things like a Wife, the Name excepted: She feign'd to listen with less Aversion than before to his Offers; but he fearing to be interrupted, for they were then in the Parlour, begg'd she would give him a meeting in some Place, where it would be less dangerous to converse in; but she would by no means be perswaded to see him abroad; pretending, that since the Adventure of *Blackheath* she had made a Vow——And, said she, I should think breaking a Vow, tho' made only to my self, the wickedest thing I could do——but, added she blushing, Sir, if you desire to take leave of me, or have any thing to say that I ought not to be ashamed to hear, I'll tell you how we might pass an Hour, at least, together without Suspicion: Where, my Angel? cry'd he impatiently. You know, Sir, answer'd she, that Sir *Thomas*, your *Mamma*, and my Lady, go all to Church next *Sunday*, and it being the first of their appearing since the Death of Lady G——, Mrs. *Brown*, Mrs. *Mary*, Mr. *Groves*, and my self are order'd to attend them, to shew our Mourning, and the Men, you know, will be all with them: Now, Sir, I can say, I have got a violent Head-ach to excuse going; and if you could find any Pretence for staying at Home, I will once more indulge my self in the dangerous Satisfaction of hearing you talk. He was quite transported with this Contrivance, and told her that nothing could have happen'd more lucky; for, my Dear, said he, I am at this Time solliciting a Place at Court, and my Lord R——, on whose Interest I chiefly depend, has really order'd me to attend him on *Sunday* Morning: Now, as his Lordships Hour of rising is usually about the time of Divine Service, Sir *Thomas* does not expect me to go to Church, and will suppose I stay to dress for this Visit. Then, cry'd she, I will be in my Lady's Chamber, because of the Convenience of the Closet, in case any of the Maids that are left at home should chance to come up for any thing—But, Sir, pursu'd she, don't you think me very forward now? Does not agreeing too soon to see you in private, look as if I were consenting in a manner to every thing——if it does, indeed I won't be there; for tho' I love to be with you, and my Heart is ready to break when I don't see you, as you know sometimes I don't, for two or three Days together, yet I won't be dishonest——I will die first. My dearest, sweetest Innocence, reply'd he, time will convince you, that I would not hurt you for the World. They had no time for farther Conversation, nor did they meet again, till the Morning equally long'd for by both, tho' for different Reasons was arrived.

The Family went to Church, little imagining, while they were in this laudable Act of Devotion, what a Scene of Mischief was preparing for them at home, by a Creature whom they took to be the most artless and innocent of her Sex. The young Deceiver was ready in the appointed Chamber to meet her expected Lover, who no sooner found the Coast clear, than he flew to her with all the Raptures of an unfeign'd Affection, after the most vigorous Pressures on the one side, and a well-acted childish Fondness, mingled with a shame-faced Simplicity on the other, he gained the utmost of his Desires, and she the Opportunity to attempt the Accomplishment of her's.

He had no sooner left the Chamber, than she tore her Hair and Cloaths, pinch'd her Arms and Hands till they became black; pluck'd down one of the Curtains from the Bed, and throw'd it on the Floor, and put her self and every thing in such Disorder, that the Room seem'd a Scene of Distraction——Then having watch'd at the Window Mr. *L*——'s going out, she rung the Bell with all her Strength, and the Maids below came running up, surpriz'd what could be the meaning, but were much more so, when they saw *Syrena* in the most pity-moving Posture imaginable——She was lying cross the Bed, her Eyes rolling as just recover'd from a Fit——She wrung her Hands——She cry'd to Heaven for Justice——Then rav'd, as if the Anguish of her Mind had deprived her of Reason.——The Girls were strangely alarm'd at so unexpected a Sight——and ask'd her the Occasion——but instead of giving any direct Answer, she only cry'd, let me be gone—O let me get out of this accursed, this fatal House——O that I had been bury'd quick before I ever set my Foot in it——and then begg'd of them, that they would send some body for a Coach or a Chair for her, but they refusing to let her go out of the house till the Family came Home, she started up, and snatching a Penknife[1] that lay upon the Table, cry'd she would run it into her Heart, if they offer'd to detain her——No, said she I will never see my Lady, Lady *L*——, nor Sir *Thomas* any more——I cannot bear it——let me go——raved she——I am sure I have taken nothing from any body——My Trunk is here——keep that and search, but as for me I will go—I will—I will, continu'd she; and in spite of all they could do, broke from them and ran down Stairs, and so into the Street, in that torn and dishevell'd Condition, where she soon got a Coach, and was carry'd to her Mother's; who highly applauded her Management in this Affair, and gave her fresh Instructions for the perfecting their most detestable Plot.

Nothing ever equall'd the Surprize that Sir *Thomas*, the Ladies, and whole Family were in, when on their coming Home they were told the Departure of *Syrena*, and the Confusion of her Behaviour ——They look'd one upon the other, as not knowing what to think of the Matter——Mrs. *Brown* and Mr. *Groves* shook their Heads, as if they apprehended somewhat they durst not speak——and all of them at once demanded who had been in the Chamber with her? The Maids answer'd, that they knew of nobody, and were certain no Person had come into the House since they went out. In fine, as 'twas impossible she could have been in such a Condition as was described without some very extraordinary Occasion, the least Mischief they could think of it was, that she had been taken suddenly mad——This unhappy Adventure engross'd not only their Thoughts, but Conversation also, and on Mr. *L*——'s return from visiting the Nobleman his Friend, and was inform'd of it, all he could do to command himself, was insufficient to prevent some part of the Concern he felt from appearing in his Countenance——He said the least, however, of any of them; and endeavour'd frequently to turn the Discourse on other Subjects——telling the Ladies, that tho' *Syrena* was a pretty modest Girl he believ'd, yet he wonder'd they should be so uneasy about her; that probably some Disorder in the Brain had seized her, which might be removed by proper Remedies; and it was pity they should give themselves so much Trouble about a Servant. But this affected Carelessness, which he Thought so politick, was very prejudicial to himself afterward; and help'd greatly to

---

1 A small knife, usually carried in the pocket, used originally for making and mending quill pens.

assist the base Designs form'd against him, tho' at present none took notice of it, or at least seem'd to do so. As soon as Dinner was over, one of the Men was order'd to go to *Syrena's* Mother, to see if she was with her, and learn, if possible, the Truth of this Affair: Mr. *Groves* desired he might be the Person employ'd, and Mrs. *Brown* and the Chambermaid who all had a great Regard for her on the score of her Youth and pretended Innocence, begg'd they might accompany him in this Errand, which was readily granted, and Sir *Thomas* told them they might have the Coach; but before it could be got ready, so industrious is Villany, Mr. *L——* was informed two Gentlemen desired to speak with him, he went to receive them in the Parlor, where they had been conducted by the Footman, who had open'd the Door. He no sooner was within the Room, than one of them coming up close to him, told him, that he was sorry he was obliged to execute the Duty of his Office on a Gentleman like Mr. *L——*, but had a Warrant against him, on account of a Rape and Assault sworn to be committed by him that Morning, on the Body of *Syrena Tricksy*.[1] Not all the Astonishment Mr. *L——* was in, and there could not be a greater, quelled the Emotions of his Rage at so vile an Accusation, and without considering the Consequences, laid his Hand on his Sword,[2] with Intention to draw it; but both the others seizing him at once, prevented what else his Passion might have prompted him to; and there ensued so great a Scuffle among them, that Sir *Thomas* and the Ladies, who were in the next Room, heard it, and ran in: The Occasion was soon discover'd, and it would be very difficult to describe the Consternation, the Terror, the Grief, the Shame, with which every one of their Faces was overspread; the Ladies fell into Fits, the Servants who assisted in recovering them, were little better themselves, and all were in the utmost Hurry and Confusion. Sir *Thomas* offer'd to engage for his Son's Appearance;[3] but the Officers said it could not be allow'd in a capital Case:[4] That

---

1 A warrant is a writ or order issued by some executive authority, empowering a ministerial officer to make an arrest. Clearly, this warrant was based on the testimony of Syrena. To prosecute rape in the eighteenth century, the woman's word or testimony (plus in this case the "physical" evidence of Syrena's bruises, etc.) were of paramount importance.

2 Although by this time primarily for decoration, Mr. L's sword is an affectation that young gentlemen followed.

3 Sir Thomas is offering himself as security for his son—he is calling on the precedence of his rank as a kind of guarantee in lieu of bail.

4 In other words, he can be executed if found guilty.

the Girl had suffer'd Violence, which perhaps might be her Death; but as they knew the Respect due to so worthy a Family, Mr. L—— should have no reason to complain of the want of any thing but Liberty, during the time he was with them; and added, that they hoped things might be made up so with the Plaintiff's Mother, that he would be restored to that also in a short time. Mr. L—— gave no answer to this Insinuation; but a Look which shewed his Contempt of coming to any Terms with such abandon'd Wretches. In fine, after some little Debate he was compell'd to obey the Order, brought against him, and quitted his Father's House with Company he little expected ever to be among.

This was the Stratagem which these pernicious Creatures had devised, and thus was it executed; the Moment *Syrena* came home, the same Coach carry'd her, in the deplorable Condition she had made her self appear, with her Mother to a Magistrate,[1] who seeing the Youth and seeming Modesty of the Girl, doubted not the Truth of their Accusation, and sent Tipstaves[2] immediately to seize on Mr. L——, which being done, Mrs. *Tricksy* congratulated her Daughter in Iniquity, as well as Blood, for the Success of their Enterprize: Now, Child, said she, you will be Lady L——, the proud Puppy will be glad to marry you now to save his Neck; and marry you he shall, or come down with a Sum sufficient to entitle you to a Husband of as good an Estate as he will have.

But the Satisfaction they had in this Event, greatly as it flatter'd their presuming Hopes, was short of the Anguish the unspeakable Horror in which it involved Sir *Thomas* and his noble Family: Dear as Mr. L—— was to them all, not one, when they consider'd Circumstances, the Time, the Place, the still believed Artlessness of *Syrena*, the Confusion he appear'd in at hearing she was gone, and which he strove to conceal, but could not—All concurr'd to make him seem as guilty as he was represented to be, and was rather an Addition, than an Alleviation of their Sorrows, especially to the Ladies.

As for the young Gentleman in Custody, Rage, Shame, and Amazement took up all his Mind, and left no room for any Thought how to disintangle himself from the Snare his Love for an unworthy Object had brought him into——He never could conceive there was so much Villany in Womankind, much less in one so young; and was ready to curse the whole Sex, for the Sake of the perfidious

---

1 A frequent synonym for justice of the peace; "any man publicly invested with authority" (Johnson).

2 An official carrying a tipped staff; in this instance, a bailiff or constable.

Syrena: So unjustly do our Passions often make us blend the worthy with the unworthy!

Sir *Thomas* in the mean time neglected nothing that might remedy this Misfortune——The best Councel was consulted in the Affair, who, on hearing the whole of the Affair, advised to make it up, if possible, with the Mother of *Syrena*; but that Monster would listen to no Proposals, and set the Virtue and Reputation of her Child at no less Price than Marriage. 'Tis impossible for Heart to conceive the Indignation of the young Gentleman when he was informed of this; he protested that he would sooner yield to all the Law inflicts in such Cases, than become the Property of those vile Serpents; for that was all the Name he could bring himself to call them by. Hard, indeed, was his Fate, when those who most endeavoured to defend him, in their Souls believ'd him guilty——His Councel, his Parents, all the Servants in the Family, even his own Man (who had been the Person who call'd the Coach for *Syrena*, when she was carry'd to *Blackheath*, and knew his Master had a Design upon her) had the matter been brought before a Court of Judicature,[1] could have said nothing but what must have tended to prove the imaginary Crime. How false and weak, therefore, is that Notion which some Men have, that they may do any thing with a Woman, but marry her, and that nothing but a Wife can make them unhappy; when, in reality, there are often more Disquiets, more Perplexities, more Dangers attend the Prosecution of an unlawful Amour, than can be met with, even with the worst of Wives; for if a Woman cannot be sincere in a State where 'tis her Interest to be so; what can be expected from her in one where 'tis her Interest to deceive: Besides, the Artifices practised to gain the Sex at first, gives them a kind of Pretence for Retaliation afterward; and Men frequently find to their Cost, they but too well know how to be even with them.

Thus Mr. *L*——, who in the Morning thought himself happy in the Possession of a beautiful innocent Creature, that loved him with the extremest Tenderness, found himself before the Sun went down, the wretched Property of a presuming, mercenary, betraying, perjur'd and abandon'd Prostitute——His Friends incensed——his Reputation blasted——his Liberty at the Disposal of the lowest and most

---

1 An assembly of judges or other persons legally appointed and acting as a tribunal to hear and determine any case; it can also refer more generally to the action of judging or the judicial process.

despised Rank of Men,[1] and his Life in Danger of the most shameful and ignominious end.

So greatly were all Appearances against him, that what a Day before his Friends would have looked upon as the heaviest Misfortune could have befallen them, they now labour'd with all their Might to bring about, as the only remaining Remedy for the present Evil; and Mr. L——, to aggravate the Horrors of his Mind, was compelled to hear every Moment, from all who wish'd him well, the distracting Solicitations, that he would Consent to make the supposed injured Girl his Wife. Whether he would at last have been prevailed upon by their Arguments; or whether he would rather have chose to endure the Sentence of the Law; or whether, to avoid both, he would not have been guilty of some Act of Desperation on himself, is uncertain; Providence thought not fit to punish him any farther, and when he least expected it, sent him a Deliverance.

The Villains who had robb'd the ★★★★★ Mail,[2] as beforementioned, after they had taken out the Bills, threw the Bag and Letters into a Ditch; but there happening to be no Water in it, the Papers receiv'd no Damage; but the Post-Man had been so beaten and cruelly used, that he was not capable of telling what had become of them; they were afterwards found by a Country-Fellow, who seeing what they were, carry'd them as directed; there being two for Sir *Thomas L*——, and one for Mrs. *Syrena Tricksy*; the Man delivered them at his Seat, but the Family being come to *London* that Morning, a Servant took them, and putting them altogether under a Cover, sent them up by the next Post. Those for Sir *Thomas* were nothing to the Purpose of this Story, but every body agreeing that it would be proper to open that for Syrena,[3] they found it from her Mother, and contained as follows:

Dear Syrena,
I Have considered on all you acquainted me with; and have been much perplex'd in my Mind how to advise you in this ticklish Affair;

---

1 When Mr. L—— is incarcerated, he is subject to his jailors who have purchased the rights to run the prison.
2 Typically, mail routes referred to the location they serviced (e.g. the Bristol Mail). Haywood obscures this reference to maintain the appearance of 'reality' in her text.
3 Because she was a servant (and a woman), the family perceives Syrena's mail as something to which they would meaningfully have access; servants do not really have private business.

but am at last come to a Resolution. Sir *Thomas*'s Proposals are very niggardly;[1] what is an hundred Pounds a Year to a Woman that would appear handsome in the World?—and then if he dies, to be reduced to Fifty—good God! I wonder how he can offer to think of having a fine Girl, and a Maid too, as he takes you for, on such poor Terms;——but it may be it would have been better for his Family, if he had bid higher; for I have a Project in my Head to force his Son to marry you, in Case all your Arts to draw him in should fail—— Nay, and to oblige Sir *Thomas* and my Lady, and all of them, to consent to it; and if he should refuse to live with you afterward, the Allowance they must give you as his Wife, will be more than his Father's pitiful hundred Pounds a Year: Besides, when Sir *Thomas* dies (and what I design to do, will go a good way towards breaking his Heart) you will be Lady L——, they can't hinder you of that; and a Title will give you such an Air among the young Fellows, that you may make what Terms you will with any of them;——the Contrivance I have formed is indeed pretty dangerous, and requires Abundance of Cunning and Courage too to go thro' with it to Purpose; but I perceive with Pleasure, you have a good share of the one; and as I shall be obliged to act a Part in it myself, I don't doubt but I shall be able to give you enough of the *other* also;——but nothing of this can be put in Practice till you come back to *London*;—all you have to do in the mean time, is to heighten the young Squire's Affection, by all the little Stratagems you can invent;——as to the Father, I would have you avoid, if you possibly can, giving him any positive Answer; but be sure not to part with the Proposals he gave you; they may be useful hereafter, in making him fearful of provoking us to expose him;——if he should ask for the Paper, you may pretend you burn'd it as soon as you had examin'd it, for fear of its being found. ——My dear Girl, my Head is always at work for thee—be careful to do as I direct; let Mr. L—— believe you love him to Madness if he will; but be still more and more tenacious of your Virtue, till I inform you the proper time for resigning it——'tis possible as he loves you so well, you may persuade him to marry you, when he finds there's no having you without; but once again depend that I have the sure Means to make him be glad to do it. So no more at present, from

Your affectionate Mother,
ANN TRICKSY.

---

1 Meanly parsimonious or stingy.

Here Mr. L——'s Parents found a full as well as a seasonable Discovery of the wicked Plot, and their Son's Innocence, as to the pretended Rape, cleared. Their Transport could not but be great, tho' somewhat allayed by the Story of Sir *Thomas* and his Proposals; the Confusion of that Gentleman, and the jealous Disdain of his Lady, a while combated with the sincere Satisfaction they would otherwise have felt——some few Upbraidings on the one side, and Excuses on the other were natural on the Occasion, but at length were wholly swallowed up in the Joy for the Deliverance of an only Son. The next thing they had to think upon, was how to proceed for the Punishment of these vile Creatures who had imposed upon them; but when they found that it could not be done without bringing the whole Affair to a public Trial;[1] their Counsel advised them rather to compromise it, and rest contented with the Disappointment *Syrena* and her Mother had met with, and not pursue a Justice which would occasion so much Town-talk of themselves; especially considering that such Practices would infallibly some time or other, draw on the Authors the publick Shame they merited, where perhaps the Avengers had not laid themselves so open to Ridicule, as Sir *Thomas* and his Son had done. The Letter therefore being produced, and the Person who brought it, detained as an Evidence, in Case they had offered to deny the Hand, the audacious Expectations of our female Plotters, were turned into Submissions; and all their Arts employed only to prevail on the Lawyer, who negotiated between them, that Sir *Thomas* and his Family would not prosecute them for Perjury and Fraud,[2] which he pretended to accomplish with a great deal of Difficulty; and so this troublesome and dangerous Business ended, and was, 'tis to be hoped, a means of preventing both Father and Son from rendring themselves liable to any future Impositions of the same Nature.

Now had the wicked Mrs. *Tricksy* and her Daughter time to reflect on the ill Success of their Stratagem; but instead of acknowledging the Justice of Divine Providence in unravelling this Affair, they only cursed Fortune, and accused themselves for having trusted the Secret of their Design to Pen and Paper: Dreadful Proof that their Hearts were total-

---

1 The family could prosecute Syrena and her mother for fraud and perjury, but not without revealing the impropriety of both Sir Thomas and his son.

2 Fraud is criminal deception; the using of false representations to obtain an unjust advantage or to injure the rights or interests of another. Perjury is the willful utterance of false evidence while on oath.

ly void of all Distinction between Vice and Virtue! The best may have fallen into Errors which they have afterwards so truly repented of, that even those Faults have contributed to the rendering them more perfect.——Others again may have been guilty of repeated Crimes, and yet have felt Remorse, even in the Moment of perpetrating them; but the Wretch, incapable either of Penitence or Remorse, one may, without Breach of Charity, pronounce irreclaimable but by a Miracle, and fit for the engaging in any Mischief where Temptation calls.

When our young Deceiver and her Mother had a little recovered from the Emotions occasioned by their Disappointment, they began to consider what they had best do: The Family *Syrena* had quitted, kept so much Company, that for her to think of getting into any other as a Servant was dangerous; as she possibly might be seen, by those she had ill treated, and by that means be exposed:[1] It therefore seem'd most prudent to get out of the way for some time, and trust to Chance for Adventures. *Greenwich*[2] was the Place they pitch'd on for a Retirement; and Mrs. *Tricksy* having sold what few Household-Goods she had, took a neat,[3] but plain ready-furnish'd Lodging, for herself and Daughter, at a House which had a Door into the Park;[4] as judging not improbable, but that by frequent walking there, the little Harpy[5] might happen on some Prey to her Advantage: The Event in part answered to their wish; her Youth, her Beauty, and seeming Innocence, soon made her be taken Notice of by several Gentlemen, whom the Season of the Year,[6] and the Pleasantness of

---

1 Because of her actions, and the prominence of Sir Thomas's family, Syrena can never work in domestic service again.

2 As a port town, Greenwich had its share of shady characters. The Royal Hospital was there and the community consisted of pensioners and their dependents. As Syrena's activities indicate, Greenwich was a place where much could happen.

3 Elegant, not tidy.

4 Greenwich Park lies between the Greenwich Hospital and Greenwich Palace. It had a reputation as a site of social mixing and rambunctious activities, but it was also an almost rural spot in 1750. It faced the Thames to the north and from that point one would have been able to see the ships sailing to the docks between London Bridge and the Tower.

5 A fabulous monster, rapacious and filthy, with a woman's face and body and a bird's wings and claws; or, more generally, a rapacious person that preys upon others.

6 People would frequent Greenwich in the spring and summer when the weather was warm. The fact that immediately before this, Sir Thomas's family retired to its estate also strongly suggests that this period is sometime between April and October.

the Place, had drawn thither; but he that seem'd most affected with her Charms, was Mr. D——, he had often seen her walking in the Park, sometimes with her Mother, and sometimes with a young Lady, who lodged in the same House with them; and had more than once fallen into such little Conversations with them, as the Freedom of a Country-Place allows, without being particular;[1] his Eyes however discovered[2] something, which did not 'scape the vigilant Observation of both Mother and Daughter, and afforded a Prospect they so much wish'd to find.

Mr. D—— was a young Gentleman of about 800*l.* a Year,[3] was contracted to a Lady called *Maria*, and shortly to be married to her, with the Consent of the Friends on both sides; but a near Relation in *Lincolnshire*, from whom she expected a considerable Augmentation of her Fortune, being taken ill, the young Lady was gone to make her Visit. During her Absence, Mr. D—— intended to pass the time at *Greenwich*, a Place he always liked, but now more especially; the solemn Prospect of the Sea indulging those Ideas, which Persons separated from those they love, are ordinarily possess'd of. The first Sight of *Syrena* struck him with a kind of pleasing Surprize;——he fancy'd he saw something in her Face, like that of her he had for many Years been accustomed to admire: he little thought how much he injured the virtuous Maid, by making any Comparison between her and this unworthy Resemblance; or that the Affection he had vow'd to *Maria*, could ever be diminish'd by an innocent Conversation with *Syrena*; yet so it was, by pleasing himself with seeing her for the Sake of another, he by degrees grew delighted with seeing her for her own——So little do we know ourselves, and so hard it

---

1 That is, away from formal rules of engagement in London that would require them to be introduced, they have conversed but not with any intimacy or familiarity—"without being particular." Later, at the masquerade, Lord R—— quickly grows "very particular" with Syrena.

2 Revealed.

3 With an income of £800, Mr. D—— is a member of the lesser gentry, an economically heterogeneous group that included esquires and gentlemen with incomes ranging from roughly £200 to the more comfortable £1000. With £800 a year, Mr. D—— is fairly comfortable although a member of the gentry with an income of less than £1000 would have been unlikely to enjoy a season in London and would have to watch his spending carefully. Indeed, as he later notes, he is marrying Maria, in part, to ensure he has the money for his sister's dowry. He has enough to support Syrena and marry handsomely, but not to live particularly luxuriously.

is to preserve Constancy in Absence. As on his first Acquaintance with *Syrena*, he had no manner of Design upon her, he made no Secret of his Affairs, and talked of his beloved *Maria* in the most tender Terms; but afterwards mentioned her Name with less and less Emotions; and from being passionately fond of talking of her, fell at last into an Uneasiness of hearing her spoken of at all.

Mrs. *Tricksy* therefore had some Reason to flatter herself, that the Impression her Daughter had made on him, had erased that of the Mistress he had so long adored; and that he wanted nothing but an Opportunity to confess it to her; on which it was contrived, that she should throw herself in his Way, at a time, when there should be no Witnesses of their Conversation. They knew he was accustomed to walk early in the Morning, on that side of the Park that has the Prospect of the Sea;[1] and there on the side of a Hill did *Syrena* place herself, leaning in a pensive Posture, her Head upon her Hand; she had not waited long before Mr. *D*—— came that way, and felt (as he afterwards called it) a guilty Flutter at his Heart, in perceiving she was alone. He accosted her at first only with the usual Salutations of the Morning; but she, with a modest Blush, downcast Eyes, and all the Tokens of an Innocent Surprize (which she before had practised in her Glass) soon allured him to entertain her in a more tender manner. I am afraid Miss, said he, I have disturbed your Contemplations, and perhaps been injurious to the happy Man who was the Subject of them; for it cannot be that a young Lady like you should chuse this solitary Place, but to indulge Ideas more agreeable than any Company can afford. It is certain, Sir, replied she, that there is a Pleasure in being alone sometimes; but I assure you that is not my Case at present: I love to rise early, the Sweetness of the Morning tempted me abroad, and the few Acquaintance I have here, are all too lazy to partake of it. Then, rejoined he, you will give me leave to be your Companion? provided, answered she gayly, your Complaisance is no Violence on your Inclination; for as you have owned yourself a Lover, it may very well be supposed you come here to indulge those Ideas, you just now accused me of. Perhaps, Miss, said he, I can no where so well indulge them as in your Presence. That's impossible, replied she, unless I had seen the Object of your Affections, and could expatiate on the Beauties of her Shape, her Air, her Face, and Wit; while you shew me your own, cried he, I need no more to inspire me with the most passionate Sentiments.——Sure none,

---

1 This refers to the Royal Park; the sea is the River Thames.

added he, catching her in his Arms, can see the charming *Syrena*, and lose a Thought on any other Object.——Hold!——hold! good Sir! said she, disengaging herself from him, you grow a little too free, and I shall be in Danger of growing too serious——what! continued she, this from a Man in love with another Woman! whatever I may have felt, for any other Woman, replied he, while I see *Syrena*, I can love nothing but her. O fie! rejoined she, what has a Man to offer, that has already disposed of his Vows. His Heart, answer'd he. O! then I find, said she, your Heart is like a ready-furnish'd Chamber, to be let to the first Comer, who must go out at a short Warning, on the Prospect of a more advantageous Lodger.

The Reader will perceive she was here acting the Coquette.—— The Reason of it was, that imagining a sprightly Behaviour would be most agreeable to a Man of his gay Temper; and as she could have no hopes of gaining him for a Husband, things having been gone so far with *Maria*, whose Fortune she had heard was to pay off his Sister's Portion,[1] she thought too great a Reserve might deter him from making any Addresses to her; and tho' she could not expect any Settlement, as her Affairs now were, it seemed better to play at a small Game, than stick out.[2]

She continu'd to rally with him for some time, and her Wit and the little Artifices she made use of, so much inflam'd his amorous Inclinations, that he was ready almost to take the Advantage of that solitary Place, and become a Ravisher for the Gratification of them; but it needed not, she received his Caresses in such a manner, as afforded him a sufficient Cause to hope, she would not be cruel.—— She promised to meet him the next Morning, at the same Place and Hour, and let fall, as if unguarded, some Hints that she wanted only to be convinc'd of his Affection, to give him the Proof of hers that he desired.

The Time of their Assignation being arrived, both were punctual, and she allow'd him yet greater Freedoms than before, but kept back that he was most eager to obtain; he was not to seek what 'twas she aim'd at, and presented her with a Diamond Ring, which she accepted on as a Proof of his Love.——The next Day he brought her a Gold Watch, and after that an embroider'd Purse with Fifty

---

1 A dowry, the portion given at marriage.
2 The gaming metaphor suggests that Syrena will be content with a small prize rather than a big score; she is going for the short rather than the long con. The imagery continues below when Syrena mentions the "after-game" she has designed to play upon him.

Broad Pieces.[1]—All which she took, without returning him any Thing in Exchange, but the liberty of Kissing and Embracing her, not that she absolutely refus'd him; but pretended she would find a fitter Opportunity, and that her *Mamma* was to go shortly to *London*, on some Business that would detain her the whole Day and Night; and that she would then contrive a Way, to get him privately into their own Lodging. This satisfied him for the present, but finding no Effect of the Promises she made him, he began to grow impatient; and was for seizing the Joy he aimed at, in a Place where the seeming Delicacy of *Syrena*, would not consent to yield it him.——She found Means, however, to prevent him, both from having any Suspicion she had a Design to jilt him, or from compassing his Intent, till she thought fit to grant it.

The Motives of her behaving in this Fashion, were two; the first was to get as much as she could of him, before she granted him any material Favour, having an After-game[2] in her Head to play upon him; and the other was, that she had another Lover whom she found her Account in managing.

This was a rich *Portuguese* Merchant,[3] who having finish'd some Business, which had brought him to *England*, was on the Point of returning to his Family, when Mrs. *Tricksy* and her Daughter came to *Greenwich*: He lodg'd at the next Door to them, and being charm'd with *Syrena*, soon got acquainted with them. The cunning Mother soon perceiv'd his Inclination, and to encourage him to discover it, in a proper Manner, was always entertaining him with the

---

1   Fifty broad pieces was fifty pounds—an extremely large amount of money. As a point of comparison, Mr. D—— has just given her two to four times the annual income for an unskilled day laborer, who would earn between 5 and 10 shillings a week or £12-30 a year; more than the most highly paid female domestic servant could ever earn in a year; and an amount that represents a comfortable annual income for a small shopkeeper.

2   A second game played in order to reverse or improve the issues of the first; hence, as Samuel Johnson describes it, "The scheme which may be laid or the expedients which are practised after the original game has miscarried; methods taken after the first turn of affairs."

3   Anglo-Portuguese trade, which originated in exchange of port wine for English woolens in 1703, was active. Portugal also profited tremendously from the trade in gold and diamonds from their colonies in Brazil. As a busy seaport, Greenwich had a considerable number of merchants who would lodge there while waiting the opportunity to sail.

trade

Misfortunes of her Family, and the Straits to which they were subjected.—He took the Hint, and gave her to understand, he was ready
to contribute to the Relief of the Necessities she complain'd of, provided he might obtain a grateful Return from the fair *Syrena*.——
In fine, the Agreement was soon struck up between them——he
gave his Gold, and *Syrena* her Person.——As he had begun to visit
them at their first coming, there was no suspicion in the House of
the Amour, which lasted for about a Month; at the End of which,
having fully satisfied his Desires, and the Necessity of his Affairs calling him to *Portugal*, he took his leave: And Syrena had now leisure
to prosecute her Intrigue with Mr. *D*——, which she could not so
well do, while the Merchant was so near her.

  She had met by Appointment this young Gentleman for several
Mornings; but she now came not according to her Promise, which did
not a little perplex him; but he saw her in the Afternoon in the Park,
accompanied by that Lady, who frequently walked with her in the
Evenings. He joined them as usual, and discoursed with them on ordinary Things; but perceived a Gloom on the Face of *Syrena*, which he
had never seen before, and found that she frequently sigh'd: He long'd
for an Opportunity to enquire the Cause, but could find none in that
Company. *Syrena* too, whenever she look'd upon him, expressed some
Impatience in her Eyes; but for what he was not able to guess; till they
turned a Corner to go down a Walk, she let her Handkerchief drop,
which he taking up, and returning to her she slipt a Paper into his
Hand at the same Time, and he convey'd into his Pocket unperceiv'd
by the other. *Syrena* after this seem'd tir'd with walking, and with her
Companion took leave of Mr. *D*——, who eager to see what his Billet[1] contain'd, made no Efforts to detain them; and as soon as they
were out of Sight, found to his great Surprize these Lines.

Dear Sir,

THAT I met you not this Morning, was owing to the Misfortune of
my Mother's finding the Presents, you were so kind to make me; and
which I had conceal'd from her, knowing how scrupulous she is in
such Things.——She would needs make me tell her how I came by
them, I had no way to conceal the Truth, and was obliged to endure
a strict Examination on what had past between us. I assur'd, as I well
might, that our Conversation had been perfectly innocent; but was
oblig'd to add, that your Addresses to me were on an honourable

---

1 A short informal letter, a "note."

Foot.——She told me she would believe nothing of it, unless she heard it confirm'd by your Mouth, and had sent for you to Day, if Company had not come from *London* to visit us, on Purpose to return the Watch and Ring; for the Purse she knows nothing of, and hear what you would say as to your Designs on me.——Therefore, dear Sir, do not contradict what I have said, unless you would for ever be deprived of the Sight, and thereby break the Heart of,

Your

SYRENA.

P. S. If you humour my *Mamma* in this Article, you will have leave to Visit me, and we may be together as much as either of us desire. *Pray burn this.*

Mr. *D——* was so much shock'd at this Proposal, that for some Moments all the Love he had for *Syrena* was converted into Contempt, imagining it a Trick contrived beween Mother and Daughter, to draw him into a Promise of Marriage; but when he reflected that the Girl had behav'd in a quite contrary Manner, the good Opinion he had of her Sincerity, soon clear'd her from having any share in it. He had great Debates within himself what to do in the Affair: He thought it base to pretend a Thing which he was far from intending; but then the exposing a young Creature who loved him, to the Rage of a Mother, whom he suppos'd she stood much in awe of; together with the thoughts of never see her any more, out-balanced the Consideration of his own Honour; and he chose, as, indeed, most do, when they are in love; to sacrifice his *Character* to his *Passion*, rather than his *Passion* to his *Character*, since he found himself in a Dilemma, where both could not be maintain'd.

The next Day, as he expected, the Servant of the House, where Mrs. *Tricksey* lodg'd, brought him a Letter, which was to this Purpose.

SIR,

I Am sorry to have Occasion to write to desire you will call on me, on an Affair which you ought to have found an Occasion of communicating to me.——I scarce think you can be Ignorant of what I mean, tho' I am as to your real Designs; but if they are of a Nature fit to be acknowledg'd, to a Person in the Circumstances I am in; you will not hesitate to come, and immediately declare to her, who wishes to be with Honour,

SIR,

Your oblig'd humble Servant,

ANN TRICKSY.

This Letter, and the Summons it contain'd, renew'd his Confusion; but he found himself under a Necessity of giving some Answer; and as he did not care to write, bid the Messenger give his Service to the Lady, and say he would wait on her as soon as he was drest. He was afterwards several Times prompted by his good Genius to break his Word on this Occasion, and go directly for *London*, without troubling himself about what *Syrena* or her Mother should think of him; but the Presents he had made, and the Happiness which they were to purchase for him, got again the better of the Dictates of his Prudence, or his Consideration for *Maria*; and he went with a Resolution to make the Mother of his new Charmer satisfied.

Few Women knew better how to behave themselves on all Occasions than Mrs. *Tricksy*; and on this 'tis not to be doubted if she exerted all her Artifice: She receiv'd him with the greatest Respect, yet at the same time mingled a certain Severity in her Air, which gave him to understand, she expected to be answer'd with Truth, to the Questions she had to ask him; the principal of which were, on what Score[1] he had made her Daughter such valuable Presents? And when he had told her on the most honourable One: Wherefore his Intentions, and the Courtship between them had been conceal'd from the Person, who as a Parent ought to have been consulted? To this he replied, that he was willing to know how far he could influence the Affections of the young Lady, without the Interposition of a Mother's Commands; and that also as he was contracted to another, it would be highly improper that the World should have any Suspicion he had made a second Choice, 'till he had found some Pretence to break entirely off with the first.

On these Declarations, Mrs. *Tricksy* seem'd perfectly easy, and telling him she depended on his Honour and Veracity, gave him leave to visit *Syrena*, as often as he pleas'd; and assured him at the same Time, that she would keep his Secret inviolably till a proper Time for revealing it; and that the Family where they liv'd should never know he came there, with any other View than to chat away a leisure Hour, as an ordinary Acquaintance.

Glad was Mr. *D——*, when he was got over this Task: He was a Man who naturally hated all kind of Deceit, and look'd on Lying, as

---

1 Mrs. Tricksy's use of economic terms here is, of course, consistent with her approach through the novel. The "score" refers to any sort of a record or account kept by means of tallies. It can, as in this case, refer to a customer's account for goods obtained on credit for which a debt will be due.

beneath the Dignity of his Specie;[1] he could not therefore utter Words so foreign to his Heart without feeling an inward Shock. Yet so great an Ascendant had the Charms of *Syrena* gain'd over him, that the unhappy Passion he had for her, corrupted even his very Morals; and made him think nothing vile that tended to the Enjoyment of her.

Mrs. *Tricksy*, in the mean time was far from believing what he said, tho' she feigned to do so, nor indeed had not yet formed any Design to draw him in to marry her Daughter; because his former Engagement, and the necessity of his Affairs requiring he should keep it, she had looked on it as an impracticable Attempt. All her Design in obliging him to pretend an honourable Passion, was only to support her own Character, and compel him afterwards to do more for *Syrena*, than perhaps his Inclinations would have excited him to; but I will not anticipate.

Mr. D——, had now all the Opportunity he could wish with *Syrena*, which he did not fail to make use of for the Gratification of his Desires; and our young Dissembler so well acted her Part, that he imagined never Woman loved to a greater height than she did: In the midst of this Intrigue, he received a Letter from *Maria*, and another from that Kinswoman at whose House she was: That Lady being recovered from her Indisposition, and loth to lose *Maria's* Company, made him an Invitation to come down, telling him as what she imagin'd would be a great Inducement, that he would have the Pleasure of Conducting to *London*, that dear Person, who was shortly to be his Companion for Life. *Maria* also desired him to come, in Terms as pressing as her Modesty would permit, and the engaging Manner in which she wrote somewhat awaked his former Tenderness; but happening to see *Syrena* the same Evening, and mentioning the Invitation, the artful Creature presently fell into Fits, crying out between her counterfeited Agonies, O! I shall never see you more——you love *Maria*——you will marry her——*Syrena* will be forgot——but I will not live to be forsaken——then run to the Window as tho' she would throw herself out; and on his taking her in his Arms, and vowing never to be ungrateful to her Love, clung about his Waste, bathed his Hands and Bosom with her Tears——then swooned again, and in fine, so well feign'd the desperate half dying Lover, that he thought he should be the most cruel of Mankind, to quit so soft, so endear-

---

1   His class. However, specie also refers to coins or coined money (clearly Syrena's primary interest) so Haywood may be punning on that as well.

ing a Creature; all he could say or do however could not pacify her, till he gave her the most solemn Assurances not to go to *Lincolnshire*; and the more to convince her of the Sincerity of what he said, wrote an Excuse to the Ladies in her Presence, for his refusal.

When *Syrena* told her Mother how much he was affected with her pretended Grief, and the Condescention[1] he had made, the old Woman began to be of Opinion that he really lov'd enough to marry her, if it were not for his Engagement with *Maria*, and from that Moment thought of nothing but how it might be broke off ——the most feasible Way she could invent was to make that Lady think him unworthy her Affection——She knew very well how far Pride and slighted Love work in the Minds of Women, and without farther delay wrote to *Maria* in the following Terms.

To Miss Maria S——, *at Mrs.* J——*'s House in* Lincolnshire.

Madam,

THE Assurances you have given Mr. *D*—— of making him happy in your Person and Fortune, might justly render any Man highly contented with his Lot; but as our Happiness consists chiefly in the Sense we have of it; I am sorry to inform you Mr. *D*—— is ignorant of his. I beg you will not suspect I give you this unwelcome Intelligence out of any sinister View, for I assure you, Madam, I am a Person who have not the least Self-interest in this Point; and nothing but the Love I bear to Truth and Justice could have prevail'd on me to let you know how void of both Mr. *D*—— is now become. You had no sooner left *London* than he went to *Greenwich*, in pursuit of a young Girl esteemed very beautiful, but I have never seen her, so take that Character of her upon Trust; I am, however, very certain that she is so in the Eyes of Mr. *D*——; that he makes honourable Addresses to her, and has assured her Mother that he only waits an Opportunity to break with you, and will then avow his Passion for her in the face of the World——I appeal to yourself for one Proof of what I say, if it be true as he gives out that you invited him to *Lincolnshire*, and he declined accepting that Favour on a frivolous Pretence——if you know this to be real, it is easy for you to convince yourself yet farther, by employing any Person to inspect into his

---

1 Condescension refers to a sense of affability to one's inferiors, with courteous disregard of difference of rank or position. This term is important because of the obvious class difference between Mr. D—— and Syrena.

Behaviour, while you are absent——It would be vain to wish you might hear it is such as would merit your Approbation——the next Blessing therefore that can attend you is, that you may be undeceived in your good Opinion before the indissoluble Knot is tied, that would put it out of your power to punish his Ingratitude, which is the sole Motive of this trouble, from

Madam,
Your unknown Friend.

This mischievous Letter Mrs. *Tricksy* sent to *Lincolnshire* by the Post, after having got it copied by a Friend in *London*, to prevent any Suspicion it was herself that wrote it, in Case *Maria* in a rage should either send it up to Mr. *D*——, or shew it him at her return. The unfortunate Gentleman little guessing what had been contrived against him, continued treating, presenting, and caressing his pretty *Syrena*, till he was sent for to *London* on the arrival of an Uncle, who had been three Years in *Antigua*;[1] and whose Absence, he being Guardian to his Nephew, alone had so long retarded the Nuptials of Mr. *D*—— and *Maria*, the Friends of that Lady insisting on Accounts being made up between them before Marriage.

Syrena no sooner heard this News, than she had recourse to all her Artifices to retain him; Tears, Complaints, and Faintings were all employed to detain him, while the Mother on the other hand plied him with Remonstrances of the Promise he had made her of breaking with *Maria*, than which she told him there could not be a fitter Time than the present, as he might easily find some way to embarrass the Accounts, so as to render it impossible to make any Settlement on a Wife to the Satisfaction of her Kindred.——To this he cooly answer'd, that she might depend he would act as became a Man of Honour; but tho' he had enough to do between the Mother and Daughter, and had a Heart relenting to the Sorrows of *Syrena*, he began now to be satiated with Enjoyment, and the virtuous Affection he had avowed to *Maria* to resume its former Dominion over his Soul.——He therefore took his leave of them with so ill-dissembled a Concern, that they easily perceived there was a Change in him no way to their Advantage. Mrs. *Tricksy* however, flatter'd herself with some Success in her Plot on *Maria*; she imagined

---

1 Antigua was colonized by English settlers in 1632 and remained a British possession. At first tobacco was grown, but by the eighteenth century it was the primary source of the extremely profitable sugar trade in England.

that if it did not absolutely break the Match it would breed a Jealousy and Uneasiness on her side, which in time would create a disgust on his; and that join'd with a Stratagem[1] she had from the beginning intended to put in Practice, would renew his Affections for her Daughter, and cement him to her more firmly than ever.

Mr. D—— being got to *London*, the Pleasure he took in the Society of an Uncle he had not seen in so long a Time, and who he looked upon as a Parent, being left very young to his Care, together with the hurry of settling his Affairs, so took up all his Mind, that there was little room for remembering his *Greenwich* Amour; he had not however left that Place above ten Days before he was reminded of it by a Letter from *Syrena's* Mother. The Contents of which were as follow:

SIR,

I AM very much surprized that you have not in all this Time found a leisure Hour for a Visit at *Greenwich*, or at least for writing a Line to let us know you remember'd that you have some Friends here, who have reason to expect that Proof of your Sincerity——I am loth to call your Honour in question, yet as I am a Mother, must beg you to reflect, how cruel it would be, to take so much Pains as you have done to gain the Affection of a poor innocent Girl, for no other purpose than to leave her to despair——I see the concern she is in through all her Care to hide it from me; and tho' I find enough to chide her for, in the course of her Conversation with you, yet I have a Mother's Heart; and cannot but tremble at the Apprehensions to what she will be reduced, if you should prove ungrateful or unkind——Put an end therefore, I beseech you, Sir, to the suspence we both are in, inform us how your Affairs are, and if you have made any Progress towards getting rid of your old Engagement——*Syrena* would fain have accompanied this with one from herself, but I would not permit it, till I had first heard from you, which I once more intreat may be with a Speed, conformable to the professions you have done her the Honour to make, and your Promises to,

SIR,
Your most Obedient Servant,
ANN TRICKSY.

This Letter put Mr. D—— into a very ill-humour, he now saw some Part of the ill Consequences attending the Prosecution of an

---

1 Any artifice or trick; a device or scheme for obtaining an advantage.

unlawful Flame, and condemned his own Inconstancy as much as any other Person could have done. He was in the utmost perplexity what to do to rid himself of this troublesome Affair, and for a long time could not decide within his Mind, whether not answering Mrs. *Tricksy* at all, or answering her in such Terms as might let her see there was nothing to be hoped from him on the score of Marriage, would most contribute to that End. At length he resolved on the latter, and wrote in this manner.

Madam,
As I have a great Opinion of your Honour, and Sense of Religion, I can scarce think you will blame me, that on mature Reflection I dare not make any Efforts to break an Engagement, into which I voluntarily enter'd.—I have the utmost Regard for your Daughter, and doubt not but she may be much happier with any other, then she could be with one, who to be hers must be perjur'd.——I ask your Pardon for having deceiv'd you; and shall rejoice in any Opportunity that shall put it my power to attone, for what I have done, by any Act of Friendship, that is consistent with the Character of a Person, who is shortly to give his Hand to another. I dare say, you have too much Prudence to make any Talk of this Adventure, which would only create Uneasiness to me, without any manner of Advantage to yourself and Daughter.——Pray make my best Wishes acceptable to her; but at the same Time let her know, that all future Correspondence between us, would be disreputable to her, and highly inconvenient to,

Madam,
Your humble Servant,
D——.

He wrote at the same Time to *Syrena*, in these Terms.

Dear Syrena,
I Suppose you are no Stranger to the Contents of your Mother's Letter; and as you very well know, there never was any real Intention of Marriage between us, and that what I said to her, was merely in Complaisance to your Request; I should have taken it kind, if you had saved me the Shock of her Remonstrances, or Upbraidings on that Score; by seeming to think me unworthy of your Affection, and pretending to her that the imaginary Courtship, broke off wholly on your Side.—Believe, dear Girl, that I shall always retain

the most grateful Sense of the Favours, I have receiv'd from you; but as I am now going to enter into a State, which allows not the Continuation of them, our Interviews hereafter must be as private as possible, for both our Sakes.—Therefore, I beg you will make yourself easy——in a little Time, perhaps, you will hear from me, more to your Satisfaction, and be convinced that I shall never cease to love you.

Yours,

D——.

Both these he sent by the Penny-Post; but directed that for *Syrena* under a Cover, to the Person at whose House he had lodg'd, while he was at *Greenwich*, that it might not fall into the Mother's Hands; and betray to her, that her Daughter had been of the Plot to deceive her: Poor Gentleman, little suspecting himself was the only Person impos'd upon, or that the Excursion he had made, would be attended with Consequences, which he soon after dreadfully experienced. But, methinks, I hear many of my fair Readers cry out, that no Punishment could be too severe for the Inconstancy of Mr. *D*——, and that the least inflicted on him, ought to be the everlasting Contempt of the Woman to whom he was false, and the Insincerity of her for whose Sake he was so. It cannot, indeed, be deny'd that he had acted an ungenerous Part; and if we may take his own Word for it, in the latter Part of his Letter to *Syrena*, had no Intention to be more constant to *Maria* after Marriage than before: 'Tis certain, however, that tho' that insinuating Creature had got but too much Possession of his Heart, he had at sometimes his repenting Moments. He was soon after involved in Perplexities from another Quarter; he had wrote three Letters to *Maria*, to none of which he had receiv'd any Answer; and the last being accompanied with one to Mrs. *J*——, he obtain'd one from that Lady, in which he found these Lines.

SIR,

YOUR Letters for my Cousin came safe to my House, but she being gone from me, I have according to her Desire, laid them by in order to send to her, when I shall receive Directions from her where to do so; for at Present, I am entirely ignorant of her Retirement.—— I know not what has happened, since she left my House, to go to that of a Relation we have Twenty Miles hence; where, she said, she intended to pass some Days; but I have heard went from thence directly in the *London* Stage.[1]——I am greatly surpriz'd you have not seen her, nor that she not has wrote to me.—She seem'd in a good deal of inward Agitation at her Departure;——but I could get nothing from her of the Motive.—I wish all is well.—I do not doubt now you have this Intelligence, but you will make a strict Enquiry, and beg as soon as 'tis in your power, you will let me know, for I am in more Concern, than I am able to express.

SIR,

Your most humble Servant,

K. J——.

'Tis a common saying, that People seldom know the Value of any Thing, till they are in danger of losing it.——Mr. *D*—— was not sensible himself how much he lov'd *Maria*, till this Letter. Jealousy, and the Fears that some Accident had befallen her, by Turns distracted him; he sent——he went himself to all the Relations and Acquaintaince she had in Town, to enquire after her; but to no Effect; whoever he spoke to on this Head, seem'd no less amaz'd and concern'd than himself, and the more he reflected on it, the more he was bewildered in his Thoughts. One Evening as he return'd to his Lodging with a Heart full of disturb'd Emotions from this fruitless Search; he was told by the People where he lodg'd, that a young Lady had waited for him some Time; as he then thought of nothing but *Maria*, he imagin'd it must be she, and flew up Stairs with all the Impatience of Love and Curiosity. But how great was his Surprize, when instead of her, he found *Syrena*: A Visit from her seem'd so presuming, and at the same Time so distant from that Modesty she had always counterfeited before him; that on his first coming into the Room, he had scarce command enough over himself, to forbear saying something, that might have been accounted too shocking to a Person of her Sex, and whom he once pretended to love. She gave him not much Time, however, to consider how he should receive her; for rising from an easy Chair into which she had thrown herself, and running to him with a most artfully assum'd Wildness in her Countenance, the Moment he enter'd the Room.——Pardon me, cry'd she, my dear, dear Mr. *D*——, that I come here an uninvited Guest.—'Tis the first and last Trouble I shall give you; but I could not die without seeing you:—All I beg is a kind Farewel, and that you will pity the unfortunate, the too tender *Syrena*. If he was before

---

1 The London Stage was the public coach to London.

amaz'd and angry at an Action, which he look'd upon as too bold; he was now more confounded and grieved at a Behaviour, which had in it so much the Appearance of Despair; and demanded hastily what had happened, and what she meant by talking of dying, and Farewell? On which she told him with a Flood of Tears, that her Mother had intercepted the Letter he wrote to her, and finding by it the Truth of their Correspondence, and that she had been of the Party to deceive her; she flew into such an Extremity of Rage, that she turned her out of Doors, with an Oath never to see her more, or own her as her Child.—Thus, added the young Dissembler, I am abandon'd to the World.——Destitute of Friends, of Lodging, or any Means of supporting a wretched Life; and what encreases my Misfortune, I fear I am with Child?——What then can I do but die? And die I will. The Minute I go from you, I will seek out some private Stairs that lead to the *Thames*,[1] and throw myself in. Mr. *D*——, who believed all she said, thought now of nothing, but disswading her from so dreadful a Resolution: He made use of all the Arguments he was master of; assur'd her of his everlasting Friendship, and swore that neither she, nor the dear little One, in case it was as she apprehended, should ever be to seek for Support. This being what she wanted to bring him to, her Distractions by little and little seem'd to abate.——He sent his Man to provide a handsome Lodging for her, gave her Twenty Guineas for her Pocket, and promised to bring her Three Pounds every Week, till something should offer more to her Advantage.

Now was *Syrena* a kept Mistress, and being by his Good-nature, settled in a commodious and reputable Lodging, found many Excuses besides her pretended Pregnancy to drain Money from him, more than her Allowance; but not all the Extravagance of Love she pretended to have for him, nor all the liking he had of her Person and Behaviour, had the Efficacy to drive *Maria* from his Mind: Her strange absenting herself from him and from all her Relations, at a Time, when it was expected their Marriage would have been celebrated, gave him Discontents, which it was in the power of no other Woman to dissipate. To aggravate his Confusion, he receiv'd by the Penny-Post an anonymous Letter, the Contents whereof were these.

---

1 Stairs that would lead down to a barge, a common form of transportation along the Thames.

SIR,

I Am no Stranger to your Engagement with Miss S——, nor to the Disquiet you at present labour under on her Account, and am enough your Friend to advise you, not to give yourself any farther Trouble in searching after one, who if found, might occasion you to be guilty of somewhat unworthy of your Character;——in fine, she is in the Arms of a Man, whom an Inconstancy natural to the Sex, makes her prefer to him intended for her Husband;——Chance discovered the Secret to me; nor would I have been so cruel to the Lady, to inform you of it, had I not thought I could not have conceal'd it without Ingratitude, having once received an Obligation from you, which I cannot forget;——I chuse, however, to stand behind the Curtain, till it is known how you relish so disagreeable an Intelligence.——If you have Love enough to forgive this false Step in Miss S——, and make her your Wife, when she thinks fit to be visible, you cannot expect to know the Person, whom you could not look upon without a Blush;——but if, thus warn'd, you take the Advantage she has given you of concealing herself to break off, you shall be made acquainted with the whole Story of her Infidelity, and also the Name of him, who now subscribes himself,

Your Well-wisher.

Mr. D—— believing *Syrena* to be the most disinterested, open and sincere Creature in the World, had been so weak as to entrust her with *Maria*'s having absented herself from all her Friends; the fruitless Enquiry both himself and they had made after her, and also some jealous Sentiments, which ever and anon rose in his Mind, that so odd an Elopement could have no other Motive, than a new and more favour'd Lover; and the artful Hypocrite appear'd always to take the suspected Lady's part, invented Excuses for her having acted in that manner, and apologized for her with so much seeming Earnestness, that Mr. D—— was perfectly charm'd with her Generosity, and in some Moments thought he should not be much concern'd to hear the worst that could be of *Maria*, since he had in *Syrena* so faithful a Friend as well as Mistress. He no sooner receiv'd the above Letter, than he flew to communicate it to her, tho' it was then very late at Night, and he had passed all the Afternoon with her; but as if since his unhappy Amour with her, he was to be continually involved in Matters of Surprize, of one kind or other, he met one here he little expected, that of being told she was abroad; as he had left her quite undrest, and she had mentioned no Occasion that should call her out, he knew not what to think of such a nocturnal

Ramble;[1] he resolved however to wait till she returned, tho' it should be all Night, and bid the Servant of the House light him up Stairs; for *Syrena* boarding with the Family, had yet taken no Maid of her own; the People durst not refuse him, and he sat down, full of various and disturbed Emotions. He had not long indulged them, before casting his Eye on the Table, he saw a seal'd Letter; he took it up, and finding it directed to Mrs. *Syrena Tricksy*, and as he thought in her Mother's Hand, he broke it hastily open, and found he was, not deceiv'd; it was indeed from Mrs. *Tricksy*, and contained these Lines:

Dear Syrena,

I Was in Town Yesterday, and should have been glad to have given you my Opinion on what you wrote; but durst not come or send for you any where, for fear of Mr. *D*——'s being with you——a little Circumspection, my Girl, may draw the Fool in to marry you at last; therefore I am vex'd you have gone so far with Captain *H*——s; if any thing should happen to discover your Intrigue with him, and Mr. *D*—— should turn you off before you have got a Settlement, the other you know has no Estate, but it is too late to advise you now, only be cautious; it is lucky your Keeper depends so much on your Sincerity, as to tell you his Suspicions of *Maria*; I took the hint you gave me, and sent him a Letter as from an unknown Person, which will make him quite confirm'd of her Falshood. That I sent to *Lincolnshire* I am positive has had a good Effect, for a Person has been at *Greenwich* since you left it, making great Enquiry concerning you and Mr. *D*——, which could be only by *Maria*'s Orders——I dare believe by this time they heartily hate one another, and as we have contrived it, can never come to a right Knowledge of the Matter; only I once more charge you to take care, that nobody has it in their power to betray your Affair with the Captain; and also, that you will get as much as you can of him soon, for I hear his Ship will sail in a Month's Time;——let your next bring me an Account how Mr. *D*—— takes my anonymous Letter, and whether *Maria* is heard of yet——I think to leave *Greenwich* soon, and then we may see one

---

1 An act of rambling or walking without definite aim other than recreation or pleasure. In his *Dictionary*, Johnson fabricates the etymology as from the Dutch word "rammelen" which he defines as "to rove loosely in lust." As Rochester's "A Ramble in St. James's Park" (1680) suggests, the term had a distinctly sexual connotation and is not unlike the modern term "cruising."

another privately, for I must not pretend to forgive your yielding to Mr. D—— yet a-while. Adieu, dear Girl. I am,

Your Loving Mother,
ANN TRICKSY.

No Man that has not loved, entrusted, and been jilted, and betray'd, like Mr. D——, can have a true Notion of what he felt at this Scene of Villany, so wonderfully laid open to him——he shudder'd to think there could be so much Wickedness in the World; but when he reflected that it had been practis'd on himself, by a Person he had so much confided in, he was all Rage and Madness. Had he follow'd the first Dictates of his Fury, he would have staid till the false *Syrena* had come home, and torn out her beguiling Eyes, and soft dissembling Tongue; but Reason afterward remonstrating, that all he could do, would be but a demeaning of himself, and fall short of what her Hypocrisy merited at his Hands, he took Pen and Paper, and wrote to her in these Terms.

Base Monster,
A Letter from your vile Mother and Accomplice of your Crimes, has fallen into my Hands; I need say no more to let you know, I am no longer a Stranger to your Treachery to me, and the injured *Maria.* ——Tremble then, curs'd Deceiver! thou abandon'd Profligate! thou hoard of complicated Crimes, at my just Resentment, and fly for ever from my Sight, lest I stamp Deformity on every Limb, and make thy Body as hideous as thy Soul.——'Tis highly probable I am not the first, but am resolv'd to be the last on whom your detestable Artifices shall take Effect—Captain *H——s* shall be immediately inform'd what a Viper he cherishes; and after, your Character shall be made Publick,[1] to warn all Mankind from falling into those Snares, so fatal to the Reputation and Peace of Mind of

D——.

This Letter he left for her on the Table, and put that from her Mother into his Pocket, as an Evidence of their confederated Base-

---

1   To make public is to make something "generally and openly known" (Johnson), possibly by publishing in print. Mr. D—— subsequently threatens to record "all the Particulars of this fatal Adventure, and desired it might be made publick, as a Warning to Gentlemen, how they inadvertently are drawn into Acquaintance with Women of *Syrena's* Character." The latter instance (which is comparable to *Anti-Pamela* itself) more strongly suggests the act of publication.

ness; he read it over several times after he got home; but tho' he plainly perceived by it, that *Maria* had been imposed upon and made uneasy, as well as himself, by their Artifices; yet he could find nothing that could give him room to think they knew what Steps she had taken, any more than that a Person enquiring after him at *Greenwich*, seem'd probably employed by her; but who this Person was, he could not guess; and his Curiosity in that Point was so great, imagining, that if he could discover this Agent of *Maria*, he might by that means be informed where she was; that he was sometimes tempted to offer old Mrs. *Tricksy* a free Pardon for herself and Daughter, if she would in the first Place turn her prolific Brain, for discovering the Person that came to *Greenwich*; and in the second, make a full Recantation of all she had put in Practice, for sowing Dissention between *Maria* and him; but tho' he would have done almost any thing to come at the Knowledge of the Truth, yet when he came to consider a second time, he could not yield ever to see or to hold any Conversation more, tho' for never so small a time, with those Wretches, who had so grosly imposed upon and betrayed him.

Much Compassion had been due to the Vexation this Gentleman was involved in, had not his Infidelity, in a manner, merited the Mischiefs it drew upon him; but what the innocent and wrong'd *Maria* suffered all this time, cannot but excite the Pity of every generous Reader.

This Lady loved Mr. *D——* with a Tenderness, which is rarely to be met with in these times of Gallantry:[1] She had from her very Infancy been taught to look upon him, as the Man who was one Day to be her Husband; and her Virtue and Duty improving the Inclination she naturally had for him, she had never indulg'd herself in those Gaities so many of her Sex are fond of—had never listen'd to the Sound of Love from any Tongue but his, nor had a Wish beyond him. He, for his part, had seem'd to center all his Hopes and his Desires in her, had never given her Cause for one uneasy Moment on his Score, nor did she even know what Jealousy meant; till that fatal Letter from the wicked Mrs. *Tricksy* awaken'd in her that poisonous Passion, and forc'd her, all soft and gentle as she was by Nature, to experience those furious Emotions, which Love ill-treated, and Confidence abused, never fail to excite. The Shock she felt at first reading the malicious Intelligence, was greater than her ten-

---

1 Amorous intercourse or intrigue. "Vicious love, lewdness or debauchery" (Johnson).

der Frame could well sustain——She strove to disbelieve it, but in vain: The racking Idea return'd, in spite of all she could do to hinder it——sleeping and waking the hated Vision of a Rival flash'd upon her Mind——She painted her in Imagination, sometimes kind and consenting to his Vows, sometimes reserv'd and haughty, repaying his Inconstancy with Scorn—In fine, *Love, Hate, Curiosity*, and what was more distracting than them all, *Suspence*, made her once tranquil Soul a perfect Chaos of Confusion: Resolving to be satisfy'd, yet unwilling to make any one privy to what she felt on the Occasion of it, she pretended to Mrs. *J*—— that she would visit a Kinswoman at some Distance, and where she knew that Lady would not offer to accompany her, on account of a little pique between them——She went, indeed, but stay'd no longer than one Night, and took the Stage for *London.* She let no Person into the Secret of her Arrival, but one who had formerly been a Servant in the Family, and was now married and kept a House for Lodgers: With her did the discontented *Maria* take up her Residence: It was her whom she sent to *Greenwich*, to enquire concerning Mr. *D*—— and *Syrena*, and from her she received an Account which seem'd to confirm the Truth of the Letter; for Mrs. *Tricksy* had taken care to spread through all that little Town, that her Daughter was about being married to Mr. *D*——. Being thus, as she imagined, fully assured of the worst that could have been suggested to her, Curiosity led her to try all possible Methods to gain a Sight of the Face that had undone her: By the Diligence of her faithful Emissary, she obtain'd that too; for Mr. *D*—— being watch'd to the House where she lodg'd, *Maria* afterward went disguised into the Neighbourhood, and saw not only her Rival, but her ungrateful Lover also, with her at the Window ——Killing Sight! All the Fortitude she had assum'd for this Adventure, was too little to enable her to endure it.——She fell immediately into Convulsions, and after into a high Fever, which from the very beginning threaten'd Death. The poor Creature who had been her Confidant, now wish'd she had been less industrious in obeying Orders, which were likely to bring on so fatal a Catastrophe; and judging it wholly improper to conceal her any longer, sent to several of her Relations, who immediately came to visit her full of Surprize, to find she was in Town,[1] and had hid herself till her Condition made it necessary to disclose the place she was in: no body, however, question'd her on that Head, believing it might encrease

---

1   That is to say, in London.

her Disorder; but they fail'd not to enquire of the Woman the Motives which had brought her thither, to which the other pleaded Ignorance, and kept inviolably the Secret committed to her trust; tho' it did not long remain so; for *Maria*, growing delirious, so often mention'd the Names of Mr. D—— and *Syrena*, that it was easy to believe that something relating to that Gentleman, had been the Cause both of her strange Behaviour, and the Condition they now found her in. As they were sensible of the Trouble he was in on her Account, they thought it best he should be sent for, which he accordingly was, tho' much against the Will of the Woman of the House, who fear'd the Sight of him would heighten her Fever.

Mr. D—— received the News where *Maria* was, and of her Indisposition, the very Morning after he had detected the Treachery of *Syrena*; and not doubting but it was to the pernicious Arts of Mrs. *Tricksy* that she owed her Illness, flatter'd himself, that his Presence, and a full Confession of what had past, would greatly contribute to her Recovery; but he found altogether the reverse; that unhappy Lady no sooner saw him in her Chamber, than she fell into such Agonies, that he was obliged to withdraw: He imputed it, however, to the Force of her Distemper, and still hoped, that if she came a little to her Senses, she would consent both to see him, and hear what he had to say; so order'd a Bed to be prepared for him in the same House, that he might be near to watch her Intervals of Reason, and endeavour to make his Peace with her. In the mean time, he was inform'd by the Confidant, of the pains *Maria* had taken to convince herself of a Truth, she had better have been eternally ignorant of; and in relating the Steps that had been taken, highly condemn'd her self for having assisted in the cruel Discovery. Mr. D—— shook his Head, and told her that he wish'd she had been enough his Friend to have given him a private Intelligence of *Maria*'s Sentiments—— Tho', added he, I cannot blame your acting in the manner you did, as Appearances were so much against me.

Two Days had Mr. D—— been under the same Roof without being able to speak to her; the Physicians having order'd she should be kept extremely quiet—but at the end of that time, being, as they thought, somewhat better, the Women ventur'd to acquaint her, who was so near her, and his true Remorse for a false Step, which Youth and Inadvertency alone had made him take, and his real Innocence as to the main Point, that of having any Inclination to breaking of with her, or of marrying *Syrena*. The disconsolate *Maria* listen'd attentively to her, without giving any other Answer than Sighs; and when the other alledg'd the Improbability there was, of his having any settled Affection for a Girl, such as *Syrena*, and expatiated on the Vileness of both her, and her Mother; so much the more unhappy is my Lot, cry'd *Maria*, to be the Sacrifize of such Wretches——However, continu'd she, I will see the still dear and guilty Man——Let him be call'd in.

He threw himself on his Knees by her Bedside, and said every thing that Love and Repentance could inspire, to assure her, that his Heart had never been but hers; however, an unlucky, as well as criminal Inclination, had for a small time made him act contrary to his Honour and his Vows——I believe Mr. *D*——, answer'd she, you are now sorry for and asham'd of your Acquaintance with *Syrena*; but, perhaps, it is more owing to the Discovery of her Baseness, than to your regard for me; and the next new Face that pleased you, would have the same Influence; at least the Passion you have had for her has destroy'd all the Confidence I had in you—I could not now be happy with you—Nor, cry'd she, in a low Voice, can I live without you. In speaking these Words she fainted away——He was obliged to ring for the People to come to her Assistance; but all they could do was ineffectual, she dying in less than an Hour, and left him, who could not but look upon himself as the Cause, in a Condition little different from Distraction.

The real Affliction Mr. *D*—— was in for this sad Accident, made *England* and the Sight of all his Friends hateful to him: He embark'd in a short time for foreign Parts; but before he went, wrote all the Particulars of this fatal Adventure, and desired it might be made publick, as a Warning to Gentlemen, how they inadvertently are drawn into Acquaintance with Women of *Syrena's* Character.

Our hypocritical Mother and Daughter had all this time Business enough upon their hands: *Syrena* no sooner came home, which was about six in the Morning, than finding Mr. *D*——'s Letter, she made no Delay, for fear he should return, and use her as she knew she merited at his hands, but pack'd up her things, quitted her Lodging, and took a Coach immediately to *Greenwich*. Mrs. *Tricksy*, on being told what had happen'd, thought that Place altogether unsafe for them; so they both return'd the same Day to *London*, and took Lodgings at *Westminister*; where, having no Acquaintance, they lived quite private for some Days, to avoid meeting with Mr. *D*—— or Capt. *H*——s, to whom they did not doubt, but that the Resentment of the other, had exposed them, as he had threaten'd in his Letter. Between the Liberality of Mr. *D*——, the *Portuguese* Merchant, and the Captain, they had made a pretty handsome Purse, which if they could have resolved to be honest, might have put them in some way of getting Bread;[1] but neither of them were of frugal Dispositions, they indulged themselves in every thing they liked, and *Syrena* sent for a Mercer, Millener, and other Trades People to equip her in a gay manner, that when she went abroad, her Charms might appear to advantage: By private Enquiries they soon heard that the Captain had sailed, and also of *Maria*'s Death, and Mr. *D*——'s voluntary Banishment from *England*; on which *Syrena* broke from her Obscurity, drest, and trod the Mall[2] with as great a Grace, and as little Concern, as the most virtuous that frequented that place; she had nothing, indeed, to apprehend; but meeting with some or other of Sir *Thomas L*——'s Family; she had, therefore, her Eyes continually on the Watch, that if she happen'd to see any of them at a Distance, she might turn away, before they came near enough to distinguish her, thus disguised as the Hussy was in Lace and Embrodery. The Season for Park-walking[3] in an Evening being far advanced, it quite past over without her being able to make one Conquest, which was no small Mortification to this fine Lady, especially as her Money was almost exhausted in Cloaths, luxurious Eating, and Chair-Hire. In short, Winter came on, without any thing being done.——She durst not go to Plays, Opera's, nor Concerts, because she very well knew, that there was seldom a Night but some or other of that Family she had so gross-

---

1 In other words, they have enough to establish some sort of business.

2 The walk bordered by trees in St. James's Park. The Mall in St. James's Park was a fashionable place for displaying oneself while walking. As such, it was frequently the site of assignations and provided the opportunity to meet individuals of the opposite sex. It was, as Dorothy Marshall notes, "a curiously mixed throng, for though in theory it was one of the royal parks, public access to it had long been a matter of right" (*Dr. Johnson's London* [New York: John Wiley & Sons, 1968] 150). However, the use of the verb "trod" suggests how this would-be ramble is in fact labor for Syrena.

3 If we follow Syrena's activities through the year, it now is becoming winter, too late in the year to walk long in the evening before it gets to be dark and cold. And, since Syrena subsequently attends a masquerade, it suggests that it is some time after October since the London social season has begun.

ly imposed upon, were at those Diversions.——The Masquerade[1] was the only place she could go to without fear of being exposed, and even there was in Danger of being accosted, either by Sir *Thomas* or his Son; she flatter'd herself, however, that she should have Penetration enough to find either of them out in any Habit, without their being able to discover her; and she happen'd in reality to be more lucky than she deserv'd on this score. She was not so, however, in her principal Intention, that of being address'd to in a particular manner. She had been there twice without having been accosted with any other than the common Salutations of the Place, as *Do you know me*, and *I know you*, and such like Stuff; or the impudent Freedoms which are used to common Women, and which some who glory in being accounted Libertines, have the Effrontery to practise in the most publick Places. The Expence of her Tickets, Dress, and Chair-Hire thus thrown away, was no small Mortification to her, as Cash began now to run very low: She adventured, however, a third time, and happening to be address'd by a Person, who, on stretching out his Arm to reach at something on one of the *Beaufets*, she perceiv'd, by his *Domine*[2] falling a little open, had a Star on his Coat;[3] she resolv'd to encourage a

---

1 Haywood discussed the dangers of the masquerade in *The Female Spectator*. "[N]othing can be more agreeable" than the private masquerade among the "neighboring Gentry;" "where every one is obliged to pluck off his Mask, and own himself for what he is, as soon as the Ball is over, nothing will be said or done improper or indecent." However, public masquerades, which Syrena frequents, are "mercenary Entertainments"; "the most abandon'd Rake, or low-bred Fellow, who has wherewithal to purchase a Ticket, may take the Liberty of uttering the grossest Things in the chastest Ears, and safe in his Disguise go off without incurring either the Shame or Punishment his Behaviour deserves. But, besides being subjected to the Insults of every pert Coxcomb, who imagines himself most witty when he is most shocking to Modesty, I wonder Ladies can reflect what Creatures of their own Sex they vouchsafe to blend with in these promiscuous Assemblies, without blushing to Death" (*The Female Spectator*, Volume I, 33).

2 "Beaufets" are buffet tables. "Domine" refers to a clergyman and marks Lord R——'s costume as a clergyman.

3 Lord R—— is a member of the order of the garter, the most prestigious of the orders of chivalry. According to Alan Mansfield, the eight-pointed star, with the Cross of St. George in red enamel as its center, was the badge of the order, worn together with the ribbon and garter on daily occasions (*Ceremonial Costume: Court, Civil and Civic Costume from 1600 to the Present Day* [London: Adam and Charles Black, 1980] 56-57). Lord R—— is the most socially elevated individual with whom Syrena interacts.

Conversation[1] with him; and keeping her Eye constantly fix'd upon him, had Artifice enough to draw him off, wherever she found he was engaging with any other of the Masks.[2] Her Wit and Manner pleas'd him extremely, and at length he grew very particular with her——She seem'd no less charm'd with his Behaviour; and, after a good deal of feign'd Reluctance, consented he should conduct her to some place, where they might discourse with more Freedom; and he accordingly carry'd her to a Bagnio in *St. James's-Street*.[3] If she had appear'd agreable to him before, she was much more so now, when she had an Opportunity of revealing those Beauties in full, which in the Ball-Room could but be shewn in Part, and that too, but by stealth.

After a Supper, and some amorous Conversation, he entreated she would stay with him all Night; but tho' she pretended to have been struck with an irresistable Passion for him, the first Moment she saw his Face, and had it not in her power to refuse him any thing; yet said, she would sooner die than be guilty of an Injustice to one of her own Sex; so begg'd to know if he were married. He told her, on his Honour, that he was not.——She then insisted on his Name, and he made no Scruple of letting her know, he was Lord *R*——.

They past the Time till Morning in mutual Endearments, and indeed mutual Dissimulation——*Syrena* artfully mingling with her pretended Fondness certain modest Shocks to heighten his good Opinion of her, and he affecting to be possest of a more than ordinary Passion, for the more emboldning her to meet his amorous Desires with equal Warmth. The Night being past, and his Lordship fully gratify'd, he made her a Present of ten Guineas, which she at first refused with an Air of Disdain, telling him that he injured her greatly if he imagin'd she had yielded from any motive but Love. But he forced her to accept this Token, as he call'd it of his Affection; on those Terms, said she, I take it from my dear Lord; but were every Piece a Thousand I would reject them with Scorn if offer'd as the

---

1 In the eighteenth century, conversation could refer not only to a verbal exchange, but to sexual intimacy as well.

2 Other women in costume; however "mask" also marked any woman wearing a visor and was often slang for prostitute. In either sense, these women are identified as Syrena's sexual competition.

3 A bagnio is a brothel or a house where a room could be rented for an assignation. St. James's Street, right off Pall Mall and near St. James's Palace, is a highly fashionable area, consistent with Lord R——'s social position.

purchase of my Virtue——I am no Prostitute, continued she, and if I thought you look'd on me as such, and having accomplish'd your Desires would never see me more, I would this Instant undeceive you, by running your Sword through my too fond, too easily charm'd Heart. Lord R—— smiled within himself to hear her talk in this romantick Stile; but willing to humour her in it, made her as many promises of Constancy as she desired, and assured her in a very small Time, he would write to appoint a second Meeting, and they would then settle Things so as to see each other often.

Thus they parted, and *Syrena* went home somewhat better satisfied with the Effects of this Masquerade than she had been with the two former, tho' she did not flatter herself with securing the Heart of this Nobleman, as she had done those of Mr. *L*—— and Mr. *D*——; she feared he knew the Town too well to be drawn into any serious Engagement with a Woman he had come acquainted with in that manner, but expected however, that he would send to her, and that she should have further Presents from him.

The first Part of her Conjectures she soon found were but too true for her, but the other greatly deceiv'd her; for his Lordship thought little of her after they were parted, and less desired a second Interview: He judged by her Behaviour that if he were to encourage her Expectations by making any future Assignations she would become a troublesome Dependant, and be a kind of Bur not easily shaken off. Beside he had a Mistress whose Love and Fidelity he had for many Years experienced; by whom he had several fine Children, and who was at that Time lying-in at his Seat in the Country.[1] He would have been loth to give any Cause of discontent to a Woman he loved, and had Reason to do so, by any settled Intrigue with another, and tho' meeting with *Syrena* (at a Time when *Christians* as well as *Jews* think they may indulge an amorous Inclination without breach of Constancy) he had toyed away a Night, it never entered into his Head to continue an Acquaintance with her.

Four Days being past over, *Syrena's* impatience would suffer her to wait no longer, and having enquir'd where Lord R—— lodged, for he kept no House in Town, drest herself in as alluring a manner as she could, and went to make him a Visit.

His Lordship was strangely surprized when his Gentleman told him a Lady in a Chair, who said her Name was *Tricksy*, desired to

---

1 His mistress is pregnant; "lying-in" refers to a woman's confinement during the later months of pregnancy.

speak with him; he looked on her coming to his Lodging as a Piece of Impudence altogether inconsistent with the Modesty she affected to be Mistress of; however he ordered she should be admitted, but resolved to behave to her in such a manner as should prevent her from ever troubling him again.

This was certainly a very wrong step in *Syrena,* and what her Mother would fain have dissuaded her from; she told her that none but those who were not ashamed to be thought common, ever went to visit Men at their Lodgings; and that if Lord *R*—— were a Man of Sense, or had but the least Knowledge of the World, he must contemn her for it; but our young Deluder was of a quite different Opinion; she imagined that going to him in that manner, would give him a high Idea of the extreme Passion she had flatter'd him with, and that also it would make her seem to act without Disguise, and that she was too innocent even to know there was any indecency in what she did. So all the Arguments Mrs. *Tricksy* made use of were to no purpose; the pert Baggage told her she was capable of managing now for herself, and would walk with Leading-Strings no longer.[1]

This is a Favour I little expected Madam, said his Lordship, as soon as she was introduced. Then, my Lord, answer'd she, you were ignorant of the Power you have over me; but it is not to be wonder'd at, that you should not expect any Effects of Love from me, when you are so insensible of that Passion yourself——what, continued she, to be four long Days without seeing me or sending to me——I have had Business, return'd he coldly. O ungrateful! cried she, can you have any Business of equal Moment to the peace of one who adores you as I do, who have given you the greatest Proof of it a Woman can do, and who cannot live without you?——Hush, Madam, interrupted he, we may be overheard—this is not a Place for Expostulations or Upbraidings,—and as I never receive Visits from your Sex, unless those who are known to be nearly related to me; I must beg you will make yours as short as possible for both our Reputations. O my Stars! cryed she, are you then asham'd of me? with these Words she burst into Tears. Fie, fie, said he, with a half Smile, which denoted his Contempt, do not spoil that pretty Face with crying—You were all Gaity when I saw you before, and good Company, and if you desire to pass three or four Hours again in the same Manner, I assure you this is not the way to charm a Man of my

---

1 Strings with which children used to be guided and supported when learning to walk; thus to be in leading-strings is to be still a child or to be in a state of dependence.

Humour.——*Syrena* now burst into a real Rage, and scrupled not to treat him in a Manner little befitting his Quality; on which he bid her leave the House, and learn better Manners. She had then Recourse to Fits, and swoon'd so naturally, that if he had not been well versed in this Artifice of the Sex, he would have taken it to be real; but he immediately saw through it, and instead of calling for any Help, only said—look you, Madam, these Airs won't pass upon me, I see your Drift—you want to pin yourself upon me——but it won't do; and instead of softning me into the Cully[1] you want, you only incur my Disdain, and inspire me with the worst Sentiments for you I can have of any Woman,——therefore put your Face into Order and be gone; for if you continue in this Posture, I shall order my Servants to put your Head in a Pail of Water, which I look upon to be the best Remedy in the World for such Disorders as yours. These Words frighted her, and not doubting by all his Behaviour to her, that he would do as he said; raised herself from the Ground, and flew down Stairs without making any farther Attempts to bring him to her Purpose.

I do not doubt but many of my fair Readers will be highly disobliged at this Nobleman's Behaviour; they will say, he ought to have carry'd with more Complaisance, at least to a pretty young Creature, who had obliged him; and some perhaps may even tax him with Savageness and Brutality; therefore to vindicate his Character from all such Aspersions, I must inform them, that he had before met with Women of *Syrena's* Stamp;—that he had for some few Years of his Life devoted himself so much to Gallantry,[2] that he was perfectly acquainted with every little Art put in Practice by those, whose Business it is to ensnare; and had more than once been imposed upon by the Pretence of a violent Affection, which made him not only presently discern, but likewise abhor those studied and counterfeited Tendernesses; but as to the rest, no Man knew more how to value real Merit in the Sex, nor paid a greater Regard to it.

The Disappointment *Syrena* had met with, made her half distracted: She was ready on her coming home to break and tear to pieces every thing that was in her way; then her Mother remonstrated to her, that she could expect no better Usage, when she pretended to pursue a Man to his Lodgings, and reproach'd her for not

---

1 One who is cheated or imposed upon; a dupe.
2 While gallantry, a word that appears seven times in this text, can have a more positive connotation of courtship or refined address to women, here it is more consistently associated with sexuality.

taking her Advice; But the other, instead of acquiescing with what she said, or acknowledging she had been to blame, flew into a greater Rage than before, and told her, that all her Misfortunes had been owing to the Rules she had prescribed. You were always preaching up Softness and Tenderness, cry'd she, but I dare swear if I had been sawcy, and given myself an Air of Insolence, as indeed is more natural to me, I should have fared better. You are a poor ignorant Fool, reply'd the Mother, if you are not used well by the Man who thinks you love him, you never will by the Man who thinks you do not. ——Softness is the most prevailing Arms we have; Beauty may attract, but that alone secures the Heart. A great Argument on this arose between them, and at length terminated in a Quarrel, in so much, that *Syrena* went directly and took a separate Lodging, and vowed she would henceforth follow no Direction, but her own Humour; but this Quarrel did not last long, each found she had need of the other, and their mutual Interest reconciled them; it was judged proper, however, they should live apart for some time; *Syrena* having embark'd in an Adventure, which could best be carry'd on without the Appearance of a Mother.

She remember'd that in the time she was kept by Mr. *D*——, happening to buy some Silk for a Short-apron, at a Shop in *Covent-Garden*, the Mercer[1] had seemed to look upon her with an Eye of Admiration, pulled down several pieces of fine Brocade, under the Pretence of tempting her to buy; but in reality, only to have the Pleasure of detaining her as long as he could; and tho' she bought only such a Trifle, would fain have sent one of his young Men home with it. All this she thought testify'd a Desire of being acquainted with her, if he could find any Means to bring it about, so she contrived it for him in this manner.

She made it her Business to walk for several Evenings by his Shop, just in the close of Day, when they were preparing to shut up; and the first time she saw him there, ran in a vast Hurry and seeming Fright up the Steps, and cried, I beg a thousand Pardons for this Trouble, Sir, but for God's Sake give me House Room for a few Minutes—for I am frighted to Death. He immediately reach'd a Chair, and having made her sit down, enquired the Cause of her Disorder——O! said she, this *Covent-Garden* is a wicked Place—I hope I have not the look of an ill Woman—but a Gentleman has fol-

---

1 One who deals in textile fabrics, especially a dealer in silks, velvets, and other costly materials.

lowed me I know not how far—I could not get rid of him for my Life; and he swore I should either go with him to a Tavern, or he would see me home.——O! what a Terror he has put me in——so I took the Liberty to run into your Shop to avoid him. The complaisant Mercer told her she was extremely welcome, and perceiving she grew pale, and ready to faint (which she could counterfeit whenever she pleased) ordered a Glass of Water, and bid his Man ask his Wife for some Drops;[1] the good Gentlewoman hearing of the Accident, ran down, and assisted in recovering the Hypocrite from her pretended Illness, exclaiming all the time against the Vileness of Mankind; who, tho' there were so many fit for their Purpose, could not suffer civil Women to pass. *Syrena* having created a good deal of Bustle,[2] began at last to come to her Senses, and then made a great many Apologies for the Trouble she had given, but begg'd they would add to the Obligation, that of letting one of the Servants call a Chair for her; this was readily granted, but not till they had made her drink a Glass of Sack,[3] and eat a bit of rich Cake; she assured them she would endeavour to return their Favours, by buying every thing she wanted in their way, and recommending the Shop to all her Acquaintance. As she was going into the Chair, she took care to give the Men Directions where to carry her, loud enough for the Mercer not to be mistaken in the Place, in case he should take it into his Head to visit her, as she imagined he would do, by some tender Looks and Pressures he gave her, while he supposed her not in a Condition to be sensible of them.

She was not deceived, indeed, for the amorous Mercer was quite charm'd with her, and the next Day came to her Lodgings, under the Pretence of enquiring how she got home, and found herself after her Fright;——she had dress'd herself in Expectation of him in a loose and most becoming Dishabillee,[4] and received him full of Sweetness and affected Modesty. Every Look she gave him, and every Word she spoke, was new Fuel to the unhappy Flame she before had kindled in his Heart;—he thought there never was so perfect, so beautiful a Creature born, and wish'd himself unmarry'd, that he might have endeavoured to gain her Affection, which he now durst not presume

---

1 Any kind of medicinal potion that could either be inhaled or imbibed.
2 Noise or commotion.
3 A general name for a class of sweet white wines formerly imported from Spain and the Canary Islands.
4 The state of being partly undressed, or dressed in a negligent or careless style.

to attempt. He thought however he might indulge himself in the Pleasure of seeing and conversing with her, without any Injury either to her or his Wife; but the Consequence proved (as indeed it always does) how fatal it is to give way to Inclinations of that sort, which, by not being nipp'd in the Bud, at length grow too sturdy to be bowed down, and extend themselves to the most dreadful and enormous Size. She asked him to drink Tea, which he too gladly complied with, and after that a Bottle of Wine; among other Chat, she led him into that of his Business, and of the Fashions, asked him many Questions concerning what Colours, and what Patterns were most in Vogue; and then told him, she should soon be his Customer for three or four Suits of Cloaths; for, said she, I have been out of Town for a considerable time, and am quite out of Gowns and Petticoats; but I must stay, continued she, till I receive a Remittance from my Husband. Husband! Madam! interrupted the Mercer, are you married then? Yes, cry'd she, with a deep Sigh; you Answer, Madam, added he, as tho' you were not so happy in that State, as I am sure you deserve to be; where Hearts are not united, replied she, there can be no solid Felicity——however, he is my Husband, and absent, neither is it owing to him if I am miserable; in speaking these Words she let fall some Tears, which gave him a Curiosity to know the Motive; and tho' he thought it would be too great a Freedom to ask it, yet he could not help dropping some Expressions which testify'd his Desire, and gave her an Opportunity of telling him a long Story that she had invented to amuse him.

As she found he was married, and that there could be no hope of drawing him in for a Husband, she thought it best, for many Reasons, to pass for a Wife; so said, that being courted very young by a Gentleman, who was Heir to a great Estate, her Mother had compelled her to marry him, but that his Friends were so enraged at it, that they had sent him to *Venice*, where he now resided; and added she, must do so till Heaven shall turn their Hearts, which I see little hope of; they allow him a very handsome Income, however, out of which he sends me sufficient to support me, in the little way you see me in—as we lived together but three Days, I do not chuse to be called by his Name, till I can appear in a Fashion more befitting his Rank in the World; and also, because I have been privately informed, that if they can bring him to consent to it, they will give me a handsome Sum of Money to renounce all Claim to him. Thus, Sir, said she, I am a Wife, and no Wife——have lost my Peace of Mind and Character, with those who know not the Truth of my unhappy Marriage, and all thro' the mistaken Care of a too covetous Parent.

The Mercer seemed much affected with her Misfortunes, but gathered more Courage for his Love, thinking there was more hope at least of being listened favourably to by a Wife in such Circumstances, than there would have been by a young Virgin of a handsome Fortune, as he at first took her for.

He made her a great many Compliments on her Beauty and Merit; highly blaming her Husband's Friends for their inexorable Behaviour; and saying, that in his Opinion, such a Woman as she would become the highest Rank of Life. He told her moreover, that as she had said she wanted some Silks, she was extremely welcome to whatever his Shop afforded, and begg'd she would come the next Day, and order what she would have sent in.

She thank'd him for his kind Offer, but seemed loth to accept it, till he press'd her over and over, and assured her, with the tenderest Air he could put on, that having it in his power to oblige her, was the happiest thing could befall him. At last she promised to come, and he took his leave, rejoiced at this Opportunity of continuing an Acquaintance with her.

She, who was perfectly sensible of the Ascendant she had gain'd over him, resolv'd to manage him, so as to command every Thing he had: She went the next Day according to Appointment; and became his Customer for three rich Suits and two Night-gowns——which she carry'd away with her in a Hackney-Coach, after having invited him and his Wife to drink Tea at her Lodging, the first Time their Leisure permitted.

It is not to be suppos'd he fail'd waiting on her; and his Wife taking her to be a Lady of strict Modesty, was so much charm'd with her, that nothing but the fear of being troublesome, kept her from being almost continually with her. She never thought herself so happy, as in her Company, and was for ever inviting her to dine and sup at their House.——*Syrena* accepted her Kindness, as often as Prudence would admit; and the Intimacy between them encreasing every Day; the Husband took the Advantage of their Familiarity, to grow more so also. He told *Syrena* that if she were a Man, he should not approve of the Affection his Wife had for her; and as she was a Woman, he thought he merited something from her in Compensation, for robbing him of so much of his Wife's Company. The sly Deluder answer'd, that she look'd upon him and his Wife as one, and therefore desired when she could not have them both, that she might not be without One.——Your Business calls you so often my Way, added she, with a most bewitching Air, that, methinks, I need not miss the Sight of you once or twice every Day.—This with some other kind Expressions she let fall, whenever she had an Opportunity, by Degrees dissipated the Awe his good Opinion of her had inspired him with; and he at length took Courage to discover his Inclinations. Never had *Syrena* given a greater Proof, how perfect a Mistress she was in the Art of Dissimulation, than by the Amazement she put on at hearing him talk to her in the Language of a Lover— a half Resentment, and a half Compliance were blended with it, so as not to dash his Hopes too much, nor lessen herself with him by approving too easily of his Addresses. In fine, she behaved in such a Fashion, as made him think her an Angel of Virtue, and at the same Time, a Woman not a little attach'd to him by a secret liking of his Person.——He was not, however, long held in Suspence, he was one Night at her Lodging——they were alone——had drank a Glass of Wine pretty freely.——He was bolder than ordinary, and she sunk into his Arms at once, and gave herself up entirely to him, without seeming to know what she did.

Never Man thought himself happier than the transported Mercer; and *Syrena* was perfectly content with what she done; not doubting but she should henceforward have the command of his Purse; as indeed, she had; he lov'd her too well to refuse her any Thing, and she had so little Conscience in the Expences she brought him into, that in three Months, there was a frightful diminution of his Substance. His lavish Love bestowed so much upon her, that had she liv'd in any frugal Decorum, she might have sav'd sufficient to have made her easy for a long time; but having nothing now to think on, farther than indulging every Luxury, she became exceedingly leud; and the Mercer not being able to give her enough of his Company, and, besides, had something of a Sobriety in his Nature, not agreeable to her present Way of thinking; she fell into an Adventure which was not a little Expensive to her.

Living in good Lodgings, appearing always rich in Dress, and conversing with none who were any Blemish to her Character, for her Intimacy with the Mercer's Wife, took off all Scandal on his Account; she visited, and receiv'd Visits from several Ladies in the Neighbourhood; with them she us'd frequently to take a Morning's Walk up *Constitution-Hill*, as it is call'd, in the *Green-Park*.[1] She was seldom there without seeing a Man of a genteel Appearance and

---

1 Constitution Hill is an avenue running through Green Park; Green Park, a 53-acre royal park, was a favored place for duels. See map in Appendix F.

agreeable Person; she was struck at first Sight of him, with something she had never felt before, and which made her uneasy to become acquainted with him. As she found he was pretty constantly there; she went one Morning alone, and had, what she thought, the good Fortune to meet him—as they drew pretty near, she tript her Foot purposely against a little Pebble, and fell down as if by Accident, as he was just by her; he ran and rais'd her, but she pretended to have sprain'd her Ancle, and was not able to walk without Support, so she lean'd upon his Arm till they got into the lower Park, where they sat down on the first Bench. As she had no farther Designs on him, than entring into an Amour, she shew'd herself without Disguise, and was all the Libertine. On his proposing to go to a Tavern, she immediately consented, and yielded herself up to his Embraces, without the least Reserve or Scruple.—If such abandon'd Inclinations can be call'd Love, she might be said to love this new Gallant to a very great Degree.—She stay'd with him the whole Day, and encroach'd some Hours on the Night; nor parted without telling him her Name and Lodgings, and exacting a Promise from him, of coming to see her the next Day.

She had no reason to doubt his Punctuality in this Point. He was of as amorous a Constitution, as her vicious Desires had made her languish for.—He was at that time free from all Engagements, and thought himself lucky, in having so young and beautiful a Mistress thrown in his Way; but what extremely added to his Satisfaction, in the Enjoyment of her was, that he was pretty secure, both by her Appearance and Temper; for she would not suffer him to pay the Reckoning, that she would be no manner of Charge to him; but on the contrary, he should be able to render his Acquaintance with her serviceable, as well to his Interest, as he had found it to his Pleasure.

Their second Interview was no less full of Rapture than the first; and they were so highly satisfied with each other, that both swore eternal Constancy, and, perhaps, at that Juncture intended to preserve it. From this time they were seldom asunder; he breakfasted with her at her Lodgings, then they went together to the *White-Eagle* in *Suffolk-Street*[1] to dine; and parted not till the Hour, in which she expected the Mercer, or his deluded, injur'd Wife; she always defraying the Expence, tho' he complain'd he was asham'd of it; but that being a young Fellow of a small Fortune, he had it not in his power to

---

1 Suffolk-Street was a fashionable short street that ran off Pall Mall and was near St. James's Square. The White Eagle is a tavern.

behave towards her in that Respect, as he could wish. She told him she had enough for both, and begg'd he would make himself easy, for his Love and Constancy, was all she expected from him; and withal told him, that he might command whatever she was Mistress of, with the same Freedom as his own. Nor was she backward in the Performance of this Promise; whenever they went abroad, she took care to put more Money in his Pocket, than the Charges of the Day could possibly amount to. So that never any Man, who could content himself with receiving Obligations of that Nature from a Woman, had more reason to be satisfied.

The Passion she had for this young Gallant, however, did not make her negligent in preserving her Interest with the Mercer. She was never out of the way, when he appointed to be with her, and received him with such an Infinity of Tenderness, that he would almost have doubted the Testimony of his own Eyes, had they told him she was false.

But being willing to prevent any Accident that might discover her Intrigue, or render it even suspected by the People of the House; she consider'd that it would be proper, he should not be much seen at her Lodgings: She had past him at first, as a Country Kinsman just come to Town; but as a Continuance of such frequent Visits, might occasion Enquiries, she henceforward met him at her Mother's; and for this Reason it was she submitted herself to her, and was reconciled. But knowing well that Mrs. *Tricksy*, being past the Pleasures of Love herself, was solely devoted to Interest; she carefully conceal'd from her the Truth of her Sentiments for her new Lover, pretending to her that he was a Man of Fortune, and allow'd her Five Guineas a Week; and to gain Credit for what she said, gave him wherewith, to make her very handsome Presents. Thus was the Instructress in Deceit, deceived herself; and tho' she did receive some Profit from her Daughter's Vices, yet it was little in Comparison of what she might have got, if the other had been as sincere to her, and to her own Interest, as she pretended. But it is generally speaking, the Fate of Prostitutes to lavish on some Indigent Favourite, who, perhaps, despises them, what they gain by the Folly of the deluded Keeper.

The Mercer at length finding her grow exorbitant in her Demands upon him, and beyond what he cou'd continue to grant without ruining his Family, began to feel some touches of Remorse for the wrong he did his Wife and Children, but the artful *Syrena*, whenever she found him slack either in his Embraces or Presents, knew so well how to win him to her Purpose, and disperse all Thoughts, but those of the Pleasures he enjoyed in her Arms, that he could not find in his Heart to refuse any Thing to so lovely, so endearing, so faithful a Creature; much less to abandon her entirely; and had certainly kept on his Correspondence with her, till his Destruction had been inevitable, had not an Accident happened to open his Eyes to her Perfidy and Ingratitude.

Early one Morning she receiv'd a Letter from her beloved, acquainting her, that he had been arrested the Night before, by his Taylor, for the Sum of an hundred Pounds,[1] and desiring she would forthwith oblige him with the Money; for he had no Bail to offer, and had other Debts, which, he fear'd, would come upon him and fix him in a Gaol for Life, if not discharg'd immediately.[2] This News gave her the utmost Concern, she had been too profuse to have half that Sum by her, and could not bear the Loss of a Lover, so well qualify'd to please her. She, therefore, sent directly to the Mercer, begging he would come to her that Moment, on a Business of equal Moment with her Life: He had too much real Tenderness not to obey so pressing a Summons, and found her lying on her Bed, half drown'd in Tears. She told him her Mother was going to be carry'd to Prison for a Debt of an old standing, and that tho' there had not been a very good Understanding between them of late, on account of her unhappy Marriage; yet she could not live and see her Parent die in a Gaol, as she must do, if the Money was not paid——It would be highly improper, both on your own Account and mine,

---

1   While 100 pounds would have been an extremely large debt to a tailor (as well as a comfortable annual income for some members of the middle station), it would have been easy to accrue that large a bill for clothing. Clothing and other articles for personal adornment were among the most expensive purchases one could make. Cloth itself was expensive and a fashionable men's suit was, as John Burnett observes, "a very expensive commodity" (151). For example, according to Burnett's sampling, during this period a man's velvet suit cost £21 10s 9d; a blue dress suit would be £11. 17s., and wigs ranged from £5-20. Even rather modest clothes would be expensive. Dorothy George cites the account of a clerk who spent £4 10s for a suit of clothes, outfitting himself "in the plainest and coarsest manner" (*London Life in the Eighteenth Century* [London: Penguin Books, 1992; originally published 1925] 170).

2   One can be imprisoned for debt. As John Brewer notes, "the least hint of unreliability could produce a debtor's collapse as his creditors unceremoniously competed with one another to ensure the security of their assets" (*The Sinews of Power: War, Money and the English State, 1688-1783* [New York: Alfred A. Knopf, 1989] 204).

said she, that you should appear in the Affair, either as to bail her yourself, or send any other Person to do it; and besides the Money must be paid at last, so that if you have any Love, Friendship, or Pity for the poor *Syrena*, let me have the Sum required, that I may fly to save from Misery, the Person to whom I owe my Being.——I would have pawn'd my Jewels, and what little Plate I have, added she, rather than have given you this Trouble; but I know not which way to go about such a Business, and also fear they would not raise so much. How moving are the Griefs of those we love; had she ask'd him for his Soul he would have given it, and tho' at that time he could very ill spare it, being going to pay a Bill drawn on him by one of his Weavers, yet he immediately took out of his Pocket-Book two fifty Pound Bank Notes[1] and gave her, bidding her dry her Tears; and go instantly to remedy the cause; with these Words, accompany'd with a thousand Kisses, he took his leave, and she order'd a Hackney Coach to carry her to the Place where her Lover was confined. As the believing Mercer was going home, he met a Taylor, with whom he had been long acquainted, and was a Customer; this Man seeing him so opportunely, told him he was going to a Spunging House,[2] to hear what Offers a Person he had arrested, had to make him: The Mercer comply'd, and they went together. On their coming to the Officer's House, they were told a Lady had just gone up to the Prisoner, and desired to wait in the Parlour till she was gone: Accordingly they did so, but the Door not being shut, what Astonishment was the Mercer in, when the Lady passing by to go into the Coach that waited for her, he saw it was his, till then, suppos'd faithful *Syrena*: She had pluck'd her Hood pretty much over her Face, not that she suspected in the least who was there, but that her Face might not

---

1 The Mercer has given her bank notes worth £100. Bills of exchange, bank notes, and other kinds of paper money could be identified by what James Thompson describes as their "individualized nature." Bills "not only held the name of the drawer and the bearer, but often a number of intermediary bearers who had endorsed the bill" (*Models of Value* [Durham: Duke UP, 1996] 137). Additionally, the bank notes the Mercer gives Syrena are numbered, and he recognizes them immediately. The bills allow the Mercer to construct a narrative about Syrena's relationship with the Gallant and, in turn, his own relationship with Syrena.

2 "A house to which debtors are taken before commitment to prison, where the bailiffs sponge upon them or riot at their cost" (Johnson). It is a mid-point between arrest, arraignment, and prison.

be known hereafter, by any one who should have seen her in such a Place: Her Cloaths, however, being the same he had just left her in, and which had come from his own Shop, her Shape, her Air, and her Voice in speaking to the Coachman, discover'd *Syrena* too plainly, to one who had so much Cause to know her, for him to be mistaken. He was scarce able to dissemble his Confusion, before the Person he was with, but their being that Moment desired to go up to the Prisoner, prevented the other from taking Notice of it. On going in he receiv'd a dreadful Confirmation of *Syrena's* Baseness, had he doubted of it——He saw the two fifty Pound Bills he had just given to her, and the Number of which he knew, paid as so much Money to his Friend, and on the Prisoner's Finger a Diamond Ring he presented her with, and which she pretended to have lost.

Those of my Readers who have some time or other in their Lives, found themselves in the Mercer's Case, need not be told what 'twas he felt at so amazing a Proof, how greatly he had all along been imposed upon by the Artifices of this wicked Woman; and those who have never been so unhappy to experience such Deceptions, ought to be warn'd by the Despair this poor Man afterwards fell into, how they enter into any Engagements with Women, whose Principles they are not acquainted with; and not like him be beguil'd and ruin'd by a fair Face and seeming affection; but, as the Poet says,

Shun the dangerous Beauty of the Wanton—.[1]

For in corrupted Morals no Sincerity can be expected, and the sacred Names of Love and Friendship are but prophan'd and prostituted for the basest ends.

The Mercer thought every Moment an Age till the Business on which his Friend had brought him there was ended, that he might go to *Syrena*, and vent some Part of his Rage in those Reproaches which her Behaviour had merited from him. He found her at home, and was received by her with such a Shew of Love and Gratitude, that his Astonishment at her Dissimulation was so great, he had not presently the power of uttering what was in his Heart; but he gave her a Look, and, at the same time push'd her from him, as she was throwing her Arms about his Waste, as sufficiently inform'd her somewhat very extraordinary was labouring in his Mind——She

---

1   Thomas Otway's *The Orphan* (1680). The correct quotation reads "Beware the dangerous Beauty of the Wanton."

trembled inwardly, but disguis'd it with her usual Artifice, and ask'd him tenderly, what had disorder'd him? As soon as he could speak there was nothing opprobrious, that he omitted saying to her; he call'd her every vile Name that his Passion could suggest, and on her having recourse to Protestations of Innocence, and falling into Faintings, he let her know he was not to be again deceiv'd, and flung out of the Room, leaving her in a pretended Swoon.

The loss of so great a Support vex'd her to the Heart; but perceiving he was not to be recover'd, and that the Proofs of her Infidelity were too plain for her to aim at any Justification of her Actions, she consoled herself with the Reflection, that he would not dare to expose her, for the sake of his own Character; and that she had Youth and Beauty enough to attract some other, who might be as much devoted to her Interest as he had been.

The Mercer after this examining into his Affairs more heedfully than he had done during the Hurry of his Passion for the infamous *Syrena*, found himself in very bad Circumstances, and that he was no less than thirteen hundred Pounds a worse Man, for his Acquaintance with her, tho' it had not lasted above four Months ——The Injury he had done his Wife and Family now glared him full in the Face, and together with the Thoughts how impossible it was for him to retrieve this false Step, made him grow extremely melancholy: His Wife perceiv'd it through all his Endeavours to conceal it, and often with the greatest Tenderness, urg'd him to reveal the Cause; but could get no other Answer from him, than that he had of late had some Losses in Trade, which hinder'd him from being so punctual in his Payments as he had been accustom'd to be; but that he hoped he should recover it in time. This he said, to keep her from the Knowledge of her Misfortune as long as he could; but finding his Creditors grow impatient, and no visible way of making things easy, but by a Statute of Bankruptcy, his Pride would not suffer him to consent to that, and, therefore, resolved to put a Period to his Life and Troubles at once. To this end he shut himself one Day in his Counting-House,[1] and clapp'd a loaded Pistol to his Ear, with an Intent to shoot himself through the Head; but Providence averted his Aim, and by a sudden shaking of his Hand just in that dreadful Moment, directed the Bullets another way, and they but graz'd on the back part of his Head, and lodg'd in a Shelf behind him. The Report of the Pistol drew all the

---

1 An office in which the book-keeping or correspondence are carried on.

Family to the Place;[1] the Door was immediately broke open, and they found him with that Instrument of Death in his Hand, about to charge it for a second Attempt——His Servants by force wrested it from him, and his Wife having made them carry it away, and leave the Room, threw herself upon her Knees before him, and conjured him, for the sake of his own Soul, and for the sake of those dear Babes, who must be left Orphans, not to harbour Thoughts so contrary to Religion and to Nature——You know, said she, that my Fortune is by our Marriage-Articles settled on me, I will give it you up entirely; dispose of it as you please to make you easy[2]——If that is not sufficient, take all my Jewels, my Cloths—And should all be ineffectual, I will go to my Father, prostrate my self before him, and never leave his Feet, till I have obtain'd wherewith to retrieve your Circumstances—It was now he found the Difference between a virtuous and a vicious Woman; and having naturally very tender and grateful Sentiments, was quite overcome with her Generosity—He could not resolve to abuse it, nor suffer her to remain longer in Ignorance.——The wrong he had done her, was a Burthen on his Soul, which he could not sustain——O cease this Goodness, said he, to an unworthy Husband—I have been base, been unfaithful, and deserve the Punishment my Crime has brought upon me.—I will not involve you in my Ruin—Live, my dear virtuous Wife, continu'd he, and enjoy what, I thank Heaven, my Creditors cannot dispossess you of; and do the best you can with it for your self, and our unhappy Children—for me, I am determin'd either not to live, or not to live in *England.* The poor Gentlewoman was ready to die at these Words; but insisted, as well as she was able, on his accepting her Offer. O, said he, you little imagine what a Villain I have been—but you shall know——Then after some small Struggles between Shame and Generosity, he made her sit down by him, and related the whole Story of his guilty Commerce, concealing not the least Article of what he had done for *Syrena,* nor the Ingratitude with which she had return'd his too sincere, tho' criminal Affection——concluding with these Words——Now my injur'd Dear, said he, judge if a

---

1 This sentence, like the previous section, reveals that the Mercer lives where he works, demonstrates just how middle class he really is.

2 His wife is willing to give up her jointure, the separate money settled on her upon their marriage, to pay his debts. For a discussion of jointure and women's property, see Susan Staves, *Married Women's Separate Property in England, 1660-1833* (Cambridge, MA: Harvard UP, 1990).

Wretch like me ought to live, much less to receive any Marks of Good-will from you, whom I have so much abus'd and deceiv'd? It was impossible for a Wife to hear such an Account of the Cause of their Misfortunes, and from a Husband's Mouth, without being seized with many different Emotions, all violent in their turns; but Jealousy, Resentment, Pride, all subsided, and gave way to Tenderness and Pity——She was a few Minutes without being able to give him any Answer for Tears, but a kind Embrace supply'd the want of Words, and when she spoke, it was in these Terms: My dearest Love, said she, I look on your making me the Confidant of your failing, as a full Attonement for it—had I been told it by any other, I could not, perhaps, so readily have forgiven it; because I cannot but think, that the Heart still takes Pleasure in a Crime which it cannot bring itself to acknowledge as such, and that there is no true *Penitence* without *Confession*.—But your having told me all, obliges me in return to pardon all, and to do all in my power to contribute to your ease——I now, more than ever, insist on your commanding my Fortune; and if you refuse taking it up, I will do it my self, and distribute it among your Creditors, as far as it will go. The Husband was confounded at a Sweetness, so rarely to be found in a Woman wrong'd in so tender a point; and the Pleasure he took in having thus eas'd his aking Heart, mingled with the just sense of Shame, for having injured a Goodness and Excellence of Nature, superior to all he ever heard of, render'd him in a manner beside himself—He could say nothing but what a blind Wretch was I?——How insensible of what was truly valuable——How could I slight the real Diamond, and set my Heart upon a common Pebble, fit only to be trod upon, spurn'd, and kick'd into the Sewer!——Come, come, no more of this, my dear, cry'd she, throwing herself upon his Breast, many Men like you, have erred where there was less Temptation to excite them; but few Men like you, have honour enough to own they have done amiss—if you think me worthy the return of your Affection, oblige me by speaking no more of this matter than I shall do, to whom it shall be as it had never happened; and let us study how to recover our little Affairs from the Perplexity they are at present involved in.

It was with the utmost Difficulty however, that she at length prevailed on him to call in her Fortune; and just as he was about to do it, News arrived of the Death of a Brother he had abroad, who left him more than ten times what was necessary for the retrieving of his Credit;——to make what Reparation he could to his Wife, he settled upon her all that remained after paying his Debts; he soon after left off Trade, and retired into the Country, where no People live more happy in each other; she blessing his Return to Virtue, and he the Goodness that had reclaim'd him.

Syrena in the mean Time soon began to feel the want of his Purse, and as her power of treating and presenting declined, found also her Favourite's Inclinations declined in Proportion: He talk'd of nothing now in her Company but the want of Money, and on her reproaching him with the change she found in him, he told her that Love was the Child of Plenty, and that for his Part he could think nothing charming that was indigent[1]—this so enraged her that she gave him a Blow on the Face, which he, who neither loved nor regarded her, but for Self-Interest, return'd with Interest, and there was a perfect Battle between them——as she found her Strength inferior to such Sort of Combats, and liking him too well for his Ingratitude to extinguish, she fell into abject submissions, beg'd his Pardon for doing what indeed he deserved from her, since vile as she was to others, she had been generous to him even to Excess; and did every thing in the Power of Woman to engage a Continuation of their Acquaintance, which however lasted not long. Debts came upon him; and she not having it in her power to discharge them, he was oblig'd to quit the Kingdom to avoid a Prison.

She was now destitute of either Friend or Lover, and having expended and made away with all had been given her by the Mercer, fell into extreme Poverty, and had nothing for her Support but the Credit, which having laid out a great deal of Money in the Neighbourhood; had given her, on this she lived some little Time, but the Shop-keepers beginning to send in their Bills, she was thinking to remove privately to some other Lodging, to prevent one being provided for her, she could by no Means approve,[2] when Chance threw an offer in her Way, which her Industry had for a good while in vain sought after. Happening to be looking at some Lodgings at a Tradesman's House in the *Strand*, she perceived as she was going home a Fellow in a very rich Livery[3] followed her till she came

---

1 Actually, in Plato's *Symposium*, Socrates asserts that Love (*Eros*) is the child of Plenty (*Poros*) and Poverty (*Penia*), and it has inherited traits from both parents; however the Gallant's restating more accurately reflects the environment Haywood is detailing.

2 That is, Syrena wants to move before she is arrested and imprisoned for debt.

3 The distinctive uniform style of dress worn by a person's male servants. The richness of the livery was often perceived as commensurate with the wealth of the employer.

home, and as soon as he had seen her enter, go to an opposite Neighbour's; she could not guess the meaning, but was informed by that Person soon after, that a Footman had enquired there her Name. And the next Day receiv'd a Letter to this Effect.

Madam,

I SAW you Yesterday at one of my Tradesmen's Houses where I call'd to pay a Bill, and at the same Time lost my Heart; if you will permit a Visit from me this Afternoon, I shall endeavour to convince you that I think you deserve a better Situation than his House can afford——favour me with your Answer by the Bearer, and believe me,

Your sincere Admirer,
M——

This was indeed wrote with the freedom of a Man of Quality, to one he thought honour'd with his Addresses; but she was not at present in a Condition to stand upon Forms, and therefore answered him in these Terms, after being informed by his Servant by what Title she should address him.

My Lord,

I AM extremely oblig'd to the Honour of your Lordship's Notice, and know too well what is owing to your Rank and Character, not to receive the Favour you are pleas'd to offer with all Submission; but must take the Liberty to acquaint your Lordship, that tho' under Misfortunes, I am a Gentlewoman, and have hitherto preserved my Reputation; so flatter myself, your Lordship has no other View in this Visit than Commiseration for the ill Fate that perhaps may have reach'd your Ears of the

Unhappy
SYRENA TRICKSY.

Having dispatch'd this Epistle, the remainder of the Day was taken up in setting herself forth to the best Advantage, and consulting in what manner she should behave; as she thought it might give him an ill Opinion of her Sincerity afterwards, if she pretended to put herself upon him for a Virgin, she resolved to tell him the same Story she had done the Mercer, only with this Addition that her Husband died abroad, and by that Means she was cut off from any Hope of future Support from that quarter.

About six in the Evening came the expected Guest, who, struck with her Beauty and seeming Innocence by seeing her only *en pas-sant*,[1] was now quite ravish'd with her Charms; as he knew well enough however that she could not be ignorant of the Intention of the Visit, he made no great Ceremony, but came directly to the point; and she seeing his Humour was not to be dallied with, prac-tised none of those Artifices to keep him in hand, which she had made use of to others: All she insisted upon was a Settlement for Life, but he stop'd her Mouth, by telling her he was under an Oath to the contrary, having been deceived by some, who after that Engagement had ill-treated him; and, said he, you, Madam, have much less Occasion than any of your Sex to desire it, since you may be certain your Charms will secure me constant while you contin-ue to be so. Finding that nothing was to be done that way, she gave over all Speech of it, and told him she would then depend entirely on his Love and Honour. So a Bargain as it might truly be call'd, was struck up between them the same Night. He made her a Present of 50 Broad Pieces, and the promise of 10 Guineas per Week to defray common Expences.[2]

Now was *Syrena* in high Spirits again, and her Lord was so fond of her, that she might have brought him almost to any Thing, if the Warmth of her Inclinations could have permitted her to content herself with his Embraces alone; but publick Affairs, or Pleasures of a different Nature took up so much of his Time, that she wanted a Companion in his Absence; and by keeping a great deal of Compa-ny, and those not of the best Sort, she soon enter'd into Intrigues in which her usual Cunning had not the least share: In fine, she became so free of her Favours, that she at length got the Disease common in such Cases, and without knowing it, made a Present of it to his

---

1 In passing.
2 Ten Guineas, or roughly 10 1/2 pounds, per week is a very handsome sum, nearly a year's income for an unskilled day laborer. That amount would especially go far if only used to defray "common expenses." Food for a basic diet was relatively inexpensive; Peter Earle estimates that members of the middling classes would spend approximately 16.50 pence or a little more than a shilling a week on a diet that would include bread, meat, dairy products, and beverages (including milk, beer and tea). Thus, Syrena would have a lot of extra pocket money under this arrangement. See Peter Earle, *The Making of the English Middle Class: Business, Society and Family Life in London 1660-1730* (Berkeley and Los Angeles: U of California P, 1989) 14.

Lordship:[1] As Persons of his Quality cannot feel the least Disorder without having immediate recourse to their Physicians, he was soon informed from what source his Ailment proceeded; and as he had no Gallantries with any Woman since the Commencement of his Amour with *Syrena*, had no room to doubt if it were she who had done him this unwelcome Favour: He accused her with it in Terms, which made her know he was convinced of her Inconstancy, and tho' she here made use of every Stratagem to perswade him she was Innocent, all her Vows, her Tears, her Imprecations were of no Force, he quitted her, and told her, if it were not more for demeaning himself than any remains of regard for her, he should resent the Injury she had done him in a severer manner.

One would imagine she should, in so terrible an Exigence, have look'd back with Shame and Confusion on her past Conduct, but she appeared rather harden'd than abashed, when her Mother, who soon discovered the Truth, remonstrated to her the Folly and Madness of her late Behaviour————'tis possible the old Woman now began to repent the having train'd up a Child in that manner; but if she did, it was of no Service, since the other was too opinionated and too obstinate to take any Advice, but such as was agreeable to her own Inclinations. 'Tis certain, that tho' she at first taught her to ensnare, to deceive, and to betray, her Aim was to enable her by those Arts to secure to herself some one Man, by whom she might make her Fortune; and never imagined she would have run such Lengths, meerly for a precarious Dependance, or to gratify Desires, which when once indulg'd, bring on inevitable Destruction; but it was too late to reflect on what was past, and she forbore saying much to her, seeing the Violence of her Temper, and unwilling to come to a downright Quarrel, hoping she might still make some Conquest, that might be of greater Service than those she had lost; and her Condition now requiring Medicine rather than Reproof, she bent all her Cares for her Cure in the most private Manner; for which Reason she made her leave the Lodging she was in, and come to hers; where,

---

1 Gonorrhea is likely the disease referred to. "Women afflicted with gonorrhea were generally unaware they had the disease, and so they were often unknowing carriers of it" (Linda E. Merians, "Introduction," *The Secret Malady: Venereal Disease in Eighteenth-Century Britain and France*, ed. Linda E. Merians [Lexington: The UP of Kentucky, 1996] 8).

by the Assistance of a skillful Surgeon and good Nurse,[1] she was perfectly recovered in a short time.

But her Circumstances were not so easily repair'd as her Health had been; the Expences of her Illness had so reduced her, that she had scarce a change of Garments to appear in; in such as she had however, she took little Rambles about the Town, in hope of captivating some admiring Fool; but nothing offering answerable to her Expectations, she grew very much mortify'd, and began to fear she had lost the Power of pleasing, tho' not yet seventeen. No Necessities could almost be greater than what Mother and Daughter were now in, yet would neither of them think of betaking themselves to any honest way of getting a lively-hood. Those Relations who had formerly been kind to them, having heard something confusedly of *Syrena's* Conduct, had for a long time withdrawn their Bounties, so they were entirely destitute of all Assistance.

In this melancholy Posture of Affairs *Syrena* went one Day into the Park, not with the view of meeting any Adventure to her Advantage, for she was now quite hopeless, but meerly to indulge her Vexation——she sate down on one of the most remote and unfrequented Benches, and no body being in Sight, vented her Spleen in real Tears, mingled with Sighs, and ever and anon an Exclamation ——What shall I do?—what will become of me? did she frequently cry, without being sensible she did so;——such was the Agony she now was in, she neither saw, nor heard the Tread of any Person approaching, till all at once she turn'd her Head, and found a grave old Gentleman, sitting by her on the same Bench. If it would not be an impertinent Question, pretty Lady, said he, I should desire to know what occasions such excessive Grief in one so young and beautiful? Overwhelm'd with Sorrow, as *Syrena* had been, she felt her Heart spring with Joy, at being accosted by a Person, who looked as if he had it in his power to redress her Grievances; so drying her Eyes, and assuming all possible Sweetness in her Countenance, alas, Sir, answered she, my Misfortunes are too great to be conceal'd; and as they are not fallen upon me through any Fault I have been guilty of, I need make no Scruple of declaring the real Cause, especially to a Gentleman, who tho' a Stranger, seems to have a Heart relenting

---

1 Treatment for gonorrhea included various liquids and purges, as well as a combination of topical and ingested forms of mercury. Syrena's use of a surgeon and a nurse suggest she seeks a higher level of care that is more expensive but also more effective. The text also suggests Syrena has sold some of her clothes to pay for her treatment.

to Distress. She then told him, that she had been married very young to a Gentleman, whose Friends having been disoblig'd on the Account of her having no Fortune, had sent him to *Venice*; whence, out of what they allowed him, he had always sent her something; but that being now dead, all her Support was lost; she having no Friends but a Mother, wholly unable to help her—adding, that she was a Gentlewoman, and had never been bred to any Business.

He seemed very much affected with her Story, but persuaded her not to give way to Despair; telling her, that the Ways of Providence were mysterious, and that frequently when things had the worst Appearance, good Fortune was nearest at hand—he talked to her in this Fashion for a considerable time, and asked her many Questions, to all which she answered with so much Sweetness and seeming Sincerity, that he grew very much taken with her; and among other Particulars, having enquired of her where she lived, and her Name, told her, he would make her a Visit, if she would give him leave; for, added he, it may be that I may think of something that will be to your Advantage.——You seem, Sir, replied she, too much the Gentleman and the Man of Honour for me to apprehend you have any Motives for this Offer, but meerly Pity for the Calamities you see me involved in; therefore shall think myself honoured in your Acquaintance. I assure you, returned he, I shall never give you any Reason to repent this Confidence; and when I see you next, and acquaint you who I am, I flatter my self the Character I bear in the World, will entirely rid you of all Scruples on my Account——in the mean time, continued he, you shall promise me to be chearful, and attend with Patience a Lot which may be happier than· you at present see any Cause to expect. She replied, that she would do her Endeavour to follow the Advice of so worthy a Person——he then took his leave, and she went home a good deal more at Ease than she went out——her Mother was rejoiced at hearing what had befallen her, and cry'd out in a sort of Transport, *Syrena*, this is the Man will make you happy! not one Woman in an hundred makes her Fortune by a young Fellow——a young Fellow thinks himself upon a Par with any of us, be we never so handsome; but when once an old Fellow takes it into his head to fall in love, he will do every thing, give every thing to render himself agreeable—there is indeed a kind of boyish Love, which begins about sixteen or seventeen, and lasts till twenty or something longer, but then it wears off, and they commonly despise the Object afterwards, and wonder at themselves for having found any thing in her to admire—from twenty to thirty they ramble from one to another, liking every new Face, and fixing on none—after thirty, they grow more settled and wary; and if they love at all, it is commonly lasting; but a Passion commenced between forty and fifty, is hardly to be worn off—'tis certainly strange, but true of that Sex, that amorous Desires grow stronger, as the power of gratifying them grows weaker, and an old Lover is the most doating fond Fool on Earth, especially if his Mistress be very young; for it is remarkable, that when a Woman is advanced in Years, I mean about Forty, she shall look more lovely in the Eyes of a young Man, than in those of one of her own Age, who at that time begin to grow fond of Girls, in so much, that I have known some forsake very agreeable Women, and take up with, nay, have been ready to ravish Creatures that have been Blear-ey'd, Hump-back'd, had pimpled Faces, and all for the Sake of dear Eighteen—so that while you are young, my Girl, chuse a Lover old enough to be your Father, and as you grow older, one who might be your Son.

With these learned Maxims did the old Jezebel[1] entertain her Daughter, who stirr'd not out all that Day nor the next, in hope of the old Gentleman's coming; but he deferr'd his Visit till the third Day, either thinking it unbecoming to his Character to appear too hasty, or perhaps not altogether determined within himself how he should act when he did come.

At last he came however, and *Syrena* seeing him from the Window, ran to tell her Mother, on which they both took up a Work-Basket:[2] *Syrena* seem'd darning a Cambrick Apron, and her Mother altering an old Velvet Mantelet.[3] These Marks of good Houswifry and Frugality were very engaging to the old Gentleman; to find them thus employ'd gave him an advantageous Idea of their Modesty and Virtue, and he did not fail to give them those Praises he thought they merited.

After some few Compliments and preparatory Discourses; I have been thinking, said he, to Mrs. *Tricksy*, on the Account your Daughter gave me of her Misfortunes, and have been ever since very much affected with them.——I should be glad, methinks, to have it in my power to alleviate them; but the way I have to propose may not, perhaps, be agreeable to either of you. O! Sir, reply'd she, I dare believe you are too worthy a Person, to offer any thing we should not

---

1　Name of the infamous wife of Ahab king of Israel (I Kings 16:31) and used allusively for a wicked, impudent, or abandoned woman.

2　A work basket typically contained implements and materials for needle-work; thus, making Syrena and her mother appear as industrious women.

3　A kind of short, loose, sleeveless cape covering the shoulders.

approve of with Joy. You might think it an under-valuing of your Family, which I hear is very good, rejoin'd he; for your Daughter to undertake the Charge of a House, I do not mean the servile Offices of it; but to overlook the Servants, and see that they did their Duty.——She seems, added he, to have a Prudence above her Years, and I imagine would be very fit for such a Trust in every Respect. I am sure she would endeavour to be so, cry'd her Mother, if you, Sir, would do her the Honour to recommend her. She needs no other Recommendation than her own, answer'd he, since it is myself, who would put the care of my Family into her Hands. He then told them, that he was call'd Mr. W——; that he was formerly a Merchant, but having acquired sufficient for his Contentment, he had retir'd from Business, and took a House in an airy Part of the Town;[1] that he was a Widower, had but two Sons, one of whom was married, and settl'd in the City, and the other a Student at Oxford.—— So that continued he, I live alone, and should be glad of a Gentlewoman to eat with me, play a Game at Picquet[2] in an Evening, and, in fine, be a Companion as well as Housekeeper.[3]

Both the Mother and Daughter seem'd very much pleas'd with his Proposal, and left it to himself, what Consideration she should have for the Trouble she was to take; telling him that he should reward her as he found she merited. This he thought was acting like

---

1   It appears that Syrena is moving west in London, to the newer and thus "airier" part of town, especially in contrast to the location of the Merchant and his wife who clearly lived in the old City of London where Mr. W——'s older son also lives.

2   A card game in which two players are each dealt 12 cards from a pack of 32 (the low cards from the two to the six being excluded). Points are scored on various groups or combinations of cards, and on tricks.

3   Syrena is supremely unqualified to serve effectively as a housekeeper given the range of responsibilities a true housekeeper would traditionally assume. The housekeeper, who would have earned about £40 p.a., is the highest ranking female servant in a household. In addition to the responsibilities Syrena mentions, such as planning menus, a housekeeper would also "supervise the whole establishment, with the exception of whatever stable servants were employed, but she also kept the provisions, dispensed them as they were needed, and kept the household accounts" (Hecht 64). She would hire servants and, typically, a housekeeper also had some special culinary duties. Usually, the position was held by a woman of age, maturity, and experience due to the range of responsibilities. Clearly, Syrena does not fulfill the qualifications. It is, perhaps, as a "companion" that Syrena is more qualified.

real Gentlewomen, and the Confidence they placed in him highly oblig'd him. It was agreed that she should come into his House, in the Station he mention'd, the ensuing Week, and he then made a Present of a Twenty Pound Bank Note to Mrs. *Tricksy*, for hers and her Daughter's Use till that Time.

After he was gone, *Syrena* communicated to her Mother some Fears she had, that he intended her for no other than a real House-keeper; but Mrs. *Tricksy* told her there was not the least Reason for such Apprehension.——Thou silly Girl, said she, would any Man, take a Stranger like you into his Family without having a more than ordinary liking to her Person; and will not that liking produce Offers of a different kind, when he becomes more acquainted?——Per-haps, he has a mind to try how you will behave before he will dis-cover his Inclinations; therefore it behoves you, indeed, to be very cautious——to keep a strict guard upon every Word and Look, and above all things to strengthen the Opinion, he now has of your Innocence and Virtue. But said, *Syrena*, if I should seem too rigidly honest, it might deter him from any Attempt upon me, and in time extinguish all amorous Inclinations, if he now has any for me. Not at all, reply'd her Mother; Men, especially rich Men, are apt enough to think their Wealth will conquer the most stubborn Virtue——beside have not I instructed you how to play at *fast* and *loose*,[1] as I call it, with the Men—sometimes kind, sometimes reserv'd.—Coy when they're free, and Tender when they seem more cold; and all as if by Accident, and as if Design had not the least share in your Conduct?

Between Lessons for her Behaviour, and preparing things neces-sary for her Departure, the time was taken up till the appointed Day; on which he came in his Chariot, and conducted her himself to his House; where they no sooner arrived, then he had all his Servants call'd into the Parlour, and told them he had brought a Gentle-woman to be in the Place of their Mistress, and they must follow her Directions in every thing. The Keys of all the Plate and Linnen were then deliver'd to her, and she took Possession of all, as tho' she had been Wife, or Daughter of the Owner of the House. As it was not thought proper her Mother should come often to visit her any more, than when she was at Sir *Thomas L*——'s; they agreed *Syrena* should write whenever any Thing material occur'd; and that her Mother

---

1   "Fast and loose" refers both to the quality of being slippery, inconstant, or shifty, as well as to an old cheating game played with a stick and a string (*OED*). Note that both senses of the term apply equally well to Syrena.

whenever it requir'd any Answer should send it by old *Sarah*, who still liv'd with her, and not trust to the Penny-Post. In three or four Days she wrote as follows.

LETTER I.

From G——— Square.[1]

THURSDAY.

Dear Mother,

I Cannot yet tell what to make of the old Gentleman's Designs: He uses me with more Respect than I could look for as a House-keeper, and with all the Freedom of a Relation; but speaks not the least Word of Love. He approves of every thing I do, and has never found the least Fault; tho' God knows I am ignorant enough how to order the Affairs of a Family. I do my best, however, to please him; and every Morning as soon as I get up, write a Bill of Fare,[2] and shew it him when he comes down to Breakfast; and I assure you he has told me more than once, that I have an elegant Taste; whether he is earnest or not, I don't know; and I am sometimes afraid he should think me too delicate, but I bring myself off: For Yesterday having set down *Green Pease*, are there any yet said he, pretty hastily, as I thought? yes, Sir, I reply'd, I saw some Yesterday, but they are dear; I set them down only to shew you, that I know they are to be had, if you should have a Fancy to any; for you see the second Course is full without them, and they may be omitted. You are very obliging, answer'd he, and I think may spare yourself the trouble of making any Bills of Fare hereafter, since you are so good a Judge yourself, of what would become my Table. I told him that I could not be easy, unless he saw how his Money was to be laid out: Well, said he, if it must be so; but, I believe, you'll seldom find me either add or diminish to what you shall contrive for me. I play'd at Cards with him last Night, till Twelve o'Clock, and he had a Bowl of Rack Punch[3]

---

1 Given the previous reference to living in the "airy" part of town, this seems possibly to refer to Grovesnor Square.

2 The menu for the day.

3 "Rack punch" is a beverage composed of wine or spirits (arrack) mixed with hot water or milk and flavored with sugar, lemons, and some spice or cordial. Rack or arrack is distilled liquor from the West Indies. Johnson notes that "punch," like "bishop," is a cant word.

made, and set by us on a Dumb Waiter; but tho' he prest me very much to drink Glass for Glass with him; yet I begg'd to be excus'd, telling him I had a weak Head, and had never been accustom'd to drink any thing strong.—Indeed, I could have drank the whole Quantity, myself; and you know how well I love that Liquor; but I tell you this, to shew you what a Command I have over myself—— if he intends to make me either a Wife or a Mistress, I find 'tis necessary to give him a very high Opinion of me; for he is devilish wary and observing; so I must lead the Life of a Vestal,[1] tho' cruelly against my Inclinations, till I have got the upper Hand of him; and then— but I won't build Castles in the Air.[2]—As soon as I know any thing farther, I will write again, and am,

Dear Mother,
Your dutiful Daughter,
SYRENA TRICKSY.

P. S. Just as I had finish'd the above, he sent for me to tell me To-morrow is his Birth Day, and he shall have his Son in the City, and his Wife, and several other Relations to dine with him; so bid me order a Dinner accordingly. I wonder whether I shall sit at Table or not, or what he will say of me to them.—Pray Heaven none of them know me.

LETTER II.

From G—— Square.

SATURDAY.

Dear Mother,
Yesterday was, as I expected it would be, a very hurrying Day, we had a vast deal of Company indeed, and a very noble Entertainment I provided for them. A little before they came, the old Gentleman sent for me into the Parlour, and said, Mrs. *Tricksy*[3] as I shall have so many People here to Day, and your Youth and Beauty may possibly occasion some Raillery, or if not some Conjectures at least that I dare say your Modesty would not willingly excite; I hope you will not take

---

1   A reference to the Vestal Virgin priestesses who took care of the sacred fire in the Temple of Vesta in Rome. The adjective means chaste, virginal or pure.

2   To form unsubstantial or visionary projects.

3   Once Syrena becomes his housekeeper, he refers to her by the honorific title "Mrs. Tricksy" in deference to her status in the household.

it ill, if I desire you to dine alone,———I say *alone*, for I will not have you dine with the Servants by any Means———I am sorry I did not think of bidding you invite your Mother to keep you Company———but it is too late now—when any other such Occasion falls out I shall be more considerate. I told him nothing could be more agreeable to my Inclinations than to avoid being seen by so many Persons to whom I was an utter Stranger, and not at present in a rank of Life to entitle me to such Conversation. As to that, replied he, you are Company for any body; and when you have been here a little longer, it may be, I may introduce you; in the mean time you must be content. I made him a low Curtesy in token of being perfectly satisfied with his goodness, and was going out of the Room, but he called me back and said, I had like to have forgot to tell you that I insist upon it, that you order a Part of whatever you like best to be carried into your own Chamber, and not let any Thing come to your Table after it has been on mine———I have my Reasons, continued he, for this Injunction, and shall not be pleased if you do not observe it. I made him all the Acknowledgements so great a Mark of his Respect deserved from me, but would have declined accepting it till I found he was resolved upon it.

At Night after they were all gone, which was not till almost 12 o'Clock, I went in to him to ask if Things had been ordered to his Satisfaction: Nothing could be more so, my pretty Manager, said he, with a Look that I thought had something very amorous in it, but I perceived he had been drinking pretty freely; so I asked a great many Questions on purpose to give him an Opportunity of opening his Mind, and I imagined he was going to say something two or three Times, but whatever it was he restrained himself, only as I was taking my leave he gave me a gentle pull by the Gown, and said, I must not omit making you a small Acknowledgement for the Care you have taken to Day, and put 5 Guineas into my Hand, and at the same Time kissed me with a good deal of Eagerness three or four Times, then push'd me from him as it were, and cried go your ways, you little Temptation you! I neither seemed frighted, nor yielding all the time, but affected a little Confusion, and once more wish'd him a good Repose: He did not call me back again, as I was in hopes he would; and this Morning at Breakfast he behaved to me no otherwise than usual; so whether he has forgot, or repented of the Freedom he took with me last Night, I know not, but it vexes me that he comes on no faster———I hate Suspence of all Things, and begin to grow weary of this dull insipid Life, yet I am resolved to endure it a little longer—I long to see you and have some talk about this

Matter——I have never stirr'd out since I have been here, and I find it pleases him wonderfully to think that I love home so well—I am sure it would not be improper for you to come to see me some Day next Week, so if you don't hear from me before I shall expect you, who am,

Your Dutiful Daughter,
SYRENA TRICKSY.

Her Mother came as she desired the *Wednesday* following, but *Syrena* having nothing of Consequence to inform her their Conversation is of no moment to the Reader. But on the *Monday* following she wrote a third Letter to this Effect.

LETTER III.

From G——— Square.

MONDAY.

I Have now the Satisfaction of acquainting you, part of the Secret which we so much wish'd to know is at last reveal'd—I will tell you how it came out.——Last *Saturday* Night I was sitting in the Parlour reading the Play call'd the *Conscious Lovers*,[1] when the old Gentleman came home—I laid down the Book as soon as I saw him enter, which he perceiving, cried, don't let me disturb you—pray what is the Subject of your Entertainment, and then look into it——O! the *Conscious Lovers*, continued he; this is accounted a very good Play— pray what's your Opinion? I told him I was no judge, but it pleased me. So it does most People, said he, and indeed is a good Performance, but yet, methinks, there is somewhat in the Characters of *Bevil* and *Indiana* not quite agreeable to Nature.——The Gentleman is very generous, Sir, cried I; ay, replied he, and less self-interested

---

1   A sentimental comedy by Richard Steele, produced in 1722. *The Conscious Lovers* is the story of the apparently orphaned Indiana and her relationship with the honorable Bevil who, though in love with Indiana, is about to marry Lucinda, daughter of the wealthy Mr. Sealand. Indiana's true identity as Sealand's daughter is revealed when the bracelet she wears is recognized by her father, and she and Bevil marry. The reference draws both on Haywood's knowledge of the theatre as well as the popularity of this sentimental comedy and the change in theatrical tastes it suggests. The play also endorses a sentimental and sincere attitude toward romantic relationships that is the antithesis of Syrena's.

than we Men are capable of being to the Object we love. I could not help looking a little surprized at these Words, and cried, I thought, Sir, that Love had inspired Generosity. Yes, answered he, it does inspire what is commonly called Generosity, we are ready enough to give every thing, and do every thing for the Person we love; but then that Passion that makes us so liberal, makes us also desire something in return——we cannot content ourselves with rendring happy the Object of our Affections, but languish for something more than Gratitude.——Indeed, pretty Mrs. *Tricksy*, continued he, taking my Hand and pressing it, these are all Romantick Notions; and as charming as you are, you will never find a Man who loves you for your own sake alone. I cannot expect it Sir, said I, without I had as much Merit as *Indiana*: You have as much, and perhaps more, replied he, at least in my Eyes, than ever Woman had—yet sweet Creature, my Heart is far from feeling any Platonick Sentiments[1] for you.

Here I pretended to be in a vast Confusion, and hung down my Head as ashamed to hear him talk so——don't blush, said he, whatever Liberty I may take in thought, my Actions shall never be such as shall give you cause to fear me—I am an old Man now, and cannot hope to make myself any way equal with your Youth and Beauty——then perceiving I made no reply, but seemed more and more ashamed—is not what I said too sad a truth for me, pursued he? I know not what you mean Sir, answered I, but I am sure the Goodness you have been pleased to shew me, deserves all the regard I can pay you. Well, well, resumed he, that's all I expect at present—But it may be that in time I shall grow more covetous and over-rate my Services in hope of greater reward—but come let us go to Cards, for I find you are more at a loss in Conversation of this kind than any other. I made him no Answer, but rung the Bell for a Servant to set a Table, and we went to play——I won every Game, for I found he lost to me on purpose, and was a gainer above 50 Shillings[2]—when we left off, you know how to conquer me every way, said he, but I must have a small Revenge, and kissed me with an infinity of warmth—I cannot help loving you, he cried, two or three times over, but you must not be angry, then went up to his Chamber without staying to hear what I would say. I went soon after to Bed, but

---

1 Applied to love or affection for one of the opposite sex of a purely spiritual character and free from sensual desire.

2 Fifty shillings was almost three pounds—again, a nice sum of money at a time when a woman in domestic service would usually be able to earn little more than £4 p.a.

could not sleep all Night for thinking of his odd Behaviour——yesterday Morning at Breakfast he look'd more than usually earnest upon
me, and after being silent some time, ask'd how long it was since I
heard of my Husband's Death; the Question a little startled me lest he
should happened to have been told something of me that had made
him suspect the Truth of what I had said; but I disguised my Confusion well enough, and answered about eighteen Months. I wonder,
said he, you have not been tempted to make a second venture: On
which I replied with a Smile, that it must be something very extraordinary indeed, that could tempt me to enter again into a State which
had cost me so much disquiet. Indeed, pursued he, there are so many
things requisite to make a happy Marriage, that if Passion did not get
the better of Reason much fewer would engage in it than do. These
Words were uttered with a Sort of Coldness, which I knew not to
what Cause to attribute: Nor has he since spoke to me but on ordinary Things——I very plainly see he loves me, but for what End I
know not, and fancy that he has also a kind of struggle within himself
what he shall do concerning me—I wish therefore that there could be
something contrived to put him in fear of losing me.—I would have
him think I had some offer of Marriage much to my Advantage, if
such a Thing could be artfully brought about——I wish you would
consider of it, and help me out—it would certainly make him declare
what he would be at sooner than he seems willing to do at present;
and my Patience is almost worn out I assure you. For tho' I live well,
want for nothing, and am treated with the greatest Respect; yet you
must be sensible, my Youth and Inclinations are not to be satisfy'd with
such a sort of Life; besides I should be glad to be at some certainty
——I shall not fail to acquaint you with every thing that happens, but
in the mean time think of my Request, and believe me,

Dear Mother,
Your dutiful Daughter,
SYRENA TRICKSY.

LETTER IV.

From G—— *Square.*
THURSDAY.

Dear Mother,
MY old Spark comes on a little, tho' not so fast as I would have
him.——He both din'd and supp'd abroad Yesterday, and did not
come home till very late—I would not go to bed, thinking he would

take it as a Mark of my Respect; and so, indeed, he did, and seem'd mightily pleas'd with it, tho' he said he was sorry to have been the cause of breaking my Rest—He was in a very gay Humour, and I found had been drinking pretty hard, tho' he was not what one may call fuddled neither: He told me, they had been very merry with him upon my account, and will need have it, said he, that I should not have made choice of so young a House-keeper, if I had not lik'd her for the Management of other Affairs besides those of the Family—So, continued he, I am at a loss what Reparation to make you for the Scandal the living with me is like to bring upon you. O, Sir, answered I, putting on a very troubled Countenance, I fear these are People who envy me the Happiness of your Favour, and invent this Ridicule on purpose to make you part with me.——No, no, no such matter, said he, they rather envy me.—But let their Designs be what they will, if you ever leave me, it shall not be my Fault—I am only afraid you will grow tir'd of an old Man's Company, and I shall lose you by your own Inclination. I then assured him, with an Earnestness that came pretty near to Tenderness, that I thought my Lot extremely blest in being with him—that I looked upon him as my good Angel—that nothing could be more perfectly satisfy'd than I was with my Condition; and would not quit his Service, for any Consideration whatever. He was so much transported with what I said, that he catch'd me in his Arms, and held me there for some Minutes, then kiss'd me, and cry'd, My dear Creature, you shall never quit me—I could not live without you.—Good God! what a Neck, what Breasts are here! added he, putting my Handkerchief back with one Hand, and laying the other upon my Breast[1]——I drew a little back—but he pull'd me to him, and forc'd me to sit by him on a Couch, where he took me about the Waste, and kiss'd me till my Breath was almost gone; I struggled, and begg'd him to desist; but he pursuing what I found gave him an Infinity of Pleasure; I fell a weeping, and cry'd, O, Sir, do not compel me to call back the Words, I just now said, and make me fearful of the Lot I so lately blest—I am unhappy, it is true; but I am virtuous, and will be always so. He seem'd very much affected with the counterfeit Terror I was in, and wiping away my Tears with his Handkerchief, forgive me, said he, I

---

1   At this time, a woman in domestic dress would have worn a relatively low-necked dress that was covered by a kerchief (which Mr. W—— is trying to remove). Mrs. Jervis does the same thing in *Shamela*: "he shall see those pretty, little, white, round, panting—and offer'd to pull off my Handkerchief" (246).

told you there were times when we Men could not command our Passions—but I will never do any thing to your real Prejudice—I love you too well for that—indeed I do—love you much more than you imagine—and——here he stop'd, and after having paus'd a while——But I won't keep you any longer from your Repose, good Night, my dear Creature, permit me one more Kiss, in token of Forgiveness, with these Words he gave me another tender Embrace, tho' less vehement than the former, and so retir'd.

Now, my dear Mother, I think this looks as if he had kind of Inclination to make me his Wife, only the Fear of the World's Censure, and the Dissatisfaction it would be to his Children, hinders him from coming to any Resolution about it.——I am almost sure, if he could be made to believe I refused some good Offer for the sake of living with him, Jealousy and Gratitude would spur him up to a Determination in my Favour——'Tis worth trying for, at least—so I beg you'll think on't—I know you have a good working Brain, and can do any thing when set about it. Consider that if I get him for a Husband, we are both of us made forever—but I won't urge you any farther, I dare say, you will not neglect what shall be as much your own Interest, as that of,

Your Dutiful Daughter,
SYRENA TRICKSY.

To this her Mother return'd the following Answer by old *Sarah*.

FRIDAY.

Dear Syrena,

I Have been considering of what you wrote, of hastning the old Gentleman to come to a Resolution, ever since your first Letter.——There are several Stratagems; but that which seems most likely to prevent Suspicion, is my writing to you, concerning some Person that has been in love with you a long time, and has a good Fortune; if you can any way contrive that my Letter might fall into his hands—but this is a nice point, and must be manag'd very delicately, or it would Ruin all.—Old Men are naturally wary, and apt to think every thing has a Design in it; and if he should once imagine you went about to deceive or trick him, he would never endure you more—So without you can order it so, that he may see what I write, without your knowing he does so, I would not advise you to attempt it—I cannot but say, if it could be done cleverly, it would bind him very much to you, and also oblige him to declare himself sooner than, perhaps, he otherwise will——Therefore weigh the matter well, and when you have resolved, let me hear from you again, and you may be sure of all the Assistance in the power of,

Your affectionate Mother,
ANN TRICKSY.

LETTER V.

From G—— Square.

MONDAY.

Dear Mother,

I Have been racking my Brains ever since I received yours, for some expedient to assist my Project; but can think of nothing, but what may give room for Suspicion, and I am of your Mind so far, that the least doubt of my Sincerity would ruin all: However, I would have you write in the manner you speak of, and send it to me. Some Opportunity may happen, that I do not yet foresee——In the mean time I must acquaint you, that he now makes no Scruple of telling me he loves me, whenever we are alone; but he has never yet put the Question to me, and all his Words are so ambiguous, that I cannot, for Soul of me, discover what he would be at; nor dare I ask him for fear of offending him.——If he means *honourable*, it would be making myself cheap to seem to imagine he could have any other Designs upon me; and if he intends me for a *Mistress*, to give any Hints that I thought my self deserving of being his *Wife*, would look too presuming, and perhaps at the same time, hinder him from making any Proposals at all; so that I am in a strange Dilemma.—— However, since my last to you, I have met with something that a little sweetens the tastless insipid Hours I used to pass here—I mean, the Thoughts of one of the most agreeable pretty young Fellows I was ever acquainted with——Don't be alarm'd; for I have taken such care, that the old Gentleman can never come to the Knowledge of the matter——I met with him by accident the other Day, when I went to buy some things for our Cook, who had begg'd that favour of me—It happen'd to rain while I was abroad, and believing it would be but a small Shower, I stood for shelter under a Porch, my Spark came there also, we fell into a Chat, and a mutual liking of each other carry'd us into a Tavern—We pass'd two or three Hours as agreeably as any two young People equally gay, could do——In fine, this one Interview made us know we were fitted by Nature for each other, and, I hope, we shall always continue to think as we now do.—I told him I was a young Widow, had a small Fortune, and an unblemish'd Reputation.—Swore he was the first Man, with whom I had ever made a false Step, and that I liv'd with my Mother.—So 'tis to your Lodgings I have appointed him to direct a Letter; which pray let me have the Moment you receive it, and only say to the Messenger that brings it, that I am abroad; but you will deliver it to me as soon I come home, and for the rest leave it me; I know how to order it, so that if he sends never so often, he will never find out, that I do not live with you. Now, methinks, I see you all in a tremble, for fear this Intrigue should undo me with the old Gentleman; but I beg you will make yourself easy, for I will engage it shall never be discover'd, and as for anything else you ought not to blame me; consider I have liv'd like a Nun for three Months, including the time I was sick.——So dear Mother don't think of chiding my Pleasures; but do your best to help forward my Interest: Let me have the Letter I mention'd, and wrote with as much Artifice as you can; if I can find no plausible Occasion to make use of it, it will be only a little Labour lost, which I flatter myself, you will not grudge to

Your obedient Daughter,
SYRENA TRICKSY.

P. S. If any Letter comes from my dear new Gallant, I beg you'll send it me the same Moment, for I am half mad with Impatience to see him again.

This Epistle was answer'd as soon as receiv'd by Mrs. *Tricksy*, with another inclos'd, which on first opening, *Syrena* flatter'd herself had been from her young Spark; but her Conjecture this time deceiv'd her: They were both from her Mother, the one for her private Perusal, and the other for the old Gentleman's, if it could be brought about. That which contain'd her real Sentiments was to this Purpose.

Dear Child,
YOU see I have not been idle in complying with your Desires: I had wrote a Letter, such as I think proper to excite the old Gentlemen to be more hasty in his Resolution, before your last came to my Hand; and will add nothing to the Cautions I before gave you on *that* Score; because I think you do not seem to stand in need of it. I wish there were no greater Danger of your Inadvertency on *another* Score; and that the Inclination you have for the *young* Lover, may not be fatal to our Designs on the *old* One.——However, if any Letter or Message comes from him, Sarah shall bring it directly.——I neither blame, nor wonder at your liking a pretty Fellow; I would only

have you keep it ever in your Thoughts, that you never were in so fair a Way of making your Fortune as at present, and not do any thing that might even give a Possibility of reversing it.——Remember the Mercer who was so good a Friend to you; and Mr. *D*——, who I don't know but might have married you, if the Discovery of your Amour with Capt. *H*——, had not ruin'd you with him.—'Tis true that was an Affair of my own promoting; but, however, it should be a Warning to you.——Nothing has contributed more to establish you in the good Opinion of Mr. *W*—— than your staying so much at Home; and if your Passion for this new Gallant, should take you too frequently abroad, who knows what Jealousies, such a Change in your Behaviour might occasion.——He might send to watch where you went, and with what Company; or if he should not go such Lengths, may you not chance to be seen by some Person or other who may inform him of it.——A thousand Accidents may happen, which is not in the power of Prudence to prevent. But I am very sensible, who reasons with a Person in love, talks to the Wind. So I shall say no more than to remind you, how much it behoves you to be upon your guard.—I am far from being an *Enemy* to your *Pleasures*; but would have you a *true Friend* to your *Interest*; and that you may be so, is the sole Aim of,

Your indulgent Mother,
Ann Tricksy.

The enclos'd contain'd these Lines.

Dear Syrena,

I Have for these three Weeks been strangely persecuted with the Importunities of Mr. *Smith*; I would not have you vain; and you know very well, have always caution'd you against putting too great a Faith in Mankind; but I think that I may venture to say, he loves you with a Passion rarely to be found in one of his Sex, especially in these Days. He behav'd like a Mad-man, when he first heard you had left me; but when I refus'd letting him know where he might see you, or direct a Letter, his Desperation encreas'd to such a Degree, that I trembled for the Consequence. He would not believe but you were married, and on my protesting you were not, seem'd more outrageous than before; whether it was that he was under some Apprehensions you had dispos'd of yourself a worse Way, or that he thought I deceiv'd him, I cannot tell: He is still extremely melancholy, and I could not forbear letting you know the Proofs he gives of his Sincerity; tho' I don't expect you will ever be perswaded to reward it.

Yet after all, *Syrena*, 'tis strange you should be so blind to your own Interest.——If ever you design to marry again, 'tis not to be expected you should have a better Offer as to Fortune; and as to Character, 'tis unexceptionable.—His Person is agreeable enough, I think for any Woman to love; and you know very well, he might have had Wives long ago, who are accounted pretty Women, and handsome Portions.——But if you would not resolve to have him, when you were under such Distresses as you have been; I can neither flatter him, nor myself, that you will do so now, when you want for nothing, and have such a good Master. However, Child, Service is no Inheritance, a thousand Accidents may happen to throw you out, and our Friends who you found were weary enough of assisting us before; will do nothing at all if you persist in this obstinate denying the good that Providence seems to point out for you.[1]—I dare answer even Mr. *W*—— himself, would very much blame you if he knew the Story; and as he has pity'd you, and been so kind to take you into his House, would rejoice to see you have one of your own; which tho' mean in Comparison with his, is yet what no Gentlewoman need be asham'd to call herself the Mistress of—— therefore, *Syrena*, I would have you consider seriously of it——'Tis very childish and silly in you, to cry you can't love him; such an honourable and constant Affection as his for you, would bring you to love him in time, especially, if it be true as you say, that your Heart is not prejudic'd in Favour of any other Man: But I have so often press'd you on this Score, and with such small Success, that I think 'tis lessening my Character, as your Mother to say any thing farther; nor had I done it now, but the poor Gentleman extorted a Promise from me to write.—I wish you never may have Cause to repent the Ingratitude, you are guilty of to him, or the Injustice you do yourself; which, with my Blessing, is all at present from,

Your affectionate Mother,
ANN TRICKSY.

P. S. Your Aunt longs very much to see you, I believe, to talk to you concerning Mr. *Smith*; so if you continue resolv'd to refuse his Offers, it will be best for you not to go.

---

1 While the whole letter is based in deception with the hope of making Mr. W—— marry Syrena, Mrs. Tricksy rightly alludes to the precarious nature of domestic service, especially if one lacks familial support.

Syrena had scarce time to consider on these Letters, before old *Sarah* return'd with another, which had been left for her by a Porter, at Mrs. *Tricksy's* Lodgings, while she was abroad. This was the dear expected Billet, she had entreated her Mother to be so careful of, and contain'd these Lines.

Dear Creature,

YOU must be too sensible of the Pleasure your Conversation affords, not to believe whoever has once enjoy'd it, must languish for a second Interview.——You told me other Engagements would detain you for some Days, so have deferr'd Writing as long as my Impatience would permit; but, now I hope my charming *Syrena* will no longer hold herself from me. I shall be at my Cousin's To-morrow about four; and earnestly entreat nothing may disappoint me of a Pleasure, I till then shall live in the most eager Expectation of, who am,

> *Lovely Widow,*
> *Your sincerely devoted*
> *Friend and Admirer,*
> HARRIOT MANLY.

The Reader will doubtless be at a loss for the meaning of this Epistle; but never had *Syrena* given a greater Proof of her Cunning, than in the Management of this Intrigue; to prevent his making any Enquiry after her at Mr. *W*——'s; she had told him, that being left a very young Widow, without any Children, she lived with her Mother, and to give him a good Opinion of her Mother's Virtue, and Care of her, as well as to hinder him from knowing she had deceived him in the Place of her Abode, she told him he must never visit her; and when he wrote, as she desir'd he would often do, to appoint a Meeting, it must be in a Woman's Name, whom she said she would pretend to have commenced an Acquaintance with, at the House of some female Friend. She made him believe also, that whenever he desired to see her, he must send the Day before at least, for that Mrs. *Tricksy* was so fearful of her entring into any Correspondence with a Man, that she made her be denied to all that came, unless Relations, or such as she had an Intimacy with herself, nor ever gave her any Letter till she had first open'd it, and examin'd the Contents; so that, said she, you must not be surprized, if the Messenger you send with your Billets, never finds me at home; but when she reads them, and supposes them wrote by a Woman, which I shall take care to mention before, as a mighty agreeable young Lady, who has taken a

Fancy to me, she will make no Scruple of permitting me to come out.

Thus having settled every thing, as she thought, beyond a Possibility of Discovery, she flew to the Rendezvous, his Cousin's as he term'd it, which indeed was no other than a common Bagnio, with a Pleasure which attends the Gratification of any Passion whatever; but more especially that which more or less is inherent to all animated beings, and for that Reason called the most natural.

To keep Mr. *W*——'s Servants from suspecting any thing by old *Sarah's* coming twice in one Day; she pretended her Mother had been taken suddenly ill, after she sent the first Message; and that the second was to desire to see her immediately; she back'd this Excuse with so much seeming Grief, that nobody had the least doubt of the Truth of what she said; and the old Gentleman coming home before her, and being told the Story, was very much concerned at the supposed Indisposition of so good a Woman.

After passing four or five Hours in a manner perfectly agreeable to her Inclinations, she came home in a Hackney-Coach about Eleven o'Clock, with a Countenance, conformable to the melancholy Visit she pretended to have made. Mr. *W*—— not being gone to Bed, enquired concerning her Mother's Condition, in a most tender and obliging Manner; and the Hypocrite dropping some well dissembled Tears, answered, that she had found her so ill, that she had ventured to intrude on his Goodness so far, as to promise to go again the next Day; by all Means, cried the worthy Gentleman, and I will send a Physician with you. I most humbly thank you, Sir, replied she, but my Mother has one, who has always attended our Family, and is acquainted with her Constitution. Well then, resumed he, I desire she may want nothing else proper for her;—— you shall go to her as early as you please in the Morning;——and pray, continued he, give her this, with my best Wishes for her Recovery; with these Words he put five Guineas into her Hand. *Syrena* affected to receive this Favour with an equal share of Gratitude for his Goodness, and Grief for the Danger of a much esteemed and lov'd Parent. Their Conversation, till he retir'd to his Chamber, was that Night wholly taken up with Mrs. *Tricksy*; Mr. *W*—— imagining any gayer Subjects would be little pleasing to a Person, under the Affliction *Syrena* seemed to be.

She went early in the Morning in reality to her Mother's, and gave her the five Guineas, with a full Recital of the Occasion of that Present; Mrs. *Tricksy* was very well pleased with her Management of his Intrigue, and they both laughed heartily at the ease with which a Woman beloved, could impose on a Man of the best Understanding. They breakfasted together, and then *Syrena* took her leave, and went to the Bagnio, having promised her young Lover to dine with him there, in Confidence, that the Story she had to tell Mr. *W*—— would render it no Difficulty for her to come out.

In fine, she carry'd on the Deception of her Mother's Illness, for above a Fortnight;[1] so that in all that time, she never miss'd seeing her Gallant one Day; nay, staid with him two whole Nights, under the Pretence that her Mother being expected to expire every Moment, she waited to pay the last Duties of a Child. Mr. *W*—— was always extremely indulgent, sent her ten Guineas more, and some Phials of rich Cordials, which they drank together with a good deal of Mirth and Ridicule on the Donor.

But now Mrs. *Tricksy* began to think it was high time for her to be on the mending hand, lest a too long counterfeiting, might at length raise some Suspicion; and also, because that while she was supposed to continue in this dangerous way, *Syrena's* Affair with Mr. *W*—— seemed to stand still, that Gentleman having forborn his amorous Chat, out of Decency to her Grief; but the young Wanton would scarce have been prevailed upon by her Mother's Remonstrances, to have given any Intermission to a Conversation so pleasing to her, had she not been compelled to it by the young Gentleman, who told her a Business of the most urgent Nature called him into the Country. Her Grief at parting with him was really sincere, and she omitted nothing that she thought might detain him, but tho' he had an extreme Compassion for the Agonies she threw herself into, yet there was a Necessity he should quit her at least for a time; she made him swear to write to her, and urged to know the exact Place to which he was going; but it being highly inconvenient for him to comply with either of these Requests, he yielded not to the one without a mental Reservation, and wholly deceiving her as to the other; and told her a County as distant as North from South, from that he went to, which, together with his having passed with her by a feign'd Name, render'd it altogether impossible for her to hear any thing of him, tho' on finding he did not write to her, she afterwards strenuously endeavoured.

Well, Mrs. *Tricksy* recover'd, and *Syrena* at home as before this Adventure; the old Gentleman began to renew a Conversation, which with a good deal of Pain to himself, he had so long stifled in

---

1 Two weeks.

his Breast, what he said to her on the first Opportunity, will be seen in the following Letter, wrote by her to her Mother.

LETTER VI.

Dear Mother,

MY old Gentleman, tho' I allow him to be the most compassionate and best natur'd Creature in the World, had certainly a great Share of Self-Interest in the Concern he express'd for your imagin'd Sickness; in the first Place it deprived him of my Company for the most part, and when I was with him, the Sorrow that it was necessary for me to assume, obliged him to restrain the Dictates of his Heart; but now he thinks you out of Danger, he seems to give a loose to his gayer Inclinations. I never go out, nor come into the Room, without being saluted by him in the most tender manner, which I suffer as a Person who has no Aversion to such a Behaviour, but what proceeds from my Modesty; and also, as one who thinks herself too much obliged to his Bounties, not to refuse any Freedoms that are consistent with Virtue; so that by behaving to him in a tender affectionate manner, I give him room to think I am far from having any dislike to his Person; and by a seeming Struggle within myself, and half Sentences thrown in *a-propo*, whenever he takes any extraordinary Liberties, to think my Gratitude alone hinders my Resentment.—I can see he is more and more charm'd with me, and I flatter myself will soon break his Mind to me——that is, let me know what it is I am to expect from him;—Yesterday at Breakfast, as I was going to fill the Tea-pot, the Man being out of the Room on some Occasion, he snatch'd the Kettle from my Hand, no, my Dear, said he, tho' I am an old Man, I know better the Regard that ought to be paid Persons of your Sex, especially such a one as you, to suffer that. O! Sir, cried I, you are too good, and forget I am but your Servant ——I never have treated you as such, replied he; and should be sorry you should ever think of me as Master—methinks it is more natural, pursued he, smiling, for you to look upon yourself as my *Mistress*, than my Servant. God forbid Sir! cried I, I do not mean naughtily, rejoined he, but as the Mistress of my Affections; and indeed if you imagine I can place them on any other Woman you do me wrong. He had perhaps added something more which might have explained what he meant by the word *Mistress*, but the officious fool of a Footman came unluckily in and prevented any farther Discourse on that

Head. I saw him no more till Night, for he dined abroad, and then at Supper, as I was helping him to a Bit of Rasberry Tart; I think, said he, these same Pies are a kind of an Emblem of the Passion of Love, where the sweet and sour seem to strive with each other, and both together are so grateful to the Palate that one cannot wish to be without them; what do you think, pretty Mrs. *Tricksy*, is not the comparison just. Indeed Sir, answered I, the little Experience I am Mistress of, does not qualify me to form any Sort of Judgment on that Passion; and as for Tarts I seldom eat any: Yet you have loaded my Plate, cried he, and may I not also infer from thence that you would wish to see me taste all the Sweets and Sours alone, while you are unmoved at either? I carried on the Raillery, and affected not to conceive he had any other meaning in what he said than meerly literal. But he soon obliged me to be more serious, by telling me, that he would have me henceforward look upon him as a Man whose very Soul was devoted to me. These Words so uncommon with Men of his grave and sober Deportment, and utter'd with the greatest Vehemence, made me regard him with some Astonishment, and indeed render'd me incapable of replying for some Moments. During my Silence he took hold of my two Hands, and pressing them between his, said with a deep Sigh, O! that there were less disparity between us! I then perhaps might have been happy![1] I know not, Sir, answered I, any thing that can be wanting to your Happiness; but this I know, that I should be very miserable if any way the cause of giving you one Moment's Pain—you are, Sir, my Patron, my Friend, my Benefactor, my Guardian Angel, and when I cease to acknowledge your generous Goodness, may my Ingratitude be punish'd with some dreadful Mark.——Hold, dearest Creature, interrupted he, I know thy sweet, thy tender, grateful Soul—but—but what cried I, for Heaven's sake, Sir, inform me in what I am wanting——in nothing, said he, that's in your power—yet I could wish there were a possibility of—don't ask me what—it is irremediable, and becomes me not to mention—I cannot do it yet at least—good Night——with these Words he rose from the Table, called his Man, and went immediately to Bed.

Now Mother to what can this Inconsistency of Behaviour be imputed, but to an excess of Love and to some Obstacle within himself that makes him fearful of indulging it——'tis strange he conceals

---

1   Like Mr. L——'s comment, this too echoes *Pamela*; see footnote 1, p. 109.

it in this manner, but there is no getting it out of him, till he pleases himself—something sure extraordinary will be the Event, but what I know not; when I do, you shall not be a Moment in ignorance. I am

Your Dutiful Daughter,
SYRENA TRICKSY.

LETTER VII.

From G—— Square.

Congratulate me, my dear Mother, congratulate your happy Daughter—all my Fears and my Suspence are over——Mr. *W——* has at last brought himself to confess an honourable Passion for me—He will soon come to acquaint you with it, and then make me his Wife—O! how I shall roll in Riches and Plenty—How I shall indulge every Wish—enjoy every Pleasure, and despise all Restraint—The very thought of what I shall be is Extasy and Transport—O! that the joyful Time were come—I'll make him settle a Jointure[1] upon me, get possession of his Plate[2] and Jewels, turn them all into ready Money, that the Heirs may not come upon me, and then break the old Fool's Heart, and shine out the Belle of the Town——but I must tell you what brought this fortunate Catastrophe about, and of what infinite Service your Letter concerning the imaginary Mr. *Smith* was to me——you know 'tis more than a Week since I wrote to you, nor indeed had I any thing pleasing to acquaint you with—Mr. *W——* after the Conversation I repeated in my last grew more than ordinarily thoughtful—spoke but seldom, and when he did, it was either on Family Affairs, or other Subjects altogether foreign to Love——I was very uneasy in my Mind, but appeared before him as usual, tho' indeed I began to imagine I had small Hopes, not that he either gave me any Words or Looks that testified he had conceived the least disgust against me; but his whole Carriage seemed to tell me, he had conquer'd himself so far as not to make me any offers of being in a better Situation with him than he had placed me in at first. But when I thought my good Fortune farthest

---

1 Jointure is the money that Syrena would have settled on her that she alone could control (comparable to the money the Mercer's wife offers to turn over to him); it is designed to be used by a woman after her husband's death.

2 Utensils for table and domestic use; originally of silver or gold.

removed from me, it happened to be nearest—as you shall hear——
He came home last Night about an Hour before the Time of light-
ing Candles, and asking for me; one of the Servants said he believed
I was in my own Room, and was coming to call me; but Mr. *W*——
told him it was no matter, he was going up, and would speak to me
above. He found me in a musing Posture, leaning my Head upon my
Arm, and indeed discontented enough at his late Behaviour: What,
Melancholly, pretty Mrs. *Tricksy*! said he, as soon as he came into the
Chamber. I was a little surprized at seeing him there, tho' very well
pleased, especially as he seemed more chearful than he had done for
several Days. Not at all, Sir, answered I, but there are Times when
one cannot help being more than ordinarily serious. There are so,
resumed he, nor am I sorry to see you so now, because I am come
to talk with you on a very serious Matter. With these Words he made
me take my Seat again, which I had quitted on his coming in, and
placing himself in another Chair as close to me as he could, I have
been reflecting for some Days past, said he, on the Pleasure your
agreeable Company has afforded me ever since you came into my
House, and how forlorn I shall be whenever you leave it. I hope, Sir,
said I, that I have been guilty of nothing that should lay you under
a Necessity of obliging me to leave it? No, no, cried he, far from any
such Thing—I have already told you, and I now repeat it, that it will
be yourself alone can ever take you from me—but, my dear Creature, I should be unreasonable to desire a young Person like you, to
live always in the manner you now do—there is no doubt but you
will have offers of bettering your Fortune—and you will marry——
here he ceased; and I took the Opportunity of telling him that I preferred the Honour of living with him as I now did, to being the Wife
of any Man in the World: And on his seeming to question my Sincerity in that Point, as he well might; I endeavoured to convince him
by all the Asseverations befitting a modest Woman to make; but he
stopped my Mouth with a Kiss, and told me, that tho' what I said
was vastly obliging, yet he could not think I could be so much an
Enemy to myself. I then thought I had a fine pretence for shewing
him your Letter, and running to the *Buroe*[1] brought it in my Hand,
and presenting it to him, Sir, said I, tho' I should die with blushing
to make you the Confidante of such an Affair, yet I cannot help
doing it, to clear myself from all Deceit—so beg, Sir, you will give
yourself the trouble to read this——He made no reply, but did as I

---

1 Bureau.

desired, and I could see while thus employed a good deal of Impatience in his Eyes. As soon as he had finished the perusal—he gave me the Letter again, and ask'd me several Questions concerning Mr. *Smith*; to all which I gave him such ready and natural Answers, that he had no room to imagine I was amusing him with a fictitious Story. After he had nothing farther to inform himself of, he told me he should be extremely happy if he could be sure that I refused Mr. *Smith*, merely because I chose to live with him, to which I replied to give him still a greater Opinion of my Sincerity, that I could not say I had refused Mr. *Smith* altogether on his Account, because I had resolved not to marry him before I ever had the Happiness of living with so excellent a Master, but that since I had enjoyed so great a Blessing, and had the Experience of his Goodness; not only Mr. *Smith*, but all Mankind beside were perfectly my Aversion——He seemed overjoyed to hear me speak in this manner—kiss'd me, and embraced me a Hundred Times I believe, before he was able to make me any Answer; at last, well but, my dear Love, cried he, there yet remains one Proof of your preferring my Society above all others of my Sex, and if you deny to give me that, you must give me leave to disbelieve all others?—in fine, you must consent to put it out of either of our Powers to part—you must be my Wife. Judge, my dear Mother, how much I was transported at these Words, but I concealed it under a modest Surprize, and hanging down my Head, said, you are pleas'd to sport, Sir, with your unworthy Servant. No my Dear, reply'd he, the Offer I make you is not only serious, but well weigh'd, the Result of a long Consideration—the first Moment I saw you, I entertained a Thought of it, but was willing to wait till some Proofs of my Friendship had in part compensated for a Disparity of Years— what say you then?—Is it possible for you to yield that Youth and Beauty to the Embraces of an old Man, without Reluctance?—Can you love me as a Husband? answer me, continued he, with your usual Sincerity; if you can love me as a Husband (I again repeat it) I shall be happy—if you cannot, I will endeavour to make you so, either with any other more agreeable to your Years; or if you chuse a single Life, by settling an Annuity upon you; on this I replied, that his excessive Generosity had entirely overcome all my Timidity and natural Bashfulness; and that since he was so good to make me three Offers, the first, and infinitely the best, must be my choice. It would be endless to repeat what he said on this Occasion; had I been a Queen, and he my Subject, rais'd by me to a Throne, he could not have express'd greater Joy. I did not fail, however, to represent to him, the Fears I had, that his Sons and his other Relations, would not be satisfied with our Marriage; but he seem'd to slight all I urg'd on that Head, and told me, he had not liv'd so long in the World, to place his Felicity in other People's Opinions; and as for his Children, they were too well acquainted with their Duty to repine at any thing he thought fit to approve.

Thus is every thing agreed between us, and we shall come this Afternoon or To-morrow to acquaint you with the Affair, and ask your Consent for our Marriage, which he intends to solemnize as soon as a new Coach and Liveries can be got ready; for he resolves it shall be in as much Splendor, as if I brought him a Fortune equal to his own.[1] Well, after all, he is very good to me, but 'tis all to please himself; and I shall follow his Example, in doing every thing to please myself—O! I shall live a rare Life—but I must conclude, for I expect him to Dinner every Moment. Dear Mother rejoice for the good Fortune of

Your happy Daughter,
SYRENA TRICKSY.

P. S. I send this by a Porter, for fear the Penny-Post should not have come time enough to apprise you of our coming, for you to get every thing in order—once more, farewell.

Mr. *W*—— having determined, and indeed desired nothing more than to make *Syrena* his Wife, fulfill'd the Contents of her Letter to her Mother, in going to ask her Consent in form, which it would be needless to say was readily granted; after this he made no Secret of his Intentions, but declared to every body that he was going to alter his Condition——accordingly he bespoke a fine new Coach, ordered rich Liveries for his Men, and made some Additions to his Furniture—omitted nothing that he thought might shew his Regard for his designed Bride, who he took abroad with him in his Chariot almost every Day, either for the Air, or to buy things for her Appearance as his Wife.

His eldest Son, tho' doubtless not well pleas'd in his Mind, was oblig'd to treat her with all imaginable Respect; and his other Relations contented themselves with condemning his Conduct among

---

1   Another echo of *Pamela*. Immediately before their wedding, Mr. B. says "I have Possessions ample enough for us both; and you deserve to share them with me; and you shall do it, with as little Reserve, as if you had brought me what the World reckons an Equivalent" (336–37).

themselves, and did not pretend to dissuade or to argue with him on a thing, which they found he was absolutely bent upon.

Mr. *W——* resolving however to make all his Family as easy as possible, in this unexpected Change of his Condition, sent for his Son from *Oxford*, in order to settle a handsome Fortune upon him before his Marriage; and thereby prevent any Apprehensions he might otherwise have had, of being a Sufferer by a future Issue.[1]

By some Accident the Letter was delayed at the Post-House, so that the young Gentleman came not so soon as expected, and arriv'd at his Father's but the Evening before the Day prefix'd for the Wedding; but happy was it for the whole Family he came when he did, as will presently appear.

The old Gentleman happening to be at home when he came, took him directly to his Closet, and entertained him there a considerable time, telling him, that tho' he was about being married a second time, as it was to a Woman, whose Virtue and Good-Nature would rather make her an Advocate for his Children, than the contrary; none of them ought to repine at his Conduct in this Affair. The Son assur'd him with a great deal of Submission, but how much Veracity I cannot take upon me to determine, that he did not think it became a Son to call his Father's Actions in Question; and that whoever he had made choice of, he, for his part, should not have the least Reluctance, in paying her all those Duties she could expect from a Son of her own, if it should please Heaven to favour her with any; which, added he, I sincerely wish. Well said, my Boy, replied Mr. *W——*; I assure thee, thy Disinterestedness shall lose thee nothing— I sent for thee to Town, for no other Purpose, than to make over to thee now, what I intended for thee at my Death; and as near as my Marriage is, thy Settlement shall be made before it——I will immediately send for my Lawyer, and the Writings shall be drawn To-night—in the mean time you shall see the Lady, I shall make your Mother To-morrow Morning, and who has been some time in my House——so that, my dear Boy, continued he, it is not one whose Humour I am unacquainted with, that I am going to make my Partner for Life; but one, whose uncommon Virtues and Goodness I have experienced, and am perfectly convinced of; with these Words he led him the way to *Syrena's* Chamber, who rose to receive them with her accustomed Sweetness, and well affected Innocence. But on his

---

1 In other words, Mr. W—— will provide his son with his inheritance now in case he has a son with Syrena.

approaching to salute[1] her, presented by his Father, never was so odd a Meeting——the young Gentleman started back as if he had seen a Gorgon,[2] nor could the reality of that Fiction have been more shocking to him. *Syrena* lost all her Presence of Mind, and gave a great Shriek——Mr. *W*—— seem'd thunderstruck at seeing them so——in fine, never did three People appear in a greater Consternation——all of them were in a profound Silence for some Minutes——during which time, the Father cast his Eyes from *Syrena* to his Son; then from his Son to *Syrena* again, as expecting to be inform'd either by the one or the other, of what at present seem'd so mysterious. At last, is this the Lady, Sir, you intend for my Mother? said the young Gentleman, with a faultring Voice: Yes, answered Mr. *W*——, I told you so before I brought you here; have you any thing to object against my Choice? or have you, *Syrena*, continued he, turning to her, any Motives for being dissatisfied with this young Man? No, Sir, reply'd she, by this time having recollected what was best for her to do, but he is so very like a Brother I once had, that the first Sight gave me a Surprize, I could not presently overcome; and you, Madam, cry'd the young Gentleman, are so like a Mistress of mine, and I doubt not but of half the Town beside, that I could not with Patience look on you as the Person intended for my Father's Wife. How! cry'd Mr. *W*——; with an angry Tone! your Pardon, Sir, reply'd his Son, putting one Knee to the Ground; that I presume to own before you the Folly of my Youth——on any other Occasion I could not hope Forgiveness; but here 'tis absolutely necessary——yes, Sir, I confess, that without your Permission I came about a Month past to *London*, indeed to give a loose to some Extravagancies, which I will never henceforward repeat——in my Rambles I met with this Woman—we fell into Conversation—she affected in Words to appear a modest Woman; but her Actions were altogether the reverse—in fine, Sir, she is no other than a common Creature——he was going on, but *Syrena* had now no Card but one to play, and interrupted by saying——O! barbarous Aspersion! O! that I had died, rather than lived to hear my Reputation thus cruelly traduced—and to my Face—by one I never saw before, Heaven is my Witness, tho' the likeness of Faces at first deceived me—with

---

1 A kiss, by way of salutation.
2 Originally, the term referred to one of three mythical female personages with snakes for hair whose look turned the beholder into stone. It can more generally refer to a repulsive woman.

these Words she fell into Fits, nor could all the old Gentleman's Endeavours bring her to herself;——the Servants were called in to assist, but she no sooner seemed to recover from one Convulsion, than she fell into another; insomuch, that all present, excepting the young Gentleman, who had experienced her Artifices, imagined she would die.——Mr. *W——*, who yet knew not what to make of what his Son had said, was too generous and humane to let her perish for want of proper help, even tho' she should be proved guilty of all she was accused of; order'd the Maids to take care of her, and sent immediately for a Physician. Having given these Directions, he withdrew into another Room, taking his Son with him; he questioned him very closely concerning the time of his Acquaintance with *Syrena*——the Places where they met, and every Particular that he thought might inform him of the Truth; for tho' he could not entertain so bad an Opinion of the young Gentleman, as to imagine he had forged this Story on Purpose to break the Match; yet he could not tell how to bring himself to think he could have been so grossly imposed upon by a Woman, whose Temper, Inclinations, and Conduct, he had observed with the utmost Strictness, ever since she came into his House.

I believe the Reader by this time guesses the Truth, and that the Son of Mr. *W——* was no other, than the last Gallant she had; and for whom, to meet with the greater Freedom, she had pretended her Mother's Indisposition. This Article it was, which more than any thing convinced the old Gentleman, that the seeming modest *Syrena*, was the infamous Wretch his Son had described her; for not only her Name, and the young Gentleman's positiveness as to her Person, but the times of their being so frequently together, agreeing exactly with those of her pretended Visits to Mrs. *Tricksy*, at length opened his Eyes to the Villany of both Mother and Daughter; and tho' he had loved the fair Deceiver, with too much Tenderness to endure this Detection without Pain, yet he thought himself bound to thank Heaven for so timely a Discovery of her Guilt; which, had it happened but a Day after, had made him from the most happy, the most miserable Man on Earth. The Frailty of his Son also deserved his Pardon; not only because of the Temptation that had misled him, but likewise, because he could no other way have received a Confirmation of her Crimes. After much Talk upon this Head, Mr. *W——* burst out into an Exclamation, Good God! cry'd he, what a Fiend must this be under an Angel's Form! She knew herself a Prostitute to the Son, yet would have marry'd the Father! Monstrous incestuous

Strumpet![1] Hold, Sir, interrupted the Son, compound as she is of Leudness and Deceit, let us not wrong her——She knew not till this Hour, I was your Son; for the better to conceal my being in Town from you, I pass'd with her, and wherever I went, by a different Name. But she is now no longer ignorant of that Secret, reply'd the Father, yet would she have persuaded me, you either had mistook her for some other, or had Malice enough to asperse her without Cause.—O what Punishment is great enough for such a Wretch! The Physician that Moment came in and broke off their farther Discourse, by telling them the Lady was dangerously ill—that he had prescrib'd for her, but much fear'd the Success. Young Mr. *W*—— shook his Head in token of Contempt, and after he was gone could not forbear saying, some severe things on the Gentlemen of that Profession; but in this he was guilty of some little Injustice; for the Truth was, that tho' *Syrena's* Fits were only counterfeited, yet the Surprize she had been in, and the Apprehension which immediately follow'd of losing that great Fortune, she had but a few Minutes before thought her self secure of, gave her real Agonies, which put her whole Frame into such Disorders, as, joyn'd with the artificial ones she put on, might well puzzle the Physician's Skill.

The old Gentleman, however, not being able to suffer so vile a Creature under his Roof, made her be told she must quit his House; and that if she were as ill as she pretended, her Mother was the most proper Person to take care of her; and if she were not, it would be doing her a good Office, to send her where she would no longer have any need of feigning.——She begg'd with Floods of Tears to see him, protested her Innocence, and left nothing undone to deceive him once more, and throw the Odium of all upon his Son's Dislike of their Marriage; but he was now too well assured of her Baseness, and remain'd inexorable to all her Messages; so that with a Heart full of Rage, and a Tongue full of Imprecations, she took an everlasting leave of a House she was so near being Mistress of, after having been obliged to resign all the fine Jewels that had been presented to her when intended for a Bride.

It would be needless to repeat the Distraction that both Mother

---

1 A strumpet is a debauched or unchaste woman. "Incest" refers to any sort of "unnatural and criminal conjunction of persons within degrees prohibited" (Johnson), a slightly broader understanding than we have now.

and Daughter were involved in at this sudden turn in their Fate; neither could it be pleasing to a virtuous Ear to hear those shocking and prophane Exclamations, which 'tis easy to suppose Persons of their abandon'd Principles make use of, when any way cross'd by Providence in the Pursuit of their wicked Designs. It must be confest, indeed, that *Syrena* had very ill Luck in being so often on the very Point of compassing all her Avarice, Ambition, or Pride could aim at; and then, by the most unforeseen Accidents, thrown from the height of all her Hopes. And here, methinks, it is worth remarking, how the indulging one Vice, destroy'd all the Success she might have expected from the other; for had she been less leud, her Hypocrisy, in all Probability, had obtain'd its end, at least, in this last Pursuit it had done so: But it is generally the Fate of such Wretches, who, while they go about ensnaring and deceiving all they can, to be themselves ensnar'd and deceived, either by others, or their own headstrong and ungovern'd Appetites.

In a short Space of time they again began to feel the want of what before they had profusely lavished. *Syrena* was not idle in spreading her Nets; but none as yet had the ill Fortune to fall into them, and the first that did, proved little to her Advantage, as well as to his own.——Their Acquaintance began in this manner.

She was walking one Day through the *Strand*,[1] equipp'd for Adventures in a modish Dishabillee, with a little Hat on her Head, and a Cane in her Hand, when she saw at a Bookseller's Door a Gentleman, whom she no sooner cast her Eye upon, than she imagin'd fit for her purpose: He was in the prime of his Age, well proportion'd, genteel, and had somewhat in his Looks that denoted him to be of a more than ordinary amorous Constitution: She perceived he had his Eye upon her as she past, and the Street being pretty dirty, and the Kennel[2] of a great breadth just in that Part, she either had,

---

1 The Strand, originally named for the "strand" or shore of the Thames between the cities of London and Westminster, was a relatively salacious area of London. Dorothy George notes "Many courts off the Strand bore an infamous character" (92); Boswell recounts a number of sexual adventures off the Strand. In the *London Journal* Boswell recounts "I picked up a girl in the Strand; went into a court with intention to enjoy her in armour [a condom]…"(49). In addition to the lascivious character the Strand acquired, it was also London's principal shopping street. As Hugh Phillips notes, "it consisted solely of shops from end to end with no private residences apart from Somerset and Northumberland House" (*Mid-Georgian London; a topographical and social survey of central and western London about 1750* [London: Collins, 1964] 119).

2 The gutter.

or seem'd to have an Occasion to cross the way——The Coaches driving backward and forward very fast, it being Term time,[1] made her often obliged to stop, and return, then go on again, and all this opposite to where the Gentleman stood; so that he had a full Opportunity of seeing and admiring all the pretty Airs she put on; the Distress she affected, in not being able to prosecute her little Journey, gave him a Pretence of offering to assist her——He step'd hastily to her, and taking her under the Arm with one Hand, and with the other extending his Cane to keep off the Horses, like a true Knight-Errant, lifted his Dulcinea[2] over the muddy Brook, and safely bore her to the farther Shore——when arriv'd, she made a Curtesy, and thank'd him with so bewitching a Softness in her Eyes and Voice, as wholly compleated the Conquest she desired.——He entreated Permission to attend her to the Place where she was going, and telling her it was altogether unfit a Lady of her Appearance should walk the Streets, without some Person who might guard her, both from the Insults of the undistinguishing Populace, and the Dangers also, such uncommon Charms might lay her under, from Men of more elevated Rank——To these obliging Offers and Compliments, she made him such Answers, as gave him an Opinion she had been brought up in high Life, and had conversed only with People of the greatest Fashion; but seemed to decline accepting his Protection, any farther, saying there was no need of his giving himself that Trouble, since she was only going home, and there were no more such ugly Places to pass over in her way thither—adding, that she was already under too great an Obligation to his care to consent to receive any Addition; since conscious there was nothing in her Conversation capable of compensating for his Loss of time. This naturally drew a great many fine things from him; nor would he be perswaded to quit her, tho' she often desired he would; but how sincerely the Reader may imagine.

They walk'd on together talking in this manner, when just as they pass'd by a Tavern, he perceiv'd her Colour change, and a sudden Trembling seize all her Limbs, which, as I have in many Instances explain'd, she could bring on herself whenever she found it necessary for her purpose——He was surpriz'd and troubled at this Alteration, and was about to ask the Cause, when she catch'd hold of his

---

1 One of the four terms during which the courts are in session.
2 A reference to Cervantes' *Don Quixote* (1605) and the eponymous hero's imagined lover.

Arm, as if to save her self from falling; roll'd her Eyes with a half dying Languor, then closed them, and appear'd quite fainting.———— He little suspecting all this for Artifice, was extremely frighted, and supporting her as well as he could, led her into the Tavern, where having call'd for Hartshorn[1] and Water, she soon became reviv'd, but seem'd not presently to recollect her Senses enough to know where she was, or what had happen'd to her; but when she did, O Heaven! cry'd she, how strange an Accident is this!————Bless me, how can I answer to my self or the World, being in a Tavern with a Gentleman, I never saw before!—or how, Sir, can I ever retaliate the Favours I have received from you this Day! Besides the common Compliments on such Occasions, as thinking it an Honour to be any way service-able to a Lady who seem'd so much to deserve it, he being a Man of great Wit and Gallantry, added a thousand infinitely more elegant and obliging;————his natural Complaisance and Respect to the fair Sex, being now heighten'd by a Passion he had never felt before, tho' frequently what is called a Lover, he expressed himself in a manner, which might have charm'd a Woman less susceptible than her he now address'd— 'Tis certain she was transported with him, and had no need of feigning to make him see his Behaviour had made an Impression on her.————All her Subject for Dissimulation, was to pass it on him for the first, which she was too perfect a Mistress of, not to succeed in.

On his asking her if she had been accustomed to these Fainting? ————No, Sir, answer'd she, calling to her Cheeks a most becoming Blush, I never before knew what it was to lose my Senses, even for a Moment—few Women, I thank Heaven, are blest with a better Con-stitution, or a more easy and chearful Mind.————I know not what to think of the Accident that has just now happen'd, nor to what Cause to impute it—and were I inclin'd to be superstitious, should be appre-hensive it was the Fore-runner of some very extraordinary Event. If we pay any Regard to History or Tradition, said the Gentleman, whatever happens out of the common Course of Nature, as your Dis-order, Madam, seems to have been, has ever been look'd upon as a Presage of some unexpected Change in Fortune.—But you have not the least Reason to imagine it an ill Omen; since it would be calling in question the Justice of Providence, to suppose it had created an Excellence like yours, for any thing but to give and receive the high-

---

1 Hart's horn, which actually came from the horn of a male deer, could be used in many ways—something inhaled or imbibed. "It is used to bring people out of faintings by its pungency" (Johnson).

est Good this World at least can bestow.———But I suspect, continued he, with a Sigh, that as so many Charms cannot be without an adequate Number of Adorers, it was the Commiseration for Woes, you cannot bring yourself to redress, that overwhelm'd your gentle Heart, and for a Moment depriv'd you of yourself.

Here he ceas'd, and look'd stedfastly on her with a kind of enquiring, yet imploring Eye; and she who easily saw into his Thoughts, and found with Pleasure the Influence she had gain'd, made no immediate Reply; and when she did, assuming a half Smile, by the manner of your talking, said she, I fancy you take me for a Maid— but, Sir, I have been married, and as I was so without feeling for him who was my Husband, much less any other Man; those Emotions, Lovers talk of, I can not have much Compassion for what I always look'd on fictitious, and meer Words of Course.———How, Madam, cry'd he, have you been married, and are so long a Widow, as to be out of Mourning, at your Years? On this she told him the same Story, she had done her former Lovers; only with this Difference, that as she knew not his Circumstances, it seem'd most proper to keep him ignorant of hers, till time should discover, if it were best to affect Poverty or Riches.

After having past about two Hours with him; she thought it time to pretend being perfectly recover'd; nor could all his Persuasions, nor her own secret Inclinations, induce her to stay longer.———She could not now, however, refuse giving him leave to go home with her, which he did; and on her telling her Mother before him, the Civilities she had receiv'd from him; he was treated with the utmost Respect and Gratitude, by the seemingly good Mrs. *Tricksy*. And from her as well as *Syrena*, had Permission to wait on them again.

When he was gone, and these Ensnarers had Liberty to consult together, judging by his Garb and Appearance, that he was a Man of a Fortune sufficient to maintain her as a Wife; they set all their Wits to work to make a Husband of him; for in the way of Discourse to them both, he had declar'd himself neither married nor under any Engagements of that kind.———Schemes were therefore contriv'd between them to delude him; which they afterward had but too much Opportunity to put in Practice; and which his own Temper and Circumstances contributed to assist in.

He was a Gentleman whose Father had been possess'd of a plentiful Estate, but by giving too much into the Gallantries of the Times had dissipated it so far, that at his Decease he had not an Acre to bequeath; and young Mr. *P——* was only left with a small Fortune in Money, for which the last Acre had been dispos'd of: His Education had been the *best* for a Man of an *Estate*, but the *worst* for a Man of *Business*: He had too much Pride to descend to any thing for Bread, which he thought unbefitting his Birth; and tho' he had many powerful Friends, whose Interest might have procur'd him a Place at Court, or a Commission in the Army, either of which he would gladly have accepted, whenever such a Thing was in Agitation, some cross Accident interven'd, and disappointed his Hopes; when they seem'd nearest the Accomplishment.——Several Years having past over since the Death of his Father; and nothing succeeding according to his Expectations, his little Stock of Money almost exhausted, and Years coming on, for he was now turn'd of Thirty; he could think of nothing to retrieve himself but Marriage.——He was, therefore, on his Acquaintance with *Syrena*, looking out for some elderly Widow or Maid, whose Substance might support him in the Eve of Life, in a decent manner; and as he was a Man perfectly agreeable both in his Person and Conversation, 'tis not to be doubted, but he might easily have succeeded in that View, had he not unhappily met with this fair, and more base Deceiver, whose Arts engross'd his whole Attention, on herself, and render'd him *incapable* because *unwilling*, to apply where his good Genius call'd him.

He imagin'd by *Syrena's* Appearance, and the manner in which her Mother and she liv'd, that she must have either a good Fortune in her own Hands, or a Jointure; and tho' he was enough infatuated with her, to have marry'd her without a Shilling, could his Affairs have admitted of it; yet the Belief, that she had sufficient for them both, was no small Spur to his Inclinations. With the view therefore of making his Addresses to her, did he visit her the next Day; where every thing he saw, serving the more to confirm him in the good Opinion he had conceiv'd of their Circumstances; for they took care to put on the best Outside; he after two or three Visits more declar'd himself a Lover. *Syrena* receiv'd his Suit with the greatest Shew of Modesty; but blended with a certain Languor in her Eyes, which gave him to understand, as if against her Will, that she felt the highest Satisfaction on it.——Every time he entertain'd her on this Topick, she grew less and less reserv'd, and at last confess'd, that she lov'd him from the first Moment she beheld him; and that it was wholly owing to the Emotions he had occasion'd in her; that she fell into those Disorders which gave Rise to their Acquaintance. How pleasing are the Thoughts of being belov'd by one who seems worthy of being lov'd! Mr. *P——* thought himself the happiest of all created Beings; blest in the purest and tenderest Affections of the most beautiful, most engaging, and most virtuous of her Sex; and one who had also a handsome Competency[1] at least, to make smooth the rugged Road of Life. Tho' he was by Nature a Man of very warm Inclinations, and had been the Destruction of many fine Women's Virtue and Reputation; so great was the Respect he bore *Syrena*; that tho' he had unnumber'd Opportunities he never took the Advantage of any of them, or approach'd her with Liberties beyond a Kiss, which considering her Constitution, and the real liking she had to him, was not, perhaps, so agreeable to her as he imagin'd.——He all this time, however, never came directly to the point, and tho' he courted her on honourable terms, and she had acknowledged the greatest Passion for him, he had not press'd the Consummation of his Happiness; had not entreated her to fix the Day that should give her forever to him.——This very much surprized both Mother and Daughter, and made them begin to fear there was some Mystery in his being so silent on that head; and having consider'd on what means would be best for obliging him to explain himself, Mrs. *Tricksy* one Day, when *Syrena* on purpose had left the Room, took an Occasion to tell him, that as she found he and her Daughter had settled their Affections on each other, she hoped he would not think it an improper Question if she desir'd to be inform'd of some Particulars relating to his Fortune. On which he seem'd a little confounded; but answer'd, that his Estate at present did not exceed four hundred Pounds *per Annum*;[2] but that he expected more on the Death of a Relation. Well, resum'd Mrs. *Tricksy*, four hundred Pounds a Year frugally manag'd, may keep a little Table for a time——Mr. P—— thought he had now an Excuse for expressing a Desire of knowing in what manner *Syrena* was left in her Widowhood; his Ignorance of that having been, indeed, the cause he had not been more eager for the Knot being ty'd; for tho' he lov'd her with an Extremity of Passion, he had no Notion of living with a Wife in a mean and penurious manner. Madam, said he, in answer to Mrs. *Tricksy*'s last Words, my Estate is much too small to maintain your Daughter in a fashion worthy of her, and I should be asham'd to be

---

1 A sufficiency, without superfluity, of the means of life; he believes Syrena is financially solvent.
2 As Syrena slips downward, the relative worth of the men she is involved with also declines; while £400 a year is not an insignificant amount for a single man to live on (for example Boswell had an allowance of £200 p.a. when he went to London in 1762), it is not enough to comfortably support a wife or mistress. It places Mr. P—— in the lower level of the lesser gentry.

too much indebted to a Wife's Purse: I would, therefore, indeavour
to bring my Kinsman to add something before his Death to what I
at present enjoy. If you can do so it will be well, reply'd Mrs. *Tricksy*,
but if not, you must be content————perhaps when you are marry'd
and Children come, he may be prevailed upon.————In the mean
time, you may make some small Settlement out of what you have
upon my Daughter.————Gladly, Madam, cry'd he, and whatever the
young Lady is possess'd of, shall also be settled on herself. This was
enough to let her see he expected a Fortune with her, and as it was
impossible to deceive him in that point, thought best not to attempt
it; but to seem entirely open in what could not be conceal'd, that he
might the more readily believe those things in which she had it in
her power to impose on him. Sir, said she, what I have to tell you
will be a certain test of the Sincerity of that Affection you profess.
————I do assure you, *Syrena* has at present no Fortune; but lives
dependant on me who have a tolerable good Jointure, and is all that
is preserved out of a large Estate her Father once enjoy'd; but which,
at my Decease goes also to an eldest Son————Not that she will
always be a Beggar————she is set down six thousand Pounds[1] in the
Will of a rich Cousin, who by the Course of Nature cannot live
many Years, being now more than Ninety.—Several others also of
our Kindred have promised to leave her handsomely; so that, as I
observ'd before, if you both live frugally for a while, you may hereafter indulge what want of Fortune, at present, will not suffer you to
enjoy with Prudence.

Mr. *P*———— found a shivering at his Heart from the time Mrs.
Tricksy had said her Daughter was no more than a Dependent on
her; but he conceal'd the Shock it gave him as much as possible,
and told her, he was only concerned, that he had not more to lay at
Syrena's Feet.

Notwithstanding all his Efforts to behave with the same Gaiety as
usual, he could not conceal from the piercing Eyes of *Syrena* and her
Mother, his inward Discontent; and reasoning upon it after he was
gone, they both were of Opinion he would not marry without a
Portion, which was not a little Disappointment to them both, as they
doubted not the Truth of his being possest of some Estate, if not altogether so much as he pretended.

---

1   By contrast, if Syrena really possessed this amount, the interest on that
    sum, roughly £180 assuming a 3% rate of return, would supplement Mr.
    P————'s income nicely.

He, on his part, when the Hour came in which it was proper for him to retire, went home to his Lodgings with an aking Heart: He loved *Syrena*, too well to be able to live without her in any tollerable degree of Peace, and the Impossibility of maintaining her as a Wife, made him pass the Night in the most grievous Aggitations—— He curs'd Fate and his Friends, whose Endeavours to get him a Place had been unsuccessful; for as he doubted not the Truth of what Mrs. *Tricksy* had told him concerning the six thousand Pounds, and other Legacies, he thought if he could any way have supported her till that time, he might very well venture to marry her—but as things stood now with him, that was entirely out of the Question, and how to proceed he could not determine.

He went to visit her the next Day, however, and several succeeding ones as before this *Eclaircissement* had been made; but tho' he could not forbear talking to her as a Lover, he mention'd not the least Word of Marriage, which confirming *Syrena* and her Mother in their Conjectures, that he intended no such thing, made them resolve to push the matter home; but in what manner they could not yet determine; and were thinking of various Stratagems, without being able to fix on any, when Fortune presented *Syrena* with an Adventure, which furnish'd her with one, that, besides being agreeable in itself, promised Success.

She was walking cross the Park one Morning, after having breakfasted with a Friend at *Westminster*, when she saw a Gentleman go before her, whose Shape and Air she fancy'd she was not unacquainted with——She, therefore, mended her Pace, and tho' he went not slow came up with him, and pulling her Hat as low as she could to conceal her Face, if it should chance to be any of those she had reason to avoid, look'd full on him as she past, and found it was *Vardine*, the Man who had triumph'd over her Virgin Beauties, and betray'd her Innocence, if a Creature so early bred up in Wiles, can be said to remember she ever had any. It presently came into her Head, that he might be of Service in her Designs on Mr. P——, and accosted him with a Tap on the Arm with her little Cane.——He started and turned to her taking her at first for one of those Ladies of Pleasure who frequent that Place; for he knew her not immediately, being grown fatter and somewhat more plump, tho' far from fat; but she soon by her Voice, and discovering her Face more fully, let him see who she was—He was a little confounded at first, and was beginning to make Excuses for his Behaviour; but she would not suffer him to go on, telling him she had forgot and forgiven all that was disagreeable to her in his Conduct— that she was now glad to see him, and had a Favour to ask of him, which it would cost him nothing to grant——He took this as a sort of Reproach for the little he had done for her; but made her no other Answer, than that he should rejoice in an Opportunity of obliging her with any thing in his power. After some Conversation relating to their former Intimacy, they adjourned to a Tavern, where finding by him that he was still but a Lieutenant, and had as little Money to spare in matters of Gallantry as ever, she attempted not to impose on him in any Shape, affected not Virtue, nor refused, on his desiring it, a renewing of those Endearments he before had experienc'd from her, tho' then given with more Artifice than she now took the Trouble to put in practice——She told him she was endeavouring to draw in a Gentleman to marry her, and that if he would assist her, he should command her in every thing.——He readily comply'd to do any thing she desired on that Score, and thought he owed her a greater Service, if in his power, for the Favours she had conferr'd on him.—— She carry'd him home to Dinner, and having presented him to her Mother, and told her his Name, soon reconciled her to him, by informing her also, what he was to do for her; they then all three enter'd into a Consultation, and as he was a graceful young Fellow and well dress'd, it seem'd probable, that the very sight of him would create a Jealousy in Mr. P——, that might serve to quicken his Love; it was, therefore, agreed upon, that he should stay till the other came, which was generally about the Hours of six or seven——and then take his Leave with a seemingly dejected Air.

Vardine acted his Part as naturally as they could wish, and Mr. P—— made no doubt but he had a Rival, which, as he truly loved her, was no small Addition to his Inquietudes——He complain'd of it to *Syrena* in the most tender Terms, and she confest, blushing, that indeed that young Officer had made Pretensions to her almost ever since her Widowhood; but that he was always her Aversion, and that having been oblig'd to go into the Country to his Regiment, she had hoped to have been rid of his Importunities, and was sorry to find he still continued his Passion for her; but, said she, I had not seen him today, if by Chance I had not been at the Window when he knock'd, and am resolved to be deny'd to him henceforward, if he comes ever so often—be easy and satisfy'd, therefore, continued she, for as I loved him not when my Heart was wholly unengaged, 'tis impossible to endure him now, so full as it is of your Idea. The believing Lover appear'd transported with Joy and Gratitude; and had it not been for the Thoughts of not being able at present to make so excellent a Woman his own, his Extasy had been beyond all Bounds.

Some few Days after this they contrived it so, that when Mr. P—— was in the Dining-Room with Mrs. *Tricksy* and her Daughter, a great Sound of Voices was heard below, and the old Deceiver feigning a Surprize, open'd the Door, as to listen what it meant, having stood a Moment, Heavens! cry'd she, 'tis Capt. *Vardine*! he is quite outrageous on your being deny'd to him——I must go down my self, and put a stop to the Clamours of his Despair——With speaking this she ran hastily out of the Room, and the Door being purposely left open, Mr. P—— heard him say——I have nothing wherewith to accuse the cruel Charmer, nor the happy Gentleman I am told she has made choice of—I only would beg once more to see her——to take my last Farewell, and die before her Eyes. Mrs. *Tricksy* seem'd expostulating with him; but he continued his Exclamations for some time, and *Syrena* pretended the utmost Terror, lest he should force his way up Stairs, and there should be a Quarrel between him and Mr. P——; at length, however he departed, and Mrs. *Tricksy*, return'd, full of a well-counterfeited Concern for his Condition.

To refuse a Man who lov'd her with such an Excess of Passion and unweary'd Constancy, they thought would lay a kind of Obligation on Mr. P——'s Honour, as well as his Love to make her his Wife; but to strengthen her Claim to him they also had recourse to another Artifice, which was this:

They had several worthy and good Relations, as has been before mention'd, who had formerly been very kind and beneficent to them; but some Whispers concerning the Conduct of *Syrena*, which the manner in which she was supported without following any Business, served to confirm, having reached their Ears, they had not seen either her or her Mother for a long time; but on this Juncture, that crafty Woman ventur'd to approach them, saying, that her Daughter was now about being married to a Gentleman of an Estate, and that there wanted nothing to hasten the Marriage, but their vouchsafing to own her as a Relation, without which, continu'd she, he may imagine she has been guilty of some Mismanagement, and break off. To retrieve the Character, therefore, and settle in the World a young Person ally'd to them, the greatest Part of them consented to visit her; and now there seldom past an Evening, without his seeing some or other of his intended Wife's Kindred: They all approved highly of his Person and Behaviour, and he was invited to all their Houses by turns, which, not knowing how to avoid accepting, he went with *Syrena* and her Mother: The Fashion in which they lived, and the Entertainments they made for him, would have convinced him, if he had not been so before, that she was no mean Person. But all this served only to make him more unhappy, by reflecting, that he had acted dishonourably, by pretending to have what he had not; and that he appear'd guilty of Ingratitude, by not doing what, as his Affairs were, he had not power to do, without bringing to the utmost Misery, both himself and the Person he loved.

No Offers yet being made by him, of bringing the Matter to a Conclusion, Mrs. *Tricksy* and her Daughter began to despair of ever compassing their point; but to ascertain themselves of the Truth, if possible, they try'd one more Expedient in the following manner.

Pretty early one Morning as he was dressing to go out, the Servant of the House where he lodged, told him, a Lady desired to speak with him. He was a little alarmed, imagining it a young Creature with whom he had commenced an Amour, before he saw the fatal Face of *Syrena*, and who he knew was with Child by him; as his new Passion had render'd him wholly neglectful of her of late, he doubted not but she was come to reproach him, and endeavoured to prevail on the Servant to say he was not at home: How can I do that, Sir, said she, when I have already told the Lady you were? Pish, cry'd he, can't you pretend you were mistaken, and that I went out without your seeing me——as they were arguing, *Syrena's* Impatience at being made wait so long, with a little mixture of Jealousy, that some other Woman might be with him, made her fly up Stairs without being ask'd; he was agreeably surpriz'd to find it was she, and begg'd a thousand Pardons for not coming down to receive her. I have no Reason, said she, to be offended at your want of Ceremony; for as I did not send up my Name, I believe I was the last Person you could think of, that was come to disturb you. He was beginning to make some Compliments on the Favour she did him, but she put a stop to them, as soon as the Maid had left the Room, by saying, the Affair I come upon deserves not these civil things.——I am come, continued she, bursting into Tears, to forbid you our House—you must see me no more—my Mother has resolved it, and is prepared to tell you so at your next Visit—I thought the News would be less shocking from my Mouth; and therefore in spite of all the Considerations that might have restrained me, am come to take my everlasting leave;— and to tell you, that tho' I cannot think you love me with that Tenderness you have profest, you are too dear to me, for me to be able to resent any thing you do, and that you ever will be so to the last Moment of my wretched Life.

These Words, and the manner in which they were spoke, touched him to the very Soul,——he was ready to keep her Company in Tears; and tho' he did not absolutely weep, his Eyes were full, and it was not without great Difficulty he withheld the swelling Grief from falling down his Cheeks;——ah, Madam, cried he, what is it you tell me?— what can have made this sudden Alteration in your Mother's Sentiments? that, replied she, which ought to have had the same Effect on mine——your Deceit in pretending to love me only for my Person and Mind, when in reality you regarded nothing but the Fortune you supposed me Mistress of. Here he made a thousand Asseverations to the contrary of what she accused him of; and that no Woman in the World, though endowed with all that could glut the Avarice of the most sordid Man, could have the power to alienate his Affection from her; and concluded what he said with a solemn Vow, never to marry any other, unless she first should lead the way; to this she made no Answer, but Sighs, and he resumed his Protestations; had I Millions, said he, I would devote them all, with myself, to the Service of the charming, the adorable *Syrena*; but as the little, the very little I am at present Master of, is insufficient to give her even ease in Life, is it not a greater Proof of Love, to restrain the burning Wishes she has inspir'd me with, and delay my Happiness till Fate shall put it in the power of one of us, to make Marriage comfortable, than to desire she should be Partaker of my abject Fortune?

Syrena was too penetrating not to see into the Fallacy of this Argument, but as she was resolved to pin herself upon him any way, she forbore to urge the Matter farther, and said, I should readily agree with you; that it is better to wait till the Death of this old Impediment of my Happiness, shall make me Mistress of my Fortune, but my Mother will never be brought to think as we do——she presses me to marry the young Officer, and though I am resolved never to yield to that, and could sooner die than suffer the Embraces of any but him, to whom I have given my Heart; yet I must, terrible as it is to me, forbear your Sight and Conversation, till better times——if you can be constant in Absence— and preserve your Heart for me, as I shall do mine for you, we may hereafter find a Recompence for our present Pains. This Mr. P—— was ready enough to consent to, but could not tell how to bring himself to think of not seeing her till the Time should arise, of claiming the Performance of her Promise; and he expressing the impossibility there was for him to live without her Society, she aimed not to render him more satisfied on that Head, but pretended that whatever she had said, she doubted not but he would soon hear she was no more, when she no more enjoyed his Presence.

Nothing could be more tender than their Conversation; but he still persisting in his first Resolution of not marrying yet a-while, she fell into violent Fits, the People of the House were called up, but as she seemed a little recovered, withdrew——she then wept, and hung upon him with Agonies, such as threatned Distraction;—he kiss'd, embraced, said all he could to comfort her, and these Endearments continuing for a long time, rendered both, according to all Appearance, in the end forgetful of themselves, and sinking into each others Arms, they enjoyed the Pleasures of Matrimony without the Ceremony. But *Syrena*, whose every Word and Look during the whole time of her being with him, was studied Artifice, and before concerted with her Mother, seemed so shocked at what she had done, that she begg'd he would that Moment run his Sword through her Heart; for Life after the Loss of Honour, cried she, would be a perfect Hell——he endeavoured to reconcile her to an Act, which he said could not be criminal between two People, whose Souls were already married, and who had resolved never to receive any other Idea, than those with which they were at present fill'd—she began by Degrees to seem convinced by his Reasons, but told him, that after what had happened, she could not think of being absent from him even a Day——that she now looked upon him as her Husband, and conscious of her own Integrity, regarded not what Opinion the World might have of her Conduct—and in fine, said she would live with him as a *Mistress*, till Circumstances should admit of her being made a *Wife*.

An Offer, such as this, from a Woman of her supposed Modesty, could not but surprize him—he took it however as a Proof of the most exalted and disinterested Passion that ever was——but when he reflected, that to support her as a *Mistress*, would be little less inconvenient than maintaining her as a *Wife*, it very much puzzled him—but he loved her, and that overcame all other Considerations; she staid with him at his Lodgings—shared the same Bed, and they lived together in every Respect, as if they had been married.

So full an Enjoyment did not in the least abate his Tenderness; and tho' after she had been with him some few Days, he was told by Persons who happened to see her at his Window, that she was a Woman of an infamous Character, and made up of Deceit, he looked upon it all as Malice or Envy, and even quarrelled with the dearest Friend he had on Earth, for but seeming to doubt of her Sincerity.——Have I not Proofs both of her Love and Honour, cry'd he, such

Proofs as never Woman but herself ever gave, nor never Man but me was ever bless'd with?—O! she is all Charms, both Mind and Body! till I knew her, I knew not what real Happiness was, and vainly searched for it in various Pleasures; but in my dear *Syrena* is all that's excellent compriz'd.

Those who loved him, pitied and lamented his Infatuation; and those to whom he was Indifferent, ridicul'd it—all who knew his Circumstances stood amazed, that a Man of so fine an Understanding in other things, should neglect all Opportunities of making his Fortune, dissipate the little Substance he had left, and devote his whole time to a Woman, who, had she been as much an *Angel*, as she was really a *Devil*, had it not in her power either to serve him or herself.

In the mean time, *Syrena* was not idle in providing against a Change, or more properly speaking, *for a Change*; she liked Mr. P—— indeed, but liked Interest better; and frequently pretending to go to some or other of her Kindred, where till they were married, it was improper he should accompany her, went abroad in hope of meeting with something more to her Advantage, than she now began to suspect he could ever be; and continued with him but till she could be better provided for.

Her expensive way of living, and the Pleasure he took in indulging her every Wish, together with the Shame he found in himself, whenever he attempted to let her know how ill he could afford it, had exhausted his little Stock of Money in a short time—he then borrowed of all who would lend—and went in Debt wherever he could—so that soon he found himself without either Money, Friends, or Credit; shunn'd by his Acquaintance, and in Danger of a Gaol—this made him very melancholy, but did not make him love the less—— he cursed his Fate, but bless'd the Wretch who had undone him—she took Notice of the Alteration in his Countenance, and press'd him in so endearing a manner to let her know the Cause, that he at last confess'd his Misfortunes, concealing nothing from her of the Truth; she hid the Vexation it gave her, with her accustomed Artifice, and said, well my Dear, be as patient as you can——I love you not the less for having no Estate; and this old Creature of a Kinsman cannot live for ever, and my six thousand Pounds will at least procure you a Place.

From this time, however, she thought of nothing but how to get a new Gallant; but none offering their Service, she chose rather to remain with him, till he had made away with the last things, that would even purchase a Dinner, than go home to her Mother, where she must have been put to those Straits herself, which he alone at present sustained.

A Gentleman who had been an old Friend of Mr. P——'s Father, hearing of his Misfortunes, made him an Invitation to his House, which he told him should be to him as his own, till he could get into some Employment; but this unhappy and deluded Man refused to accept so kind an Offer, on *Syrena's* falling into Fits, when he but barely mention'd it; and chose rather to starve with her, than forsake her without her own Consent; and sure a greater Act of Barbarity and Ingratitude was never practis'd, than by this base Wretch in still hanging on a Man, who to support her was obliged to be guilty of Meanesses which his Soul on any other Occasion would have abhorred; and Heaven only knows to what Extremes, he might have been driven, had not Providence discovered to him her Perfidy in too full a Manner for all her Dissimulation to evade, had she attempted it; but indeed having now run in a Manner, the last length she could go with him, she took not any Pains about it.

As he was taking a solitary Walk one Afternoon in *Chelsea-Fields*,[1] indulging his melancholy Contemplations, he met an Acquaintance, who would needs make him go into the next House of Entertainment;[2] where being seated and discoursing of ordinary Affairs, their Conversation was interrupted by the loud laughing of some Persons in the next Room; and there being only a Wainscot[3] Partition between them, they heard distinctly these Words, *by G—d, my Dear, if ever Fortune throws a rich Fool in my Way, you shan't want a better Commission.* This was a Woman's Voice, and sounded so like *Syrena's*, that Mr. P—— could not forbear growing as red as Scarlet; not that he imagin'd it could be she, whom he had left at Home undrest, and hard at Work, for she pretended to be a good Housewife; but he was enrag'd that any vile Woman, as he perceiv'd this was, by other Words he heard her say; should have any thing in her like his dear modest Creature. The Gentleman, who knew not his Emotions, cry'd, we have got a loving Couple near us, I find.——Prithee, let's try if we can see who they are. In speaking this, he went to the side of the Room, and found a Crevice large enough for the Eye to take in all that was done within—the fond Pair by this time were silent, or what they spoke was in

---

1 Likely the area surrounding Chelsea Waterworks just slightly west and south of St. James's Park and the open fields behind Buckingham House that Syrena has frequented in the past.

2 A building for the entertainment of travelers or of the public generally; the equivalent to an inn or tavern.

3 Panel-work of oak or other wood, used to line the walls of an apartment; in this case, a thin partition.

a lower Accent, and, indeed, they were otherwise employ'd, as Mr. *P——* who going also out of Curiosity, saw to his Confusion.—He not only found the Voice, but the Cloaths and Person of the Woman, were the same with *Syrena's*, in fine, 'twas she herself; and in a Posture such as he would have stabb'd any one, who should have told him, she could have been in with any other Man than himself.

He was naturally of a warm and sanguine Disposition, impatient of Injuries, and incapable of Reflection in the first Moments of his Passion: He made but one Step from the Room he was in to the next, burst open the Door, which tho' lock'd gave way to the Violence he us'd; drew his Sword, and had certainly destroy'd them both in the Act of Shame, had not his Friend been quick enough to prevent him, by catching hold of his Arm behind.—*Vardine*, for it was he, was ill-prepar'd for a Combat of this kind, but snatch'd up his Sword which lay in the Window, and stood on his Defence.——The People of the House hearing the Noise, by this time came into the Room, and with the Assistance of Mr. *P——*'s Friend secur'd both their Swords, and prevented the Mischief which must otherwise have happen'd; with much-a-do they got Mr. *P——* out of the Room, tho' not till after he had loaded the vile Wanton with all the Reproaches her Treachery merited.——*Vardine* and she went out of the House together; and she return'd no more to Mr. *P——*'s Lodgings—a happy Riddance, and a Day which he has since vow'd to celebrate every Year, as the most fortunate One, that he had ever seen.

The next Morning he receiv'd a Letter by a Porter, the Contents whereof were these.

SIR,

THO' I think it little worth my while to demand any Satisfaction on the Score of the Woman you found me with Yesterday; yet it would ill become my Character, to put up with your forcing into the Room where I was, and disturbing my Pleasures.—I shall therefore expect you will meet me Tomorrow Morning in the Field behind Montague-house,[1] to decide with the Points of our Swords, which of us has been to blame.

J. VARDINE.

---

1 Montague House, on Great Russell Street, was the site of what is now the British Museum. It was taken over by the government in 1755 and opened as the British Museum then. The area behind it opened onto Lamb's Conduit-Fields. The area to the north of the house was a frequent site for duels.

The Gentleman who had been with Mr. P———, at the discovery of *Syrena's* Falshood, came to see how he did after this Disorder, and was at Breakfast with him when this Letter was brought. Mr. P——— would have conceal'd the Contents, but the other guessing the Business, would needs see it; and having read it, you shall not go, said he, How! not go, cry'd Mr. P——— would you have me posted for a Coward? Not so, replyed the other, but if you will give me leave to take this Letter with me, I will go along with the Porter to him, and shall engage to order matters to the Satisfaction of you both; which I am sure is much better, than losing your Blood in a Cause so unworthy of it.

It was with great Difficulty Mr. P——— was persuaded; but knowing his Friend to be a Man who hated a mean thing, as much as himself, he at last consented he should act in it as he thought proper; only bid him be carefull of his Honour, and his Friend assuring him he would be so, went with the Porter to the Place where the Letter had been given to him, and where *Vardine* still waited his Return in Expectation of an Answer.

It was a Coffee-House, but few People being there, the Gentleman had opportunity enough to say what he intended, without Interruption. He told him that not having quitted Mr. P——— since the Skirmish, and happening to rise first, he took the Letter instead of him to whom it was directed; and suspecting the Purport open'd it, and was come to reason with him on the Affair, before Mr. P——— knew any thing of it; and also, if he could to prevent the fatal Consequences which else might possibly ensue. *Vardine* did not seem displeased in the least at his Proceeding; and when they came to argue on the Provocation Mr. P——— had received, and the almost unparalled Deceit and Ingratitude of *Syrena*, *Vardine* acknowledged that he could not be expected to act otherwise than he had done; and concluded with saying, that he thought now, that they ought to exchange Pardons with each other, for added he, I was prevailed on by the Entreaties of that Woman to joyn in the Deception put upon Mr. P———, in order to draw him in to marry her; and have as much Occasion for his Forgiveness on that Score, as he has of mine for forcing into my Room. The Friend of Mr. P——— then proposed a Meeting between them three, the same Evening to conclude all Animosities over a Bottle, the other agreed to it, and Mr. P——— at hearing what had past was perfectly satisfyed with the Gentleman's Conduct, and went with him to the Appointment, at the time prefix'd, with as much Chearfullness as his Circumstances would admit of——— all the Love he had bore *Syrena*, while he believed her sincere, was now turn'd into as great a Contempt, and *Vardine* expressing the same, and protesting never to see her more, added to his Satisfaction.

Thus ended an Affair, which tho' much to the Prejudice of Mr. *P*——, had it not been for the prudent Management of his Friend, might have been much worse, and afforded Business for the *Old Bailey*;[1] and ought to be a Warning to all Gentlemen how they suffer themselves to be beguiled in the Manner he was, or expect Sincerity from Persons whom they commence an Acquaintance with in the Street.

Syrena was now once more at Home with her Mother, who knowing how little was to be got either by Mr. *P*—— or *Vardine* who resolved to see her no more as well as the other, was not much troubled at what had happened; but her Daughter was of a different Way of thinking; she had for a long time been accustomed to be admired and caress'd; and to live without the Conversation of a Man was wretchedly irksome, and what her gay and amorous Constitution could not endure with any tollerable degree of Patience—she made some Efforts to retain *Vardine*, but that young Gentleman finding what a consummate Jilt[2] she was grown, and fearful of being brought into more Broils on her Account, declined any farther Acceptance of her Favours; this, together with the Poverty to which she was reduced, made her almost distracted; the Notion she had been bred up in, that a Woman who had Beauty to attract the Men, and Cunning to manage them afterwards, was secure of making her Fortune, appeared now altogether fallacious; since she had not been able to do it in four Years incessant Application, and such a Variety of Adventures, as in that time she had been engaged in. This naturally led her to reproach her Mother for having given her ill Advice; and the Mother retorted that the Misfortunes and Disappointments she had met with, had not been owing to her Advice, but to her own ill Conduct—what, said she, hindred you from being married to Mr. *W*—— but your Amour with his Son? or what from being still the Darling of Mr. *P*—— but your renewing your Acquaintance with *Vardine*? by which you have lost both, and will always do so while you are silly enough to love any Man.——And pray, interrupted *Syrena*, whom may I thank for losing Mr. *D*—— but you, first for

---

1 The Old Bailey in London was (and is) the seat of the Central Criminal Court.

2 A woman who gives her lover hopes, and deceives him; or one who capriciously casts off a lover after giving him encouragement. It is a term of contempt.

counselling me to be Captain *H*——'s Mistress, and then by your unlucky Letter betraying it to the other——Thus with mutual Upbraidings did they add to their ill Fate, and as there can be neither true Duty or Affection where Interest presides, that prevailing Guide being at present suspended, whoever had seen them together, and heard the bitter things they said, without knowing who they were would little have imagined, how near they were by Blood.

The manner in which *Syrena* had lived, entitled her not to keep any reputable Company of her own Sex, and as for Women of the Town, she always avoided any Acquaintance with them, as being too much addicted to tattling, and also malicious to a Face prefer'd before their own; so that whenever she went to the Play or Opera, or walk'd in the Park, she had been always obliged to dress up, some Tirewoman,[1] Sempstress, or such like Person to accompany her; but she had now a very poor Stock of Cloaths, most of those as well as her Watch and Jewels being gone to satisfy Demands of a more pressing Nature; so that she had no Opportunity to shew herself to advantage; for a Woman can give herself a thousand enticing Airs, when she has somebody to talk to, which cannot be practis'd when alone. To stay at home, however, she knew could be of no Service to her, so she went out every Day, sometimes to Church, and sometimes to Shops, cheapening Goods,[2] and to all the Auctions[3] she could hear of.

It was at one of these last Places, she had the Good-Luck, as she then thought it, to be taken particular notice of by Mr. *E*——, a Gentleman of a vast Estate, and most agreeable Person: He had seen her in the Park some Months before, and then languished for an Opportunity to entertain her; but a Relation of his Wife, for he was married, being with him, he was obliged to put a Constraint upon

---

1   A woman who assists at a lady's toilet or a woman employed in the making or sale of women's clothing. Johnson specifies it even further as "a woman whose business it is to make dresses for the head."

2   She is trying to lower the price or haggle with the tradesman. Swift uses the term in "City Shower" (1727): "To shops in crowds the daggled females fly, / Pretend to cheapen goods, but nothing buy" (lines 33-34).

3   Auctions were an important site of social interaction drawing men and women from a wide social spectrum into the participatory spectacle of competitive bidding for various kinds of property. It is an appropriate metaphor for Syrena's related activities for it is another example of the ways in which sites of consumer culture merge with the sexual marketplace.

his Inclinations, at that time, and Fortune had never since thrown her in his way. To meet with her, therefore, in a Place where the most reserved of either Sex, make no Scruple of speaking to each other, was an infinite Satisfaction to him: He went round the Room with her, as if examining the Value of the Goods; but in reality telling her how handsome she was, and how much he admired her: To give her some Proof, that what he said were not Words of course, a fine *India* Cabinet[1] being put up to sale, which she seem'd to praise, he out-bid all the Company, and made her a Present of it.——This he did in hope of knowing by that means, where he might wait upon her; and she, no less desirous that he should do so, took care to give very exact Directions to the Auctioneer where it should be sent. Tho' she affected to receive a Favour of this kind, from a Gentleman who was a perfect Stranger to her, with a great deal of Reluctance; yet she omitted not to let fall Hints, as if she accepted the Donation mere-ly for the sake of the Donor; having found by Experience, that Men, as well as Women have Vanity enough to be delighted, with the Belief they have any thing in them capable of charming at first Sight, she call'd so much Tenderness into her Voice and Eyes, whenever she look'd upon him, or spoke to him; yet at the same time blended with it such an Innocence, as made him, while he flatter'd himself with having inspired her with the softest Passion, imagine also, that she was asham'd of her own Thoughts, and was endeavouring all she could to suppress the rising Inclination: He fancy'd he saw in every Glance, Desire struggling with Modesty, and the sweet Contest, which he fancy'd he found there, so heighten'd the Idea of her Charms, that he look'd upon himself as the happiest Man alive.

As she was about leaving the Room, I would attend you to your Chair, Madam, said he; but, as I know how to direct, will give you the Trouble of a Line, if I may be permitted to hope you will allow it the Favour of a Perusal. I am too fond of improving the little Genius I owe to Nature, answer'd she, with the most seemingly art-less Blush, not to read with Pleasure whatever falls from the Pen of a Gentleman like you. She waited not to hear how he would reply; but believing he would think she had said enough, turn'd hastily away, in an admirably well dissembled Confusion, and went home to acquaint her Mother with what had happen'd.

---

1 An India cabinet was a wooden cabinet, likely with extensive carving and multiple drawers. Given England's commercial relationship with India, commodities like this would have been increasingly available and not tremendously expensive.

Early the next Morning a Porter brought a Letter directed to Miss *Tricksy*; her Orders to the Auctioneer being to carry the Cabinet to Mrs. *Tricksy* at Mr. *N*——'s in *H*—— street; and her Youth and seeming Innocence making Mr. *E*—— suppose her unmarried, occasion'd him to write the Superscription in that manner. She open'd it with Impatience enough, and found in it these Words:

Charming Miss,
As it is impossible to see you without feeling a Mixture of Love and Admiration, I fear you are too much accustom'd to Declarations of this Nature, to have that Compassion which is necessary to save the Life of your Votaries;—permit me, however, to tell you, that I have a Claim beyond what yet you have been sensible of, which is having adored you for a great length of time—Yes, most angelic Creature! I have languish'd in a hopeless Flame for many Months—One Sight of you at a Distance, made me your everlasting Slave; and tho' I have taken all imaginable Pains, I never since that fatal Moment could gain a second interview; till Yesterday, Chance, more favourable than my Industry, restor'd you to my longing Eyes.—What Agonies I have sustain'd till then, you cannot be able to comprehend, nor am I to describe—But as I have already past those Sufferings, which are a kind of Probation that Love exacts from all those who profess themselves his Votaries; if you are equally just as fair, you will allow some little Recompence is due from one who is an *old Lover*, tho' a *new Acquaintance*——that of being permitted to visit you sometimes, and to sigh my Wishes at your Feet, is all I yet presume to implore, who am,

> *Divinest of your Sex,*
> *Your most humble,*
> *Most passionate, and*
> *most faithful Adorer.*

P. S. If I have your leave to visit you, I will inform you, not only who I am, but every thing you shall ask; and also endeavour to give you greater Proofs than Words of the Sincerity of my Flame. In the mean time, favour me with an Answer directed to *A. Z.*[1]

There was something so particular in the Stile of this Letter, that neither *Syrena* nor her Mother knew how to form a Judgment of it;

---

1 A common way to mark one as anonymous.

by some Expressions they would have imagin'd, he took her for a Girl of Virtue, and intended to address her on the most honourable Score, had not others again contradicted that Belief——As they yet were ignorant of the Circumstances of him who wrote it, there was, indeed, no Possibility of fathoming his Design; but as there was a Necessity of giving an Answer, and the Porter waited, they contrived one between both, which should encourage him to be more open, and at the same time leave him as much in the dark concerning their Affairs, as they were at present on the Account of his.

To Mr. A. Z.

SIR,

THO' without ever having been what they call, in Love my self, I have suffered so much from that Passion, that I have Reason to tremble at the very Name; yet as I cannot be vain enough to imagine what is meant by it in yours, any more than mere Gallantry, I shall make no Difficulty of receiving the Visits of a Person who has so much the Appearance of a Man of Honour, and whose Civilities to me demand somewhat as an Acknowledgement from a grateful Mind; which is all the Merit to be boasted of by,

Sir,
Your most oblig'd, and
Humble Servant,
SYRENA TRICKSY.

Mr. *E——* was too impatient to defer any longer than the Evening of the same Day waiting on the admired Object, but was a little startled when he found there was a Mother in the way; and who, in the midst of the Civilities she received him with, mingled a certain Severity, which render'd him very much at a loss how to behave: *Syrena*, however, said a thousand obliging things to him, and whenever she had an Opportunity, gave him Looks sufficient to have encouraged a Man who had a less Opinion of himself. Tea was not over when a pretended Messenger came to inform Mrs. *Tricksy* her Company was desired on a Business of great Importance——She made an Apology for being oblig'd to leave him, which he very readily excused, rejoiced to be rid of the Company of one, who seem'd not likely to favour the purpose he came there upon.

She was no sooner gone, than he declared himself in the most passionate manner to *Syrena*, who reply'd to all he said with a well-affected Modesty; but with a Kindness also, which confirmed the

Hopes her Glances had before inspired him with. She told him the same Story of her Marriage and Widowhood, as she had done others, and gave him to understand her Circumstances were none of the best.——He, in return for her suppos'd Sincerity, acquainted her that he was married, obliged by his Friends to enter into that State when he was very young; but that he never loved his Lady, nor, indeed, any other Woman, till he saw the Object before him.——*Syrena* seem'd shock'd at hearing he had a Wife, and gave him an Opportunity of discovering, as he imagin'd, that she lik'd him infinitely.——She told him, her Mother would never permit her to receive his Visits when she should know it; and as it was impossible it could be long kept a Secret from her, she could not but look on herself as very unhappy in being deprived of the Company of a Man, who by an irresistable Impulse, she could not help wishing to be eternally with. All this she spoke as in the first Emotions of her Surprize, and as thô' it 'scaped her without Design——then afterwards appeared confounded at having so far betrayed herself.

Mr. *E*——, who by this Behaviour had Reason to believe she loved him to a very great Excess, was transported, and used many more Arguments than he need to have done, to persuade her to leave her Mother, and retire to Lodgings of his preparing for her.

Syrena thought it not proper to yield to these Proposals immediately, but did not seem altogether averse to them; and in this first Visit he had Cause to expect every thing he could wish, so departed highly satisfied; not that he imagined he had to deal with a Woman of that strict Virtue she pretended; but his Opinion of her was, that if she had fallen, it was merely for the Sake of Interest, and that if he gain'd any Favours, they would be the Effect of Love: In effect, he languish'd not long; the Circumstances *Syrena* and her Mother were in at this Juncture, would not permit them time for the Artifices they might otherwise have practised on this Gentleman, so thought it best to accept of his Offer, and trust to his future Generosity and their own Management, for a Settlement.

In fine, the Agreement in a few Days was concluded between the amorous Pair, and *Syrena* went to an Apartment he had provided, the Elegance of which shew'd both his Love and Liberality; he made her a Present of 500*l.*[1] the Moment she set her Foot in it; and assured

---

1 Since Mr. *P*——'s annual income was only £400, it is clear to the reader that £500 is an enormous amount of money by any measure. This is also the amount Mr. B. offers Pamela in his proposals to her (see Appendix C.2.v.).

her, that whatever he was Master of she should command; Mrs. *Tricksy* was to seem ignorant of all this, to the End, that finding it out afterwards, the Reproaches of a Mother might oblige him to do something farther to appease her.

Many Stratagems they had in Embrio, in order to impose upon him, but they were all rendred abortive, by a Misfortune which fell upon them when they least expected it, and from a Quarter they little dream'd of.

Syrena had now provoked a Woman no less cunning, tho' more virtuous than herself, the Wife of Mr. E——, who being informed by some Spies, she ever kept upon his Actions, of his Fondness of this new Favourite, resolved to break off the Intimacy between them, and affected it by this Means.

She had among her Acquaintance a Lady extremely jealous of her Husband, and of a Temper too violent and outrageous to forgive the least Infringement on her Rights; this Person she contrived to make her Instrument of Revenge on *Syrena*, without being seen in it herself, or giving Mr. E—— any Reason to imagine she even knew of the Injury he did her.

Mr. C—— was a Man of a very amorous Constitution, tho' secret in his Amours, on Account of his Wife's excessive tenaciousness that way; to him did Mrs. E—— contrive a Letter should be sent, containing these Lines.

To Mr. C——.

SIR,

LOVE being a Passion that admits of no Controul, the Custom that obliges Women to conceal it, is cruel and unjust; and what I hope you'll excuse the breach of, when made in Favour of yourself.—In fine, Sir, there is a Lady in the World, who for a long time has looked on you with the Eyes of Tenderness—the Circumstances both of you are in, will not permit her to take any other Steps, than she now does to let you know it; but if you will venture to meet her at the *King's-Arms* in —— *Street*, To-morrow at Six in the Evening, I believe you will not think your Time ill bestowed——she is a Woman of Reputation, young, and accounted handsome—as to the rest, a few Hours of her Conversation will enable you to judge better, than any Description can be given by

Sir,
Your unknown humble Servant.

P. S. Enquire for Number I.

Mrs. *E——* took care to make the Appointment, contained in this Letter, at a time when she knew her Husband was too deeply engaged with other Company, to be able to see his Mistress; and early in the Morning sent a Porter to *Syrena*, as from Mr. *E——*, to tell her, that an extraordinary Accident had made it improper for him to come to her Lodgings any more; and that he desired to see her to inform her of it, at the *King's-Arms* Tavern in —— *Street*. Every thing happened as Mrs. *E——* wish'd——*Syrena* told the Porter she would come; and the subtle Wife having a Letter ready prepar'd, sent it directly to Mrs. *C——*, the Contents of it were as follows.

To Mrs. C——.

Madam,

I Am sorry to acquaint you that you are injured in the most tender Part—Mr. *C——* has long kept Company with one of the most leud, expensive, insinuating Women about Town, who if not timely prevented, will be the ruin of his Estate, as she has already been of his Honour and Fidelity, to so excellent a Wife——to accuse him will be of little Consequence; he is too firmly attached to the Creature, to break off with her by any moderate Measures; but if you think proper to assert the Prerogative the Law allows a Wife wrong'd in this Manner, and take a Warrant and proper Officers with you;[1] you will find her with your Husband at Six this Evening, at the *King's-Arms* in —— *Street:*—Slight not this Intelligence, because it comes from one you know not, but convince yourself of the Truth, and at the same time punish the Wretch who dares to invade your Right—her Name is *Syrena Tricksy*, she passes for a Widow, and at this time lodges in *Maiden-Lane*;[2] but as Mr. *C——* seldom sees her at home, you can never have an Opportunity like the present of doing yourself Justice, and reclaiming the Man, whom both divine and human Laws ought to bind entirely to you. I am,

Madam,
Your sincere Well-wisher.

P. S. If you enquire for Number I, you will be shew directly to the Scene of Guilt and Shame.

---

1   The wife plans to sue for alienation of affections.
2   This location places Syrena where she began, near Covent Garden. Maiden Lane, about a block south and west of Covent Garden, ran parallel with Henrietta Street and the Strand.

The Rage this Lady was in at the Receipt of this, was not at all inferior to what Mrs. *E——* imagined——she went immediately to a Justice of Peace,[1] obtained a Warrant, and had a Constable[2] ready to attend her when the Hour should arrive.

Mrs. *E——* in the mean time was not idle, she knew her Husband was engaged the whole Day with his Lawyers on some Business relating to an Estate in Debate between him, and a near Relation. So she disguised herself, and went to the Tavern, resolving to be a Witness how her Plot succeeded. Having placed herself in a convenient Room, she saw Mr. *C——* come in, and soon after him the deceiving, but now deceived *Syrena*. What would she have given for the gratification of her *Curiosity* in hearing what passed between them, but that was impossible, and she was obliged to content herself with that of her Revenge which she soon saw compleated to her Wish.

The Reader however, must not be left in Ignorance; when *Syrena* first came into the Room, and found a strange Gentleman instead of him she expected; she guess'd the Drawer who shew'd her up, had made some Mistake, and was turning to go out of again, but Mr. *C——* taking it as Modesty or Affectation prevented her, by saying, Sure Madam you do not already repent of your Goodness, and would leave me before I tell you how happy I think myself in meeting you here. Sir, answered she, I ask'd for Number I, being to see a Friend here by that Token, but perhaps it may so have happened, that there may be two who left that Direction at the Bar——I know not that, Madam, replyed he, but I was made to hope, I should here meet with a Lady young, beautiful, but one altogether a Stranger to me; so whether you are the Person who design'd me that Favour or not, I am certain you have all the Marks, and must at least detain you till another more agreeable than yourself (which is altogether impossible) shall come and relieve you.——*Syrena* was at a Loss what to make of this Adventure, she could have like'd well enough to stay with him, but she feared some Trick in the Case: She was apprehensive that Mr. *E——* had form'd this Contrivance to make tryal of her Constancy, and might be in the next Room a Witness of her Behaviour; so with all the Appearance of a virtuous Indignation, she told Mr. *C——* who had fast hold of her Hand, that she was surprized

---

1 A justice of peace was an inferior magistrate appointed to preserve the peace in a county, town, or other district, and discharge other local magisterial functions.
2 An officer of the peace.

at the Accident which had brought two Persons together, in such a Place, who were entire Strangers to each other—that she came there to meet a near Relation and Friend on Business, which since she was disappointed in, begged he would not pretend to enforce her Stay, nor imagine she was a Woman who would submit to any thing, that the most strict Modesty would not allow of.

She spoke this with so serious and resolute an Air, that Mr. *C*—— began indeed to fear this was not the Person from whose Kindness he had so much to expect——to convince himself he took the Letter had been sent him out of his Pocket, and shew'd it to her, which made her more than before imagine that there was something in Agitation against her——she assured him, as indeed she well might, that she knew nothing of the sending it—had never seen him before to her Knowledge; or if I had, continued she, blushing, have a Heart already too much taken up to entertain the Thoughts of any other, tho' ever so deserving. As she still was possess'd of the Opinion, that this Gentleman was a Friend of Mr. *E*——, and would report to him every thing she said, she spoke this the more to ingratiate herself with him, when he should be told it; but the Amazement Mr. *C*—— was in, and the Vexation he express'd to find he had been impos'd upon, a little stagger'd her former Conjecture—I wish, Sir, said she, there is not some Treachery put in Practice against us both; but for what End, or from what Quarter, I cannot guess.—But, added she, the surest way to disappoint it, is immediately to separate—therefore, I beg Sir, you'll not offer to detain me longer. With these Words she endeavoured to draw back her Hand; but he, whose Desires had been raised by the Expectation of a different Entertainment, and were now quite enflamed by so pleasing an Object, could not tell how to let her go so easily; and instead of quitting his hold, threw his other Arm about her Neck, and in that defenceless Posture almost smother'd her with Kisses.——She was no less susceptible than himself of the strenuous Embrace; and beginning now to believe, that if there was a Plot, he at least had no Hand in it, made but faint Efforts to oblige him to desist what was equally pleasing to her as to himself, till quite overcome with the dangerous Temptation, he found her Lips not only yield, but return Kiss for Kiss——the amorous Pair thus equally dissolved, had not stopp'd here, but were proceeding to much greater Liberties, when Mrs. *C*—— rush'd into the Room more like a Fury than a Woman—she flew upon *Syrena*, call'd her all the Names that jealous Rage could suggest; then turning to her Husband, ungrateful Monster, cry'd she! Is this the Reward of all my Love and Virtue?—— was it for this I slighted so many noble Matches, and brought you such a Fortune? he was beginning to protest his Innocence, but the very mention made her more outrageous.——O! horrid Impudence, said she, have I not caught you almost in the odious Act! dare you deny it.—But I forbear saying farther to you at present—your Strumpet here shall curse the Hour she ever tempted you to wrong my Bed——as she spoke these Words she stamp'd with her Foot, and immediately came up the Constable, and other Persons she had placed in a Room under that where they were——do your Office, Man, cry'd she, and carry that filthy Creature, where your Warrant directs. Mr. C—— begg'd she would not expose herself and him; and *Syrena* frighted almost to Death, fell on her Knees, and entreated her Mercy and Forgiveness—but all Attempts to quell her Fury, were like fencing the Sea with a Battledor,[1] when it was Mountains high—the more they humbled themselves, the more insolent and impetuous she became; and Mrs. E——, who in her Disguise was now mingled with the crowd of Servants, Porters, and others, whom the Noise drew together, had the Satisfaction to see her hated Rival in Mr. E——'s Affections, dragg'd away like the lowest and most common Prostitute, that plies the Streets for the poor Pittance of a Half-Crown[2] Fare; a Fate, indeed, she long since had deserv'd, tho' fallen on her when she gave the least Occasion.

How Mr. C—— and his Spouse made up this Quarrel between themselves, is not to our present Purpose; but Mrs. E—— who knew not but *Syrena* might have the Confidence to send to her Husband, even from the Place she now was in, in hopes of being set at Liberty; did not here give over. She had by Bribes and incessant Application, made herself thoroughly acquainted with every Circumstance of *Syrena*'s Family and Circumstances; she knew she had pretty near Kindred in the City, who were Men of Worth and Character, and very rich: To one of these she went, and having made an Apology for coming on a Business, which she knew could not but be shocking, told him that *Syrena*, was at that time a Prisoner in the House of Correction:[3] The Lady whose Resentment confines her there, said she, is my particular Friend; but having suf-

---

1   The paddle of a canoe.

2   A coin (latterly silver) of Great Britain, of the value of two shillings and sixpence; sometimes used for the equivalent sum, which is regularly expressed by half-a-crown. More significantly, it suggests the lower levels of sexual labor to which Syrena is potentially headed.

3   A building for the confinement and punishment of offenders, especially with a view to their reformation through work (typically beating hemp). Hogarth's illustration of Bridewell Prison in Plate 4 of *The Harlot's Progress* (1731-32) provides a good visual example.

fer'd a great deal from her Husband's Intimacy with loose Women, all I can say in Favour of your unhappy Cousin, will not prevail on her to give her a Release; unless she could be certain of her being removed too far from *London*, for her Husband to continue any Correspondence with her.——Now, Sir, added she, tho' she alone is guilty, her Brother's unfortunate in being so, will share in her Disgrace——they are young, and might be eminent Men in time; but what sober Person will match his Daughter, where so near a Relative as a Sister is, every Day, nay every Hour, guilty of Actions, which render her a Shame, not only to her Family, but her whole Sex?—besides, Sir, if she continues in the wretched Place she now is, the horrid Society she in time will there become acquainted with, may excite her to Crimes worthy of her second Removal to *Newgate*,[1]—in fine, there is no knowing to what Lengths, Crimes will extend in a Person of abandon'd Morals; so that for the sake of her Family, I could wish she were dispos'd of, so as not to bring herself to farther Infamy, nor her Friends to trouble by the hearing it.

The Person to whom this Speech was address'd, seem'd infinitely shock'd, tho' by some things he had heard of his Kinswoman's Behaviour, he had dreaded to receive some such Intelligence for a long time. He thank'd Mrs. *E——* however, with the utmost Civility, and told her he would consult with some others of the Family; and she might depend upon it, order the Affair, so that the Lady her Friend, should receive no farther Injury from his abandoned Relative.

This worthy Citizen, in effect, summon'd all who were unhappy enough to be nearly ally'd to the wicked *Syrena*, and having made them a brief Recital of what Crimes had come to his Knowledge, committed by her, and the shameful Situation she now was in, they all agreed, that to avoid hearing any thing farther of her Viciousness, it was best to send her to some remote Place, where she should be strictly confined, till time, and a just Sensibility of her Infamy, should bring her to an Abhorrence of her past Life. One of them having a handsome Estate in the farther part of *Wales*,[2] proposed sending her

---

1 Newgate was the most famous London prison and the stock destination for criminals. For example, Act Three of John Gay's *The Beggar's Opera* takes place at Newgate, where the rakish hero Macheath is incarcerated.

2 Wales, which has been referred to as a "dark corner of the land," would have been an extremely unpleasant place to be sent. Communities were small, isolated, and reluctant to change; the language was different; life was harsh, class difference pronounced, transportation bad, and the bulk of the population was the laboring classes. Eighteenth-century Wales would have offered no opportunities for a woman like Syrena and would have deprived her of all kinds of "conversation"—social, sexual or verbal.

to a Tenant he had there; to which the others readily comply'd and each promis'd to contribute somewhat towards her keeping there.

This being agreed upon, the Person to whom Mrs. E—— had spoke, having the Directions, waited on her, and begg'd she would now perform her Promise in exerting her whole Interest with Mrs. C——, for the Discharge of *Syrena*; and he would engage in return, that the unhappy Girl should never wrong her more. Mrs. E—— assured him, she would undertake the Office.——She did so, and Mrs. C—— was easily enough prevail'd upon, on the Conditions her Friend mentioned.

All that remain'd now was to let *Syrena* know what had been done for her, who, glad to submit to any thing that would deliver her from the Place she was in, made a thousand Vows never to return to *London* any more.

Thus was *Syrena* taken from the first Captivity[1] she had ever been in; but when she consider'd, she was going to a second, which, tho' less shameful, would in all Probability deprive her entirely from all Conversation with Mankind, she was almost inconsolable——Fatal Necessity, however, must be obey'd, and she was sent under the Conduct of an old Servant of one of her Kinsmen to *Wales*, where what befel her, must be the Subject of future Entertainment.

F I N I S.

---

1 Again, Haywood is ironically appropriating the language Richardson uses in *Pamela*. Once Pamela is taken to Lincolnshire estate and switches from letters to her journal, she records the time there as her time in "captivity."

AN
APOLOGY
FOR THE
LIFE
OF
Mrs. SHAMELA ANDREWS.
In which, the many notorious FALSHOODS and
MISREPRSENTATIONS[1] of a Book called
PAMELA,
Are exposed and refuted; and all the matchless ARTS of that
young Politician, set in a true and just Light.

Together with
A full Account of all that passed between her and Parson *Arthur
Williams*; whose Character is represented in a manner something different from that which he bears in *PAMELA*. The
whole being exact Copies of authentick Papers delivered to
the Editor.

Necessary to be had in all FAMILIES.

By Mr. *CONNY KEYBER*.[2]

LONDON:

Printed for A. DODD,[3] at the *Peacock*, without *Temple-bar*.
M. DCC. XLI.

---

1 These typographical errors appear, uncorrected, in the second edition.
2 The title, like certain elements of the book, parody Colley Cibber's autobiography, *An Apology for the Life of Colley Cibber*, published in 1740. The
   created name on the title page, like most of the puns in the text, works on
   many levels. First, "Conny," a corruption of Colley, suggests both the term
   "cony" or "coney," a simpleton, and "cunny," a slang term for pudendum
   (Partridge). The name Keyber similarly functions as a corruption of Cibber. Additionally, "Conny" sounds similar to the first name of Conyers
   Middleton, whose dedication to *The Life of Cicero* Fielding also parodies.
3 This colophon refers to Anne Dodd Jr., the daughter of Anne Dodd who
   was a leading distributor of pamphlets and newspapers in Westminster.
   While both women were associated with the sale of scurrilous materials
   (such as those published by Edmund Curll), it is increasingly clear that
   they were important in disseminating opposition papers such as the *Crafts-
   man* and the Jacobite *Mist's Weekly Journal*. The appearance of her name
   serves Fielding's purpose in at least two ways: it aligns this parody—and
   thus *Pamela* itself—with the ephemeral texts of lower prestige; it also sig-
   nals the opposition to Walpole implicit, and at times explicit, in this satire.

To Miss *Fanny*, &c.[1]

MADAM,

IT will be naturally expected, that when I write the Life of *Shamela*, I should dedicate it to some young Lady, whose Wit and Beauty might be the proper Subject of a Comparison with the Heroine of my Piece. This, those, who see I have done it in prefixing your Name to my Work, will much more confirmedly expect me to do; and, indeed, your Character would enable me to run some Length into a Parallel, tho' you, nor any one else, are at all alike the matchless *Shamela*.[2]

You see, Madam, I have some Value for your Good-nature, when in a Dedication, which is properly a Panegyrick, I speak against, not for you; but I remember it is a Life which I am presenting you, and why should I expose my Veracity to any Hazard in the Front of the Work, considering what I have done in the Body. Indeed, I wish it was possible to write a Dedication, and get any thing by it, without one Word of Flattery; but since it is not, come on, and I hope to shew my Delicacy at least in the Compliments I intend to pay you.

First, then, Madam, I must tell the World, that you have tickled up and brightned many Strokes in this Work by your Pencil.

---

1 "Fanny" was the sobriquet commonly applied to John, Lord Hervey, Baron Ickworth (1696-1743) to whom Conyers Middleton dedicated *The Life of Cicero* (1741). A successful courtier, a supporter of Walpole and an infamous bi-sexual, Hervey was also the subject of Pope's satire, most notably the portrait of Sporus in *Epistle to Dr. Arbuthnot* (cf. lines 305-333). Like Pope, Fielding viewed Hervey as emblematic of the debasement of political culture, morality, and taste. "Fanny," a diminutive of Frances, was also slang for the female pudendum and is one in a continuing series of complex and intricate allusions and puns that Fielding uses throughout the text. And, as Hawley observes, "Fielding's '&c.' underlines the sexual suggestion (cf. Tickletext's 'a poor Girl's little, &c,' below), while also mocking the formality of Middleton's address: "To the Right Honourable John Lord Hervey, Lord Keeper of His Majesty's Privy Seal." Fielding mocks the dedication, which appears in Appendix C.3, in almost every paragraph.

2 Middleton writes, "The public will naturally expect, that in chusing a Patron for *the Life of* CICERO, I should address myself to some person of illustrious rank, distinguished by his parts and eloquence, and bearing a principal share in the great affairs of the Nation; who, according to the usual stile of Dedications, might be the proper subject of a comparison with the Hero of my piece."

Secondly, You have intimately conversed[1] with me, one of the greatest Wits and Scholars of my Age.

Thirdly, You keep very good Hours, and frequently spend an useful Day before others begin to enjoy it. This I will take my Oath on; for I am admitted to your Presence in a Morning before other People's Servants are up;[2] when I have constantly found you reading in good Books; and if ever I have drawn you upon me, I have always felt you very heavy.

Fourthly, You have a Virtue which enables you to rise early and study hard, and that is, forbearing to over-eat yourself, and this in spite of all the luscious Temptations of Puddings and Custards, exciting the Brute (as Dr. *Woodward*[3] calls it) to rebel. This is a Virtue which I can greatly admire, though I much question whether I could imitate it.

Fifthly, A Circumstance greatly to your Honour, that by means of your extraordinary Merit and Beauty; you was carried into the Ball-Room at the *Bath*, by the discerning Mr. *Nash*;[4] before the Age that other young Ladies generally arrived at that Honour, and while your Mamma herself existed in her perfect Bloom. Here you was observed in Dancing to balance your Body exactly, and to weigh every Motion with the exact and equal Measure of Time and Tune; and though you sometimes made a false Step, by leaning too much to one Side;[5] yet

---

1 To have sexual intercourse. Each of the points uses sexual, at times masturbatory, imagery to suggest the inappropriate reaction to the text.

2 Middleton writes, "in those early hours, when all around You are hushed in sleep, seize the opportunity of that quiet, as the most favourable season of study, and frequently spend an usefull day, before others begin to enjoy it."

3 Dr. John Woodward (1665-1728) wrote an oft-ridiculed treatise, *The State of Physic and of Diseases, with an Inquiry into the Causes of the late Increase of Them* (1718), in which he traced "all the evils of civilization—sickness, stupidity, poverty, faction, rebelliousness, atheism—to one cause: the rich pastries and seasoned meats and sauces of 'the New Cookery' (See *State of Physic*, Section 47)" (Battestin). Fielding is also mocking Middleton, who (with an implicit reference to Woodward) praises Hervey for his "singular temperance in diet ... superior to every temptation, that can excite an appetite to rebel."

4 Richard "Beau" Nash (1674-1762) was appointed the master of ceremonies in the resort town of Bath in 1704 and in that capacity he had a profound effect on fashion and on social interactions.

5 An allusion to Hervey's politics. Fielding substitutes dancing for politics, while suggesting that Hervey votes too often in favor of Walpole. By contrast, Middleton claims Hervey was successful "in maintaining the rights of the people, yet asserting the prerogative of the Crown; measuring them both by the equal balance of the laws."

every body said you would one Time or other, dance perfectly well, and uprightly.

Sixthly, I cannot forbear mentioning those pretty little Sonnets, and sprightly Compositions, which though they came from you with so much Ease, might be mentioned to the Praise of a great or grave Character.[1]

And now, Madam, I have done with you; it only remains to pay my Acknowledgments to an Author, whose Stile I have exactly followed in this Life, it being the properest for Biography. The Reader, I believe, easily guesses, I mean *Euclid's Elements*;[2] it was *Euclid* who taught me to write. It is you, Madam, who pay me for Writing.[3] Therefore I am to both,

A most Obedient, and
obliged humble Servant,

CONNY KEYBER.

LETTERS
TO THE
EDITOR.

The EDITOR to *HIMSELF*.[4]

Dear SIR,

HOWEVER you came by the excellent *Shamela*, out with it, without

---

1 Middleton praises Hervey for "the sprightly compositions of various kinds, with which Your Lordship has often entertained."

2 Euclid wrote the *Elements*, a thirteen-book treatise in which he compiled and systematically arranged many of the major mathematical results known in his day. Beginning with a list of definitions, postulates, and axioms, he proved one proposition after another, basing each proof only on those results that had preceded it. This axiomatic method—basing each proof only on those results that had preceded it—is the essence of biography to which "Keyber" refers. The reference to Euclid also underscores a frequent complaint about *Pamela*—that she never changed, that assumptions about her subsequent action were made exclusively on her previous action. Additionally, as Goldberg observes (274-5), Fielding was also alluding to the lack of clarity in Euclid's prose.

3 Middleton writes, "it was Cicero who instructed me to write; Your Lordship, who rewards me for Writing."

4 The first edition of *Pamela* contained a series of "puffs," inflated praise or commendation, written to influence public estimation. Fielding insinuates Richardson wrote them; Reverend William Webster is also thought to be the author. The second edition, published 14 February 1741, contained an introduction that drew on letters Aaron Hill sent to Richardson. Richardson was widely criticized for these self-congratulatory pieces that Fielding parodies so effectively.

Fear or Favour, Dedication and all; believe me, it will go through many Editions, be translated into all Languages, read in all Nations and Ages, and to say a bold Word, it will do more good than the C——y have done harm in the World.[1]

I am, Sir,
Sincerely your Well-wisher,
YOURSELF.

JOHN PUFF, *Esq; to the* EDITOR.

SIR,

I HAVE read your *Shamela* through and through, and a most inimitable Performance it is. Who is he, what is he that could write so excellent a Book? he must be doubtless most agreeable to the Age, and to *his Honour* himself; for he is able to draw every thing to Perfection but Virtue. Whoever the Author be, he hath one of the worst and most fashionable Hearts in the World, and I would recommend to him, in his next Performance, to undertake the Life of *his Honour.* For he who drew the Character of Parson *Williams,* is equal to the Task; nay he seems to have little more to do than to pull off the Parson's Gown, and *that* which makes him so agreeable to *Shamela,* and the Cap will fit.

I am, Sir,
Your humble Servant,
JOHN PUFF.

Note, Reader, several other COMMENDATORY LETTERS and COPIES of VERSES will be prepared against the NEXT EDITION.[2]

---

1 C——y is "clergy." Allegedly Pope observed that *Pamela* "will do more good than many volumes of sermons," a remark conveyed to Richardson by James Leake and circulated subsequently in the coffee houses (James Leake to Richardson, February 1741, quoted in McKillop, *Samuel Richardson,* 50). In another February 1741 letter to Richardson, George Cheyne similarly reported that Pope "read *Pamela* with great Approbation and Pleasure. . .and says it will do more good than a great many of the new Sermons" (Cheyne quoted in McKillop, 50).

2 A reference to Richardson's inclusion of the additional letters and puffs in the second edition published 14 February 1741. Three more editions were published within the year (third edition in March, fourth edition in May, and fifth edition in September), with a sixth octavo edition published in 1742.

AN
APOLOGY
For the LIFE of
Mrs. SHAMELA ANDREWS.[1]

Parson TICKLETEXT *to Parson* OLIVER.[2]

Rev. SIR,

HEREWITH I transmit you a Copy of sweet, dear, pretty *Pamela*, a little Book which this Winter hath produced; of which, I make no
Doubt, you have already heard mention from some of your Neighbouring Clergy; for we have made it our common Business here, not
only to cry it up, but to preach it up likewise: The Pulpit, as well as
the Coffee-house,[3] hath resounded with its Praise, and it is expect-

---

1   The title is a parody of Colley Cibber's autobiography, *An Apology for the
    Life of Colley Cibber* (1740). For an excerpt from *An Apology*, see Appen-
    dix C.4. The substitution of the name "Shamela" for Pamela, like the
    substitution of "vartue" for virtue, goes to the heart of Fielding's satiric
    enterprise. A "sham" is any kind of trick or fraud; something devised to
    impose upon, delude, or disappoint expectation (*OED*). The counterfeit
    nature of "sham," and the reasons for shamming, often places it in a
    commercial context (which is, of course, appropriate here). Pamela her-
    self uses the word "sham": "Perchance, some Sham-marriage may be
    design'd, on purpose to ruin me:" (179) (cf. also 228, 241, et. al.).

2   These names, like most of the allusions in this satire, have multiple layers
    of meaning. Grose and Partridge both note that tickle-text is a (rather
    obscure) term for a parson, but Fielding seems to also be probing the
    multiple meanings of tickle. To tickle is to "puzzle" or decipher a text,
    but it also suggests a kind of excitement or pleasant stimulation (*OED*).
    If one is easily tickled, one is easily moved to feeling, easily affected, or
    not firm or steadfast. Those possibilities suggest both the quasi-masturba-
    tory way Tickletext reads *Pamela* and the credulity with which he
    engages the text. Oliver is a common surname and was, in fact, the sur-
    name of Fielding's childhood Latin teacher. As discussed in the Introduc-
    tion, this sequence of letters parodies the numerous commendations
    Pamela received from the clergy that appeared in revised editions of the
    text.

3   The pervasive popularity and the secular and religious communities'
    endorsement of *Pamela* (with obvious commercial benefits for Richard-
    son and those who joined the *Pamela*-frenzy) were central to Fielding's
    satire.

ed shortly, that his L——p will recommend it in a —— Letter to our whole Body. [1]

And this Example, I am confident, will be imitated by all our Cloth in the Country: For besides speaking well of a Brother, in the Character of the Reverend Mr. *Williams*, the useful and truly religious Doctrine of *Grace* is every where inculcated. [2]

This Book is the "SOUL of *Religion*, Good-Breeding, Discretion, Good-Nature, Wit, Fancy, Fine Thought, and Morality. There is an Ease, a natural Air, a dignified Simplicity, and MEASURED FULLNESS in it, that RESEMBLING LIFE, OUT-GLOWS IT. The Author hath reconciled the *pleasing* to the *proper;* the Thought is every where exactly cloathed by the Expression; and becomes its Dress as *roundly* and as close as *Pamela* her Country Habit; or *as she doth her no Habit,* when modest Beauty seeks to hide itself, by casting off the Pride of Ornament, and displays itself without any Covering;"[3] which it frequently doth in this admirable Work, and presents Images to the Reader, which the coldest Zealot cannot read without Emotion.

For my own Part (and, I believe, I may say the same of all the Clergy of my Acquaintance) "I have done nothing but read it to others, and hear others again read it to me, ever since it came into my

---

1   "His Lordship is Edmund Gibson (1669-1748), a pious and conscientious divine who, after his appointment as Bishop of London in 1723, wrote frequent 'pastoral' letters to the clergy of his diocese" (Battestin 368). Gibson was not alone in his endorsement. Dr. Benjamin Slocock had recommend *Pamela* to his congregation at St. Saviour's Southwark; in reaction, in January 1741 Aaron Hill wrote Richardson "I am charmed by ye brave Independence of Taste in this generous Doctor!"(quoted in McKillop 47).

2   "...Grace was a key term in the Evangelical or Methodist movement of the 1730s led by George Whitefield (1714-70) and Charles (1707-80) and John (1703-91) Wesley. The Calvinist Whitefield, even more than the Wesleys, maintained that God bestowed saving Grace on the Elect, or those who had faith in him, regardless of works (good deeds). Fielding asserted that this inward-looking doctrine sanctioned immorality; he repeatedly attacks Whitefield and dwells on the opposition between faith and works" (Hawley). Grace also appears repeatedly in *Pamela,* especially in Pamela's letters from her parents.

3   Here, and throughout these faux letters, Fielding is using, verbatim, parts of the letters and other prefatory material added to the second edition of *Pamela*. Fielding recontextualizes and selectively excerpts in order to highlight the absurdity of the puffs and heighten the innuendo implicit in Richardson's text (and laid bare in Fielding's).

Hands; and I find I am like to do nothing else, for I know not how long yet to come: because if I lay the Book down *it comes after me.* When it has dwelt all Day long upon the Ear, it takes Possession all Night of the Fancy. It hath Witchcraft in every Page of it."—Oh! I feel an Emotion even while I am relating this: Methinks I see *Pamela* at this Instant, with all the Pride of Ornament cast off.[1]

"Little Book, charming *Pamela*, get thee gone; face the World, in which thou wilt find nothing like thyself." Happy would it be for Mankind, if all other Books were burnt, that we might do nothing but read thee all Day, and dream of thee all Night. Thou alone art sufficient to teach us as much Morality as we want. Dost thou not teach us to pray, to sing Psalms, and to honour the Clergy? Are not these the whole Duty of Man?[2] Forgive me, O Author of *Pamela*, mentioning the Name of a Book so unequal to thine: But, now I think of it, who is the Author, where is he, what is he, that hath hitherto been able to hide such an encircling, all-mastering Spirit, "he possesses every Quality that Art could have charm'd by: yet hath lent it to and concealed it in Nature. The Comprehensiveness of his Imagination must be truly prodigious! It has stretched out this diminutive mere Grain of Mustard-seed (a poor Girl's little, *&c.*) into a Resemblance of that Heaven, which the best of good Books has compared it to."[3]

To be short, this Book will live to the Age of the Patriarchs, and like them will carry on the good Work many hundreds of Years hence, among our Posterity, who will not HESITATE their Esteem

---

1 While Fielding is indicating Tickletext's prurient interest (and his ability to envisage Pamela naked "with all the Pride of Ornament cast off"), Fielding is again paraphrasing Richardson's own words from the preface to the second edition: "When modest Beauty seeks to hide itself by casting off the *Pride of Ornament*, it but displays itself without a Covering." The attitudes expressed in this letter capture Fielding's worst fear regarding the cultural willingness to abandon appropriate conduct books and embrace the questionable moralizing of *Pamela*.

2 Richard Allestree (1619-1681), *The Whole Duty of Man*. The following line alludes to the common attitude that *Pamela*, as a conduct book, had the force of Richard Allestree's text, *The Whole Duty of Man*. For representative excerpts, see Appendix D.1.

3 This section is quoted exactly from the second edition of *Pamela* except for the substitution of "(a poor Girl's little, *&c.*)" for "(a poor Girl's little, innocent Story)." Here, and throughout *Shamela*, "Etc." in its many forms (&c, Et caetera) alludes to a slang term for female genitalia making a bawdy parenthetical that suggests the male readers' real interests.

with Restraint. If the *Romans* granted Exemptions to Men who begat a *few* Children for the Republick, what Distinction (if Policy and we should ever be reconciled) should we find to reward this Father of Millions, which are to owe Formation to the future Effect of his Influence.—I feel another Emotion.

As soon as you have read this yourself five or six Times over (which may possibly happen within a Week) I desire you would give it to my little God-Daughter, as a Present from me. This being the only Education we intend henceforth to give our Daughters. And pray let your Servant-Maids read it over, or read it to them.[1] Both your self and the neighbouring Clergy, will supply yourselves for the Pulpit from the Booksellers, as soon as the fourth Edition is published. I am,

> *Sir,*
> *Your most humble Servant,*
> THO. TICKLETEXT.

Parson OLIVER *to Parson* TICKLETEXT.

Rev. SIR,

I Received the Favour of yours with the inclosed Book, and really must own myself sorry, to see the Report I have heard of an epidemical Phrenzy now raging in Town, confirmed in the Person of my Friend.

If I had not known your Hand, I should, from the Sentiments and Stile of the Letter, have imagined it to have come from the Author of the famous Apology, which was sent me last Summer; and on my reading the remarkable Paragraph of *measured Fulness, that resembling Life out-glows it,* to a young Baronet, he cry'd out, C——ly C—b—r by G— .[2] But I have since observed, that this, as well as many other Expressions in your Letter, was borrowed from those remarkable Epistles, which the Author, or the Editor hath prefix'd to the second Edition which you send me of his Book.

Is it possible that you or any of your Function can be in earnest, or think the Cause of Religion, or Morality, can want such slender Sup-

---

1 Fielding is both alluding to the pervasive popularity of Richardson's text and to its particular (and to his mind, inappropriate) appeal to female domestics who had marginal literacy rates. Similarly, the earlier claim to be able to read the novel five or six times in a week aligns it with amatory fiction which was ephemeral, briefer, and more easily consumed.

2 "Colley Cibber by God."

port? God forbid they should. As for Honour to the Clergy, I am sorry to see them so solicitous about it; for if worldly Honour be meant, it is what their Predecessors in the pure and primitive Age, never had or sought. Indeed the secure Satisfaction of a good Conscience, the Approbation of the Wise and Good, (which never were or will be the Generality of Mankind) and the extatick Pleasure of contemplating, that their Ways are acceptable to the Great Creator of the Universe, will always attend those, who really deserve these Blessings: But for worldly Honours, they are often the Purchase of Force and Fraud, we sometimes see them in an eminent Degree possessed by Men, who are notorious for Luxury, Pride, Cruelty, Treachery, and the most abandoned Prostitution; Wretches who are ready to invent and maintain Schemes repugnant to the Interest, the Liberty, and the Happiness of Mankind, not to supply their Necessities, or even Conveniencies, but to pamper their Avarice and Ambition. And if this be the Road to worldly Honours, God forbid the Clergy should be even suspected of walking in it.

The History of *Pamela* I was acquainted with long before I received it from you, from my Neighbourhood to the Scene of Action. Indeed I was in hopes that young Woman would have contented herself with the Good-fortune she hath attained; and rather suffered her little Arts to have been forgotten than have revived their Remembrance, and endeavoured by perverting and misrepresenting Facts to be thought to deserve what she now enjoys: for though we do not imagine her the Author of the Narrative itself, yet we must suppose the Instructions were given by her, as well as the Reward, to the Composer. Who that is, though you so earnestly require of me, I shall leave you to guess from that *Ciceronian* Eloquence, with which the Work abounds; and that excellent Knack of making every Character amiable, which he lays his hands on.[1]

But before I send you some Papers relating to this Matter, which will set *Pamela* and some others in a very different Light, than that in which they appear in the printed Book, I must beg leave to make some few Remarks on the Book itself, and its Tendency, (admitting it to be a true Relation,) towards improving Morality, or doing any good, either to the present Age, or Posterity: which when I have done, I shall, I flatter myself, stand excused from delivering it, either into the hands of my Daughter, or my Servant-Maid.

The Instruction which it conveys to Servant-Maids, is, I think, very plainly this, To look out for their Masters as sharp as they can. The

---

1 Another allusion to Middleton's dedication to Hervey.

Consequences of which will be, besides Neglect of their Business, and the using all manner of Means to come at Ornaments of their Persons, that if the Master is not a Fool, they will be debauched by him; and if he is a Fool, they will marry him. Neither of which, I apprehend, my good Friend, we desire should be the Case of our Sons.

And notwithstanding our Author's Professions of Modesty, which in my Youth I have heard at the Beginning of an Epilogue, I cannot agree that my Daughter should entertain herself with some of his Pictures; which I do not expect to be contemplated without Emotion, unless by one of my Age and Temper, who can see the Girl lie on her Back, with one Arm round Mrs. *Jewkes* and the other round the Squire, naked in Bed, with his Hand on her Breasts, *&c.* with as much Indifference as I read any other Page in the whole Novel.[1] But surely this, and some other Descriptions, will not be put into the hands of his Daughter by any wise Man, though I believe it will be difficult for him to keep them from her; especially if the Clergy in Town have cried and preached it up as you say.

But, my Friend, the whole Narrative is such a Misrepresentation of Facts, such a Perversion of Truth, as you will, I am perswaded, agree, as soon as you have perused the Papers I now inclose to you, that I hope you or some other well-disposed Person, will communicate these Papers to the Publick, that this little Jade may not impose on the World, as she hath on her Master.

The true name of this Wench was SHAMELA, and not *Pamela*, as she stiles herself. Her Father had in his Youth the Misfortune to appear in no good Light at the *Old-Bailey*;[2] he afterwards served in the Capacity of a Drummer in one of the *Scotch* Regiments in the *Dutch* Service;[3]

---

1 This passage, with its use of the obscene allusion &c., contains detail that also suggests that even a man of Oliver's "age and temper" can't contemplate *Pamela* "without emotion." The attempted rape in *Pamela* appears in Appendix B.1.

2 The Old Bailey is England's most important crown court and became known as the Central Criminal Court. To identify Shamela's father as someone who was tried at the Old Bailey is to identify him as a thief.

3 "In 1665, when war broke out between England and the Netherlands, the Dutch Republic compelled the British regiments that had been serving them to swear allegiance to Holland against their native land, or be cashiered. The English refused, but the Scotch complied and remained in the Dutch service for a century. The allusion here thus, in effect, makes Shamela's father a traitor to his country" (Battestin 369). Note too that he is a "drummer," not an actual soldier making him a traitor, a mercenary and, possibly, a coward.

where being drummed out, he came over to *England*, and turned Informer against several Persons on the late Gin-Act;[1] and becoming acquainted with an Hostler at an Inn, where a *Scotch* Gentleman's Horses stood, he hath at last by his Interest obtain'd a pretty snug Place in the *Custom-house*.[2] Her Mother sold Oranges in the Play-House;[3] and whether she was married to her Father or no, I never could learn.

After this short Introduction, the rest of her History will appear in the following Letters, which I assure you are authentick.

---

1 Parliament passed Gin Acts in 1733, 1736, 1737, and 1738. All relied on informers for enforcement. The Acts of 1736, 1737, and 1738 provided sufficient financial incentive to recruit professional informers. As Warner and Ivis detail, "In the case of the Gin Acts of 1733, 1736, 1737, and 1738, informers received £5 for each conviction. This was, by contemporary standards, a small fortune, exceeding the annual wages of many female domestics in the capital" (303). Parliament enacted two supplemental Gin Acts, in June 1737, and in June 1738. "The two Acts specifically targeted 'persons of little or no substance,' toward which end they authorized the commissioners of Excise to pay informers £5 when convicted retailers refused to do so themselves. . . . The Gin Act of 1738 also made it a felony to attack an informer, the punishment for which was seven years' transportation to the colonies in America." Jessica Warner and Frank Ivis, "'Damn You, You Informing Bitch.' *Vox Populi* and the Unmaking of the Gin Act of 1736," *Journal of Social History* 33.2 (1999): 306.

2 The Custom-house, the site of the customs office, offered many opportunities for bribery and other profitable, albeit illegal, activity.

3 The orange-girls were a fixture in the Restoration and eighteenth-century playhouse. They sold oranges at concessions in the pit of the theatre, occupying a marginal position that equated them with prostitutes, which they often were. Indeed, during the Restoration, "orange" became slang for the female pudendum.

LETTER I.

Shamela Andrews *to Mrs.* Henrietta Maria Honora
Andrews *at her Lodgings at the* Fan *and* Pepper-Box *in*
Drury-Lane.[1]

Dear Mamma,

This comes to acquaint you, that I shall set out in the Waggon on
Monday, desiring you to commodate me with a Ludgin, as near you
as possible, in *Coulstin's-Court,* or *Wild-Street,* or somewhere there-
abouts; pray let it be handsome, and not above two Stories high:[2]
For Parson *Williams* hath promised to visit me when he comes to
Town, and I have got a good many fine Cloaths of the Old Put[3]
my Mistress's, who died a wil ago; and I beleve Mrs. *Jervis* will
come along with me, for she says she would like to keep a House
somewhere about *Short's-Gardens,* or towards *Queen-Street;* and if
there was convenience for a *Bannio,* she should like it the better;
but that she will settle herself when she comes to Town.[4]—O! *How*

---

1   Although Mrs. Andrews shares her name with Charles I's wife, Queen
    Henrietta Maria of France (1609-69), she shares an address with the
    prostitutes that haunted London's subculture. Drury Lane, like Covent
    Garden, was a notorious location for prostitutes, and everything about
    the address builds on that idea. "Box" was slang for a small drinking
    place, or a compartment partitioned off in the public room of a coffee-
    house or tavern. "To pepper" is to infect with venereal disease. "Pepper-
    box" is a phrase contemptuously applied to a small turret or cupola, per-
    haps alluding to the size of Mrs. Andrews's dwelling. To "fan" is slang for
    either "to beat" or "to feel, handle" (Partridge)—either one suggesting
    the kinds of services a prostitute could provide. Additionally "fan" sug-
    gests "fanny," discussed above, as well a fan a woman would use as an
    object of adornment and an instrument of flirtation.
2   Anticipating her return to London, Shamela (in her broken spelling)
    reveals a plan to find lodgings ("Ludgin") in the area of Drury Lane.
    "Coulstin's Court" is likely Colson's Court, which runs between Drury
    Lane and Great Wild Street; "Wild Street" *per se,* did not exist, but Great
    Wild Street, Little Wild Street, and Wild Court were all near Drury Lane.
    Her desire for a room no more than two stories high is, of course, to
    facilitate visits from Parson Williams.
3   Fool.
4   Mrs. Jervis, who will become a procuress ("keep a house") when she
    arrives in London, will also reside in Drury Lane. "Short's Gardens" and
    "Queen Street" (known as Great Queen Street) both intersect Drury
    Lane and share the same milieu. In distinguishing between a "house" of
    prostitution and a "bannio" or bagnio, Mrs, Jervis is tapping into the

I long to be in the Balconey at the Old House[1]—so no more at present from

> *Your affectionate Daughter,*
> SHAMELA.

LETTER II.

SHAMELA ANDREWS *to* HENRIETTA MARIA HONORA ANDREWS.

Dear Mamma,

O WHAT News, since I writ my last! the young Squire hath been here, and as sure as a Gun he hath taken a Fancy to me; *Pamela*, says he, (for so I am called here) you was a great Favourite of your late Mistress's; yes, an't please your Honour, says I; and I believe you deserved it, says he; thank your Honour for your good Opinion, says I; and then he took me by the Hand, and I pretended to be shy: Laud, says I, Sir, I hope you don't intend to be rude; no, says he, my Dear, and then he kissed me, 'till he took away my Breath—and I pretended to be Angry, and to get away, and then he kissed me again, and breathed very short, and looked very silly; and by Ill-Luck Mrs. *Jervis* came in, and had like to have spoiled Sport.—*How troublesome is such Interruption!* You shall hear now soon, for I shall not come away yet, so I rest,

> *Your affectionate Daughter,*
> SHAMELA.

LETTER III.

HENRIETTA MARIA HONORA ANDREWS *to* SHAMELA ANDREWS.

Dear Sham,

YOUR last Letter hath put me into a great hurry of Spirits, for you

---

hierarchy of eighteenth-century prostitution. While a bagnio is, essentially, a house of prostitution, the name also refers to a kind of bathing house, especially one with hot baths, vapor-baths, and appliances for sweating, cupping, and other operations (*OED*). These were often run with great propriety, with separate entrances for men and women. In *Pamela*, B. taunts Pamela with the profits she could make from "Members of Parliament" if she were in a "house" in London (see p. 286). Additionally, in *Shamela*, Mrs. Jervis repeatedly alludes to keeping a house of prostitution in London (e.g., pp. 248, 249).

1 The "Old House" refers to the Theatre Royal, Drury Lane (presumably where her mother was an orange girl).

have a very difficult Part to act.[1] I hope you will remember your Slip with Parson *Williams*, and not be guilty of any more such Folly. Truly, a Girl who hath once known what is what, is in the highest Degree inexcusable if she respects her *Digressions*;[2] but a Hint of this is sufficient. When Mrs. *Jervis* thinks of coming to Town, I believe I can procure her a good House, and fit for the Business; so I am,

Your affectionate Mother,
HENRIETTA MARIA HONORA ANDREWS.

LETTER IV.

SHAMELA ANDREWS *to* HENRIETTA MARIA HONORA ANDREWS.

MARRY come up, good Madam, the Mother had never looked into the Oven for her Daughter, if she had not been there herself. I shall never have done if you upbraid me with having had a small One by *Arthur Williams*, when you yourself—but I say no more. *O! What fine Times when the Kettle calls the Pot.* Let me do what I will, I say my Prayers as often as another, and I read in good Books, as often as I have Leisure; and Parson *William* says, that will make amends.—So no more, but I rest

Your afflicted Daughter,
S——.

LETTER V.

HENRIETTA MARIA HONORA ANDREWS to SHAMELA ANDREWS.

Dear Child,

WHY will you give such way to your Passion? How could you imagine I should be such a Simpleton, as to upbraid thee with being thy Mother's own Daughter! When I advised you not to be guilty of Folly, I meant no more than that you should take care to be well paid

---

1   Thomas Lockwood suggests that Shamela is decidedly and self-consciously theatrical in her self-representation and fashions herself as "acting" the part of "Pamela." Mrs. Jervis later claims she "never saw any thing better acted than your part." Lockwood attributes this language, which appears consistently in the text, to Fielding's own theatrical experience. See Thomas Lockwood, "Theatrical Fielding."

2   Giving way to wayward inclinations.

before-hand, and not trust to Promises, which a Man seldom keeps, after he hath had his wicked Will. And seeing you have a rich Fool to deal with, your not making a good Market will be the more inexcusable; indeed, with such Gentlemen as Parson *Williams*, there is more to be said; for they have nothing to give, and are commonly otherwise the best Sort of Men. I am glad to hear you read good Books, pray continue so to do. I have inclosed you one of Mr. *Whitefield's* Sermons, and also the Dealings with him,[1] and am

Your affectionate Mother,
HENRIETTA MARIA, &c.

LETTER VI.

SHAMELA ANDREWS *to* HENRIETTA MARIA HONORA ANDREWS.

O Madam, I have strange Things to tell you! As I was reading in that charming Book about the Dealings, in comes my Master—to be sure he is a precious One. *Pamela*, says he, what Book is that, I warrant you *Rochester's* Poems.[2]—No, forsooth, says I, as pertly as I could; why how now Saucy Chops, Boldface, says he—Mighty pretty Words, says I, pert again.—Yes (says he) you are a d——d, impudent, stinking, cursed, confounded Jade, and I have a great Mind to kick your A——.[3] You, kiss —— says I. A-gad, says he, and so I will; with that he caught me in his Arms, and kissed me till he made my Face all over Fire. Now this served purely you know, to put upon the

---

1   George Whitefield (1714-70) was an important figure in the Evangelical or Methodist movement of the 1730s. He allegedly preached more than 18,000 sermons in his lifetime, many of which were published. By having Mrs. Andrews recommend his sermons to Shamela, Fielding is continuing his attack on the principles of Methodism. Fielding is also alluding to the so-called "Trapp Controversy" in which Whitefield was a central figure. Here, and in the next letter, Shamela and her mother refer to Whitefield's spiritual autobiography, *A Short Account of God's Dealings with the Reverend Mr. George Whitefield, from his infancy, to the time of his entering into holy orders* (1740).

2   John Wilmot, Earl of Rochester, (1647-80) was a courtier, libertine, and poet. While his poetry ranged from the deeply philosophical to the frankly sexual, his work was more consistently associated with the latter.

3   Among the terms Mr. B. uses to describe Pamela are "Idle Slut," "Foolish Slut," "Sawcy Slut," "Foolish Hussy," "Boldface," "Sawcebox," "Silly Girl," "Pretty Fool," and "Witch." He also says "D—n you!" on more than one occasion.

Fool for Anger. O! What precious Fools Men are! And so I flung from him in a mighty Rage, and pretended as how I would go out at the Door; but when I came to the End of the Room, I stood still, and my Master cryed out, Hussy, Slut, Sauce-box, Boldface, come hither—Yes to be sure, says I; why don't you come, says he; what should I come for says I; if you don't come to me, I'll come to you, says he; I shan't come to you I assure you, says I. Upon which he run up, caught me in his Arms, and flung me upon a Chair, and began to offer to touch my Under-Petticoat. Sir, says I, you had better not offer to be rude; well, says he, no more I won't then; and away he went out of the Room. I was so mad to be sure I could have cry'd.

Oh what a prodigious Vexation it is to a Woman to be made a Fool of.

Mrs. *Jervis* who had been without, harkening, now came to me. She burst into a violent Laugh the Moment she came in. Well, says she, as soon as she could speak, I have Reason to bless myself that I am an Old Woman. Ah Child! if you had known the Jolly Blades of my Age, you would not have been left in the lurch in this manner. Dear Mrs. *Jervis*, says I, don't laugh at one; and to be sure I was a little angry with her.——Come, says she, my dear Honey-suckle, I have one Game to play for you; he shall see you in Bed; he shall, my little Rose-bud, he shall see those pretty, little, white, round, panting——and offer'd to pull off my Handkerchief.—Fie, Mrs. *Jervis*, says I, you make me blush, and upon my Fackins,[1] I believe she did: She went on thus. I know the Squire likes you, and notwithstanding the Aukwardness of his Proceeding, I am convinced hath some hot Blood in his Veins, which will not let him rest, 'till he hath communicated some of his Warmth to thee my little Angel; I heard him last Night at our Door, trying if it was open, now to Night I will take care it shall be so; I warrant that he makes the second Trial; which if he doth, he shall find us ready to receive him. I will at first counterfeit Sleep, and after a Swoon; so that he will have you naked in his Possession: and then if you are disappointed, a Plague of all young Squires, say I.—And so, Mrs. *Jervis*, says I, you would have me yield myself to him, would you; you would have me be a second Time a Fool for nothing. Thank you for that, Mrs. *Jervis*. For nothing! marry forbid, says she, you know he hath large Sums of Money, besides abundance of fine Things; and do you think, when you have inflamed him, by giving his Hand a Liberty, with that charming Person; and that you know he may easily think he obtains against your

---

1 "Upon my Faith."

Will, he will not give any thing to come at all——.This will not do, Mrs. *Jervis*, answered I. I have heard my Mamma say, (and so you know, Madam, I have) that in her Youth, Fellows have often taken away in the Morning, what they gave over Night. No, Mrs. *Jervis*, nothing under a regular taking into Keeping, a settled Settlement, for me, and all my Heirs, all my whole Lifetime, shall do the Business[1] ——or else cross-legged, is the Word, faith, with *Sham*; and then I snapt my Fingers.

Thursday Night, Twelve o'Clock.

Mrs. *Jervis* and I are just in Bed, and the Door unlocked; if my Master should come——Odsbobs! I hear him just coming in at the Door. You see I write in the present Tense,[2] as Parson *Williams* says. Well, he is in Bed between us, we both shamming a Sleep, he steals his Hand into my Bosom, which I, as if in my Sleep, press close to me with mine, and then pretend to awake.—I no sooner see him, but I scream out to Mrs. *Jervis*, she feigns likewise but just to come to herself; we both begin, she to becall, and I to bescratch very liberally. After having made a pretty free Use of my Fingers, without any great Regard to the Parts I attack'd, I counterfeit a Swoon. Mrs. *Jervis* then cries out, O, Sir, what have you done, you have murthered poor *Pamela*: she is gone, she is gone.——[3]

O what a Difficulty it is to keep one's Countenance, when a violent Laugh desires to burst forth.

The poor Booby frightned out of his Wits, jumped out of Bed, and, in his Shirt, sat down by my Bed-Side, pale and trembling, for the Moon shone, and I kept my Eyes wide open, and pretended to fix them in my Head. Mrs. *Jervis* apply'd Lavender Water, and Hartshorn,[4] and this, for a full half Hour; when thinking I had carried it on long enough, and being likewise unable to continue the Sport any longer, I began by Degrees to come to my self.

---

1 Like Syrena, Shamela wants a legal financial arrangement or "settlement" before she will consummate her relationship with Booby.

2 "Odsbobs" is an eighteenth-century reduction and corruption of "Ods Bodkins," literally "God's little body" (Partridge). Here Fielding is also parodying Richardson's description of "writing, to the moment" (Richardson to Lady Bradshaigh, 14 February 1754, *Selected Letters*, 289).

3 For the comparable scene in *Pamela*, see Appendix C.2.ii.

4 Both used as smelling salts.

The Squire who had sat all this while speechless, and was almost really in that Condition, which I feigned, the Moment he saw me give Symptoms of recovering my Senses, fell down on his Knees; and O *Pamela*, cryed he, can you forgive me, my injured Maid? by Heaven, I know not whether you are a Man or a Woman, unless by your swelling Breasts. Will you promise to forgive me: I forgive you! D——n you (says I) and d——n you says he, if you come to that. I wish I had never seen your bold Face, saucy Sow, and so went out of the Room.

O what a silly Fellow is a bashful young Lover!

He was no sooner out of hearing, as we thought, than we both burst into a violent Laugh. Well, says Mrs. *Jervis*, I never saw any thing better acted than your Part: But I wish you may not have discouraged him from any future Attempt; especially since his Passions are so cool, that you could prevent his Hands going further than your Bosom. Hang him, answer'd I, he is not quite so cold as that I assure you; our Hands, on neither side, were idle in the Scuffle, nor have left us any Doubt of each other as to that matter.

Friday Morning.

My Master sent for Mrs. *Jervis*, as soon as he was up, and bid her give an Account of the Plate and Linnen in her Care; and told her, he was resolved that both she and the little Gipsy (I'll assure him) should set out together. Mrs. *Jervis* made him a saucy Answer; which any Servant of Spirit, you know, would, tho' it should be one's Ruin; and came immediately in Tears to me, crying, she had lost her Place on my Account, and that she should be forced to take to a House, as I mentioned before; and that she hoped I would, at least, make her all the amends in my power, for her Loss on my Account, and come to her House whenever I was sent for. Never fear, says I, I'll warrant we are not so near being turned away, as you imagine; and, i'cod,[1] now it comes into my Head, I have a Fetch[2] for him, and you shall assist me in it. But it being now late, and my Letter pretty long, no more at present from

Your Dutiful Daughter,
SHAMELA.

---

1   "I'cod" is a trivial oath; a Cockney corruption of "egad" or "in God."
2   A contrivance, dodge, stratagem, or trick (*OED*).

LETTER VII.

MRS. LUCRETIA JERVIS *to* HENRIETTA MARIA HONORA ANDREWS.

Madam,

MISS *Sham* being set out in a Hurry for my Master's House in *Lincolnshire*, desired me to acquaint you with the Success of her Stratagem, which was to dress herself in the plain Neatness of a Farmer's Daughter, for she before wore the Cloaths of my late Mistress, and to be introduced by me as a Stranger to her Master. To say the Truth, she became the Dress extremely, and if I was to keep a House a thousand Years, I would never desire a prettier Wench in it.[1]

As soon as my Master saw her, he immediately threw his Arms round her Neck, and smothered her with Kisses (for indeed he hath but very little to say for himself to a Woman). He swore that *Pamela* was an ugly Slut, (pardon, dear Madam, the Coarseness of the Expression) compared to such divine Excellence. He added, he would turn *Pamela* away immediately, and take this new Girl, whom he thought to be one of his Tenant's Daughters, in her Room.

Miss *Sham* smiled at these Words, and so did your humble Servant, which he perceiving, looked very earnestly at your fair Daughter, and discovered the Cheat.

How, *Pamela*, says he, is it you? I thought, Sir, said Miss, after what had happened, you would have known me in any Dress. No, Hussy, says he, but after what hath happened, I should know thee out of any Dress from all thy Sex. He then was what we Women call rude, when done in the Presence of others; but it seems it is not the first time, and Miss defended herself with great Strength and Spirit.

The Squire, who thinks her a pure Virgin, and who knows nothing of my Character, resolved to send her into *Lincolnshire*, on Pretence of conveying her home; where our old Friend *Nanny Jewkes*[2] is Housekeeper, and where Miss had her small one by Parson *Williams* about a Year ago. This is a Piece of News communicated to us by *Robin* Coachman, who is intrusted by his Master to carry on this Affair privately for him: But we hang together, I believe, as well as any Family of Servants in the Nation.

---

1 For the comparable scene in *Pamela*, see Appendix C.2. See also the scene from Eliza Haywood's *Fantomina* in Appendix A.4.
2 Nanny is also slang for a whore (Partridge).

You will, I believe, Madam, wonder that the Squire, who doth not want Generosity, should never have mentioned a Settlement all this while, I believe it slips his Memory: But it will not be long forgot, no doubt: For, as I am convinced the young Lady will do nothing unbecoming your Daughter, nor ever admit him to taste her Charms, without something sure and handsome before-hand; so, I am certain, the Squire will never rest till they have danced *Adam* and *Eve's* kissing Dance together. Your Daughter set out Yesterday Morning, and told me, as soon as she arrived, you might depend on hearing from her.

Be pleased to make my Compliments acceptable to Mrs. *Davis* and Mrs. *Silvester*, and Mrs. *Jolly*, and all Friends, and permit me the Honour, Madam, to be with the utmost Sincerity,

> *Your most Obedient,*
> *Humble Servant,*
> LUCRETIA JERVIS.

If the Squire should continue his Displeasure against me, so as to insist on the Warning he hath given me, you will see me soon, and I will lodge in the same House with you, if you have room, till I can provide for my self to my Liking.

LETTER VIII.

HENRIETTA MARIA HONORA ANDREWS *to* LUCRETIA JERVIS.

Madam,

I Received the Favour of your Letter, and I find you have not forgot your usual Poluteness, which you learned when you was in keeping with a Lord.

I am very much obliged to you for your Care of my Daughter, am glad to hear she hath taken such good Resolutions, and hope she will have sufficient Grace to maintain them.

All Friends are well, and remember to you. You will excuse the Shortness of this Scroll; for I have sprained my right Hand, with boxing three new made Officers.—Tho' to my Comfort, I beat them all. I rest,

> *Your Friend and Servant,*
> HENRIETTA, *&c.*

LETTER IX.

SHAMELA ANDREWS *to* HENRIETTA MARIA HONORA ANDREWS.

Dear Mamma,

I Suppose Mrs. *Jervis* acquainted you with what past 'till I left *Bedfordshire*; whence I am after a very pleasant Journey arrived in *Lincolnshire*, with your old Acquaintance Mrs. *Jewkes*, who formerly helped Parson *Williams* to me; and now designs I see, to sell me to my Master; thank her for that; she will find two Words go to that Bargain.

The Day after my Arrival here, I received a Letter from Mr. *Williams*, and as you have often desired to see one from him, I have inclosed it to you; it is, I think, the finest I ever received from that charming Man, and full of a great deal of Learning.

O! What a brave Thing it is to be a Scholard, and to be able to talk Latin.[1]

Parson WILLIAMS *to* PAMELA ANDREWS.

Mrs. Pamela,

HAVING learnt by means of my Clerk, who Yesternight visited the Rev^d. Mr. *Peters* with my Commands, that you are returned into this County, I purposed to have saluted your fair Hands this Day towards Even: But am obliged to sojourn this Night at a neighbouring Clergyman's; where we are to pierce a Virgin Barrel of Ale, in a Cup of which I shall not be unmindful to celebrate your Health.

I hope you have remembered your Promise, to bring me a Leaden Canister of Tobacco (the Saffron Cut) for in Troth, this Country at present affords nothing worthy the replenishing a Tube with.[2] ———Some I tasted the other Day at an Alehouse, gave me the Heart-Burn, tho' I filled no oftner than five Times.

I was greatly concerned to learn, that your late Lady left you nothing, tho' I cannot say the Tidings much surprized me: For I am too intimately acquainted with the Family; (myself, Father, and

---

1 Shamela does not realize that, as a dead language, Latin cannot be spoken, only written or read.

2 Saffron-cut is a desirable tobacco; in "troth" is a corruption of "truth," revealing Williams's regional origins. A tube is a tobacco pipe. The whole episode, like the letter, reveals the exploitive nature of Williams's relationship with Shamela, as well as his own pursuit of personal pleasure.

Grandfather having been successive Incumbents on the same Cure,[1] which you know is in their Gift) I say, I am too well acquainted with them to expect much from their Generosity. They are in Verity, as worthless a Family as any other whatever. The young Gentleman I am informed, is a perfect Reprobate; that he hath an *Ingenium Versatile*[2] to every Species of Vice, which, indeed, no one can much wonder at, who animadverts[3] on that want of Respect to the Clergy, which was observable in him when a Child. I remember when he was at the Age of Eleven only, he met my Father without either pulling off his Hat, or riding out of the way. Indeed, a Contempt of the Clergy is the fashionable Vice of the Times; but let such Wretches know, they cannot hate, detest, and despise us, half so much as we do them.

However, I have prevailed on myself to write a civil Letter to your Master, as there is a Probability of his being shortly in a Capacity of rendring me a Piece of Service; my good Friend and Neighbour the Rev^d. Mr. *Squeeze-Tithe* being, as I am informed by one whom I have employed to attend for that Purpose, very near his Dissolution.[4]

You see, sweet Mrs. *Pamela*, the Confidence with which I dictate these Things to you; whom after those Endearments which have passed between us, I must in some Respects estimate as my Wife: For tho' the Omission of the Service was a Sin; yet, as I have told you, it was a venial One,[5] of which I have truly repented, as I hope you have; and also that you have continued the wholesome Office of reading good Books, and are improved in your Psalmody,[6] of which I shall

---

1   The spiritual charge of parishioners, the office of a curate (*OED*).
2   The phrase, which means versatile genius or versatile intelligence, initially appears in Livy's *History of Rome* to describe Cato (Book XXXIX, xl, 5). The phrase appears again in Bacon's *Essays*, published in 1597 and newly written in 1625, as well as letters by Montaigne. It is used ironically here to suggest that Booby has a great facility with vice.
3   To comment critically on (*OED*).
4   Williams hopes to receive Squeeze-Tithe's position from Booby. Note how the language and action of the entire paragraph reveal the mercenary and patronage-based nature of the church and of Williams's relationships.
5   A venial sin is a lesser, or "minor" sin; a cardinal sin is a more significant transgression.
6   The practice or art of singing psalms (or sacred vocal music in general), especially in public worship. Much is made of psalmody in *Pamela*. Pamela's father "learnt Psalmody formerly, in his Youth, and had constantly practiced it in private, at home, of Sunday Evenings, (as well as endeavour'd to teach it in the little School he so unsuccessfully set up ...)," so she is "in no Pain for his undertaking it" in Williams's congregation (313).

have a speedy Trial: For I purpose[1] to give you a Sermon next *Sunday*, and shall spend the Evening with you, in Pleasures, which tho' not strictly innocent, are however to be purged away by frequent and sincere Repentance. I am,

> *Sweet Mrs.* Pamela,
> *Your faithful Servant,*
> ARTHUR WILLIAMS.

You find, Mamma, what a charming way he hath of Writing, and yet I assure you, that is not the most charming Thing[2] belonging to him: For, tho' he doth not put any Dears, and Sweets, and Loves into his Letters, yet he says a thousand of them: For he can be as fond of a Woman, as any Man living.

Sure Women are great Fools, when they prefer a laced Coat to the Clergy, whom it is our Duty to honour and respect.

Well, on *Sunday* Parson *Williams* came, according to his Promise, and an excellent Sermon he preached; his Text was, *Be not Righteous over-much*;[3] and, indeed, he handled it in a very fine way; he shewed us that the Bible doth not require too much Goodness of us, and that People very often call things Goodness that are not so. That to go to Church, and to pray, and to sing Psalms, and to honour the Clergy, and to repent, is true Religion; and 'tis not doing good to one another, for that is one of the greatest Sins we can commit, when we don't do it for the sake of Religion. That those People who talk of Vartue and Morality, are the wickedest of all Persons. That 'tis not what we do, but what we believe, that must save us, and a great many other good Things; I wish I could remember them all.

As soon as Church was over, he came to the Squire's House, and drank Tea with Mrs. *Jewkes* and me; after which Mrs. *Jewkes* went out

---

1 Propose (*OED*).
2 "Thing" is also slang for genitals.
3 "Be not righteous over much, neither make thyself over wise: why shouldest thou destroy thyself?" *Ecclesiastes* 7:16. The admonition is directed toward Richardson and what might be seen as his self-righteous attitude toward his novel; it also parodies Richardson's own use of the proverb in the "Introduction" to the second edition. Here Williams is using it inappropriately as a license for immorality. However, the phrase is also a key text in the Methodist controversy to which Fielding alludes. Williams preaches on a text that had been first used by Dr. Joseph Trapp in an anti-Methodist (and anti-Whitefield) sermon delivered in April 1739 entitled *The Nature, Folly Sin and Danger of Being Righteous Over-much.*

and left us together for an Hour and half—Oh! he is a charming Man.

After Supper he went Home, and then Mrs. *Jewkes* began to catechize[1] me, about my Familiarity with him. I see she wants him herself. Then she proceeded to tell me what an Honour my Master did me in liking me, and that it was both an inexcusable Folly and Pride in me, to pretend to refuse him any Favour. Pray, Madam, says I, consider I am a poor Girl, and have nothing but my Modesty to trust to. If I part with that, what will become of me. Methinks, says she, you are not so mighty modest when you are with Parson *Williams*; I have observed you gloat[2] at one another, in a Manner that hath made me blush. I assure you, I shall let the Squire know what sort of Man he is; you may do your Will, says I, as long as he hath a Vote for Pallamant-Men,[3] the Squire dares do nothing to offend him; and you will only shew that you are jealous of him, and that's all. How now, Mynx, says she; Mynx! No more Mynx than yourself, says I; with that she hit me a Slap on the Shoulder and I flew at her and scratched her Face, i'cod, 'till she went crying out of the Room; so no more at Present, from

Your Dutiful Daughter,
SHAMELA.

LETTER X.

SHAMELA ANDREWS *to* HENRIETTA MARIA HONORA ANDREWS.

O Mamma! Rare News! As soon as I was up this Morning, a Letter was brought me from the Squire, of which I send you a Copy.

Squire BOOBY *to* PAMELA.

Dear Creature,
I HOPE you are not angry with me for the Deceit put upon you, in conveying you to *Lincolnshire*, when you imagined yourself going to *London*. Indeed, my dear *Pamela*, I cannot live without you; and will

---

1 To question or take to task (*OED*).
2 To gaze with intense or passionate satisfaction, usually implying a lustful pleasure (*OED*).
3 Parliament Men; Booby is campaigning to be elected as a Member of Parliament, and needs Williams's vote. It implicitly demonstrates the way votes were obtained in the rural areas.

very shortly come down and convince you, that my Designs are better than you imagine, and such as you may with Honour comply with. I am,

> My Dear Creature,
> Your doating Lover,
> BOOBY.

Now, Mamma, what think you?—For my own Part, I am convinced he will marry me, and faith so he shall. O! Bless me! I shall be Mrs. *Booby*, and be Mistress of a great Estate, and have a dozen Coaches and Six, and a fine House at *London*, and another at *Bath*, and Servants, and Jewels, and Plate, and go to Plays, and Opera's, and Court; and do what I will, and spend what I will. But, poor Parson *Williams*! Well; and can't I see Parson *Williams*, as well after Marriage as before: For I shall never care a Farthing[1] for my Husband. No, I hate and despise him of all Things.

Well, as soon as I had read my Letter, in came Mrs. *Jewkes*. You see, Madam, says she, I carry the Marks of your Passion about me; but I have received Order from my Master to be civil to you, and I must obey him: For he is the best Man in the World, notwithstanding your Treatment of him. My Treatment of him; Madam, says I? Yes, says she, your Insensibility to the Honour he intends you, of making you his Mistress. I would have you to know, Madam, I would not be Mistress to the greatest King, no nor Lord in the Universe. I value my Vartue more than I do any thing my Master can give me; and so we talked a full Hour and a half, about my Vartue; and I was afraid at first, she had heard something about the Bantling,[2] but I find she hath not; tho' she is as jealous, and suspicious, as old Scratch.[3]

In the Afternoon, I stole into the Garden to meet Mr. *Williams*; I found him at the Place of his Appointment, and we staid in a kind of Arbour, till it was quite dark. He was very angry when I told him what Mrs. *Jewkes* had threatned——Let him refuse me the Living, says he, if he dares, I will vote for the other Party; and not only so, but will expose him all over the Country. I owe him 150*l*. indeed,

---

1 The quarter of a penny, or a very small piece of anything.
2 Her child by Williams. Bantling is a synonym of bastard; it refers to a child begotten on a bench, and not in the marriage-bed (Partridge).
3 The Devil.

but I don't care for that by that Time the Election is past, I shall be able to plead the *Statue of Lamentations*.[1]

I could have stayed with the dear Man forever, but when it grew dark, he told me, he was to meet the neighbouring Clergy, to finish the Barrel of Ale they had tapped the other Day, and believed they should not part till three or four in the Morning——So he left me, and I promised to be penitent, and go on with my reading in good Books.

As soon as he was gone, I bethought myself, what Excuse I should make to Mrs. *Jewkes*, and it came into my Head to pretend as how I intended to drown myself; so I stript off one of my Petticoats, and threw it into the Canal; and then I went and hid myself in the Coal-hole, where I lay all Night; and comforted myself with repeating over some Psalms, and other good things, which I had got by heart.

In the Morning Mrs. *Jewkes* and all the Servants were frighted out of their Wits, thinking I had run away; and not devising how they should answer it to their Master. They searched all the likeliest Places they could think of for me, and at last saw my Petticoat floating in the Pond. Then they got a Drag-Net, imagining I was drowned, and intending to drag me out; but at last *Moll* Cook coming for some Coals, discovered me lying all along in no very good Pickle.[2] Bless me! Mrs. *Pamela*, says she, what can be the Meaning of this? I don't know, says I, help me up, and I will go in to Breakfast, for indeed I am very hungry. Mrs. *Jewkes* came in immediately, and was so rejoyced to find me alive, that she asked with great Good-Humour, where I had been? and how my Petticoat came into the Pond. I answered, I believed the Devil had put it into my Head to drown my self; but it was a Fib; for I never saw the Devil in my Life, nor I don't believe he hath any thing to do with me.[3]

So much for this Matter. As soon as I had breakfasted, a Coach and Six came to the Door, and who should be in it but my Master.

I immediately run up into my Room, and stript, and washed, and drest my self as well as I could, and put on my prettiest round-ear'd

---

1 She means, of course, statute of limitations. The Statute of Limitations of 1623 required legal action to recover a debt be brought within six years. Because Booby wants Williams's votes, he won't press him for the £150 until after the election, by which point it will be too late. For a member of the lower clergy like Williams, a debt of £150 is large and an amount that could easily be more than twice his annual salary.

2 Condition or situation (*OED*).

3 See Appendix C.2.iv for the "drowning" scene from *Pamela*.

Cap, and pulled down my Stays, to shew as much as I could of my Bosom, (for Parson *Williams* says, that is the most beautiful part of a Woman) and then I practised over all my Airs before the Glass, and then I sat down and read a Chapter in the Whole Duty of Man.

Then Mrs. *Jewkes* came to me and told me, my Master wanted me below, and says she, Don't behave like a Fool; No, thinks I to my self, I believe I shall find Wit enough for my Master and you too.

So down goes me into the Parlour to him. *Pamela*, says he, the Moment I came in, you see I cannot stay long from you, which I think is a sufficient Proof of the Violence of my Passion. Yes, Sir, says I, I see your Honour intends to ruin me, that nothing but the Destruction of my Vartue will content you.

O what a charming Word that is, rest his Soul who first invented it.

How can you say I would ruin you, answered the Squire, when you shall not ask any thing which I will not grant you. If that be true, says I, good your Honour let me go Home to my poor but honest Parents; that is all I have to ask, and do not ruin a poor Maiden, who is resolved to carry her Vartue to the Grave with her.

Hussy, says he, don't provoke me, don't provoke me, I say. You are absolutely in my power, and if you won't let me lie with you by fair Means, I will by Force. O La, Sir, says I, I don't understand your paw[1] Words.——Very pretty Treatment indeed, says he, to say I use paw Words; Hussy, Gipsie, Hypocrite, Sauce-box, Boldface, get out of my Sight, or I will lend you such a Kick in the — I don't care to repeat the Word, but he meant my hinder part. I was offering to go away, for I was half afraid, when he called me back, and took me round the Neck and kissed me, and then bid me go about my Business.

I went directly into my Room, where Mrs. *Jewkes* came to me soon afterwards. So Madam, says she, you have left my Master below in a fine Pet, he hath threshed two or three of his Men already:[2] It is mighty pretty that all his Servants are to be punished for your Impertinence.

Harkee, Madam, says I, don't you affront me, for if you do, d——n me (I am sure I have repented for using such a Word) if I am not revenged.

---

1 Improper, obscene, or nasty.
2 A pet is a fit of ill-humor or peevishness.

How sweet is Revenge: Sure the Sermon Book is in the Right, in calling it the sweetest Morsel the Devil ever dropped into the Mouth of a Sinner.[1]

Mrs. *Jewkes* remembered the Smart of my Nails too well to go farther, and so we sat down and talked about my Vartue till Dinnertime, and then I was sent for to wait on my Master. I took care to be often caught looking at him, and then I always turn'd away my Eyes and pretended to be ashamed. As soon as the Cloth was removed, he put a Bumper of Champagne into my Hand, and bid me drink—— O la I can't name the Health.[2] Parson *Williams* may well say he is a wicked Man.

Mrs. *Jewkes* took a Glass and drank the dear *Monysyllable*;[3] I don't understand that Word, but I believe it is baudy. I then drank towards his Honour's good Pleasure. Ay, Hussy, says he, you can give me Pleasure if you will; Sir, says I, I shall be always glad to do what is in my power, and so I pretended not to know what he meant. Then he took me into his Lap.— O Mamma, I could tell you something if I would—and he kissed me—and I said I won't be slobber'd about so, so I won't, and he bid me get out of the Room for a saucy Baggage, and said he had a good mind to spit in my Face.

Sure no Man ever took such a Method to gain a Woman's Heart.

I had not been long in my Chamber before Mrs. *Jewkes* came to me and told me, my Master would not see me any more that Evening, that is, if he can help it; for, added she, I easily perceive the great Ascendant you have over him; and to confess the Truth, I don't doubt but you will shortly be my Mistress.

What says I, dear Mrs. *Jewkes*, what do you say? Don't flatter a poor Girl, it is impossible his Honour can have any honourable Design upon me. And so we talked of honourable Designs till Supper-time. And Mrs. *Jewkes* and I supped together upon a hot buttered Apple-Pie; and about ten o' Clock we went to Bed.

We had not been a Bed half an Hour, when my Master came pit a pat into the Room in his Shirt as before, I pretended not to hear him, and Mrs. *Jewkes* laid hold of one Arm, and he pulled down the

---

1   Shamela's version of a passage from Robert South (1633-1716), a divine whom Fielding greatly admired. South's original wording reads "Revenge is certainly the most luscious morsel that the devil can put into the sinner's mouth" (Battestin).
2   That is, Booby has made an obscene toast.
3   "A polite slang way of referring to the vulgar name for the female pudendum" (Goldberg).

Bed-cloaths and came into Bed on the other Side, and took my other Arm and laid it under him, and fell a kissing one of my Breasts as if he would have devoured it; I was then forced to awake, and began to struggle with him, Mrs. *Jewkes* crying why don't you do it? I have one Arm secure, if you can't deal with the rest I am sorry for you. He was as rude as possible to me; but I remembered, Mamma, the Instructions you gave me to avoid being ravished, and followed them, which soon brought him to Terms, and he promised me, on quitting my hold, that he would leave the Bed.[1]

O *Parson* Williams; *how little are all the Men in the World compared to thee.*

My Master was as good as his Word; upon which Mrs. *Jewkes* said, O Sir, I see you know very little of our *Sect*, by parting so easily from the Blessing when you was so near it. No, Mrs. *Jewkes*, answered he, I am very glad no more hath happened, I would not have injured *Pamela* for the World. And to-morrow Morning perhaps she may hear of something to her Advantage. This she may be certain of, that I will never take her by Force, and then he left the Room.

What think you now, Mrs. *Pamela*, says Mrs. *Jewkes*, are you not yet persuaded my Master hath honourable Designs? I think he hath given no great Proof of them to-night, said I. Your Experience I find is not great, says she, but I am convinced you will shortly be my Mistress, and then what will become of poor me.

With such sort of Discourse we both fell asleep. Next Morning early my Master sent for me, and after kissing me, gave a Paper into my Hand which he bid me read; I did so, and found it to be a Proposal for settling 250*l*.[2] a Year on me, besides several other advantagious Offers, as Presents of Money and other things. Well, *Pamela*, said he, what Answer do you make me to this. Sir, said I, I value my Virtue more than all the World, and I had rather be the poorest Man's Wife, than the richest Man's Whore. You are a Simpleton, said he; That may be, and yet I may have as much Wit as some Folks, cry'd I; meaning me, I suppose, said he; every Man knows himself best, says I. Hussy, says he, get out of the Room, and let me see your saucy Face no more, for I find I am in more Danger than you are, and therefore it shall be my Business to avoid you as much as I can; and it shall be mine, thinks I, at every turn to throw my self in your way. So I went out, and as I parted, I heard him sigh and say he was bewitched.

---

1 See Appendix B.1 for attempted rape scene in *Pamela*.
2 See Appendix C.2.v. for B.'s original proposals to *Pamela*.

Mrs. *Jewkes* hath been with me since, and she assures me she is convinced I shall shortly be Mistress of the Family, and she really behaves to me, as if she already thought me so. I am resolved now to aim at it. I thought once of making a little Fortune by my Person. I now intend to make a great one by my Vertue. So asking Pardon for this long Scroll, I am,

Your dutiful Daughter,
SHAMELA.

LETTER XI.

HENRIETTA MARIA HONORA ANDREWS *to* SHAMELA ANDREWS.

Dear Sham,
I RECEIVED your last Letter with infinite Pleasure, and am convinced it will be your own Fault if you are not married to your Master, and I would advise you now to take no less Terms. But, my dear Child, I am afraid of one Rock only, That Parson *Williams*, I wish he was out of the Way. A Woman never commits Folly but with such Sort of Men, as by many Hints in the Letters I collect him to be: but, consider my dear Child, you will hereafter have Opportunities sufficient to indulge yourself with Parson *Williams*, or any other you like. My Advice therefore to you is, that you would avoid seeing him any more till the Knot is tied. Remember the first Lesson I taught you, that a Married Woman injures only her Husband, but a Single Woman herself. I am in hopes of seeing you a great Lady,

Your affectionate Mother,
HENRIETTA MARIA, &c.

The following Letter seems to have been written before *Shamela* received the last from her Mother.

LETTER XII.

SHAMELA ANDREWS *to* HENRIETTA MARIA HONORA ANDREWS.

Dear Mamma,
I LITTLE feared when I sent away my last that all my Hopes would be so soon frustrated; but I am certain you will blame Fortune and not me. To proceed then. About two Hours after I had left the Squire, he sent for me into the Parlour. *Pamela*, said he, and takes me gently by the hand, will you walk with me in the Garden; yes, Sir,

says I, and pretended to tremble; but I hope your Honour will not be rude. Indeed, says he, you have nothing to fear from me, and I have something to tell you, which if it doth not please you, cannot offend. We walked out together, and he began thus, *Pamela*, will you tell me Truth? Doth the Resistance you make to my Attempts proceed from Vartue only, or have I not some Rival in thy dear Bosom who might be more successful? Sir, says I, I do assure you I never had a thought of any Man in the World. How says he, not of Parson *Williams*! Parson *Williams*, says I, is the last Man upon Earth; and if I was a Dutchess, and your Honour was to make your Addresses to me, you would have no reason to be jealous of any Rival, especially such a Fellow as Parson *Williams*. If ever I had a Liking, I am sure—but not worthy of you one Way, and no Riches should ever bribe me the other. My Dear, says he, you are worthy of every Thing, and suppose I should lay aside all Considerations of Fortune, and disregard the Censure of the World, and marry you.[1] O Sir, says I, I am sure you can have no such Thoughts, you cannot demean your self so low. Upon my Soul, I am in earnest, says he,——O Pardon me, Sir, says I, you can't persuade me of this. How Mistress, says he, in a violent Rage, do you give me the Lie? Hussy, I have a great mind to box your saucy Ears, but I am resolved I will never put it in your power to affront me again, and therefore I desire you to prepare your self for your Journey this Instant. You deserve no better Vehicle than a Cart; however, for once you shall have a Chariot, and it shall be ready for you within this half Hour; and so he flung from me in a Fury.

What a foolish Thing it is for a Woman to dally too long with her Lover's Desires; how many have owed their being old Maids to their holding out too long.

Mrs. *Jewkes* came me to presently, and told me, I must make ready with all the Expedition imaginable, for that my Master had ordered the Chariot, and that if I was not prepared to go in it, I should be turned out of Doors and left to find my way Home on Foot. This

---

1 Cf. *Pamela* (213). "Consider the Pride of my Condition. I cannot endure the Thought of Marriage, even with a Person of equal or superior Degree to myself; and have declin'd several Proposals of that kind: How then, with the Distance between us, and in the World's Judgment, can I think of making you my Wife?—Yet I must have you; I cannot bear the Thoughts of any other Man supplanting me in your Affections. And the very Apprehension of that, has made me hate the Name of Williams, and use him in a manner unworthy of my Temper."

startled me a little, yet I resolved, whether in the right or wrong, not to submit nor ask Pardon: For that know you, Mamma, you never could your self bring me to from my Childhood: Besides, I thought he would be no more able to master his Passion for me now, than he had been hitherto; and if he sent two Horses away with me, I concluded he would send four to fetch me back. So, truly, I resolved to brazen it out, and with all the Spirit I could muster up, I told Mrs. *Jewkes* I was vastly pleased with the News she brought me; that no one ever went more readily than I should, from a Place where my Vartue had been in continual Danger. That as for my Master, he might easily get those who were fit for his Purpose; but, for my Part, I preferred my Vartue to all Rakes whatever———And for his Promises, and his Offers to me, I don't value them of a Fig———Not of a Fig, Mrs. *Jewkes*; and then I snapt my Fingers.

Mrs. *Jewkes* went in with me, and helped me to pack up my little All, which was soon done; being no more than two Day-Caps, two Night-Caps, five Shifts, one Sham, a Hoop, a Quilted-Petticoat, two Flannel-Petticoats, two pair of Stockings, one odd one, a pair of lac'd Shoes, a short flowered Apron, a lac'd Neck-Handkerchief, one Clog, and almost another,[1] and some few Books: as, *A full Answer to a plain and true Account*, &c. *The Whole Duty of Man*, with only the Duty to one's Neighbour, torn out. The Third Volume of the *Atalantis*. *Venus in the Cloyster: Or, the Nun in her Smock. God's Dealings with Mr. Whitefield. Orfus and Eurydice.* Some Sermon-Books; and two or three Plays, with their Titles, and Part of the first Act torn off.[2]

So as soon as we had put all this into a Bundle, the Chariot was ready, and I took leave of all the Servants, and particularly Mrs.

---

1 For the comparable scene in *Pamela*, see Appendix C.2.iii.
2 Shamela's books reveal the peripatetic nature of her morality and reading habits. *A full Answer to a Plain and True Account &c.*, is likely one of the many works written in reply to *A Plain Account of the Nature and End of the Sacrament of the Lord's Supper* (1735). Richard Allestree's extremely popular *The Whole Duty of Man* (see Appendix D.1) was an important conduct book which contrasts strikingly with "Atalantis" which refers to Delarivier Manley's political *roman à clef, Secret Memoirs and Manners of Several Persons of Quality of Both Sexes. From the New Atalantis* (originally published in 1709, but republished in 1736). *Venus in the Cloister; or, The Nun in her Smock* (1683, translated from the French in 1724) caused publisher Edmund Curll to be tried for obscenity in 1725. *Orpheus and Eurydice* was a 1739 opera-pantomime by Lewis Theobald, who was satirized in Pope's 1728 *Dunciad*.

Jewkes, who pretended, I believe, to be more sorry to part with me than she was; and then crying out with an Air of Indifference, my Service to my Master, when he condescends to enquire after me, I flung my self into the Chariot, and bid *Robin* drive on.

We had not gone far, before a Man on Horseback, riding full Speed, overtook us, and coming up to the Side of the Chariot, threw a Letter into the Window, and then departed without uttering a single Syllable.

I immediately knew the Hand of my dear *Williams*, and was somewhat surprized, tho' I did not apprehend the Contents to be so terrible, as by the following exact Copy you will find them.

Parson WILLIAMS to PAMELA.

Dear Mrs. Pamela,

THAT Disrespect for the Clergy which I have formerly noted to you in that Villain your Master, hath now broke forth in a manifest Fact. I was proceeding to my Neighbour *Spruce's* Church, where I purposed to preach a Funeral Sermon, on the Death of Mr. *John Gage*, the Exciseman;[1] when I was met by two Persons who are, it seems, Sheriffs Officers, and arrested for the 150*l.* which your Master had lent me; and unless I can find Bail within these few Days, of which I see no likelihood, I shall be carried to Goal.[2] This accounts for my not having visited you these two Days; which you might assure yourself, I should not have fail'd, if the *Potestas*[3] had not been wanting. If you can by any means prevail on your Master to release me, I beseech you so to do, not scrupling any thing for Righteousness sake. I hear he is just arrived in this Country, I have herewith sent him a Letter, of which I transmit you a Copy. So with Prayers for your Success, I subscribe my self

Your affectionate Friend,
ARTHUR WILLIAMS.

Parson WILLIAMS to Squire BOOBY.

Honoured Sir,

I Am justly surprized to feel so heavy a Weight of your Displeasure, without being conscious of the least Demerit towards so good and

---

1 An officer employed to collect excise duties and prevent infringement of the excise laws.
2 Booby can have Williams imprisoned for failure to pay his debt.
3 Power, with a pun on the idea of sexual potency.

generous a Patron, as I have ever found you: For my own Part, I can truly say,

Nil conscire sibi nullae pallescere culpae.[1]

And therefore, as this Proceeding is so contrary to your usual Goodness, which I have often experienced, and more especially in the Loan of this Money for which I am now arrested; I cannot avoid thinking some malicious Persons have insinuated false Suggestions against me; intending thereby, to eradicate those Seeds of Affection which I have hardly travailed to sowe in your Heart, and which promised to produce such excellent Fruit. If I have any ways offended you, Sir, be graciously pleased to let me know it, and likewise to point out to me, the Means whereby I may reinstate myself in your Favour: For next to him, whom the Great themselves must bow down before, I know none to whom I shall bend with more Lowliness than your Honour. Permit me to subscribe myself,

Honoured Sir,
Your most obedient, and most obliged,
And most dutiful humble Servant,
ARTHUR WILLIAMS.

The Fate of poor Mr. *Williams* shocked me more than my own: For, as the *Beggar's Opera* says, *Nothing moves one so much as a great Man in Distress.*[2] And to see a Man of his Learning forced to submit so low, to one whom I have often heard him say, he despises, is, I think, a most affecting Circumstance. I write all this to you, Dear Mamma, at the Inn where I lie this first Night, and as I shall send it immedi-

---

1   Horace, Epistle I. *nil conscire sibi, nulla pallescere culpa:* "To be conscious of no fault, to turn pale at no accusation." It seems possible that Fielding is also making an off-handed slight against Walpole. In 1741 Sir Robert Walpole, defending himself in Parliament against an impeachment proceeding brought by William Pulteney, concluded with this line from Horace. "*Nil conscire sibi nulli pallescere culpae,*" transposing the dative and the ablative. Pulteney leapt at once—but to correct the grammar of the Horatian tag: "Your Latin is as bad as your logic: *nullA pallescere culpA!*"

2   In Act Three, scene 15, of John Gay's *The Beggar's Opera* (1728), Lucy Lockit observes: "There is nothing moves one so much as a great Man in Distress." While Lucy is referring to Macheath's imprisonment, any references to "the Great Man" during this period also refer to Prime Minister Robert Walpole. "Great Man" was his moniker among the satirists and is certainly part of Fielding's commentary as well.

ately, by the Post, it will be in Town a little before me.——Don't let my coming away vex you: For, as my Master will be in Town in a few Days, I shall have an Opportunity of seeing him; and let the worst come to the worst, I shall be sure of my Settlement at last. Which is all, from

Your Dutiful Daughter,
SHAMELA.

P. S. Just as I was going to send this away a Letter is come from my Master, desiring me to return, with a large Number of Promises.—I have him now as sure as a Gun, as you will perceive by the Letter itself, which I have inclosed to you.

This Letter is unhappily lost, as well as the next which *Shamela* wrote, and which contained an Account of all the Proceedings previous to her Marriage. The only remaining one which I could preserve, seems to have been written about a Week after the Ceremony was perform'd, and is as follows:

SHAMELA BOOBY *to* HENRIETTA MARIA HONORA ANDREWS.

Madam,
IN my last I left off at our sitting down to Supper on our Wedding Night,★ where I behaved with as much Bashfulness as the purest Virgin in the World could have done. The most difficult Task for me was to blush; however, by holding my Breath, and squeezing my Cheeks with my Handkerchief, I did pretty well. My Husband was extreamly eager and impatient to have Supper removed, after which he gave me leave to retire into my Closet for a Quarter of an Hour, which was very agreeable to me; for I employed that time in writing to Mr. *Williams,* who, as I informed you in my last, is released, and presented to the Living, upon the Death of the last Parson. Well, at last I went to Bed, and my Husband soon leap'd in after me; where I shall only assure you, I acted my Part in such a manner, that no Bridegroom was ever better satisfied with his Bride's Virginity. And to confess the Truth, I might have been well enough satisfied too, if I had never been acquainted with Parson *Williams.*

O what regard Men who marry Widows should have to the Qualifications of their former Husbands.

★   This was the Letter which is lost. [Fielding's note.]

We did not rise the next Morning till eleven, and then we sat down to Breakfast; I eat two Slices of Bread and Butter, and drank three Dishes of Tea, with a good deal of Sugar, and we both look'd very silly. After Breakfast we drest our selves, he in a blue Camlet Coat, very richly lac'd, and Breeches of the same; with a Paduasoy Waistcoat,[1] laced with Silver; and I, in one of my Mistress's Gowns. I will have finer when I come to Town.[2] We then took a Walk in the Garden, and he kissed me several times, and made me a Present of 100 Guineas, which I gave away before Night to the Servants, twenty to one, and ten to another, and so on.

We eat a very hearty Dinner, and about eight in the Evening went to Bed again. He is prodigiously fond of me; but I don't like him half so well as my dear *Williams*. The next Morning we rose earlier, and I asked him for another hundred Guineas, and he gave them me. I sent fifty to Parson *Williams*, and the rest I gave away, two Guineas to a Beggar, and three to a Man riding along the Road, and the rest to other People. I long to be in *London* that I may have an Opportunity of laying some out, as well as giving away. I believe I shall buy every thing I see. What signifies having Money if one doth not spend it.

The next Day, as soon as I was up, I asked him for another Hundred. Why, my Dear, says he, I don't grudge you any thing, but how was it possible for you to lay out the other two Hundred here. La! Sir, says I, I hope I am not obliged to give you an Account of every Shilling; Troth, that will be being your Servant still. I assure you, I married you with no such view, besides did not you tell me I should be Mistress of your Estate? And I will be too. For tho' I brought no Fortune, I am as much your Wife as if I had brought a Million——yes, but, my Dear, says he, if you had brought a Million, you would spend it all at this rate; besides, what will your Expences be in *London*, if they are so great here. Truly, says I, Sir, I shall live like other Ladies of my Fashion; and if you think, because I was a Servant, that I shall be contented to be governed as you please, I will shew you, you are mistaken. If you had not cared to marry me, you might have let it alone. I did not ask you, nor I did not court you. Madam, says he, I don't value a Hundred Guineas to oblige you; but this is a Spir-

---

1 Camblet or camlet is the name originally applied to a beautiful and costly eastern fabric, and afterwards to imitations of the same. Paduasoy is a strong corded or gross-grain silk fabric. In *Pamela*, Mr. B. wears "a fine laced silk Waistcoat, of blue Paduasoy" (487).

2 Go to London.

it which I did not expect in you, nor did I ever see any Symptoms of it before. O but Times are altered now, I am your Lady, Sir; yes to my Sorrow, says he, I am afraid—and I am afraid to my Sorrow too: For if you begin to use me in this manner already, I reckon you will beat me before a Month's at an End. I am sure if you did, it would injure me less than this barbarous Treatment; upon which I burst into Tears, and pretended to fall into a Fit. This frighted him out of his wits, and he called up the Servants. Mrs. *Jewkes* immediately came in, and she and another of the Maids fell heartily to rubbing my Temples, and holding Smelling-Bottles to my Nose. Mrs. *Jewkes* told him she fear'd I should never recover, upon which he began to beat his Breasts, and cried out, O my dearest Angel, curse on my passionate Temper, I have destroy'd her, I have destroy'd her!—would she had spent my whole Estate rather than this had happened. Speak to me, my Love, I will melt my self into Gold for thy Pleasure. At last having pretty well tired my self with counterfeiting, and imagining I had continu'd long enough for my purpose in the sham Fit, I began to move my Eyes, to loosen my Teeth, and to open my Hands, which Mr. *Booby* no sooner perceived than he embraced and kissed me with the eagerest Extacy, asked my Pardon on his Knees for what I had suffered through his Folly and Perverseness, and without more Questions fetched me the Money. I fancy I have effectually prevented any farther Refusals or Inquiry into my Expences. It would be hard indeed that a Woman who marries a Man only for his Money should be debarred from spending it.

Well, after all things were quiet, we sat down to Breakfast, yet I resolved not to smile once, nor to say one good-natured, or good-humoured Word on any Account.

Nothing can be more prudent in a Wife, than a sullen Backwardness to Reconciliation; it makes a Husband fearful of offending by the Length of his Punishment.

When we were drest, the Coach was by my Desire ordered for an Airing, which we took in it. A long Silence prevailed on both Sides, tho' he constantly squeezed my Hand, and kissed me, and used other Familiarities, which I peevishly permitted. At last, I opened my Mouth first.—And so, says I, you are sorry you are married?—Pray, my Dear, says he, forget what I said in a Passion. Passion, says I, is apter to discover our Thoughts than to teach us to counterfeit. Well, says he, whether you will believe me or no, I solemnly vow, I would not change thee for the richest Woman in the Universe. No, I warrant you, says I; and yet you could refuse me a nasty hundred Pound. At these very Words, I saw Mr. *Williams* riding as fast as he could across a Field; and I looked out, and saw a Lease[1] of Greyhounds coursing a Hare, which they presently killed, and I saw him alight, and take it from them.

My Husband ordered *Robin* to drive towards him, and looked horribly out of Humour, which I presently imputed to Jealousy. So I began with him first; for that is the wisest way. La, Sir, says I; what makes you look so Angry and Grim? Doth the Sight of Mr. *Williams* give you all this Uneasiness? I am sure, I would never have married a Woman of whom I had so bad an Opinion, that I must be uneasy at every Fellow she looks at. My Dear, answer'd he, you injure me extremely, you was not in my Thoughts, nor, indeed, could be, while they were covered by so morose a Countenance; I am justly angry with that Parson, whose Family hath been raised from the Dunghill by ours; and who hath received from me twenty Kindnesses, and yet is not contented to destroy the Game in all other Places, which I freely give him leave to do; but hath the Impudence to pursue a few Hares, which I am desirous to preserve, round about this little Coppice.[2] Look, my Dear, pray look, says he; I believe he is going to turn Higler.[3] To confess the Truth, he had no less than three ty'd up behind his Horse, and a fourth he held in his Hand.

Pshaw, says I, I wish all the Hares in the Country were d——d (the Parson himself chid me afterwards for using the Word, tho' it was in his Service.) Here's a Fuss, indeed, about a nasty little pitiful Creature, that is not half so useful as a Cat. You shall not persuade me, that a Man of your Understanding, would quarrel with a Clergyman for such a Trifle. No, no, I am the Hare, for whom poor Parson *Williams* is persecuted; and Jealousy is the Motive. If you had married one of your Quality Ladies, she would have had Lovers by dozens, she would so; but because you have taken a Servant-Maid, forsooth! You are jealous if she but looks (and then I began to Water) at a poor P—a—a—rson in his Pu—u—u—lpit, and then out burst a Flood of Tears.

My Dear, said he, for Heaven's sake dry your Eyes, and don't let him be a Witness of your Tears, which I should be sorry to think

---

1 Three.
2 A small wood or thicket consisting of underwood and small trees grown for the purpose of periodical cutting. Booby is suggesting that Williams is trying to poach the hares. For a comprehensive discussion of poaching, and the gravity with which it was taken, see E.P. Thompson, *Whigs and Hunters: The Origin of the Black Act* (New York: Pantheon, 1975).
3 A peddler, specifically of game, poultry or produce.

might be imputed to my Unkindness; I have already given you some Proofs that I am not jealous of this Parson; I will now give you a very strong One: For I will mount my Horse, and you shall take *Williams* into the Coach. You may be sure, this Motion[1] pleased me, yet I pretended to make as light of it as possible, and told him, I was sorry his Behaviour had made some such glaring Instance, necessary to the perfect clearing my Character.

He soon came up to Mr. *Williams*, who had attempted to ride off, but was prevented by one of our Horsemen, whom my Husband sent to stop him. When we met, my Husband asked him how he did with a very good humoured Air, and told him he perceived he had found good Sport that Morning. He answered pretty moderate, Sir; for that he had found the three Hares tied on to the Saddle dead in a Ditch (winking on me at the same Time) and added he was sorry there was such a Rot[2] among them.

Well, says Mr. *Booby*, if you please, Mr. *Williams*, you shall come in and ride with my Wife. For my own part, I will mount on Horseback; for it is fine Weather, and besides, it doth not become me to loll[3] in a Chariot, whilst a Clergyman rides on Horseback.

At which Words, Mr. *Booby* leap'd out, and Mr. *Williams* leap'd in, in an Instant, telling my Husband as he mounted, he was glad to see such a Reformation, and that if he continued his Respect to the Clergy, he might assure himself of Blessings from above.

It was now that the Airing began to grow pleasant to me. Mr. *Williams*, who never had but one Fault, *viz.* that he generally smells of Tobacco, was now perfectly sweet; for he had for two Days together enjoined himself as a Penance not to smoke till he had kissed my Lips. I will loosen you from that Obligation, says I, and observing my Husband looking another way, I gave him a charming Kiss, and then he asked me Questions concerning my Wedding-night; this actually made me blush: I vow I did not think it had been in him.

As he went along, he began to discourse very learnedly, and told me the Flesh and the Spirit were too distinct Matters, which had not the least relation to each other. That all immaterial Substances (those were his very Words) such as Love, Desire, and so forth, were guided by the Spirit: But fine Houses, large Estates, Coaches, and dainty Entertainments were the Product of the Flesh. Therefore, says he, my

---

1 Proposal.
2 A virulent liver disease usually affecting sheep.
3 To rest or recline in a relaxed attitude.

Dear, you have two Husbands, one the Object of your Love, and to satisfy your Desire; the other the Object of your Necessity, and to furnish you with those other Conveniencies. (I am sure I remember every Word, for he repeated it three Times; O he is very good whenever I desire him to repeat a thing to me three times he always doth it!) as then the Spirit is preferable to the Flesh, so am I preferable to your other Husband, to whom I am antecedent in Time likewise. I say these things, my Dear, (said he) to satisfie your Conscience. A Fig for my Conscience, said I, when shall I meet you again in the Garden?

My Husband now rode up to the Chariot, and asked us how we did—I hate the Sight of him. Mr. *Williams* answered very well, at your Service. They then talked of the Weather, and other things, I wished him gone again, every Minute; but all in vain I had no more Opportunity of conversing with Mr. *Williams*.

Well; at Dinner Mr. *Booby* was very civil to Mr. *Williams*, and told him he was sorry for what had happened, and would make him sufficient Amends, if in his power, and desired him to accept of a Note for fifty Pounds; which he was so *good* to receive, notwithstanding all that had past, and told Mr. *Booby*, he hop'd he would be forgiven, and that he would pray for him.

We make a charming Fool of him, i'fackins;[1] Times are finely altered, I have entirely got the better of him, and am resolved never to give him his Humour.

O how foolish it is in a Woman, who hath once got the Reins into her own Hand, ever to quit them again.

After Dinner Mr. *Williams* drank the Church *et caetera*; and smiled on me; when my Husband's Turn came, he drank *et caetera* and the Church; for which he was very severely rebuked by Mr. *Williams* it being a high Crime, it seems, to name any thing before the Church. I do not know what *Et cetera* is, but I believe it is something concerning chusing Pallament Men; for I asked if it was not a Health to Mr. *Booby*'s Borough, and Mr. *Williams* with a hearty Laugh answered, Yes, Yes, it is his Borough we mean.[2]

I slipt out as soon as I could, hoping Mr. *Williams* would finish the Squire, as I have heard him say he could easily do, and come to me; but it happened quite otherwise, for in about half an Hour,

---

1   In faith.
2   Throughout this paragraph, as throughout the text as a whole, Shamela not only misses the punning language Williams and Booby use about her (not recognizing that she is the butt of this linguistic joke), but also lacks control of her sexuality about which they joke.

Booby came to me, and told me he had left Mr. *Williams*, the Mayor of his Borough, and two or three Aldermen heartily at it, and asked me if I would go hear *Williams* sing a Catch,[1] which, added he, he doth to a Miracle.

Every Opportunity of seeing my dear *Williams*, was agreeable to me, which indeed I scarce had at this Time; for when we returned, the whole Corporation were got together, and the Room was in a Cloud of Tobacco; Parson *Williams* was at the upper End of the Table, and he hath pure round cherry Cheeks, and his Face look'd all the World to nothing like the Sun in a Fog. If the Sun had a Pipe in his Mouth, there would be no Difference.

I began now to grow uneasy, apprehending I should have no more of Mr. *Williams's* Company that Evening, and not at all caring for my Husband, I advised him to sit down and drink for his Country with the rest of the Company; but he refused, and desired me to give him some Tea; swearing nothing made him so sick, as to hear a Parcel of Scoundrels, roaring forth the Principles of honest Men over their Cups, when, says he, I know most of them are such empty Blockheads, that they don't know their right Hand from their left, and that Fellow there, who hath talked so much of *Shipping*, at the left Side of the Parson, in whom they all place a Confidence, if I don't take care, will sell them to my Adversary.[2]

I don't know why I mention this Stuff to you; for I am sure I know nothing about *Pollitricks*,[3] more than Parson *Williams* tells me,

---

1 Originally, a short composition for three of more voices which sing the same melody as a round. Subsequently, especially applied to rounds in which the words are so arranged as to produce ludicrous effects, one singer catching at the words of another (*OED*). Here, and throughout, Williams's professional and political ambitions take precedence over his relationship with Shamela.

2 "An allusion to a recent disaster for the opposition. Six weeks before the publication of *Shamela*, a motion to remove Walpole failed overwhelmingly when many Tories deserted the opposition. Some of them actually voted against the motion, but the departure before the vote of veteran Jacobite leader William Shippen (1673-1743) and thirty-four followers caused more comment. The widely respected and incorruptible though not always sober, Shippen (who sat with other opposition leaders on the left of the Speaker) was suspected by some of taking a bribe. Sheridan Baker points out that Walpole's son Horace wrote 'Shippen' here in the margin of his copy" (Goldberg 302).

3 Politics.

who says that the Court-side are in the right on't, and that every Christian ought to be on the same with the Bishops.

When we had finished our Tea, we walked in the Garden till it was dark, and then my Husband proposed, instead of returning to the Company, (which I desired, that I might see Parson *Williams* again,) to sup in another Room by our selves, which, for fear of making him jealous, and considering too, that Parson *Williams* would be pretty far gone, I was obliged to consent to.

O! what a devilish Thing it is, for a Woman to be obliged to go to Bed to a spindle-shanked young Squire, she doth not like, when there is a jolly Parson in the same House she is fond of.

In the Morning I grew very peevish, and in the Dumps, notwithstanding all he could say or do to please me. I exclaimed against the Priviledge of Husbands, and vowed I would not be pulled and tumbled about. At last he hit on the only Method, which could have brought me into Humour, and proposed to me a Journey to *London*, within a few Days. This you may easily guess pleased me; for besides the Desire which I have of shewing my self forth, of buying fine Cloaths, Jewels, Coaches, Houses, and ten thousand other fine things, Parson *Williams* is, it seems, going thither too, to be *instuted*.[1]

O! what a charming Journey I shall have; for I hope to keep the dear Man in the Chariot with me all the way; and that foolish Booby (for that is the Name Mr. Williams *hath set him) will ride on Horseback.*

So as I shall have an Opportunity of seeing you so shortly, I think I will mention no more Matters to you now. O I had like to have forgot one very material thing; which is that it will look horribly, for a Lady of my Quality and Fashion, to own such a Woman as you for my Mother. Therefore we must meet in private only, and if you will never claim me, nor mention me to any one, I will always allow you what is very handsome. Parson *Williams* hath greatly advised me in this, and says, he thinks I should do very well to lay out twenty Pounds, and set you up in a little Chandler's Shop:[2] but you must remember all my Favours to you will depend on your Secrecy; for I am positively resolved, I will not be known to be your Daughter; and if you tell any one so, I shall deny it with all my Might, which Parson *Williams* says, I may do with a safe Conscience, being now a married Woman. So I rest

Your humble Servant
SHAMELA.

---

1 Instituted, i.e. into his new benefice that has been given to him by Booby.

2 A chandler is one who makes or sells candles.

P. S. The strangest Fancy hath enter'd into my Booby's Head, that can be imagined. He is resolved to have a Book made about him and me; he proposed it to Mr. *Williams*, and offered him a Reward for his Pains; but he says he never writ any thing of that kind, but will recommend my Husband, when he comes to Town, to a Parson *who does that Sort of Business for Folks*, one who can make my Husband, and me, and Parson *Williams*, to be all great People; for he *can make black white*, it seems. Well, but they say my Name is to be altered, Mr. *Williams*, says the first Syllabub[1] hath too comical a Sound, so it is to be changed into *Pamela*; I own I can't imagine what can be said; for to be sure I shan't confess any of my Secrets to them, and so I whispered Parson *Williams* about that, who answered me, I need not give my self any Trouble: for the Gentleman *who writes Lives*, never asked more than a few Names of his Customers, and that he made all the rest out of his own Head; you mistake, Child, said he, if you apprehend any Truths are to be delivered. So far on the contrary, if you had not been acquainted with the Name, you would not have known it to be your own History. I have seen a *Piece of his Performance*, where the Person, whose Life was written, could he have risen from the Dead again, would not have even suspected he had been aimed at, unless by the Title of the Book, which was superscribed with his Name. Well, all these Matters are strange to me, yet I can't help laughing, to think I shall see my self in a printed Book.

So much for Mrs. *Shamela*, or *Pamela*, which I have taken Pains to transcribe from the Originals, sent down by her Mother in a Rage, at the Proposal in her last Letter. The Originals themselves are in my Hands, and shall be communicated to you, if you think proper to make them publick; and certainly they will have their Use. The Character of *Shamela*, will make young Gentlemen wary how they take the most fatal Step both to themselves and Families, by youthful, hasty and improper Matches; indeed, they may assure themselves, that all such Prospects of Happiness are vain and delusive, and that they sacrifice all the solid Comforts of their Lives, to a very transient Satisfaction of a Passion, which how hot so ever it be, will be soon cooled; and when cooled, will afford them nothing but Repentance.[2]

---

1 Shamela confuses syllable, which is intended, with syllabub, a drink or dish made of milk or cream, curdled by the admixture of wine or cider, often sweetened and flavored.
2 This echoes one of Haywood's main points in *Anti-Pamela*.

Can any thing be more miserable, than to be despised by the whole World, and that must certainly be the Consequence; to be despised by the Person obliged, which it is more than probable will be the Consequence, and of which, we see an Instance in *Shamela*; and lastly to despise one's self, which must be the Result of any Reflection on so weak and unworthy a Choice.

As to the Character of Parson *Williams*, I am sorry it is a true one. Indeed those who do not know him, will hardly believe it so; but what Scandal doth it throw on the Order to have one bad Member, unless they endeavour to screen[1] and protect him? In him you see a Picture of almost every Vice exposed in nauseous and odious Colours; and if a Clergyman would ask me by what Pattern he should form himself, I would say, Be the reverse of *Williams*:[2] So far therefore he may be of use to the Clergy themselves, and though God forbid there should be many *Williams*'s amongst them, you and I are too honest to pretend, that the Body wants no Reformation.

To say the Truth, I think no greater Instance of the contrary can be given than that which appears in your Letter. The confederating to cry up a nonsensical ridiculous Book, (I believe the most extensively so of any ever yet published,) and to be so weak and so wicked as to pretend to make it a Matter of Religion; whereas so far from having any moral Tendency, the Book is by no means innocent:[3] For,

---

1 For an eighteenth-century reader the term "screen" would immediately summon thoughts of Robert Walpole, who earned the title "screenmaster general" for his ability to screen his political allies, particularly from the fallout of the South Sea Bubble in 1720.

2 In *The Champion* (19 April 1740) Fielding includes a description of what a clergyman is *not* that resembles Williams: "a Man of loose Morals, proud, malevolent, vain, rapacious, and revengeful; not grieving at, but triumphing over the Sins of Men, and rejoicing, like the Devil, that they will be punished for them; deaf to the Cries of the Poor; shunning the Distress'd; blind to Merit; a Magnifier and Spreader of Slander; not shunning the Society of the Wicked for Fear of Contamination, but from Hypocrisy and Vain Glory; hating not Vice but the Vicious; resenting not only an Injury, but the least Affront with Inveteracy. Let us suppose this Man feasting himself luxuriously at the Tables of the Great, where he is suffered at the Expense of flattering their Vices, and often too, as meanly submitting to see himself and his Order, nay often Religion itself, ridiculed, whilst, that he may join in the Burgundy, he joins in the Laugh, or rather is laughed at by the Fools he flatters."

3 One of Fielding's key points.

First, There are many lascivious Images in it, very improper to be laid before the Youth of either Sex.

2dly, Young Gentlemen are here taught, that to marry their Mother's Chambermaids, and to indulge the Passion of Lust, at the Expence of Reason and Common Sense, is an Act of Religion, Virtue, and Honour; and, indeed the surest Road to Happiness.

3dly, All Chambermaids are strictly enjoyned to look out after their Masters; they are taught to use little Arts to that purpose: And lastly, are countenanced in Impertinence to their Superiors, and in betraying the Secrets of Families.

4thly, In the Character of Mrs. *Jewkes* Vice is rewarded; whence every Housekeeper may learn the Usefulness of pimping and bawding for her Master.

5thly, In Parson *Williams*, who is represented as a faultless Character, we see a busy Fellow, intermeddling with the private Affairs of his Patron, whom he is very ungratefully forward to expose and condemn on every Occasion.

Many more Objections might, if I had Time or Inclination, be made to this Book; but I apprehend, what hath been said is sufficient to persuade you of the use which may arise from publishing an Antidote to this Poison. I have therefore sent you the Copies of these Papers, and if you have Leisure to communicate them to the Press, I will transmit you the Originals, tho' I assure you, the Copies are exact.

I shall only add, that there is not the least Foundation for any thing which is said of Lady *Davers*, or any of the other Ladies; all that is merely to be imputed to the Invention of the Biographer. I have particularly enquired after Lady *Davers*, and don't hear Mr. *Booby* hath such a Relation, or that there is indeed any such Person existing. I am,

> *Dear Sir,*
> *Most faithfully and respectfully,*
> *Your humble Servant,*
> J. OLIVER.

Parson TICKLETEXT *to Parson* OLIVER.

Dear SIR,

I Have read over the History of *Shamela*, as it appears in those authentick Copies you favour'd me with, and am very much ashamed of the Character, which I was hastily prevailed on to give that Book. I am equally angry with the pert Jade herself, and with the Author of her Life: For I scarce know yet to whom I chiefly owe an Imposition, which hath been so general, that if Numbers could defend me from Shame, I should have no Reason to apprehend it.

As I have your implied Leave to publish, what you so kindly sent me, I shall not wait for the Originals, as you assure me the Copies are exact, and as I am really impatient to do what I think a serviceable Act of Justice to the World.

Finding by the End of her last Letter, that the little Hussy was in Town, I made it pretty much my Business to enquire after her, but with no effect hitherto: As soon as I succeed in this Enquiry, you shall hear what Discoveries I can learn. You will pardon the Shortness of this Letter, as you shall be troubled with a much longer very soon: And believe me,

Dear Sir,
Your most faithful Servant,
THO. TICKLETEXT.

P. S. Since I writ, I have a certain Account, that Mr. *Booby* hath caught his Wife in bed with *Williams*; hath turned her off, and is prosecuting him in the spiritual Court.[1]

FINIS.

---

1 A court having jurisdiction in matters of religion or ecclesiastical affairs; matrimonial matters would also come under its authority.

Appendix A: Women's Work

1. **Richard Campbell, from** *The London Tradesman.* **Being a** *Compendious View of All the Trades, Professions, Arts, both Liberal and Mechanic, now practiced in the Cities of London and Westminster* **(London: 1747)**

From Chapter 39: *Of the Milliner*

[This description of the profession and apprenticing of milliners suggests the intersection of professional work and the threats of sexual work that woman forced to earn a wage regularly encountered. It also suggests some of the negative associations with milliners.]

The Milliner, though no Male Trade, has a just Claim to a Place on this Occasion, as the Fair Sex, who are generally bound to this Business, may have as much Curiosity to know the Nature of their Employment before they engage in it, and stand as much in need of sound Advice in the Choice of an Occupation, as the Youth of our own Sex.

The Milliner is concerned in making and providing the Ladies with Linen of all sorts, fit for Wearing Apparel, from the Holland Smock to the Tippet and Commode; but as we are got into the Lady's Articles, which are so very numerous, the Reader is not to expect that we are to give an exact List of every thing belonging to them; let it suffice in general, that the Milliner furnishes them with Holland, Cambrick, Lawn and Lace of all sorts, and makes these Materials into Smocks, Aprons, Tippits, Handerchiefs, Necaties, Ruffles, Mobs, Caps, Dressed-Heads, with as many *Etceteras* as would reach from *Charing-Cross* to the *Royal Exchange.*

They make up Cloaks, Manteels, Mantelets, Cheens and Capucheens, of Silk, Velvet, plain or brocaded, and trim them with Silver and Gold Lace, or Black Lace: They make up and sell Hats, Hoods, and Caps of all Sorts and Materials; they find them in Gloves, Muffs, and Ribbons; they sell quilted Petticoats, and Hoops of all Sizes, & c. and lastly, some of them deal in Habits for Riding, and Dresses for the Masquerade; In a word, they furnish every thing to the Ladies, that can contribute to set off their Beauty, increase their Vanity, or render them ridiculous.

....They have vast Profits on every Article they deal in; yet give but poor, mean Wages to every Person they employ under them: Though a young Woman can work nearly in all manner of Needle Work, yet she cannot earn more than Five or Six Shillings a Week, out of which she is to find herself in Board and Lodging. Therefore, out of Regard to the Fair Sex, I must caution Parents, not to bind their Daughters to this Business: the vast Resort of young Beaus and Rakes to Milliner's Shops, exposes young Creatures to many Temptations, and insensibly debauches their Morals before they are capable of Vice. A young Coxcomb no sooner is Master of an Estate, and a small Share of Brains, but he affects to deal with the most noted Milliner: If he chances to meet in her Shop any thing that has the Appearance of Youth, and the simple Behaviour of undesigning Innocence, he immediately accosts the young Sempstress with all the little Raillery he is Master of, talks loosely, and thinks himself most witty, when he has cracked some obscene Jest upon the young Creature. The Mistress, tho' honest, is obliged to bear the Wretch's Ribaldry, out of Regard to his Custom, and Respect to some undeserved Title of Quality he wears, and is forced to lay her Commands upon the Apprentice to answer all his Rudeness with Civility and Complaisance. Thus the young Creature is obliged every Day to hear a Language, that by degrees undermines her Virtue, deprives her of that modest Delicacy of Thought, which is the constant Companion of uncorrupted Innocence, and makes Vice become familiar to the Ear, from whence there is but a small Transition to the grosser Gratification of the Appetite.

I am far from charging all Milliners with the Crime of Connivance at the Ruin of their Apprentices; but fatal Experience must convince the Public, that nine out of ten of the young Creatures that are obliged to serve in these Shops, are ruined and undone: Take a Survey of all the common Women of the Town, who take their Walks between Charing-Cross and Fleet-Ditch, and, I am persuaded, more than one Half of them have been bred Milliners, have been debauched in their Houses, and are obliged to throw themselves upon the Town for Want of Bread, after they have left them. Whether then it is owing to the Milliners, or to the Nature of the Business, or to whatever Cause it is owing, the Facts are so clear, and the Misfortunes attending their Apprentices so manifest, that it ought to be the last Shift a young Creature is driven to. But if Parents will needs give their Daughters this kind of Education, let them avoid your private Hedge Milliners; those who pretend to deal only with a few select Customers, who scorn to keep open Shop, but live in some remote Corner: These are Decoys for the Unwary; they are but Places for Assignations, and take the Title of Milliner, a more polite Name for a Bawd, a Procuress, a Wretch who lives upon the Spoils of Virtue, and supports her Pride by robbing the Innocent of Health, Fame, and Reputations: They are the Ruin of private Families, Enemies to conjugal Affection, promote nothing but Vice, and live by Lust.

2. **Richard Steele, *The Spectator* no. 155 (28 August 1711), *The Spectator*, edited by Donald F. Bond (Oxford at the Clarendon Press, 1965) Vol. 2, 110**

[This letter from a "milliner" suggests the intersection of sexual and mercantile commerce central to *Anti-Pamela*.]

I shall end this Speculation with a Letter I have received from a pretty Milliner in the City.

Mr. SPECTATOR,

"I HAVE read your Account of Beauties, and was not a little surprized to find no Character of my self in it. I do assure you I have little else to do but to give Audience as I am such. Here are Merchants of no small Consideration, who call in as certainly as they go to 'Change to say something of my Roguish Eye: And here is one who makes me once or twice a week Tumble over all my Goods, and then owns it was only a Gallantry to see me act with these pretty Hands; then lays out three Pence in a little Ribband for his Wristbands, and thinks he is a Man of great Vivacity. There is an ugly Thing not far off me whose Shop is frequented only by People of Business, that is all Day long as busy as possible. Must I that am a Beauty be treated with for nothing but my Beauty? Be pleased to assign Rates to my kind Glances, or make all pay who come to see me, or shall I be undone by my Admirers for want of Customers. *Albacinda, Eudosia,* and all the rest would be used just as we are, if they were in our Condition; therefore pray consider the Distress of us the lower Order of Beauties, and I shall be
Your oblig'd humble Servant."

3. **Samuel Johnson, *Idler* no. 26 (14 October 1758) and no. 29 (4 November 1758), *The Yale Edition of the Works of Samuel Johnson, Volume II. The Idler and The Adventurer,* edited by W. J. Bate, John M. Bullitt, and L.F. Powell (New Haven and London: Yale UP, 1963) 80-83, 89-92**

[This excerpt details the career of "Betty Broom," a serving girl who, like Pamela, possesses skills in reading and writing that distinguish her from her fellow servants. These essays highlight the complicated inter-section of class and literacy for domestic servants, as well as the exces-sive demands placed on servants. Additionally, they offer an interesting perspective on the hierarchy within service, as well as servants' peri-patetic and fundamentally unstable situation. These two essays were reprinted at least six times and informed contemporary perceptions of the servant class. For another perspective on the treatment of a servant, see Lady Sarah Pennington, Appendix D.2.]

Mr. Idler,

....I am a poor girl. I was bred in the country at a charity school, main-tained by the contributions of wealthy neighbours. The ladies our patronesses visited us from time to time, examined how we were taught, and saw that our cloaths were clean. We lived happily enough, and were instructed to be thankful to those at whose cost we were educated. I was always the favourite of my mistress; she used to call me to read and shew my copybook to all strangers, who never dismissed me without commendation, and very seldom without a shilling.

At last the chief of our subscribers having passed a winter in Lon-don, came down full of an opinion new and strange to the whole country. She held it little less than criminal to teach poor girls to read and write. They who are born to poverty, she said, are born to igno-rance, and will work the harder the less they know. She told her friends, that London was in confusion by the insolence of servants, that scarcely a wench was to be got "for all work," since education had made such numbers of fine ladies, that nobody would now accept a lower title than that of a waiting maid, or something that might qual-ify her to wear laced shoes and long ruffles, and to sit at work in the parlour window. But she was resolved, for her part, to spoil no more girls; those who were to live by their hands should neither read nor write out of her pocket; the world was bad enough already, and she would have no part in making it worse....

....in less than a year the whole parish was convinced, that the nation would be ruined if the children of the poor were taught to read and write.

Our school was now dissolved....

My reputation for scholarship, which had hitherto recommended me to favour, was, by the adherents to the new opinion, considered as a crime; and, when I offered myself to any mistress, I had no other answer, than, "Sure, child, you would not work; hard work is not fit for a penwoman; a scrubbing brush would spoil your hand, child!"

....I was resolved to try my fortune, and took my passage in the next week's waggon to London. I had no snares laid for me at my arrival, but came safe to a sister of my mistress, who undertook to get me a place. She knew only the families of mean tradesmen; and I, having no high opinion of my own qualifications, was willing to accept the first offer.

My first mistress was wife of a working watchmaker, who earned more than was sufficient to keep his family in decency and plenty, but it was their constant practice to hire a chaise on Sunday, and spend half the wages of the week on Richmond-Hill; of Monday he commonly lay half in bed, and spent the other half in merriment; Tuesday and Wednesday consumed the rest of his money; and three days every week were passed in extremity of want by us who were left at home, while my master lived on trust at an alehouse. You may be sure that of the sufferers the maid suffered most, and I left them, after three months, rather than be starved.

I was then maid to a hatter's wife. There was no want to be dreaded, for they lived in perpetual luxury. My mistress was a diligent woman, and rose early in the morning to set the journeymen to work; my master was a man much beloved by his neighbours, and sat at one club or other every night. I was obliged to wait on my master at night, and on my mistress in the morning. He seldom came home before two, and she rose at five. I could no more live without sleep than without food, and therefore entreated them to look out for another servant.

My next removal was to a linen draper's, who had six children. My mistress, when I first entered the house, informed me that I must never contradict the children, nor suffer them to cry.... I could not keep six children quiet, who were bribed to be clamorous, and was therefore dismissed, as a girl honest, but not good-natured.

I then lived with a couple that kept a petty shop of remnants and cheap linen. I was qualified to make a bill, or keep a book, and being therefore often called, at a busy time, to serve the customers, expected that I should now be happy, in proportion as I was useful. But my mistress appropriated every day part of the profit to some private use, and, as she grew bolder in her theft, at last deducted such sums, that my master began to wonder how he sold so much, and gained so little. She pretended to assist his enquiries, and began, very gravely, to hope that "Betty was honest, and yet those sharp girls were apt to be light fingered." You will believe that I did not stay there much longer....

Having left the last place in haste to avoid the charge or the suspicion of theft, I had not secured another service, and was forced to take a lodging in a back street. I had now got good cloaths. The woman who lived in the garret opposite to mine was very officious, and offered to take care of my room and clean it, while I went round to my acquaintance to enquire for a mistress. I knew not why she was so kind, nor how I could recompense her, but in a few days I missed some of my linen, went to another lodging, and resolved not to have another friend in the next garret.

In six weeks I became under-maid at the house of a mercer, in Cornhill, whose son was his apprentice. The young gentleman used to sit late at the tavern, without the knowledge of his father, and I was ordered by my mistress to let him in silently, to his bed under the counter, and to be very careful to take away his candle. The hours which I was obliged to watch, whilst the rest of the family was in bed, I considered as supernumerary, and having no business assigned for them, thought myself at liberty to spend them my own way: I kept myself awake with a book, and for some time liked my state the better for this opportunity of reading. At last, the upper-maid found my book and shewed it to my mistress, who told me that wenches like me might spend their time better; that she never knew any of the readers that had good designs in their heads; that she could always find something else to do with her time, than to puzzle over books; and did not like that such a fine lady should sit up for her young master.

This was the first time that I found it thought criminal or dangerous to know how to read. I was dismissed decently, lest I should tell tales, and had a small gratuity above my wages.

I then lived with a gentlewoman of a small fortune. This was the only happy part of my life; my mistress, for whom publick diversions were too expensive, spent her time with books, and was pleased to find a maid who could partake her amusements. I rose early in the morning, that I might have time in the afternoon to read or listen, and was suffered to tell my opinion, or express my delight. Thus fifteen months stole away, in which I did not repine that I was born to servitude. But a burning fever seized my mistress, of whom I shall say no more than that her servant wept upon her grave.

I had lived in a kind of luxury, which made me very unfit for another place; and was rather too delicate for the conversation of a kitchen; so that when I was hired in the family of an East India director, my behaviour was so different, as they said, from that of a common servant, that they concluded me a gentlewoman in disguise, and turned me out in three weeks, on suspicion of some design which they could not comprehend.

I then fled for refuge to the other end of the town, where I hoped to find no obstruction from my new accomplishments, and was hired under the house-keeper in a splendid family. Here I was too wise for the maids, and too nice for the footmen; yet I might have lived on without much uneasiness, had not my mistress, the house-keeper, who used to employ me in buying necessaries for the family, found a bill which I had made of one day's expences. I suppose it did not quite agree with her own book, for she fiercely declared her resolution, that there should be no pen and ink in that kitchen but her own.

She had the justice, or the prudence, not to injure my reputation; and I was easily admitted into another house in the neighbourhood, where my business was to sweep the rooms and make the beds. Here I was, for some time, the favourite of Mrs. Simper, my lady's woman, who could not bear the vulgar girls, and was happy in the attendance of a young woman of some education. Mrs. Simper loved a novel, tho' she could not read hard words, and therefore when her lady was abroad, we always laid hold on her books. At last, my abilities became so much celebrated, that the house-steward used to employ me in keeping his accounts. Mrs. Simper then found out that my sauciness was grown to such a height that no body could endure it, and told my lady, that there never had been a room well swept, since Betty Broom came into the house.

I was then hired by a consumptive lady, who wanted a maid that could read and write. I attended her four years, and tho' she was never pleased, yet when I declared my resolution to leave her, she burst into tears, and told me that I must bear the peevishness of a sick-bed, and I should find myself remembered in her will. I complied, and a codicil was added in my favour; but in less than a week, when I set her gruel before her, I laid the spoon on the left side, and she threw her will into the fire. In two days she made another, which she burnt in the same manner because she could not eat her chicken. A third was made and destroyed, because she heard a mouse within the wainscot, and was sure that I should suffer her to be carried out alive. After this I was for some time out of favour, but as her illness grew upon her, resentment and sullenness gave way to her kinder sentiments. She died and left me five hundred pounds; with this fortune I am going to settle in my native parish, where I resolve to spend some hours every day, in teaching poor girls to read and write.

I am, Sir,
Your humble servant,
BETTY BROOM.

4. Eliza Haywood, from *Fantomina; or, Love in a Maze. Being a Secret History of an Amour Between Two Persons of Condition* (London: 1724)

[Haywood's 1724 novel, *Fantomina*, records the adventures of a woman who completely changes her identity four times in order to seduce repeatedly the same man, Beauplaisir. One of these identities is that of Celia, a serving maid. Her description provides insight into the situation for female domestics, with the danger of "amorous violence," and the character anticipates both Richardson's Pamela and Haywood's Syrena Tricksy.]

She no sooner heard he had left the Town than making a Pretence to her aunt that she was going to visit a Relation in the Country went towards *Bath*, attended but by two Servants, who she found Reasons to quarrel with on the Road and discharged: Clothing herself in a Habit she had brought with her, she forsook the Coach and went into a Wagon in which Equipage she arrived at *Bath*. The Dress she was in, was a round eared Cap, a short Red Petticoat and a little Jacket of Grey Stuff; all the rest of her Accoutrements were answerable to these and joined with a broad Country Dialect, a rude unpolished Air, which she, having been bred in these Parts, knew very well how to imitate, with her Hair and Eye-brows blackened, made it impossible for her to be known or taken for any other than what she seemed. Thus disguised did she offer herself to Service in the House where *Beauplaisir* lodged, having made it her Business to find out immediately where he was. Notwithstanding this Metamorphosis she was still extremely pretty; and the Mistress of the House happening at that Time to want a Maid, was very glad of the Opportunity of taking her. She was presently received into the Family; and had a Post in it, (such as she would have chosen, had she been left at her Liberty,) that of making the Gentlemen's Beds, getting them their Breakfasts, and waiting on them in their Chambers. Fortune in this Exploit was extremely on her side; there were no others of the Male-Sex in the House, than an old Gentleman, who had lost the Use of his Limbs with the Rheumatism and had come thither for the Benefit of the Waters, and her beloved *Beauplaisir*; so that she was in no Apprehensions of any Amorous Violence, but where she wished to find it. Nor were her Designs disappointed: He was fired with the first Sight of her; and tho' he did not presently take any farther Notice of her than giving her two or three hearty Kisses, yet she, who now understood that Language but too well, easily saw they were the Prelude to more substantial joys.—Coming the next

Morning to bring his Chocolate as he had ordered, he caught her by the pretty Leg, which the Shortness of her Petticoat did not in the least oppose: then pulling her gently to him, asked her, how long she had been in Service? ——How many Sweethearts she had? If she had ever been in Love? and many other such Questions, befitting one of the Degree she appeared to be: All which she answered with such seeming Innocence, as more enflamed the amorous Heart of him who talked to her. He compelled her to sit in his Lap; and gazing on her blushing Beauties, which, if possible, received Addition from her plain and rural Dress, he soon lost the Power of containing himself. ——His wild Desires burst out in all his Words and Actions: he called her little Angel, Cherubim, swore he must enjoy her, though Death were to be the Consequence, devoured her Lips, her Breasts with greedy Kisses, held to his burning Bosom her half-yielding, half-reluctant Body, nor suffered her to get loose, till he had ravaged all and glutted each rapacious Sense with the Sweet Beauties of the pretty *Celia*, for that was the Name she bore in this second Expedition. ——Generous as Liberality itself in all who gave him Joy this way, he gave her a handsome Sum of Gold, which she dare not now refuse for fear of creating some Mistrust and losing the Heart she so lately had regained; therefore taking it with an humble Curtsy, and a well counterfeited Show of surprize and Joy, cried O Law, Sir ! what must I do for all this? He laughed at her Simplicity, and kissing her again, tho' less fervently than he had done before, bade her not be out of the Way when he came home at Night. She promised she would not and very obediently kept her Word.

5. Samuel Richardson, from *Pamela; or, Virtue Rewarded* (1740), edited by Thomas Keymer and Alice Wakely (Oxford: Oxford UP, 2001)

[Though Pamela is a servant girl, there is a limited amount of time devoted to discussions of the kinds of work she is (or should be) doing. The following passage details what she did for Mr. B.'s mother, the kinds of sexual labor that is an implicit alternative to domestic service, and Pamela's own descriptions of "work." For more selections from *Pamela*, see Appendix B.1, and C.2.]

from Letter I.
Dear Father and Mother,
I Have great Trouble, and some Comfort, to acquaint you with. The Trouble is, that my good Lady died of the Illness I mention'd to you, and left us all much griev'd for her Loss; for she was a dear good Lady,

and kind to all us her Servants. Much I fear'd, that as I was taken by her Goodness to wait upon her Person, I should be quite destitute again, and forc'd to return to you and my poor Mother, who have so much to do to maintain yourselves; and, as my Lady's Goodness had put me to write and cast Accompts, and made me a little expert at my Needle, and other Qualifications above my Degree, it would have been no easy Matter to find a Place that your poor *Pamela* was fit for: But God, whose Graciousness to us we have so often experienc'd at a Pinch, put it into my good Lady's Heart, on her Death-bed, just an Hour before she expir'd, to recommend to my young Master all her Servants, one by one; and when it came to my Turn to be recommended, for I was sobbing and crying at her Pillow, she could only say, My dear Son!—and so broke off a little, and then recovering,— Remember my poor *Pamela*!—And these were some of her last Words! O how my Eyes run!—Don't wonder to see the Paper so blotted!

Well, but God's Will must be done!—and so comes the Comfort, that I shall not be oblig'd to return back to be a Clog upon my dear Parents! For my Master said, I will take care of you all, my Lasses; and for you, *Pamela*, (and took me by the Hand; yes, he took me by the Hand before them all) for my dear Mother's sake, I will be a Friend to you, and you shall take care of my Linen (11).

from Letter X.

... I have not been idle.... For he will see I was resolv'd to be honest, and glory'd in the Honesty of my poor Parents. I will tell you all, the next Opportunity; for I am watch'd, and such-like, very narrowly; and he says to Mrs. *Jervis*, This Girl is always scribbling; I think she may be better employ'd. And yet I work all Hours with my Needle, upon his Linen, and the fine Linen of the Family; and am besides about flowering him a Waistcoat.—But, Oh! my Heart's broke almost; for what am I likely to have for my Reward, but Shame and Disgrace, or else ill Words, and hard Treatment! I'll tell you all soon, and hope I shall find my long Letter (22).

from Letter XXVII.

Well, said he, you are an ungrateful Baggage; but I am thinking it would be Pity, with these fair soft Hands, and that lovely Skin (as he call'd it) that you should return again to hard Work, as you must, if you go to your Father's; and so I would advise her to take a House in *London*, and let Lodgings to us Members of Parliament, when we come to Town, and such a pretty Daughter as you may pass for, will always fill her House, and she'll get a great deal of Money (69).

from Letter XXIX.

My dear Father and Mother,

I Must write on, tho' I shall come so soon; for now I have hardly any thing else to do. For I have finish'd all that lay upon me to do, and only wait the good Time of setting out. Mrs. *Jervis* said, I must be low in Pocket, for what I had laid out; and so would have presented me with two Guineas of her Five; but I could not take them of her, because, poor Gentlewoman! she pays old Debts for her Children that were extravagant, and wants them herself. This, tho', was very good in her.

I am sorry, I shall have but little to bring with me; but I know you won't; you are so good!—and I will work the harder when I come home, if I can get a little Plain-work, or any thing to do. But all your Neighbourhood is so poor, that I fear I shall want Work; but may-be Dame *Mumford* can help me to something, from some good Family she is acquainted with.

Here, what a sad Thing it is! I have been brought up wrong, as Matters stand. For, you know, my Lady, now with God, lov'd Singing and Dancing; and, as she would have it I had a Voice, she made me learn both; and often has she made me sing her an innocent Song, and a good Psalm too, and dance before her. And I must learn to flower and draw too, and to work fine Work with my Needle; why, all this too I have got pretty tolerably at my Finger's End, as they say, and she us'd to praise me, and was a good Judge of such Matters.

Well, now, what is all this to the Purpose, as Things have turn'd about?...

So I shall make a fine Figure with my Singing and my Dancing when I come home to you. Nay, even I shall be unfit for a May-day Holiday-time; for these Minuets, Rigadoons, and *French* Dances, that I have been practising, will make me but ill Company for my rural Milkmaid Companions that are to be. Be sure I had better, as Things stand, have learn'd to wash and scour, and brew and bake, and such-like. But I hope, if I can't get Work, and can get a Place, to learn these soon, if any body will have the Goodness to bear with me, till I can learn. For I bless God! I have an humble, and a teachable Mind, for all what my Master says; and, next to his Grace, that is all my Comfort: For I shall think nothing too mean that is honest. It may be a little hard at first, but woe to my proud Heart, if I shall find it so, on Tryal! for I will make it bend to its Condition, or will break it.

I have read of a good Bishop that was to be burnt for his Religion; and he try'd how he could bear it, by putting his Fingers into the lighted Candle: So I, t'other Day, try'd, when *Rachel's* Back was turn'd, if I could not scour the Pewter Plate she had begun. I see I could do't by Degrees; tho' I blister'd my Hand in two Places.

All the Matter is, if I could get Needle-work enough, I would not spoil my Fingers by this rough Work. But if I can't, I hope to make my Hands as red as a Blood-pudden, and as hard as a Beechen Trencher, to accommodate them to my Condition.—But I must break off, here's some-body coming!— (75-77).

6. Eliza Haywood, from *A Present for a Servant-Maid* (London: 1743)

[Like *Anti-Pamela*, *A Present for a Servant-Maid* sought to capitalize on the *Pamela* craze by offering a kind of *vade mecum* for female servants. Published anonymously in June 1743, the title page advertizes the price as "*One Shilling, or 25 for a Guinea for those who give them away.*" In his forthcoming *Bibliography of Eliza Haywood*, Patrick Spedding notes that *A Present for a Servant-Maid* was Haywood's "fastest-selling title, going through at least seven editions in six years" (Ab.58). It was also published in the American colonies. It is a kind of anti-*Anti-Pamela* for it admonishes servant-maids to avoid nearly every kind of behavior in which Syrena indulges. The commonality between the two texts is the representation of the sexual vulnerability of female servants to the advances of their masters. It also, in the section discussing the appropriate behavior with an amourous single master, implicitly holds up *Pamela* as a model to follow.]

[Haywood advises the servant to stay in the employ of one family.]

As the first Step therefore towards being happy in Service, you should never enter into a Place but with a View of *staying in it*; to which End I think it highly necessary, that (as no Mistress worth serving will take you without a Character) you should also make some Enquiry into the Place before you suffer yourself to be hired. There are some Houses which appear well by *Day*, that it would be little safe for a modest Maid to sleep in at *Night*: I do not mean those Coffee-houses, Bagnio's &c. which some Parts of the Town, particularly *Covent-Garden*, abounds with; for in those the very Aspect of the Persons who keep them are sufficient to shew what manner of Trade they follow; but Houses which have no public Shew of Business, are richly furnished, and where the Mistress has an Air of the strictest Modesty, and perhaps affects a double Purity of Behaviour: Yet under such Roofs, and under the Sanction of such Women as I have described, are too frequently acted such Scenes of Debauchery as would startle even the Owners of some common Brothels.

[She has a list of tendencies against which one should guard.]

Sloth.] One of the greatest Impediments to the Practice of this Lesson is *Sloth*; which tho' it proceeds at first from a Heaviness in the Blood, and is no more than a Distemper, if indulg'd grows up into a Vice, and renders you incapable of doing your Duty either to God or Man ... it is, as I may say, the principal Source of all the Evils a Person in any Station can be guilty of, but more especially in yours. *Sloth* occasions a falling-off from every thing that is commendable, and a general Defection of the Animal Spirits; so that you become unable as well as unwilling to perform even what would otherwise be most pleasing to you. Take care, therefore, how you give way to the Love of Idleness, or too much Sleep, both which dull the Spirits, and fill the Body full of gross Humours; you shou'd therefore make use of your utmost Endeavours against these potent Enemies of your Health, your Happiness, your Virtue.

Staying when sent on Errands.] Another very great Fault I have observed in many of you, which, if not proceeding always from downright Sloth, does from something so like it, that the Effect is scarce to be distinguish'd from the Cause: It shews at least a *Sloth of the Mind*, a Want of Diligence, a Carelessness of pleasing, which, as I have already said, is the Source of almost all the Faults you can be guilty of; and this is staying when you are sent on an Errand; a Croud gather'd about a Pickpocket, a Pedlar, a Mountebank, or a Ballad-Singer, has the Power to detain too many of you, tho' when sent on the most important Business to those you serve; and which, perhaps, may greatly suffer by a Moment's Delay. How cruel, therefore, how unjust is it to sacrifice to a little impertinent Curiosity the Interest of those who give you Bread! But supposing the Affair you go upon is in itself immaterial, it is not so to those who send you: No body sends for any thing they do not want, nor on any Message which they would not have immediately deliver'd; and the Suspence they are in while waiting beyond the Time they might expect you back, creates an Uneasiness of Mind which no considerate Person would give to any one, much less to a Master or Mistress. Sometimes, perhaps, you have the Excuse of meeting an Acquaintance, a Friend, or one who knows the Family you lived in before, and has a thousand Things to tell you concerning what happened since you went away, and what is said of yourself; but you ought to remember, that no Intelligence that detains you from your Business can be worth your while to hear, or an Equivalent for disobliging those you serve; and that none are truly your Friends that would hold you by the Ears with any idle Story; for while you are in the Condition of a Servant, your Time belongs to those who pay you for it; and all you waste from the Employment they set you about, is a Robbery from them.

Listening to Fortune-tellers.] ... It must be confessed a Desire of prying into future Events is very much ingrafted in human Nature, especially in your Sex; yet sure nothing can be more silly than an Endeavour to penetrate into them by looking into a Cup, as if the Decrees of Heaven were written in the Grounds of Coffee, and intelligible to such poor ignorant Wretches as those who make a Practice of this pretended Art. It is no Excuse for you, that you see your Betters sometimes guilty of this Weakness; you are not to imitate them in their Errors: Besides, what they do of this Kind is only for Amusement; they cannot but have more Sense than to place any Dependance on the absurd things foretold them by these People, nor can run the Hazards you do by bringing them into the House, where, when you happen to be called away, they are often left alone in a Room, and, as I said before, 'tis great Odds if they do not make use of that Opportunity to pilfer something, for which afterwards you will have the Blame. Tho' I have only mentioned the Prognosticators in Coffee-grounds, the Calculators of Nativity, Resolvers of Horory Questions, Palmistry, Geomancy-mongers, Card-cutters, Gipsies, and all the other Pretenders to Divination, come under the same Head, and are in general to be discouraged and avoided by all discreet and honest Servants.

Temptations from your Master.] Being so much under his Command, and obliged to attend him at any Hour, and at any Place he is pleased to call you, will lay you under Difficulties to avoid his Importunities, which it must be confessed are not easy to surmount; yet a steady Resolution will enable you; and as a vigorous Resistance is less to be expected in your Station, your persevering may, perhaps, in Time, oblige him to desist, and acknowledge you have more Reason than himself: It is a Duty, however, owing to yourself to endeavour it.

Behaviour to him, if a single Man.] If he happens to be a single Man, and is consequently under less Restraint, be as careful as you can, Opportunities will not be wanting to prosecute his Aim; and as you cannot avoid hearing what he says, must humbly, and in the most modest Terms you can, remonstrate to him the Sin and Shame he would involve you in; and omit nothing to make him sensible how cruel it is to go about to betray a Person whom it is his Duty to protect; add that nothing shall ever prevail on you to forfeit your Virtue; and take Care that all your Looks and Gestures correspond with what you say: Let no wanton Smile, or light coquet Air give him room to suspect you are not so much displeased with the Inclination he has for you as you wou'd seem; for if he once imagines you deny but for the sake of Form, it will the more enflame him, and render him more pressing than ever. Let your Answers, therefore, be delivered with the greatest Sedateness; shew that you are truly sorry, and more ashamed than vain, that he finds any thing in you to like: How great will be your Glory, if, by your Behaviour, you convert the base Design he had upon you, into an Esteem for your Virtue! Greater Advantages will accrue to you from the Friendship he will afterwards have for you, than you would ever have obtained from the Gratification of his wild Desires, even tho' he should continue an Affection for you much longer than is common in such Intrigues. But if you fail in this laudable Ambition, if he persists in his Importunities, and you have Reason to fear he will make Use of other Means than Persuasions to satisfy his brutal Appetite, (as what may not Lust seconded by Power attempt, and there is no answering for the Honour of some Men on such Occasions) you have nothing to do, but, on the first Symptom that appears of such a Design, to go directly out of his House: He will not insist on your forfeiting a Month's Wages for his own Sake, for fear you should declare the Cause of your quitting his Service; and if he should be even so harden'd in Vice, as to have no Regard for his Character in this Point, it is much better you should lose a Month's Wages, than continue a Moment longer in the Power of such a one.

If a married Man.] Great Caution is still to be observ'd, if he is a married Man: As soon as he gives you the least Intimation of his Design, either by Word or Action, you ought to keep as much as possible out of his Way, in order to prevent his declaring himself more plainly; and if, in spite of all your Care, he finds an Opportunity of telling you his Mind, you must remonstrate the Wrong he would do his Wife, and how much he demeans both himself and her by making such an Offer to his own Servant. If this is ineffectual, and he continues to persecute you still, watching you wherever you go, both abroad and at home, and is so troublesome in his Importunities, that you cannot do your Business quietly and regularly, your only Way then is to give Warning; but be very careful not to let your Mistress know the Motive of it: That is a Point too tender to be touch'd upon even in the most distant Manner, much less plainly told: Such a Discovery would not only give her an infinite Uneasiness, (for in such Cases the Innocent suffer for the Crimes of the guilty) but turn the Inclination your Master had for you into the extremest Hatred.

Temptations from your Master's Son.] But there is yet a greater Trial of your Virtue than these I have mentioned, which you may probably meet with; and that is when your young Master happens to take a Fancy to you, flatters your Vanity with Praises of your Beauty; your Avarice with Presents; perhaps, if his Circumstance countenance such a Proposal, the Offer of a Settlement for Life, and, it may be, even a Promise of marrying you as soon as he shall be at his own Disposal. This last Bait has seduced some who have been Proof against all the others: It behoves you therefore to be extremely on your Guard against it, and not flatter yourselves, that because such Matches have sometimes happened, it will be your Fortune: Examples of this kind are very rare, and as seldom happy.

7. **Mary Collier, from "The Woman's Labour: An Epistle to Mr. Stephen Duck; In Answer to his late Poem, called The Thresher's Labour" (1739),** *Eighteenth-Century Poetry: An Annotated Anthology,* **edited by David Fairer and Christine Gerrard (London: Blackwell, 1999) 257–62**

[This excerpted reply to Stephen Duck's "The Thresher's Labour" (1730) enumerates in great detail the labor of a washer-woman (which is how Collier identifies herself in the subtitle to the poem). Posed as a dialogue with Duck, Collier compares the never-ending work of women, responsible both for their own homes and someone else's, with the more segmented work of men (referred to as "you" in the poem). In the Advertisement to the poem, Collier plainly states that she sees writing poetry as another form of employment: "I think it no Reproach to the Author, whose Life is toilsome, and her Wages inconsiderable, to confess honestly, that the View of her putting a small Sum of Money in her Pocket, as well as the Reader's Entertainment, had its Share of Influences upon this Publication." She adds that though the poem may have its "Faults and Imperfections," she hopes that the reader will "judge it to be something considerably beyond the common Capacity of those of her own Rank and Occupation." The detail with which she describes both the labor required and the payment rendered

(6 or 8 pence) contrast sharply with the kind of "sexual labor" required by Syrena or the domestic labor of Shamela (or even Pamela).]

Immortal Bard! thou Fav'rite of the Nine!
Enrich'd by Peers, advanc'd by CAROLINE!
Deign to look down on One that's poor and low,
Remembring you yourself was lately so;
Accept these Lines: Alas! what can you have
From her, who ever was, and's still a Slave?
No Learning ever was bestow'd on me;
My Life was always spent in Drudgery:
And not alone; alas! with Grief I find,
It is the Portion of poor Woman-kind.
Oft have I thought as on my Bed I lay,
Eas'd from the tiresome Labours of the Day,
Our first Extraction from a Mass refin'd,
Could never be for Slavery design'd;
'Till Time and Custom by degrees destroy'd
That happy State our Sex at first enjoy'd.
When Men had us'd their utmost Care and Toil,
Their Recompense was but a Female Smile;
When they by Arts or Arms were render'd Great,
They laid their Trophies at a Woman's Feet,
They, in those Days, unto our Sex did bring
Their Hearts, their All, a Free-will Offering;
And as from us their Being they derive,
They back again should all due Homage give....
But now, alas! that Golden Age is past,
We are the Objects of your Scorn at last....

'Tis true, that when our Morning's Work is done,
And all our Grass expos'd unto the Sun,
While that his scorching Beams do on it shine,
As well as you, we have a Time to dine:
I hope, that since we freely toil and sweat
To earn our Bread, you'll give us Time to eat.
That over, soon we must get up again,
And nimbly turn our Hay upon the Plain;...

When Ev'ning does approach, we homeward hie,
And our domestic Toils incessant ply:

Against your coming Home prepare to get
Our Work all done, our House in order set;
Bacon and *Dumpling* in the Pot we boil,
Our Beds we make, our Swine we feed the while;
Then wait at Door to see you coming Home,
And set the Table out against you come:
Early next Morning we on you attend;
Our Children dress and feed, their Cloathes we mend;
And in the Field our daily Task renew,
Soon as the rising Sun has dry'd the Dew.

When Harvest comes, into the Field we go,
And help to reap the Wheat as well as you;
Or else we go the Ears of Corn to glean;
No Labour scorning, be it e'er so mean;
But in the Work we freely bear a Part,
And what we can, perform with all our Heart.
To get a Living we so willing are,
Our tender Babes into the Field we bear,
And wrap them in our Cloathes to keep them warm,
While round about we gather up the Corn;
And often unto them our Course do bend,
To keep them safe, that nothing them offend:
Our Children that are able, bear a Share
In gleaning Corn, such is our frugal Care.
When Night comes on, unto our Home we go,
Our Corn we carry, and our Infant too;
Weary, alas! but 'tis not worth our while
Once to complain, or *rest at ev'ry Stile*;
We must make haste, for when we Home are come,
Alas! we find our Work but just begun;
So many Things for our Attendance call,
Had we ten Hands, we could employ them all.
Our Children put to Bed, with greatest Care
We all Things for your coming Home prepare:
You sup, and go to Bed without delay,
And rest yourselves till the ensuing Day;
While we, alas! but little Sleep can have
Because our froward Children cry and rave;....

The Harvest ended, Respite none we find;
The hardest of our Toil is still behind:

Hard Labour we most chearfully pursue,
And out, abroad, a Charing often go:
Of which I now will briefly tell in part,
What fully to declare is past my Art;
So many Hardships daily we go through,
I boldly say, the like *you* never knew....
Heaps of fine Linen we before us view,
Whereon to lay our Strength and Patience too;
Cambricks and Muslins, which our Ladies wear,
Laces and Edgings, costly, fine, and rare,
Which must be wash'd with utmost Skill and Care;
With Holland Shirts, Ruffles and Fringes too,
Fashions which our Fore-fathers never knew.
For several Hours here we work and slave,
Before we can one Glimpse of Day-light have;
We labour hard before the Morning's past,
Because we fear the Time runs on too fast....
Now we drive on, resolv'd our Strength to try,
And what we can, we do most willingly;
Until with Heat and Work, 'tis often known,
Not only Sweat, but Blood runs trickling down
Our Wrists and Fingers; still our Work demands
The constant Action of our lab'ring Hands.

Now Night comes on, from whence you have Relief,
But that, alas! does but increase our Grief;
With heavy Hearts we often view the Sun,
Fearing he'll set before our Work is done;
For either in the Morning, or at Night,
We piece the *Summer's* Day with Candle-light.
Tho' we all Day with Care our Work attend,
Such is our Fate, we know not when 'twill end:
When Ev'ning's come, you Homeward take your Way,
We, till our Work is done, are forc'd to stay;
And after all our Toil and Labour past,
Six-pence or Eight-pence pays us off at last;
For all our Pains, no Prospect can we see
Attend us, but *Old Age* and *Poverty.*

The *Washing* is not all we have to do:
We oft change Work for Work as well as you.
Our Mistress of her Pewter doth complain,

And 'tis our Part to make it clean again.
This Work, tho' very hard and tiresome too,
Is not the worst we hapless Females do:
When Night comes on, and we quite weary are,
We scarce can count what falls unto our Share;
Pots, Kettles, Sauce-pans, Skillets, we may see,
Skimmers and Ladles, and such Trumpery,
Brought in to make complete our Slavery.
Tho' early in the Morning 'tis begun,
'Tis often very late before we've done;
Alas! our Labours never know an End;
On Brass and Iron we our Strength must spend;
Our tender Hands and Fingers scratch and tear:
All this, and more, with Patience we must bear.
Colour'd with Dirt and Filth we now appear;
Your threshing *sooty Peas* will not come near.
All the Perfections Woman once could boast,
Are quite obscur'd, and altogether lost....

  So the industrious Bees do hourly strive
To bring their Loads of Honey to the Hive;
Their sordid Owners always reap the Gains,
And poorly recompense their Toil and Pains.

Appendix B: Sexuality

1. Attempted rape scene from Samuel Richardson, *Pamela; or, Virtue Rewarded* (1740), edited by Thomas Keymer and Alice Wakely (Oxford: Oxford UP, 2001)

[A scene parodied by both Fielding and Haywood was the attempted rape of Pamela by her master Mr. B.]

What Words shall I find, my dear Mother, (for my Father should not see this shocking Part) to describe the rest, and my Confusion, when the guilty Wretch took my Left-arm, and laid it under his Neck, as the vile Procuress held my Right; and then he clasp'd me round my Waist!

Said I, Is the Wench mad! Why, how now, Confidence? thinking still it had been *Nan*. But he kissed me with frightful Vehemence; and then his Voice broke upon me like a Clap of Thunder. Now, *Pamela*, said he, is the dreadful Time of Reckoning come, that I have threaten'd.—I scream'd out in such a manner, as never any body heard the like. But there was nobody to help me: And both my Hands were secured, as I said. Sure never poor Soul was in such Agonies as I. Wicked Man! said I; wicked, abominable Woman! O God! my God! this *Time*, this *one* Time! deliver me from this Distress! or strike me dead this Moment; and then I scream'd again and again.

Says he, One Word with you, *Pamela*; one Word hear me but; and hitherto you see I offer nothing to you. Is this nothing, said I, to be in Bed here? To hold my Hands between you? I will hear, if you will instantly leave the Bed, and take this villainous Woman from me!

Said she, (O Disgrace of Womankind!) What you do, Sir, do; don't stand dilly-dallying. She cannot exclaim worse than she has done. And she'll be quieter when she knows the worst.

Silence, said he to her; I must say one Word to you, *Pamela*; it is this: You see, now you are in my Power!—You cannot get from me, nor help yourself: Yet have I not offer'd any thing amiss to you. But if you resolve not to comply with my Proposals, I will not lose this Opportunity: If you do, I will yet leave you.

O Sir, said I, leave me, leave me but, and I will do any thing I ought to do.—Swear then to me, said he, that you will accept my Proposals!—And then, (for this was all detestable Grimace) he put his Hand in my Bosom. With Struggling, Fright, Terror, I fainted away quite, and did not come to myself soon; so that they both, from the cold Sweats that I was in, thought me dying—And I remember no more than that, when, with great Difficulty, they brought me to myself, she was sitting on one side of the Bed, with her Cloaths on; and he on the other with his, and in his Gown and Slippers.

Your poor *Pamela* cannot answer for the Liberties taken with her in her deplorable State of Death. And when I saw them there, I sat up in my Bed, without any Regard to what Appearance I made, and nothing about my Neck; and he soothing me, with an Aspect of Pity and Concern, I put my Hand to his Mouth, and said, O tell me, yet tell me not, what I have suffer'd in this Distress! And I talked quite wild, and knew not what; for, to be sure, I was on the Point of Distraction (203-4).

2. James Boswell, from *The London Journal 1762-63*, edited by Frederick A. Pottle (New Haven: Yale University Press, 1950)

[These excerpts from James Boswell's *London Journal* recount his sexual adventures as a single man (and self-fashioned rake) in London, 1762-63. They detail the kinds of sexual commerce common in the parts of the city that Syrena frequents. Boswell describes his activities in the Strand, Covent Garden, St. James's Park, and the taverns, courts, and bagnios of the same. The passages also make clear the sexual availability of a certain group of women, as well as the risks involved in such activity. Boswell, concerned about venereal disease, frequently wears a prophylactic or "armour" if he thinks he's not with a "safe girl."]

THURSDAY 25 NOVEMBER. ... I went to Love's [a family friend] and drank tea. I had now been some time in town without female sport. I determined to have nothing to do with whores, as my health was of great consequence to me. I went to a girl with whom I had an intrigue at Edinburgh, but my affection cooling, I had left her. I knew she was come up. I waited on her and tried to obtain my former favours, but in vain. She would by no means listen. I was really unhappy for want of women. I thought it hard to be in such a place without them. I picked up a girl in the Strand; went into a court with intention to enjoy her in armour. But she had none. I toyed with her. She wondered at my size, and said if I ever took a girl's maidenhead, I would make her squeak. I gave her a shilling, and had command enough of myself to go without touching her. I afterwards trembled at the danger I had escaped. I resolved to wait cheerfully till I got some safe girl or was liked by some woman of fashion.

TUESDAY 14 DECEMBER. It is very curious to think that I have now been in London several weeks without ever enjoying that delightful sex, although I am surrounded with numbers of free-hearted ladies of all kinds: from the splendid Madam at fifty guineas a night, down to the civil nymph with white-thread stockings who tramps along the Strand and will resign her engaging person to your honour for a pint of wine and a shilling.

FRIDAY 25 MARCH. ...As I was coming home this night, I felt carnal inclinations raging through my frame. I determined to gratify them. I went to St. James's Park, and, like Sir John Brute, picked up a whore. For the first time I did engage in armour, which I found but a dull satisfaction. She who submitted to my lusty embraces was a young Shropshire girl, only seventeen, very well-looked, her name Elizabeth Parker. Poor being, she has a sad time of it!

THURSDAY 31 MARCH. ...At night I strolled into the Park and took the first whore I met, whom I without many words copulated with free from danger, being safely sheathed. She was ugly and lean and her breath smelt of spirits. I never asked her name. When it was done, she slunk off. I had a low opinion of this gross practice and resolved to do it no more.

WEDNESDAY 13 APRIL. ...I should have mentioned last night that I met with a monstrous big whore in the Strand, whom I had a great curiosity to lubricate, as the saying is. I went into a tavern with her, where she displayed to me all the parts of her enormous carcass; but I found that her avarice was as large as her a——, for she would by no means take what I offered her. I therefore with all coolness pulled the bell and discharged the reckoning, to her no small surprise and mortification, who would fain have provoked me to talk harshly to her and so make a disturbance. But I walked off with the gravity of a Barcelonian bishop. I had an opportunity tonight of observing the rascality of the waiters in these infamous sort of taverns. They connive with the whores, and do what they can to fleece the gentlemen. I was on my guard, and got off pretty well. I was so much in the lewd humour that I felt myself restless, and took a little girl into a court; but wanted vigour. So I went home, resolved against low street debauchery.

THURSDAY 19 MAY. ...I called upon Miss Watts, whom I found by herself, neatly dressed and looking very well. I was free and easy with her, and begged that she would drink a glass of wine with me at the Shakespeare,[1] which she complied with. I told her my name was Macdonald, and that I was a Scotch Highlander. She said she liked them much, as they had always spirit and generosity. We were shown into a handsome room and had a bottle of choice sherry. We sat near two hours and became very

---

1 The Shakespeare Head tavern, in Covent Garden.

cheerful and agreeable to each other. I told her with a polite freedom, "Madam, I tell you honestly I have no money to give you, but if you allow me favours without it, I shall be much obliged to you." She smiled and said she would. Her maid then brought her a message that a particular friend from the country was waiting for her; so that I was obliged to give her up this night, as I determined to give her no money. She left me pleased, and said she hoped to have the pleasure of my company at tea when it was convenient. This I faithfully promised and took as a good sign of her willingness to establish a friendly communication with me.

I then sallied forth to the Piazzas[1] in rich flow of animal spirits and burning with fierce desire. I met two very pretty little girls who asked me to take them with me. "My dear girls," said I, "I am a poor fellow. I can give you no money. But if you choose to have a glass of wine and my company and let us be gay and obliging to each other without money, I am your man." They agreed with great good humor. So back to the Shakespeare I went. "Waiter," said I, "I have got here a couple of human beings; I don't know how they'll do." "I'll look, your Honour," cried he, and with inimitable effrontery stared them in the face and then cried, "They'll do very well." "What," said I, "are they good fellow-creatures? Bring them up, then." We were shown into a good room and had a bottle of sherry before us in a minute. I surveyed my seraglio and found them both good subjects for amorous play. I toyed with them and drank about and sung *Youth's the Season* and thought myself Captain Macheath;[2] and then I solaced my existence with them, one after the other, according to their seniority. I was quite *raised*, as the phrase is: thought I was in a London tavern, the Shakespeare's Head, enjoying high debauchery after my sober winter. I parted with my ladies politely and came home in a glow of spirits.

3. Daniel Defoe, from *Conjugal Lewdness; or, Matrimonial Whoredom. A Treatise concerning the Use and Abuse of the Marriage Bed* (London: 1727)

[In chapter five, Defoe discusses "Means physical or diabolical, to prevent Conception" (123), including the possibilities for women to terminate pregnancies and the consequences of the same. This section details the activities of a Quack and, though ostensibly detailing the dangers of abortions, catalogues some of the options available to women.]

---

1 The open area in Covent Garden.
2 "Youth's the Season" is sung by Macheath and his "ladies of the town" in a tavern near Newgate at the beginning of Act Two of John Gay's *The Beggar's Opera* (1731).

FIRST, These desperate Medicines which are usually taken for such Purposes, what are they, and of what Kind? Have they an effect only upon that particular Part which they are pointed at? Are they able to confine the Operation of the Physick to the very mathematical Point of Situation? And shall the Poisons extend no farther? Are they sure they shall affect no Part but the Conception? Shall the Physick, like a Messenger sent upon a particular Business, knock at no Doors in his Journey going or coming? Shall it affect no other Part? Shall the murthering Dart kill just the Part, strike a mortal Wound just there, and no where else, and innocently passing by every other Place, do no more than just the Errand 'tis sent about.

WHAT if you should mistake, and the Application being misplaced, the Arrow should miss the Child, and kill the Mother? I have heard of a certain Quack in this Town, and knew him too, who profess'd to prescribe in this very Case; the Villain, for he must be no other, had his Preparations of the several following particular Kinds, are for the several following Operations, and accordingly, gave the Directions to his Patients, as follows:

"N°. 1. IF the Party or Woman be young with Child, not above three Months gone, and would miscarry without Noise, and without Danger, take the Bolus herewith sent in the Evening an Hour before she goes to Bed, and thirty drops of the Tincture in the Bottle, just when she goes to Bed, repeating the Drops in the Morning before she eats; take the Drops in *Rhenish* Wine, right *Moselle*.

N°. 2. IF she is quick with Child, and desires to miscarry, take two Papers of the Powder here enclosed, Night and Morning, infused in the Draught contained in the Bottle ____—; taking it twice, shall bring away the Conception.

N°. 3. IF the Party be a Man, and he would have the Child the Woman goes with preserved against her Will, let her take the Decoction here directed every Morning for three Weeks, and one of the Pills every Night; but when her Travail approaches, leave off the Decoction, and let her take three of the Pills, the Child shall certainly be brought into the World alive, though it may be some danger to the Mother."

THAT was, in short, he would kill the Woman, and save the Child.

THERE were likewise *Recipe*'s, with these Directions: If the Party only fears she is with Child, but is not certain, take these Powders Night and Morning, as directed, her Fears shall be over in four times taking.

IF the Party is not with Child, and would not conceive, take one Paper of the Powders in a Glass of warm Ale, every Morning after the Man has been with her, and she shall be out of danger.

I need give no Vouchers for this Account; there are People still living, who sent several poor Servants to him, pretending this or that Part to be their Case, and craving his learned Advice, and so have had his hellish Preparations, and given him his Fee or Rate for them, and so brought them away, in order to have him prosecuted and punished.

[This section contains a dialogue between two married women, the "Lady" who states her aversion to having any children, and the "Cousin," who is her advisor. The Lady seeks a "physick" that will act as a contraception, an act the "Cousin" describes as "willful Murther, as essentially and as effectually, as your destroying the Child after it was formed in your Womb" (140). However, the Cousin appears to capitulate, as described below.]

HERE the Discourse stopt a-while; and the Cousin, though she had said it was against her Conscience and Judgment, was prevailed with to tell her of a Medicine, and a devilish one it was, if she had set down all the Particulars. N. B. You are to note, that it was a Medicine indeed for the wicked Purpose; but the other Lady that gave it her kept out the main and most dangerous Ingredients, and gave her, as appeared afterwards, nothing but what, if she had been with Child, she might have taken with the greatest Safety in the World. However, the other having believed she had taken other Things, her Imagination made it work other Effects than it would have done.

WHEN she had taken the Medicine it made her very sick, and, in a word, set her a Vomiting and Purging most violently, and that threw her into a high Fever.

IN her Fever she was exceedingly struck in her Conscience with the Fact; and I could give a very pleasing Account from her own Mouth, of her after Reflections upon the criminal Part, which she was then convinced of, and began to be penitent for.

[Though she continues marital relations with her husband, she fails to conceive, which causes her husband to believe that she either still uses some form of contraception or has been rendered infertile by the "physick" she previously used. The nature of this conversation makes it clear that various kinds of "physick"—no matter how imprecise— were available for use as contraceptives or abortifacient: drugs that "poisoned or vitiated her Womb, so that she could never conceive" (150).]

HER Apprehensions now were, that her Husband should suppose either that she still used Art with her self to prevent her being with Child, or to destroy a Conception after it had taken place, or that she had injured her self some Way or other, by what she had formerly done in such a manner, that now it was probable she might never be with Child at all .... she hardly knew what she had done, and what she had not done; she did not know what she had taken, except the

Names of some of the Drugs, what Effect they might have had, she was ill able to know, as any Body else was to tell her; she might have spoiled her self for ought she knew; nor was she able to give him any Assurance that it was not so.

[When queried, her Cousin admits that the "Receipt" for the alleged abortifacient she gave to the Lady was innocuous, and she "received no Damage" (148). The Cousin suggests they "go to some eminent Physician, and show him the Recipe, and tell him the plain Matter of Fact; and let us hear his Opinion" (149).]

ACCORDING to this Agreement they went to the Doctor, and he read the Particulars: He assured her, that he who gave her the Medicine to cause Abortion, or prevent Conception, or to do a breeding Woman the least harm, deceived her; for that there was nothing in it but what a Woman with Child might freely take without the least Danger, and that nothing in the Medicine could do her the least Injury.

4. Richard Steele, from *The Spectator* no. 266 (4 January 1712), *The Spectator*, edited by Donald F. Bond (Oxford: Clarendon Press, 1965) Vol. 2, 534-55

[The brief description of a young prostitute provides a telling point of contrast both to Boswell's experiences and the trajectory of Syrena Tricksy's life.]

I...begin with the Consideration of poor and publick Whores. The other Evening passing along near *Covent-Garden*, I was jogged on the Elbow as I turned into the Piazza, on the right Hand coming out of *James-street*, by a slim young Girl of about Seventeen, who with a pert Air asked me if I was for a Pint of Wine....we stood under one of the Arches by Twilight; and there I could observe as exact Features as I had ever seen, the most agreeable Shape, the finest Neck and Bosom, in a Word, the whole Person of a Woman exquisitely beautiful. She affected to allure me with a forced Wantonness in her Look and Air; but I saw it checked with Hunger and Cold: Her Eyes were wan and eager, her Dress thin and tawdry, her Mein [*sic*] genteel and childish. This strange Figure gave me much Anguish of Heart, and to avoid being seen with her I went away, but could not forbear giving her a Crown. The poor thing sighed, curtisied, and with a Blessing, expressed with the utmost Vehemence, turned from me. This Creature is what they call *newly come upon the Town*, but who, I suppose, falling into cruel Hands, was left in the first Month from her Dishonour, and exposed to pass through the Hands and Discipline of one of those Hags of Hell whom we call Bawds.

1. Title-pages (*Pamela, Anti-Pamela*, and *Mrs. Shamela Andrews*)

Title-page of *Pamela; or, Virtue Rewarded*, 1741. Reprinted with permission of the British Library.

ANTI-PAMELA:

OR,

Feign'd Innocence

DETECTED;

In a SERIES of

SYRENA's
ADVENTURES.

A NARRATIVE which has really its Foundation in Truth and Nature; and at the fame time that it entertains, by a vaſt variety of ſurprizing Incidents, arms againſt a partial Credulity, by ſhewing the Miſchiefs that frequently ariſe from a too ſudden Admiration.

Publiſh'd as a neceſſary Caution to all Young Gentlemen.

LONDON:

Printed for *J. Huggonſon*, in *Sword-and-Buckler-Court*, over againſt the *Crown-Tavern* on *Ludgate-Hill.* M.DCC.XLI.

Title-page of *Anti-Pamela; or, Feign'd Innocence Detected*, 1741.
Reprinted with permission of the British Library.

AN

APOLOGY

FOR THE

L I F E

OF

Mrs. SHAMELA ANDREWS.

In which, the many notorious FALSHOODS and
MISREPRSENTATIONS of a Book called

P A M E L A,

Are expofed and refuted; and all the matchlefs
ARTS of that young Politician, fet in a true and
juft Light.

Together with

A full Account of all that paffed between her
and Parfon *Arthur Williams*; whofe Chara&ter
is reprefented in a manner fomething different
from what he bears in *PAMELA.* The
whole being exa&t Copies of authentick Papers
delivered to the Editor.

Neceffary to be had in all FAMILIES.

By Mr. *CONNY KEYBER.*

LONDON:

Print_ed for A. DODD, at the *Peacock,* without *Temple-bar.*
M. DCC. XLI.

Title-page of *An Apology for the Life of Mrs. Shamela Andrews,* 1741.
Reprinted with permission of the British Library.

2. Samuel Richardson, from *Pamela*

[This series of scenes is directly parodied by Fielding and, in some cases, alluded to by Haywood. All quotations are from the Keymer edition of the 1740 *Pamela*.]

i. Pamela in Homespun Gown, from Letter XXIV.

And so, when I had din'd, up Stairs I went, and lock'd myself into my little Room. There I trick'd myself up as well as I could in my new Garb, and put on my round-ear'd ordinary Cap; but with a green Knot however, and my homespun Gown and Petticoat, and plain-leather Shoes; but yet they are what they call *Spanish* Leather, and my ordinary Hose, ordinary I mean to what I have been lately used to; tho' I shall think good Yarn may do very well for every Day, when I come home. A plain Muslin Tucker I put on, and my black silk Necklace, instead of the *French* Necklace my Lady gave me, and put the Ear-rings out of my Ears; and when I was quite 'quip'd, I took my Straw Hat in my Hand, with its two blue Strings, and look'd about me in the Glass, as proud as any thing.—To say Truth, I never lik'd myself so well in my Life.

O the Pleasure of descending with Ease, Innocence and Resignation!—Indeed there is nothing like it! An humble Mind, I plainly see, cannot meet with any very shocking Disappointment, let Fortune's Wheel turn round as it will.

So I went down to look for Mrs. *Jervis*, to see how she lik'd me.

I met, as I was upon the Stairs, our *Rachel*, who is the Housemaid, and she made me a low Curchee, and I found did not know me. So I smil'd, and went to the House-keeper's Parlour. And there sat good Mrs. *Jervis* at Work, making a Shift: And, would you believe it? she did not know me at first; but rose up, and pull'd off her Spectacles; and said, Do you want me, forsooth? I could not help laughing, and said, Hey-day! Mrs. *Jervis*, what! don't you know me?—She stood all in Amaze, and look'd at me from Top to Toe; Why you surprise me, said she; what! *Pamela*! Thus metamorphos'd! How came this about? As it happen'd, in stept my Master, and my Back being to him, he thought it was a Stranger speaking to Mrs. *Jervis*, and withdrew again; and did not hear her ask if his Honour had any Commands with her?—She turn'd me about and about, and I shew'd her all my Dress, to my Under-petticoat; and she said, sitting down, Why I am all in Amaze! I must sit down. What can all this mean? I told her, I had no Cloaths suitable to my Condition when I return'd to my Father's; and so it was better to begin here, as I was soon to go away, that all my Fellow-

Servants might see, I knew how to suit myself to the State I was returning to.

Well, said she, I never knew the like of thee. But this sad Preparation for going away (for now I see you are quite in Earnest) is what I know not how to get over. O my dear *Pamela*, how can I part with you!

My Master rung in the back Parlour, and so I withdrew, and Mrs. *Jervis* went to attend him. It seems he said to her, I was coming in to let you know that I shall go to *Lincolnshire*, and may-be to my Sister *Davers*'s, and be absent some Weeks. But, pray, what pretty neat Damsel was that with you? She says, she smil'd, and ask'd if his Honour did not know who it was? No, said he, I never saw her before. Farmer *Nichols*, or Farmer *Brady*, have neither of them such a tight prim Lass for a Daughter; have they?—Tho' I did not see her Face neither, said he. If your Honour won't be angry, said she, I will introduce her into your Presence; for I think, says she, she out-does our *Pamela*.

Now I did not thank her for this, as I told her afterwards (for it brought a great deal of Trouble upon me, as well as Crossness, as you shall hear). That can't be, he was pleased to say. But if you can find an Excuse for it, let her come in.

At that she stept to me, and told me, I must go in with her to my Master; but, said she, for Goodness sake, let him find you out; for he don't know you. Good Sirs! Mrs. *Jervis*, said I, how could you serve me so? Besides, it looks too free both *in me*, and *to him*. I tell you, said she, you shall come in; and pray don't reveal yourself till he finds you out.

So I went in, foolish as I was; tho' I must have been seen by him another time, if I had not then. And she would make me take my Straw-hat in my Hand.

I dropt a low Curchee, but said never a Word. I dare say, he knew me as soon as he saw my Face; but was as cunning as *Lucifer*. He came up to me, and took me by the Hand, and said, Whose pretty Maiden are you?—I dare say you are *Pamela*'s Sister, you are so like her. So neat, so clean, so pretty! Why, Child, you far surpass your Sister *Pamela*!

I was all Confusion, and would have spoken; but he took me about the Neck; Why, said he, you are very pretty, Child; I would not be so free with your *Sister*, you may believe; but I must kiss *you*.

O Sir, said I, I am *Pamela*, indeed I am: Indeed I am *Pamela, her own self!*

He kissed me for all I could do; and said, Impossible! you are a lovelier Girl by half than *Pamela*; and sure I may be innocently free with you, tho' I would not do her so much Favour.

This was a sad Bite upon me indeed, and what I could not expect;

and Mrs. *Jervis* look'd like a Fool as much as I, for her Officiousness.—
At last I got away, and ran out of the Parlour, most sadly vex'd, as you
may well think (55-57).

ii. B.'s first nocturnal visit, from Letter XXV.

I sat myself down on one side of the Bed, and she on the other,
and we began to undress ourselves; but she on that side next the
wicked Closet, that held the worst Heart in the World.... I pulled off
my Stays, and my Stockens, and my Gown, all to an Under-petticoat;
and then hearing a rustling again in the Closet, I said, God protect us!
but before I say my Prayers, I must look into this Closet. And so was
going to it slip shod, when, O dreadful! out rush'd my Master, in a rich
silk and silver Morning Gown.

I scream'd, and run to the Bed; and Mrs. *Jervis* scream'd too; and he
said, I'll do you no harm, if you forbear this Noise; but otherwise take
what follows.

Instantly he came to the Bed; for I had crept into it, to Mrs. *Jervis*,
with my Coat on, and my Shoes; and taking me in his Arms, said, Mrs.
Jervis, rise, and just step up Stairs, to keep the Maids from coming
down at this Noise; I'll do no harm to this Rebel.

O, for God's sake! for Pity's sake! Mrs. *Jervis*, said I, if I am not
betray'd, don't leave me; and, I beseech you, raise all the House. No,
said Mrs. *Jervis*, I will not stir, my dear Lamb; I will not leave you. I
wonder at you, Sir, said she, and kindly threw herself upon my Coat,
clasping me round the Waist, you shall not hurt this Innocent, said she;
for I will lose my Life in her Defence. Are there not, said she, enough
wicked ones in the World, for your base Purpose, but you must
attempt such a Lamb as this!

He was desperate angry, and threaten'd to throw her out of the
Window; and to turn her out of the House the next Morning. You
need not, Sir, said she; for I will not stay in it. God defend my poor
Pamela till To-morrow, and we will both go together.—Says he, let me
but expostulate a Word or two with you, *Pamela*. Pray, *Pamela*, said
Mrs. *Jervis*, don't hear a Word, except he leaves the Bed, and goes to
the other End of the Room. Aye, out of the Room! said I; expostulate To-morrow, if you must expostulate!

I found his Hand in my Bosom, and when my Fright let me know
it, I was ready to die; and I sighed, and scream'd, and fainted away. And
still he had his Arms about my Neck; and Mrs. *Jervis* was about my
Feet, and upon my Coat. And all in a cold, clammy Sweat was I.
Pamela, Pamela! said Mrs. *Jervis*, as she tells me since, O—h, and gave

another Shriek, my poor *Pamela* is dead for certain!—And so, to be sure, I was for a time; for I knew nothing more of the Matter, one Fit following another, till about three Hours after, as it prov'd to be, I found myself in Bed, and Mrs. *Jervis* sitting up on one side, with her Wrapper about her, and *Rachel* on the other; and no Master, for the wicked Wretch was gone. But I was so overjoy'd, that I hardly could believe myself; and I said, which were my first Words, Mrs. *Jervis*, Mrs. *Rachel*, can I be sure it is you? God be prais'd! God be prais'd!—Where have I been? Hush, my Dear, said Mrs. *Jervis*, you have been in Fit after Fit. I never saw any body so frightful in my Life! (60–64).

iii. Bundle Scene, from Letter XXIX.

...I took all my Cloaths, and all my Linen, and I divided them into three Parcels; and I said, It is now *Monday*, Mrs. *Jervis*, and I am to go away on *Thursday* Morning betimes; so, tho' I know you don't doubt my Honesty, I beg you will look over my poor Matters, and let every one have what belongs to them; for, said I, you know, I am resolv'd to take with me only what I can properly call my own....

So I said, when she came up, Here, Mrs. *Jervis*, is the first Parcel; I will spread it all abroad. These are the Things my good Lady gave me.—In the first place, said I,—and so I went on describing the Cloaths and Linen my Lady had given me, mingling Blessings, as I proceeded, for her Goodness to me; and when I had turn'd over that Parcel, I said, Well, so much for the first Parcel, Mrs. *Jervis*, that was my Lady's Presents.

Now I come to the Presents of my dear virtuous Master: Hay, you know, *Closet* for that, Mrs. *Jervis*! She laugh'd, and said, I never saw such a comical Girl in my Life. But go on. I will, Mrs. *Jervis*, said I, as soon as I have open'd the Bundle; for I was as brisk and as pert as I could be, little thinking who heard me.

Now here, Mrs. *Jervis*, said I, are my ever worthy Master's Presents; and then I particulariz'd all those in the second Bundle.

After which, I turn'd to my own, and said,

Now, Mrs. *Jervis*, comes poor *Pamela*'s Bundles, and a little one it is, to the others. First, here is a Calicoe Night-gown, that I used to wear o' Mornings. 'Twill be rather too good for me when I get home; but I must have something. Then there is a quilted Callimancoe Coat, and a Pair of Stockens I bought of the Pedlar, and my Straw-hat with blue Strings; and a Remanant of *Scots* Cloth, which will make two Shirts and two Shifts, the same I have on, for my poor Father and Mother. And there are four other Shifts, one the Fellow to that I have on;

another pretty good one, and the other two old fine ones, that will serve me to turn and wind with at home, for they are not worth leaving behind me; and here are two Pair of Shoes, I have taken the Lace off, which I will burn, and may-be will fetch me some little Matter at a Pinch, with an old Shoe-Buckle or two....

Well, let me see; aye, here is a Cotton Handkerchief I bought of the Pedlar; there should be another somewhere. O here it is! And here too are my new-bought knit Mittens. And this is my new Flannel Coat, the Fellow to that I have on. And in this Parcel pinn'd together, are several Pieces of printed Callicoe, Remnant of Silks, and such-like, that, if good Luck should happen, and I should get Work, would serve for Robings and Facings, and such-like Uses. And here too are a Pair of Pockets; they are too fine for me; but I have no worse. Bless me! said I, I didn't think I had so many good Things! (77-79).

iv. Pamela considers drowning herself.

God forgive me! but a sad Thought came just then into my Head!—I tremble to think of it! Indeed my Apprehensions of the Usage I should meet with, had like to have made me miserable for ever! O my dear, dear Parents, forgive your poor Child; but being then quite desperate, I crept along till I could get up on my Feet, tho' I could hardly stand; and away limp'd I!—What to do, but to throw myself into the Pond, and so put a Period to all my Griefs in this World!—But, Oh! to find them infinitely aggravated (had I not, by God's Grace, been with-held) in a miserable *Eternity*! As I have escap'd this Temptation, (blessed by God for it!) I will tell you my Conflicts on this dreadful Occasion, that God's Mercies may be magnify'd in my Deliverance, that I am yet on this Side the dreadful Gulph, from which there can be no Redemption.

It was well for me, as I have since thought, that I was so maim'd, as made me the longer before I got to the Water; for this gave me some Reflection, and abated that Liveliness of my Passions, which possibly might otherwise have hurry'd me, in my first Transport of Grief, (on my seeing no way to escape, and the hard Usage I had Reason to expect from my dreadful Keepers) to throw myself without Consideration; but my Weakness of Body made me move so slowly, that it gave Time for a little Reflection, a Ray of Grace, to dart in upon my benighted Mind; and so, when I came to the Pond-side, I sat myself down on the sloping Bank, and began to ponder my wretched Condition: And thus I reason'd with myself.

Pause here a little, *Pamela*, on what thou are about, before thou takest the dreadful Leap; and consider whether there be no Way yet left, no Hope, if not to escape from this wicked House, yet from the Mischiefs threatened thee in it.

I then consider'd, and after I had cast about in my Mind, every thing that could make me hope, and saw no Probability... What hast thou to do, distressed Creature, said I to myself, but throw thyself upon a merciful God, (who knows how innocently I suffer) to avoid the merciless Wickedness of those who are determin'd on my Ruin?

And then thought I, (and Oh! that Thought was surely of the Devil's Instigation; for it was very soothing and powerful with me) these wicked Wretches, who now have no Remorse, no Pity on me, will then be mov'd to lament their Misdoings; and when they see the dead Corpse of the unhappy *Pamela* dragg'd out to these slopy Banks, and lying breathless at their Feet, they will find that Remorse to wring their obdurate Hearts, which now has no Place there!—And my Master, my angry Master, will then forget his Resentments, and say, O this is the unhappy *Pamela!* that I have so causelessly persecuted and destroy'd! Now do I see she preferr'd her Honesty to her Life, will he say, and is no Hypocrite, nor Deceiver; but really was the innocent Creature she pretended to be! Then, thinks I, will he, perhaps, shed a few Tears over the poor Corse of his persecuted Servant; and, tho' he may give out, it was Love and Disappointment, and that too, (in order to hide his own Guilt) for the unfortunate Mr. *Williams*, perhaps, yet will he be inwardly griev'd, and order me a decent Funeral, and save me, or rather this Part of me, from the dreadful Stake, and the Highway Interrment; and the young Men and Maidens all around my dear Father's, will pity poor *Pamela*; but O! I hope I shall not be the Subject of their Ballads and Elegies; but that my Memory, for the sake of my dear Father and Mother, may quickly slide into Oblivion!

[....]

What then, presumptuous *Pamela*, dost thou here, thought I? Quit with Speed these guilty Banks, and flee from these dashing Waters, that even in their sounding Murmurs, this still Night, reproach thy Rashness! Tempt not God's Goodness on the mossy Banks, that have been witnesses of thy guilty Intentions; and while thou has Power left thee, avoid the tempting Evil, lest thy grand Enemy, now repuls'd by Divine Grace, and due Reflection, return to the Charge with a Force that thy Weakness may not be able to resist! And lest one rash Moment destroy all the Convictions, which now have aw'd thy rebellious Mind into Duty and Resignation to the Divine Will!

And so saying, I arose; but was so stiff with my Hurts, so cold with the moist Dew of the Night, and the wet Banks on which I had sat, as also the Damps arising from so large a Piece of Water, that with great Pain I got from the Banks of this Pond, which now I think of with Terror; and bending my limping Steps towards the House, refug'd myself in the Corner of an Out-house, where Wood and Coals are laid up for Family Use, till I should be found by my cruel Keepers, and consign'd to a wretched Confinement, and worse Usage than I had hitherto experienc'd; and there behind a Pile of Fire-wood I crept, and lay down, as you may imagine, with a Mind just broken, and a Heart sensible to nothing but the extremest Woe and Dejection.... *Nan* had the Thought to go towards the Pond, and there seeing my Coat, and Cap and Handkerchief in the Water, cast almost to the Banks by the dashing of the Waves, she thought it was me, and screaming out, run to Mrs. *Jewkes*, and said, O Madam, Madam! here's a piteous Thing!—Mrs. *Pamela* lies drown'd in the Pond!—Thither they all ran! and finding my Cloaths, doubted not I was at the Bottom;... Mrs. *Jewkes* sent *Nan* to the Men, to bid them get the Drag-net ready, and leave the Horses, and come to try to find the poor Innocent! as she, it seems, *then* call'd me, beating her Breast, and lamenting my hard Hap; but most what would become of them, and what Account they should give to my Master (171-75).

v. The articles of proposal Mr. B. offers Pamela are imitated in both *Shamela* and *Anti-Pamela*. Below are the terms Mr. B. offers, without Pamela's response.

To Mrs. PAMELA ANDREWS.

The following ARTICLES are proposed to your serious Consideration; and let me have an Answer, in Writing, to them; that I may take my Resolutions accordingly. Only remember, that I will not be trifled with; and what you give for Answer, will absolutely decide your Fate, without Expostulation or further Trouble.

I. IF you can convince me, that the hated Parson has had no Encouragement from you in his Addresses; and that you have no Inclination for him, in Preference to me; then I will offer the following Proposals to you, which I will punctually make good.

II. I will directly make you a Present of 500 *Guineas*, for your own Use, which you may dispose of to any Purpose you please: And will give it absolutely into the Hands of any Person you shall appoint to receive it; and expect no Favour in Return, till you are satisfy'd in the Possession of it.

III. I will likewise directly make over to you a Purchase I lately made in *Kent*, which brings in 250*l. per Annum*, clear of all Deductions. This shall be made over to you in full Property for your Life, and for the Lives of any Children, to Perpetuity, that you may happen to have: And your Father shall be immediately put into Possession of it, in Trust for these Purposes. And the Management of it will yield a comfortable Subsistence to him and your Mother, for Life; and I will make up any Deficiencies, if such should happen to that clear Sum, and allow him 50*l. per Annum* besides, for his Life, and that of your Mother, for his Care and Management of this your Estate.

IV. I will, moreover, extend my Favour to any other of your Relations, that you may think worthy of it, or that are valued by you.

V. I will, besides, order Patterns to be sent you for chusing four complete Suits of Cloaths, that you may appear with Reputation, as if you was my Wife. And I will give you the two Diamond Rings, and two Pair of Ear-rings, and Diamond Necklace, that were bought by my Mother, to present to Miss *Tomlins*, if the Match had been brought to Effect, that was proposed between her and me; And I will confer upon you still other Gratuities, as I shall find myself obliged, by your good Behaviour and Affection.

VI. Now, *Pamela*, will you see by this, what a Value I set upon the Free-will of a Person already in my Power; and who, if these Proposals are not accepted, shall find that I have not taken all these Pains, and risqued my Reputation, as I have done, without resolving to gratify my Passion for you, at all Adventures, and if you refuse, without making any Terms at all.

VII. You shall be Mistress of my Person and Fortune, as much as if the foolish Ceremony had passed. All my Servants shall be yours; and you shall chuse any two Persons to attend yourself, either Male or Female, without any Controul of mine; and if your Conduct be such, that I have Reason to be satisfied with it, I know not (but will not engage for this) that I may, after a Twelve-month's Cohabitation, marry you; for if my Love increases for you, as it has done for many Months past, it will be impossible for me to deny you anything.

And now, *Pamela*, consider well, it is in your Power to oblige me on such Terms, as will make yourself, and all your Friends, happy: But this will be over this very Day, irrevocably over; and you shall find all you would be thought to fear, without the least Benefit arising from it to yourself.—And I beg you'll well weigh the Matter, and comply with my Proposals; and I will instantly set about securing to you the full Effect of them: And let me, if you value yourself, experience a grateful Return on this Occasion; and I'll forgive all that's past (188-92).

3. Conyers Middleton, "Dedication" to *History of the Life of Marcus Tullius Cicero* (London: 1741)

[As discussed in the Introduction (p. 25), this dedication to Lord Hervey is parodied very closely in the dedication to *Shamela*.]

To the RIGHT HONORABLE JOHN, Lord HERVEY,
Lord Keeper of his Majesty's Privy Seal.

My Lord,
THE public will naturally expect, that in chusing a Patron for *the Life of* CICERO, I should address myself to some person of illustrious rank, distinguished by his parts and eloquence, and bearing a principal share in the great affairs of the Nation; who, according to the usual stile of Dedications, might be the proper subject of a comparison with the Hero of my piece. Your Lordship's name will confirm that expectation, and Your character would justify me in running some length into the parallel; but my experience of your good sense forbids me the attempt. For Your Lordship knows what a disadvantage it would be to any character, to be placed in the same light with that of CICERO; that all such comparisons must be invidious and adulatory; and that the following History will suggest a reason in every page, why no man now living can justly be compared with him.

I DO not impute this to any superiority of parts or genius, peculiar to the Ancients; for human nature has ever been the same in all ages and nations, and owes the difference of its improvements to a difference only of culture, and of the rewards proposed to its industry: where these are the most amply provided, there we shall always find the most numerous and shining examples of human perfection. In old *Rome*, the public honours were laid open to the virtue of every Citizen; which, by raising them in their turns to the command of that mighty Empire, produced a race of Nobles, superior even to Kings. This was a prospect, that filled the soul of the ambitious, and roused every faculty of mind and body, to exert its utmost force: whereas in modern states, men's views being usually confined to narrow bounds, beyond which they cannot pass, and a partial culture of their talents being sufficient to procure every thing, that their ambition can aspire to, a great genius has seldom either room or invitation to stretch itself to its full size.

YOU see, my Lord, how much I trust to your good nature, as well as good sense, when, in an *Epistle dedicatory*, the proper place of Panegyric, I am depreciating your abilities, instead of extolling them: but I remember, that it is an History, which I am offering to Your Lordship, and it would ill become me, in the front of such a work, to expose my veracity to any hazard: and my head indeed is now so full of antiquity, that I could wish to see the dedicatory stile reduced to that classical simplicity, with which the ancient writers used to present their books to their friends or Patrons, at whose desire they were written, or by whose authority they were published: for this was the first use, and the sole purpose of *a Dedication*; and as this also is the real ground of my present address to Your Lordship, so it will be the best argument of my Epistle, and the most agreeable to the character of an Historian, to acquaint the public with a plain fact, that it was Your Lordship, who first advised me, to undertake *the Life of* CICERO; and when, from a diffidence of my strength, and a nearer view of the task, I began to think myself unequal to the weight of it, Your Lordship still urged and exhorted me to persist, till I had moulded it into the form, in which it now appears.

Thus far Your Lordship was carried by *that love for* CICERO, which, as one of the *best Critics* of antiquity assures us, is the undoubted proof of a true taste. I wish only, that the favour, which You have since shewn to *my English* CICERO, may not detract from that praise, which is due to Your love of the *Roman*: but whatever censure it may draw upon Your Lordship, I cannot prevail with myself to conceal, what does so much honour my work; that, before it went to the Press, Your Lordship not only saw and approved, but, as the sincerest mark of Your approbation, corrected it. It adds no small credit to the History of POLYBIUS, that he professes to have been assisted in it by SCIPIO and LAELIUS; even TERENCE's stile was made the purer, for its being retouched by the same great hands. You must pardon me, therefore, my Lord, if, after the example of those excellent Authors, I cannot forbear boasting, that some parts of my present work have been brightened by the strokes of Your Lordship's pencil.

IT was the custom of those *Roman* Nobles, to spend their leisure, not in vicious pleasures, or trifling diversions, contrived, as we truly call it, *to kill the time*; but in conversing with the celebrated wits and Scholars of the age: in encouraging other people's learning, and improving their own: and here Your Lordship imitates them with success, and for love of letters and politeness may be compared with the Noblest of them. For Your house, like theirs, is open to men of parts and merit; where I have admired Your Lordship's agreeable manner of treating them all in their own way, by introducing questions of literature, and varying them so artfully, as to give every one an opportunity, not only of bearing a part, but of leading the conversation in his turn. In these liberal exercises You drop the cares of the Statesman; relieve Your fatigues in the Senate; and strengthen Your mind, while You relax it.

ENCOMIUMS of this kind, upon persons of Your Lordship's quality, commonly pass for words of course, or a fashionable language to the Great, and make little impression on men of sense, who know learning, not to be the fruit of wit or parts, for there Your Lordship's title would be unquestionable, but an acquisition of much labour and study, which the Nobles of our days are apt to look upon, as inconsistent with the ease and splendour of an elevated fortune, and generally leave to men of professions and inferior life. But Your Lordship has a different way of thinking, and, by Your education in a public School and University, has learnt from Your earliest youth, that no fortune can exempt a man from pains, who desires to distinguish himself from the vulgar; and that it is a folly in any condition of life, to aspire to a superior character, without a superior virtue and industry to support it. What time therefore others bestow upon their sports, or pleasures, or the lazy indolence of a luxurious life, Your Lordship applies to the improvement of Your knowledge; and in those early hours, when all around You are hushed in sleep, seize the opportunity of that quiet, as the most favourable season of study, and frequently spend an usefull day, before others begin to enjoy it.

I AM saying no more, my Lord, than what I know from my constant admission to Your Lordship in my morning visits, before good manners would permit me to attempt to visit any where else; where I have found You commonly engaged with the Classical writers of *Greece* or *Rome*; and conversing with those very dead, with whom SCIPIO and LAELIUS used to converse so familiarly when living. Nor does Your Lordship assume this part for ostentation or amusement only, but for the real benefit both of Yourself and others; for I have seen the solid effects of Your reading, in Your judicious reflections on the policy of those ancient Governments, and have felt your weight even in controversy, on some of the most delicate parts of their History.

THERE is another circumstance peculiar to Your Lordship, which makes this task of Study the easier to you, by giving You not only the greater health, but the greater leisure to pursue it; I mean that singular temperance in diet, in which Your Lordship perseveres with a constancy superior to every temptation that can excite an appetite to rebel; and shews a firmness of mind, that subjects every gratification of sense to the rule of right reason. Thus with all the accomplishments of the Nobleman, You lead the life of a Philosopher; and, while You shine a principal ornament of the Court, You practise the discipline of the College.

IN old *Rome* there were no hereditary honours; but when the virtue of a family was extinct, its honour was extinguished too; so that no man, how nobly soever born, could arrive at any dignity, who did not win it by his personal merit: and here again Your Lordship seems to have emulated that ancient spirit; for, though born to the first honours of Your country, yet disclaiming as it were Your birthright, and putting Yourself upon the foot of a *Roman*, You were not content with inheriting, but resolved to import new dignities into Your family; and, after the example of Your Noble Father, to open Your own way into the supreme council of the Kingdom. In this august Assembly, Your Lordship displays those shining talents, by which You acquired a seat in it, in the defence of our excellent Establishment; in maintaining the rights of the people, yet asserting the prerogative of the Crown; measuring them both by the equal balance of the laws; which by the provident care of our Ancestors, and the happy settlement at the Revolution, have so fixed their just limits, and moderated the extent of their influence, that they mutually defend and preserve, but can never destroy each other without a general ruin.

In a nation like ours, which, from the natural effect of freedom, is divided into opposite parties, though particular attachments to certain principles, or friendships with certain men, will sometimes draw the best Citizens into measures of a subordinate kind, which they cannot wholly approve; yet whatever envy your Lordship may incur on that account, You will be found, on all occasions of trial, a true friend to our constitution both in Church and State; which I have heard You demonstrate with great force, to be the bulwark of our common peace and prosperity. From this fundamental point, no engagements will ever move, or interest draw You; and though men inflamed by opposition are apt to charge each other with designs, which were never dreamt of perhaps by either side, yet if there be any, who know so little of You, as to distrust Your principles, they may depend at least on Your judgment, that it can never suffer a person of Your Lordship's rank, born to so large a share of the property, as well as the honours of the nation, to think any private interest an equivalent, for consenting to the ruin of the public.

I MENTION this, my Lord, as an additional reason for presenting You with *the Life of* CICERO: for were I not persuaded of Your Lordship's sincere love of liberty, and zeal for the happiness of Your fellow citizens, it would be a reproach to You, to put into Your Hands the Life of a man, who, in all the variety of his admirable talents, does not shine so glorious in any, as in his constant attachment to the true interests of his country, and the noble struggle that he sustained, at the expence even of his Life, to avert the impending tyranny, that finally oppressed it.

BUT I ought to ask Your Lordship's pardon for dwelling so long upon a character, which is known to the whole Kingdom, as well as to myself; not only by the high Office, which You fill, and the eminent dignity that You bear in it, but by the sprightly compositions of various kinds, with which Your Lordship has often entertained it. It would be a presumption, to think of adding any honour to Your Lordship by my pen, after You have acquired so much by Your own. The chief design of my Epistle is, to give this public testimony of my thanks for the signal marks of friendship, with which Your Lordship has long honoured me; and to interest Your name, as far as I can, in the fate and success of my work; by letting the world know, what a share You had in the production of it; and it owed its being to Your encouragement; correctness to Your pencil; and what many will think the most substantial benefit, its large subscription to Your authority. For though, in this way of publishing it, I have had the pleasure to find myself supported by a noble list of generous friends, who, without being solicited, or even asked by me, have promoted my subscription with an uncommon zeal, yet Your Lordship has distinguished Yourself the most eminently of them, in contributing not only to the number, but the splendor of the names, that adorn it.

NEXT to that little reputation, with which the public has been pleased to favour me, the benefit of this subscription is the chief fruit, that I have ever reaped from my studies. I am indebted for the first to CICERO, for the second, to Your Lordship: it was CICERO, who instructed me to write; Your Lordship, who rewards me for writing: the same motive therefore, which induced me to attempt the history of the one, engages me to dedicate it to the other; that I may express my gratitude to you both, in the most effectual manner that I am able, by celebrating the memory of the dead, and acknowledging the generosity of my living Benefactor.

I HAVE received great civilities, on several occasions, from many Noble persons, of which I shall ever retain a most gratefull sense; but Your Lordship's accumulated favours have long ago risen up to the character of obligations, and made it my perpetual duty, as it had always been my ambition, to profess myself with the greatest truth and respect,

> MY LORD,
> > Your Lordship's
> > > Most obliged and
> > > > Devoted Servant,
> > > > > CONYERS MIDDLETON.

4. Colley Cibber, from *An Apology for the Life of Mr. Colley Cibber, Comedian, and Late Patentee of the Theatre-Royal. With an Historical View of the Stage during his Own Time* (London: 1740) 1-4

YOU know, Sir, I have often told you, that one time or other I should give the Publick some Memoirs of my own Life; at which you have never fail'd to laugh, like a Friend, without saying a word to dissuade me from it; concluding, I suppose, that such a wild Thought could not possibly require a serious Answer. But you see I was in earnest. And now you will say, the World will find me, under my own Hand, a weaker Man than perhaps I may have pass'd for, even among my Enemies.—With all my Heart! my Enemies will then read me with Pleasure, and you, perhaps, with Envy, when you find that Follies, without the Reproach of Guilt upon them, are not inconsistent with Happiness.—But why make my Follies publick? Why not? I have pass'd my Time very pleasantly with them, and I don't recollect that they have ever been hurtful to any other Man living. Even admitting they were injudiciously chosen, would it not be Vanity in me to take Shame to myself for not being found a Wise Man? Really, Sir, my Appetites were in too much haste to be happy, to throw away my Time in pursuit of a Name I was sure I could never arrive at.

Now the Follies I frankly confess, I look upon as, in some measure, discharged; while those I conceal are still keeping the Account open between me and my Conscience. To me the Fatigue of being upon a continual Guard to hide them, is more than the Reputation of being without them can repay. If this be Weakness, *defendit numerus*, I have such comfortable Numbers on my side, that were all Men to blush, that are not Wise, I am afraid, in Ten, Nine Parts of the World ought to be out of Countenance: But since that sort of Modesty is what they don't care to come into, why should I be afraid of being star'd at for not being particular? Or if the Particularity lies in owning my Weakness, will my wisest Reader be so inhuman as not to pardon it? But if there should be such a one, let me, at least, beg him to shew me that strange Man who is perfect! Is any one more unhappy, more ridiculous, than he who is always labouring to be thought so, or that is impatient when he is not thought so? Having brought myself to be easy under whatever the World may say of my Undertaking, you may still ask me, why I give myself all this trouble? Is it for Fame, or Profit to myself, or Use or Delight to others? For all these Considerations I have neither Fondness nor Indifference: If I obtain none of them, the Amusement, at worst, will be a Reward that must constantly go along with the Labour. But behind all this, there is something inwardly inciting, which I cannot express in few Words; I must therefore a little make bold with your Patience.

A Man who has pass'd above Forty Years of his Life upon a Theatre, where he has never appear'd to be Himself, may have naturally excited the Curiosity of his Spectators to know what he really was, when in no body's Shape but his own; and whether he, who by his Profession had so long been ridiculing his Benefactors, might not, when the Coat of his Profession was off, deserve to be laugh'd at himself; or from his being often seen in, the most flagrant, and immoral Characters; whether he might not see as great a Rogue, when he look'd into the Glass himself, as when he held it to others....

Now, Sir, when my Time comes, lest they shou'd think it worth while to handle my Memory with the same Freedom, I am willing to prevent its being so odly besmear'd (or at best but flatly white-wash'd) by taking upon me to give the Publick This, as true a Picture of myself as natural Vanity will permit me to draw: For, to promise you that I shall never be vain, were a Promise that, like a Looking-glass too large, might break itself in the making: Nor am I sure I ought wholly to avoid that Imputation, because if Vanity be one of my natural Features, the Portrait wou'd not be like me without it. In a Word, I may palliate and soften as much as I please; but, upon an honest Examination of my Heart, I am afraid the same Vanity which makes even homely People employ Painters to preserve a flattering Record of their Persons, has seduced me to print off this *Chiaro Oscuro* of my Mind.

And when I have done it, you may reasonably ask me, of what Importance can the History of my private Life be to the Publick? To this, indeed, I can only make you a ludicrous Answer, which is, That the Publick very well knows, my Life has not been a private one; that I have been employ'd in their Service, ever since many of their Grandfathers were young Men; And tho' I have voluntarily laid down my Post, they have a sort of Right to enquire into my Conduct, (for which they have so well paid me) and to call for the Account of it, during my Share of the Administration in the State of the Theatre. This Work, therefore, which, I hope they will not expect a Man of my hasty Head shou'd confine to any regular Method: (For I shall make no scruple of leaving my History, when I think a Digression may make it lighter, for my Reader's Digestion.) This Work, I say, shall not only contain the various Impressions of my Mind, (as in *Louis the Fourteenth* his Cabinet you have seen the growing Medals of his Person from Infancy to Old Age,) but shall likewise include with them the *Theatrical History of my Own Time*, from my first Appearance on the Stage to my last *Exit*.

If then what I shall advance on that Head, may any ways contribute to the Prosperity or Improvement of the Stage in being, the Publick must of consequence have a Share in its Utility.

This, Sir, is the best Apology I can make for being my own Biographer. Give me leave therefore to open the first Scene of my Life, from the very Day I came into it; and tho' (considering my Profession) I have no reason to be asham'd of my Original; yet I am afraid a plain dry Account of it, will scarce admit of a better Excuse than what my brother *Bays* makes for Prince *Prettyman* in the *Rehearsal*, viz. *I only do it, for fear I should be thought to be no body's Son at all*; for if I have led a worthless Life, the Weight of my Pedigree will not add an Ounce to my intrinsic Value. But be the Inference what it will, the simple Truth is this.

Appendix D: Education and Conduct Books

1. Richard Allestree, from *The Whole Duty of Man, Laid Down in a Plain and Familiar Way for the Use of All, but especially the Meanest Reader* (London: 1658)

[Published in 1659, this conduct book was republished throughout the eighteenth century. A collection of seventeen lessons designed to be read on Sunday, the book could be read through three times in a year. On the title page, it advertised itself as "necessary for all families." Both *Shamela* and *Pamela* allude to the book, and the excerpts below focus on Allestree's statements regarding chastity, the duties between parents and children, and the duties between masters and servants.]

From Sunday VII. "...Of Duties which Concern our Bodies; of Chastity, &c. Helps to it; of Temperance."

.... I have now done with those VERTUES which respect our SOULS, I come now to those which concern our BODIES.

17. The first of which is CHASTITY or PURITY, which may well be set in the front of duties we owe to our Bodies, since the Apostle, I. *Cor*. 6.18 sets the contrary as the especial sin against them, *He that committeth fornication, sinneth against his own body.*

18. Now this Vertue of Chastity consists in a perfect abstaining from all kind of uncleanness, not only that of Adultery, and Fornication, but all other more unnatural sorts of it committed either upon our selves, or with any other. In a word, all acts of that kind are utterly against Chastity, save only in lawful marriage. And even there men are not to think themselves let loose to please their brutish appetites, but are to keep themselves within such rules of moderation, as agree to the ends of marriage, which being these two, the begetting of Children, and the avoiding of Fornication, nothing must be done which may hinder the first of these ends; and the second aiming only at the subduing of Lust, the keeping Men from any sinful effects of it, is very contrary to that end to make Marriage an occasion of heightning and enflaming it.

19. But this Vertue of Chastity reacheth not only to the restraining of the grosser act, but to all lower degrees; it sets a guard upon our eyes, according to that of our Saviour, *Matth*. 5.28. *He that looketh on a*

woman to lust after her, hath committed Adultery with her already in his heart; and upon our hand, as appears by what Christ adds in that place, *If thy hand offend thee cut it off*: So also upon our tongues, that they speak no immodest or filthy words, *Let no corrupt communication proceed out of your mouth, Ephes.* 4.29. Nay, upon our very thoughts and fancies, we must not entertain any foul or filthy desires, not so much as the imagination of any such thing. Therefore he that forbears the grosser act, and yet allows himself in any of these, it is to be suspected that it is rather some outward restraint that keeps him from it, than the conscience of the sin. For if it were that, it would keep him from these too, these being sins also, and very great ones in God's sight. Besides, he that lets himself loose to these, puts himself in very great danger of the other, it being much more easie to abstain from all, than to secure against the one, when the other is allowed. But above all, it is to be considered that even these lower degrees are such as make Men very odious in God's Eyes, who seeth the heart, and loves none that are not pure there.

20. The loveliness of this Vertue of Chastity needs no other way of describing, that by considering the loathsomness and mischiefs of the contrary sin, which is first, very brutish: Those desires are but the same that the beasts have, and then how far are they sunk below the nature of Men, that can boast of their sins of that kind, as of their special excellency? When, if that be the measure, a Goat is the more excellent creature. But indeed they that eagerly pursue this part of Bestiality, do often leave themselves little, besides their humane shape, to difference them from Beasts: This sin so clouds the understanding, and defaceth the reasonable Soul. Therefore *Solomon* very well describes the young Man that was going to the Harlot's house, *Prov.* 7.22. *He goeth after her as an Ox goeth to the slaughter.*

From Sunday XIV. "Of the duty of Parents to Children, &c. Of Children's duty unto Parents, &c."

....there are other things also due from the Parents to the Child, and that throughout the several States and Ages of it.

17. First, There is the care of nourishing and sustaining it, which begins from the very Birth, and continues a duty from the Parent, till the Child be able to perform it himself.... But besides this first care, which belongs to the Body of the Child, there is another, which should begin near as early, which belongs to their Souls, and that is the bringing them to the Sacrament of Baptism, thereby to procure them an early right to all those precious advantages, which that Sacrament conveighs to them....

18. Secondly, The Parents must provide for the Education of the Child, they must, as *Solomon* speaks, *Prov.* 22.6. *Train up the Child in the way he should go.* As soon therefore as Children come to the use of Reason, they are to be instructed, and that first in those things which concern their eternal well being, they are by little and little to be taught all those things which God hath commanded them as their duty to perform; as also what glorious rewards he hath provided for them, if they do it, and what grievous and eternal punishment, if they do it not. These things ought as early as is possible, to be instilled into the minds of Children, which (like new vessels) do usually keep the flavour of that which is first put into them; and therefore it nearly concerns all Parents to look they be at first thus seasoned with Virtue and Religion: 'Tis sure if this be neglected, there is one ready at hand to fill them with the contrary; the Devil will be diligent enough to instil into them all wickedness and vice, even from their Cradles; and there being also in all our Natures so much the greater aptness to evil than good, there is need of great care and watchfulness to prevent those endeavours of that enemy of Souls, which can no way be, but by possessing them at first with good things, breeding in them a love to vertue, and a hatred of vice; that so when the temptations come, they may be armed against them.... A second part of Education is the bringing them up to some employment, busying them in some honest exercise, whereby they may avoid that great snare of the Devil, Idleness: and also be taught some useful Art or Trade, whereby when they come to Age, they may become profitable to the Commonwealth, and able to get an honest living to themselves....

22. A fourth thing the Parent owes to the Child is Good Example, he is not only to set him rules of Vertue and Godliness, but he must himself give him a pattern in his own practice; we see the force of Example is infinitely beyond that of Precept, especially where the Person is one to whom we bear a reverence, or with whom we have a continual conversation; both which usually meet in a Parent. It is therefore a most necessary care in all Parents to behave themselves so before their Children, that their Example may be a means of winning them to Vertue. But alas! this Age affords little of this care, nay, so far 'tis from it, that there are none more frequently the instruments of corrupting Children, than their own Parents. And indeed how can it be otherwise! While Men give themselves liberty to all wickedness, 'tis not to be hoped, but that the Children which observe it, will imitate it; the Child that sees his Father drunk, will surely think he may be so too, as well as his Father. So he that hears him swear, will do the like, and so for all other Vices; and if any Parent that is thus wicked

himself should happen to have so much more care of his Child's Soul than his own, as to forbid him the things which himself practises, or correct him for the doing them; 'tis certain the Child will account this a great injustice in his Father, to punish him for that which himself freely does, and so he is never likely to be wrought upon by it. This consideration lays a most strict tye upon all Parents to live Christianly, for otherwise they do not only hazard their own Souls, but those of their Children also, and as it were, purchase an Estate of inheritance in Hell.

From Sunday XV. "Of Duty to our Brethren, and Relations, Husband, Wife, Friends, Masters, Servants."

25. The last relation is that between Masters and Servants, both which owe duty to each other. That of the Servant is first Obedience to all lawful commands;... And this Obedience must not be a grumbling and unwilling one, but ready and chearful....

26. The second duty of the Servant is faithfulness, and that may be of two sorts; one as opposed to Eye-service, the other to purloyning or defrauding. The first part of faithfulness is the doing of all true Service to his Master, not only when his Eye is over him, and he expects punishment for the omission, but at all times, even when his Master is not likely to discern his failing;... The second sort of faithfulness consists in the honest managery of all things instructed to him by his Master, the not wasting his Goods...whether by careless embezelling of them, or by converting any of them to his own use without the allowance of his Master....

27. A third Duty of a Servant is Patience and Meckness under the reproofs of his Master, *not answering again*, as the Apostle exhorts, *Tit.* 2.9. that is, not making such surly and rude replies, as may increase the Master's displeasure, a thing too frequent among Servants, even in the justest reprehensions....

28. A fourth duty of a Servant is Diligence: He must constantly attend to all those things, which are the duties of his place, and not give himself to idleness and sloth, nor yet to company-keeping, gaming, or any other disorderly course, which may take him off from his Master's business....

29. Now on the other side, there are some things also oweing from the Masters to their Servants: As first, The Master is bound to be just to them, in performing those conditions on which they were hired; such are commonly the giving them food and wages, and that Master that withholds these, is an Oppressor.

30. Secondly, The Master is to admonish and reprove the Servant in case of fault, and that not only in faults against them, wherein few Masters are backward, but also and more especially in faults against God, whereat every Master ought to be more troubled than at those which tend only to his own loss, or inconvenience....

31. But as it is the duty of Masters to admonish and reprove their Servants, so they must also look to do it in a due manner, that is, so as may be most likely to do good, not in passion and rage, which can never work the Servant to any thing but the despising or hating him; but with such sober and grave speeches, as may convince him of his fault, and may also assure him, that it is a kind of desire of his amendment (and not a willingness to wreck his own rage) which makes the Master thus to rebuke him.

32. A third duty of the Master is to set good example of honesty and godliness to his Servants, without which 'tis not all the exhortations or reproofs he can use will ever do good; or else he pulls down more with his example, than 'tis possible for him to build with the other, and 'tis madness for a drunken or prophane Master to expect a sober and godly Family.

33. Fourthly, The Master is to provide that his Servants may not want means of being instructed in their duty, as also that they may daily have constant times of worshipping God publickly, by having Prayers in the Family...

34. Fifthly, The Master in all affairs of his own, is to give reasonable and moderate commands, not laying greater burthens on his Servants than they are able to bear, particularly not requiring so much work, that they shall have no time to bestow on their Souls; as on the other side he is not to permit them to live so idly as may make them either useless to him, or may betray themselves to any ill.

35. Sixthly, The Master is to give his Servants encouragement in well doing, by using them with that bounty and kindness which their faithfulness and diligence, and piety deserves.

2. Lady Sarah Pennington, from *An Unfortunate Mother's Advice to her Absent Daughters* (London: 1761)

[Pennington published this "open" letter to her daughters after her estrangement from her husband. The text offers advice on all aspects of a young woman's life, from the importance of daily prayer and recommendations on clothing to the value (or lack thereof) of various kinds of needlework and considerations on choosing a husband. Tremendously popular, the book appeared in three editions the first year and at least seven more by 1800. It was also published in the American colonies. The excerpts below provide a stark contrast to the kinds of advice Shamela and Syrena receive from their mothers. The selections both highlight issues relevant to appropriate female behavior and provide insight into contemporary attitudes toward domestic management and the treatment of upper servants.]

The turn which your mind may now take, will fix the happiness or misery of your future life; and I am too nearly concerned for your welfare, not to be most solicitously anxious that you may be early led into so just a way of thinking, as will be productive to you of a prudent, rational behaviour, and which will secure to you a lasting felicity. You were old enough before our separation, to convince me that heaven has not denied you a good natural understanding. This, if properly cultivated, will set you above that trifling disposition, too common among the female world, which makes youth ridiculous, maturity insignificant, and old age contemptible. It is therefore needless to enlarge on that head, since good sense is there the best adviser; and, without it, all admonitions or directions on the subject would be as fruitless as to lay down rules for the conduct or for the actions of an ideot.

Time is invaluable; its loss is irretrievable! The remembrance of having made an ill use of it must be one of the sharpest tortures to those who are on the brink of eternity! and what can yield a more unpleasing retrospect, than whole years idled away in an irrational, insignificant manner, examples of which are continually before our eyes! Look on every day as a blank sheet of paper put into your hands to be filled up: remember the characters will remain to endless ages, and that they never can be expunged; be careful therefore not to write any thing but what you may read with pleasure a thousand years after. ...Diversions, properly regulated, are not only allowable, they are absolutely necessary to youth, and are never criminal, but when taken to excess; that is, when they engross the whole thought, when they are made the chief business of life: they then give a distaste to every valuable employment, and by a sort of infatuation, leave the mind in a state of restless impatience from the conclusion of one 'till the commencement of another. This is the unfortunate disposition of many. Guard most carefully against it, for nothing can be attended with more pernicious consequences. A little observation will convince you that there is not, among the human species, a set of more miserable beings, than those who cannot live out of a constant succession of diversions. These people have not comprehension of the more satisfactory pleasure to be found in retirement: thought is insupportable, and consequently solitude must be intolerable to them.

The management of all domestic affairs is certainly the proper business of woman; and, unfashionably rustic as such an assertion may be thought, it is not beneath the dignity of any lady, however high her rank, to know *how* to educate her children, to govern her servants; how to order an elegant table with economy, and to manage her whole family with prudence, regularity, and method.

.... Should you at any time have an upper servant, whose family and education were superior to that state of subjection to which succeeding misfortunes may have reduced her, she ought to be treated with peculiar indulgence: if she has understanding enough to be conversible, and humility enough always to keep her proper distance, lessen, as much as possible, every painful remembrance of former prospects, by looking on her as an humble friend, and making her an occasional companion. But never descend to converse with those whose birth, education, and early views in life were not superior to a state of servitude; their minds being in general suited to their station, they are apt to be intoxicated by any degree of familiarity, and become useless and impertinent.

Whatever time is taken up in dress, beyond what is necessary to decency and cleanliness, may be looked upon, to say no worse, as a vacuum in life.... Leave the study of the toilet to those who are adapted to it; I mean that insignificant set of females, whose whole life, from the cradle to the coffin, is but a varied scene of trifling, and whose intellectuals fit them not for any thing beyond it. Such as these may be allowed to pass whole mornings at their looking-glass, in the important business of suiting a set of ribands, adjusting a few curls, or determining the position of a patch; one, perhaps, of their most innocent ways of idling. But let as small a portion of your time as possible be taken up in dressing....

Of *novels* and *romances*, very few are worth the trouble of reading: some of them, perhaps, do contain a few good morals; but they are not worth the finding, where so much rubbish is intermixed. Their moral parts, indeed, are like small diamonds among mountains of dirt and trash, which, after you have found them, are too inconsiderable to answer the pains of coming at; yet, ridiculous as these fictitious tales generally are, they are so artfully managed as to excite an idle curiosity to see the conclusion, by which means the reader is drawn on, through a tiresome length of foolish adventures, from which neither knowledge, pleasure, or profit can accrue, to the common catastrophe of a wedding. The most I have met with of these writings, to say no worse, it is little better than the loss of time to peruse. But some of them have more pernicious consequences. By drawing characters that never exist in life, by representing persons and things in a false and extravagant light, and by a series of improbable causes bringing on impossible events, they are apt to give a romantic turn to the mind, which is often productive of great errors in judgment, and of fatal mistakes in conduct. Of this I have seen frequent instances, and therefore advise you scarcely ever to meddle with any of them.

The chief point, to be regarded in the choice of *a companion for life*, is a really virtuous principle, an unaffected goodness of heart. Without this, you will be continually shocked by indecency, and pained by impiety....

Let truth ever dwell upon your tongue.

Scorn to flatter any, and despise the person who would practice so base an art upon yourself.

Be honestly open in every part of your behaviour and conversation.

All, with whom you have any intercourse, even down to the meanest station, have a right to civility and good humour from you....

Examine every part of your conduct towards others by the unerring rule of supposing a change of places....

Aim at perfection, or you will never reach to an attainable height of virtue.

3. Lady Mary Wortley Montagu, from *The Complete Letters of Lady Mary Wortley Montagu*, edited by Robert Halsband, Volume 3 (Oxford: Clarendon Press, 1967)

[In these letters Montagu offers her daughter specific advice about educating her daughters; she also comments on contemporary fiction.]

i. Letter to Lady Bute (28 January 1753)

Dear Child,

You have given me a great deal of Satisfaction by your account of your eldest Daughter. I am particularly pleas'd to hear she is a good Arithmetician; it is the best proofe of understanding. The knowledge of Numbers is one of the cheif distinctions between us and Brutes. If there is any thing in Blood, you may reasonably expect your children should be endow'd with an uncommon Share of good Sense...

I will therefore speak to you as supposing Lady Mary [her granddaughter] not only capable but desirous of Learning. In that case, by all means let her be indulg'd in it. You will tell me, I did not make it a part of your Education. Your prospect was very different from hers, as you had no deffect either in mind or person to hinder, and much in your circumstances to attract, the highest offers. It seem'd your business to learn how to live in the World, as it is hers to know how to be easy out of it. It is the common Error of Builders and Parents to follow some Plan they think beautifull (and perhaps is so) without considering that nothing is beautifull that is misplac'd.... Thus every Woman endeavors to breed her Daughter to a fine Lady, qualifying her for a station in which she will never appear, and at the same time incapacitating her for that retirement to which she is destin'd. Learning (if she has a real taste for it) will not only make her contented but happy in it. No Entertainment is so cheap as reading, nor any pleasure so lasting. She will not want new Fashions nor regret the loss of expensive Diversions or variety of company if she can be amus'd with an Author in her closet. To render this amusement extensive, she should be permitted to learn the Languages. I have heard it lamented that Boys lose so many years in meer learning of Words. This is no Objection to a Girl, whose time is not so precious. She cannot advance her selfe in any proffession, and has therefore more hours to spare; and as you say her memory is good, she will be very agreably employ'd this way.

There are two cautions to be given on this subject: first, not to think her selfe Learned when she can read Latin or even Greek. Languages are more properly to be call'd Vehicles of Learning than learning it selfe, as may be observ'd in many Schoolmasters, who thô perhaps critics in Grammar are the most ignorant fellows upon Earth. True knowledge consists in knowing things, not words....

The second caution to be given her (and which is most absolutely necessary) is to conceal whatever Learning she attains, with as much solicitude as she would hide crookedness or lameness. The parade of it can only serve to draw on her the envy, and consequently the most inveterate Hatred, of all he and she Fools, which will certainly be at least three parts in four of all her Acquaintance. The use of knowledge in our Sex (beside the amusement of Solitude) is to moderate the passions and learn to be contented with a small expence, which are the certain effects of a studious Life and, it may be, preferable even to that Fame which Men have engross'd to themselves and will not suffer us to share....

At the same time I recommend Books, I neither exclude Work nor drawing. I think it as scandalous for a Woman not to know how to use a needle, as a Man not to know how to use a sword (20-22).

ii. Letter to Lady Bute (23 July 1753)

....The confounding of all Ranks and making a Jest of order has long been growing in England, and I perceive, by the Books you sent me, has made a very considerable progress. The Heros and Heroines of the age are Coblers and Kitchin Wenches. Perhaps you will say I should not take my Ideas of the manners of the times from such triffling Authors, but it is more truly to be found amongst them than from any Historian. As they write meerly to get money, they allwaies fall into the notions that are most acceptable to the present Taste. It has long been the endeavor of our English Writers to represent people of Quality as the vilest and silliest part of the Nation. Being (generally) very low born themselves, I am not surpriz'd at their propagateing this Doctrine, but I am much mistaken if this Levelling Principle does not one day or other break out in fatal consequences to the public, as it has allready done in many private Families (35-36).

Appendix E: Map of London in Anti-Pamela *and* Shamela

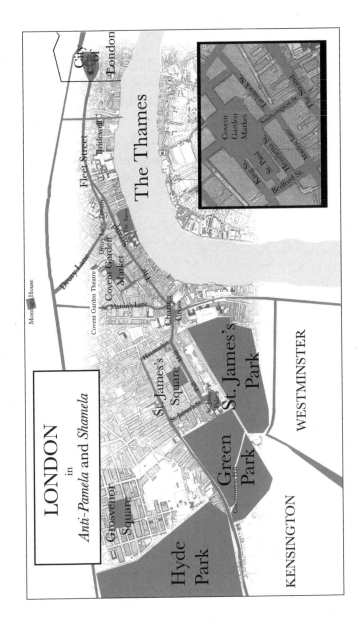

Select Bibliography

Eliza Haywood

Backscheider, Paula R. and John J. Richetti, eds. "Introduction." *Popular Fiction by Women, 1660-1730: An Anthology*. Oxford: Clarendon Press, 1996.

Backscheider, Paula R. "The Shadow of an Author: Eliza Haywood." *Eighteenth-Century Fiction* 11 (Oct. 1998): 79-100.

Ballaster, Ros. *Seductive Forms: Women's Amatory Fiction from 1684 to 1740*. Oxford: Clarendon Press, 1992.

———. "Contexts, Intertexts, Metatexts: Eighteenth-Century Prose by Women." *Eighteenth-Century Fiction* 11.3 (April 1999): 347-58.

Beasley, Jerry. "Portraits of a Monster: Robert Walpole and Early English Prose Fictions." *Eighteenth-Century Studies* 14 (1981): 405-431.

Black, Scott. "Trading Sex for Secrets in Haywood's *Love in Excess*." *Eighteenth-Century Fiction* 15.2 (2003): 207-226.

Blouch, Christine. "Eliza Haywood." *Selected Works of Eliza Haywood*, ed. Alexander Pettit. London: Pickering and Chatto, 2000. Set I, vol. 1. xxi-lxxxii.

Blouch, Christine. "Eliza Haywood and the Romance of Obscurity." *Studies in English Literature* 31 (1991): 535-52.

Bowen, Scarlett. "'A Sawce-box and Boldface Indeed': Refiguring the Female Servant in the Pamela-AntiPamela Debate." *Studies in Eighteenth-Century Culture* 28 (1999): 257-285.

Bowers, Toni. "Sex, Lies, and Invisibility: Amatory Fiction from the Restoration to Mid-Century." *The Columbia History of the British Novel*. New York: Columbia UP, 1994.

Carnell, Rachel. "It's Not Easy Being Green: Gender and Friendships in Eliza Haywood's Political Periodicals." *Eighteenth-Century Studies* 32 (1998-99): 199-214.

Elwood, John R. "Henry Fielding and Eliza Haywood: A Twenty-Year War." *Albion* 5.3 (1973): 184-92.

———. "The Stage Career of Eliza Haywood." *Theatre Survey* 5.2 (1964): 107-16.

Hollis, Karen. "Eliza Haywood and the Gender of Print." *Eighteenth-Century Theory and Interpretation* 38.1 (1997): 43-62.

Ingrassia, Catherine. *Authorship, Commerce, and Gender in Early Eighteenth-Century England: A Culture of Paper Credit*. Cambridge: Cambridge UP, 1998.

———. "Fashioning Female Authorship in Eliza Haywood's *The Tea Table.*" *Journal of Narrative Technique* 28. 3 (1998): 287-304.

King, Kathryn R. "Spying Upon the Conjurer: Haywood, Curiosity, and 'The Novel' in the 1720s." *Studies in the Novel* 30.2 (1998): 178-93.

Nestor, Deborah J. "Virtue Rarely Rewarded: Ideological Subversion and Narrative Form in Haywood's Later Fiction." *Studies in English Literature* 34 (1994): 579-98.

Oakleaf, David. "The Eloquence of Blood in Eliza Haywood's *Lasselia.*" *Studies in English Literature* 39.3 (1999): 483-98.

Richetti, John J. *The English Novel in History, 1700-1780.* London; New York: Routledge, 1999.

———. "Voice and Gender in Eighteenth-Century Fiction: Haywood to Burney," *Studies in the Novel* 19.3 (1987): 263-72.

Saxton, Kirsten T. and Rebecca P. Bocchicchio, eds. *The Passionate Fictions of Eliza Haywood: Essays on Her Life and Work.* Lexington: UP of Kentucky, 2000.

Spedding, Patrick. *A Bibliography of Eliza Haywood.* London: Pickering and Chatto, 2004.

Henry Fielding

Amory, Hugh. "*Shamela* as Aesopic Satire." *ELH* 38 (1971): 239-53.

Baker, Sheridan C. "Introduction." *An Apology for the Life of Mrs. Shamela Andrews.* Berkeley and Los Angeles: U of California P, 1953.

Battestin, Martin C. *The Moral Basis of Fielding's Art: A Study of Joseph Andrews.* Middletown, CT: Wesleyan UP, 1959.

———. *The Providence of Wit: Aspects of Form in Augustan Literature and Arts.* Oxford: Clarendon Press, 1974.

Battestin, Martin C. with Ruthe R. Battestin. *Henry Fielding: A Life.* London: Routledge, 1989.

Bell, I.A. *Henry Fielding: Authorship and Authority.* London: Longman, 1994.

Campbell, Jill. *Natural Masques: Gender and Identity in Fielding's Plays and Novels.* Stanford: Stanford UP, 1995.

Hammond, Brean. *Professional Imaginative Writing in England, 1670-1740: "Hackney for Bread."* Oxford: Clarendon Press, 1997.

Hume, Robert D. *Henry Fielding and the London Theatre 1728-1737.* Oxford: Clarendon Press, 1988.

Hunter, J. Paul *Occasional Form: Henry Fielding and the Chains of Circumstance.* Baltimore: Johns Hopkins UP, 1975.

Kreissman, Bernard. *Pamela-Shamela: a study of the criticisms, burlesques, parodies, and adaptations of Richardson's Pamela.* Lincoln: U of Nebraska P, 1960.

Paulson, Ronald. *The Life of Henry Fielding: A Critical Biography.* London: Blackwell, 2000.

Rawson, Claude. *Henry Fielding and the Augustan Ideal under Stress.* London: Routledge and Kegan Paul, 1972.

Rivero, A.J. *Critical Essays on Henry Fielding.* New York: G.K. Hall, 1998.

Rothestein, Eric. "The Framework of *Shamela.*" *ELH* 35 (1968): 381–402.

History of the Novel

Armstrong, Nancy. *Desire and Domestic Fiction.* New York: Oxford, 1987.

Beasley, Jerry C. *Novels of the 1740s.* Athens: U of Georgia P, 1982.

Davis, Lennard J. *Factual Fictions: The Origins of the English Novel.* New York: Columbia UP, 1983.

Gallagher, Catherine. *Nobody's Story: The Vanishing Acts of Women Writers in the Marketplace, 1670-1820.* Berkeley: U of California P, 1994.

Green, Katherine Sobba. *The Courtship Novel 1740-1820: A Feminized Genre.* Lexington: UP of Kentucky, 1991.

Hunter, J. Paul. *Before Novels: The Cultural Contexts of Eighteenth-Century English Fiction.* New York: W.W. Norton, 1990.

McKeon, Michael. *The Origins of the Novel.* Baltimore: Johns Hopkins UP, 1987.

Perry, Ruth. *Women, Letters, and the Novel.* New York: AMS Press, 1980.

Richetti, John J. *Popular Fiction before Richardson: Narrative Patterns 1700-1739.* Oxford: Clarendon Press, 1969.

Todd, Janet M. *The Sign of Angellica: Women, Writing and Fiction, 1660-1800.* New York: Columbia UP; London: Virago Press, 1989.

Turner, Cheryl. *Living by the Pen: Women Writers in the Eighteenth Century.* London and New York: Routledge, 1992.

Warner, William. *Licensing Entertainment: The Elevation of Novel Reading in Britain, 1684-1750.* Berkeley: U of California P, 1998.

Watt, Ian. *The Rise of the Novel: Studies in Defoe, Richardson, and Fielding.* Berkeley and Los Angeles: U of California P, 1957.

Williamson, Marilyn L. *Raising Their Voices: British Women Writers, 1650-1750.* Detroit: Wayne State UP, 1990.